ANOTHER
family
AFFAIR

ANTHOLOGY

CONTENTS

RIVALRY A. A. Davies	1
KENJI Yolanda Olson	91
COTERIE Ally Vance	177
TAKE A CHANCE JM Walker	257
HARLEY'S AERO C.L. Matthews	325
BURIED TRUTHS Faith Ryan	399
DECIET Charity. B	467

Forbidden: A RomanceAnthology
Copyright © 2020
Abigail Davies, Yolanda Olson,
C.L. Matthews, Ally Vance,
Charity B., JM Walker,
Faith Ryan.
All rights reserved.

No parts of this book may be reproduced in any form without written consent from the author. Except in the use of brief quotations in a book review.

This book is a piece of fiction. Any names, characters, businesses, places or events are a product of the author's imagination or are used fictitiously. Any resemblance to persons living or dead, events or locations is purely coincidental.

This book is licensed for your personal enjoyment only. This book may not be resold or given away to other people. If you are reading this book and have not purchased it for your use only, then you should return it to your favorite book retailer and purchase your own copy. Thank you for respecting the author's work.

Cover Design: Pink Elephant Designs
Formatting: Pink Elephant Designs

RIVALRY

BY

A. A. DAVIES

BLURB

One look.
One touch.
One decision that would change everything.

Two worlds collided the moment I laid eyes on her. I'd never known that all consuming feeling until the moment Sage came into my life.

We came from opposite worlds, but I didn't care. The bridge that separated the two sides of our town was just a roadblock I could speed through.

She was my new obsession and I was her perfect Storm.
I refused to give up.
Until buried secrets were exposed.

I was always meant to love her, I just wasn't sure in what way.

MANSION PARADISE
SAGE

"I'm not sure about this, Thalia." I bit down on my bottom lip as we drove past houses that became bigger and bigger, each one grander than the one before it. I'd never been to this side of town—never wanted to—but when Thalia had a bee in her bonnet, there was no stopping her. And tonight, that bee was her attending the prep school party.

"It'll be fun, Sage." She flicked her gaze at me where I was sitting in the passenger seat of her beat up Corolla, then looked back at the road ahead. "You only live once, right?" I grumbled under my breath, but it didn't deter her from continuing, "You can't live inside the pages of your textbooks all the time, Sage. You need to get out and have some damn fun!"

She wasn't wrong, but this didn't seem like fun, at least, not to me anyway. I was nervous. My palms were sweaty, my legs shaking and causing the car to move along with them. These houses were so much different to the two-bedroom apartment me and my mom lived in on the other side of town—the poor side.

"Here though?" I asked, staring out the window, my gut churning as I saw all of the parked cars. They weren't like the cars that sat in the small lot at the public school I'd gone to since freshman year. No. These were shinier, newer, and a hell of a lot more expensive. "How do you even know about this party?"

Thalia flipped her long auburn hair over her shoulder as she squealed to a stop and parked between two sports cars. "They always have a party after the game." *The game.* The game that they'd won tonight, just like they had every time they played our school. Sports were a big deal where I lived, football, track, baseball, but nothing compared to the basketball team. And our biggest rivals, Lakemere Prep. It may have been in the same town as Lakemere Public school, but that was where the similarities stopped.

"And you just happened to overhear where the party was going to be?" I raised a brow at her as I undid my belt. Thalia had been my best friend since grade school and we were polar opposites. Where I liked to stay safe in my bubble, she liked to jump out of it and try anything and everything she could. She was the yin to my yang, the Thelma to my Louise.

"Yep." She slicked some gloss onto her lips, smacked them together, then pushed out of the car. I followed, not wanting to be left alone in a neighborhood I didn't know.

"Wait up," I whisper shouted, rushing to catch up

with her. She laughed, the sound echoing around us, but it was soon erased by the beat of the music coming from the other side of the vast gates surrounding what could only be described as a mansion. "Holy shit."

"Agreed," Thalia said, halting at the bottom of the driveway as we both stared in awe. Neither of us moved for several minutes as we took it all in. The large lawns sat in the middle of the huge circling driveway and came to a stop in front of the biggest water feature fountain I'd ever seen. People were milling about around it, but not one person stood on the perfectly cut grass. They were respectful of the property, a complete contrast to how people behaved at public school parties.

Lights from the mansion illuminated the outside area, and as we finally took steps toward it, I felt more and more exposed. These kids were wearing what was sure to be designer clothes, and here I was in a tank top and denim shorts with my beat-up combat boots. I was out of place; not dressed at all for a party like this.

I was the odd one out, especially as Thalia was dressed to the nines, her dress gripping every inch of her body as the heels she wore clicked on the paved driveway.

"I'm not dressed right," I murmured, keeping my gaze on anything but the students gathered outside of the mansion.

"Psssh." Thalia pulled me closer. "Head up high, Sage. Show no fear."

"What?" My eyes widened. "Why are you acting as if we're about to go into the lion's den?"

"Because we are," she whispered, then pulled me through the open door that was as big as a wall in my small bedroom.

I opened my mouth, about to tell her we should leave. We shouldn't have come here in the first place. We weren't like these people; we never would be like these people. They may entertain us for a short while, but we didn't belong here.

Thalia pulled me through the vast rooms in the house, acting as if she knew exactly where she was going. The kitchen was full of people, but more than that, jampacked with alcohol. Beers sat in the porcelain sink on a bed of ice, and a refrigerated wine cellar was filled to the rafters with spirits. One thing they had in common with the Public parties were the red solo cups. Seemed like even they didn't discount the benefits of being able to throw them in the trash once they were finished with.

Thalia poured us both a drink and handed me one of the red cups, but I shook my head at her. I wasn't good with alcohol. I was a lightweight, and I knew it. So, drinking at a party where the only person we knew was each other, didn't seem like such a good idea.

"Come on, Sage. Loosen up a little." She wiggled her shoulders for effect, a giant grin on her face.

"Nope." I shook my head and took a couple of steps back, only stopping when my back hit the island in the middle of the kitchen. The cold marble cooled my palms, relaxing me a little.

"Take it," she ground out, pushing the solo cup into my chest then letting go. I had no choice but to catch it. She raised her brow at me as she swayed her hips left and right to the music blasting throughout the house. "You don't have to drink it," she continued. "Just hold onto it and make it look like you are."

I brought the red cup up to my nose, sniffed it, then nearly gagged. Whatever it was smelled disgusting, and just the thought of drinking it made me want to throw up. Thalia on the other hand downed hers and was already making herself a second drink.

I wanted nothing more than to tell her to slow down, but I stopped myself, biting down on my bottom lip. It wasn't my place to tell her what she could and couldn't do. We were seventeen-year-old high school students. We were meant to be out having fun and going to parties. This was what I should have been doing.

It was Friday night and I was out with my best friend. I didn't get to do this often, so as I watched Thalia make a beeline for the makeshift dancefloor, I decided to do exactly what she'd said—to let loose and have a little fun. It was only one night, right? How bad could it really get?

SLEEPING BEAUTY
STORM

I only had one rule when I had a party after a game: No sleeping over. But apparently whoever was snoring away in my childhood bed didn't get the memo. Her blond hair covered half of her face, her mouth parted slightly, showing her plump, soft looking lips. She was beautiful, but in that raw, natural kind of way.

Frowning, I tried to place her face. I felt like I recognized her, but I wasn't sure where from. She definitely wasn't one of the students from school.

The sun had come up several hours ago, and I'd already been for my usual workout in the gym attached to the guesthouse, which was also where my *actual* bedroom was. I hadn't slept in this room since I was thirteen years old, not since Dad had given me the guest house and let the housekeeper do all of his parenting. He was always too busy either in the office, jet setting to his latest business deal on his private plane, or entertaining his latest conquest twenty years his junior. He didn't have the time or energy to be my actual father, not unless it came to my basketball career.

I tilted my head to the side, not taking my attention off the girl as I glanced down her body. Her tank top had ridden up, showing a strip of her stomach, but it was the denim shorts showcasing her legs that had my nostrils flaring. Girls I hung out with would never have worn an outfit like that, and especially not with scuffed up combat boots.

I liked it.

She wasn't from around here, that much was clear, but I was intrigued. Curiosity waved over me, so I sat on the edge of the bed. The house was silent, the only sounds her soft snores. Everyone else had left by five am, but she hadn't. She'd stayed, and I couldn't help but wonder why she'd ended up here. Everyone knew I lived in the guesthouse next to the pool, so why would she have come up here?

I whipped my head around to face the en suite door, suddenly realizing she may not have been alone, but when all I saw was the empty bathroom, my shoulders drooped. I had no idea why the thought of her being here with someone else had me on edge, but I wasn't going to overthink it, not yet anyway.

I was captain of the basketball team, the king of my high school. I didn't want for attention from girls, but I also never really cared to give them any either. I fucked liked I shot hoops: fast and furious. I lived each day like it was the last one I was going to have on this earth, but as I stared down at Sleeping Beauty, I wondered what it would be like to live in the moment. To not worry about what everyone else thought of me. To not have to live up to expectations.

Her eyes slowly blinked open, but I didn't move my attention off her face. I needed to see if she recognized me—I needed to know who she was.

For several seconds she didn't focus on anything, just groaned and smacked her lips together, no doubt feeling the morning-after effects from the alcohol she must have drank last night. "Oh god," her raspy voice whispered. "I knew I shouldn't have—" She paused, her gaze finally landing on mine and registering. "What the fuck?" She jumped off the bed so fast she stumbled, her hip connecting with the bedside table and knocking over the nightlight I used every single night until I was nine. "Who...what...I..." She blinked over and over, but all I did was lift one side of my lips in a smirk.

"Hey," I greeted. "Have a nice sleep?"

"I..." She backed away several steps, glancing around the room in panic. "I'm sorry, I must have—"

"Fallen asleep?" I interrupted, slowly standing. I towered over her, like I did with most people. "Name?"

"Sage," she immediately replied, not missing a beat. She was responsive, something I wanted in every girl I met. The problem was, most of the girls at school faked it, they never truly wanted what I had to offer, and if I was honest, I never really wanted to give it to them. But there was something about this girl—about Sage—that had me intrigued. Who was she? Where did she come from? And how fast could I undo the button on her denim shorts and shove my hand down there?

"Why are you here?"

"I erm..." She bit down on her bottom lip and I clenched my fists to stop myself from reaching out to her. "I came with my friend, Thalia, to the party. And I was dancing and had a couple of drinks, then..." She glanced around the room again, taking in the dinosaur wallpaper and the basketball posters—like I said, this was my childhood bedroom. "I'm not sure how I got in here."

Her face paled, her green eyes glistening with unshed tears. I didn't like it. I didn't like the lost look on her face on bit. "Where's your friend now?" I asked, trying to soften my tone, but it was harder than I'd thought.

"I don't know." She audibly swallowed as she reached into the front pocket of her shorts and pulled out her cell. "I don't have any messages from her." She shot her attention to me then back to her cell as her thumb flew across the screen. She held the cell to her ear, but after several seconds, she let it drop. "She's not answering. Maybe she's still here?"

I shook my head. "Nope. Party rules, no one stays over. It's just you and me here, sugar."

She nodded, her body trying to react to what I'd said, but I could tell she wasn't concentrating on me. "I don't understand. I can't remember anything after the second drink and..." She frowned and rubbed her fingers on her temples. "This is exactly why I don't drink." Her voice became firmer. "I knew I shouldn't have taken that goddamn drink." She slammed her hands onto her hips, her gaze meeting mine again. "I hate parties."

I chuckled. "Then why did you come?"

"Thalia." She acted like the one-word name should be enough to answer, and maybe it was, but I still had no idea who this girl even was. She stared down at her cell again, bringing it to her ear a second time, but all she did was huff when there was no answer. "She's still not answering."

I didn't move my attention off her, deciding whether I should help her or not. If this would have happened with anyone else, I would have kicked them out of my house by now and not cared one bit how they got home or why they came in the first place, but there was something about the way Sage looked that had me wanting to...I didn't know...protect her?

Shaking my head at myself, I pulled my cell out of my gym shorts. "What does she look like?" I asked, not looking up at Sage.

"Long auburn hair—"

"Auburn?" I raised a brow. "What the fuck is auburn?"

"It's a color between brown and red," she answered, her voice lower now. "This is her." She handed her cell to me, showing me the image of her and her friend. I was meant to be focusing on her friend in the picture, but I couldn't help staring at Sage. The baggy T-shirt paired with skinny jeans was casual, effortless, but I couldn't help but wonder what was underneath all of that. She was trying to hide behind the clothes, but what she failed to realize was the vulnerability in her eyes. Something I saw as clear as day.

I clicked a few buttons and sent the picture to my cell then shot it off to the group text, asking if anyone had seen Thalia or knew where she went and when she left. One of my teammates was sure to know.

"I'll find out where she is. Shouldn't be long until I get an answer." I pocketed my cell. "You need a ride home?"

"Thalia's car should still be...ah shit, she's got the keys." Sage huffed out a breath, her cheeks reddening. "It's okay. I can walk." She pushed her shoulders back and licked her lips. "I'm sorry for crashing here." She glanced at the bed then back to me. "Thanks for erm... yeah...thanks."

She rushed toward the open bedroom door, but I wasn't done with her yet. "You live around here?" I asked following her down the hallway and to the grand staircase that led into the foyer. Under the stairs sat a pond with the most expensive fish my dad could have bought. Just another way for him to throw his money around as if it made an inch of difference to the man he really was.

"In Lakemere?" she asked, not turning back to look at me as she practically ran down the stairs. "Yeah. I live in Lakemere."

"Not this side, though, right?" My words had her halting at the bottom of the stairs, but I didn't let up.

"You think I don't recognize someone from the other side of town?" I grinned at the back of her head. "It'll take you at least two hours to make it across the bridge." I paused, waiting to see how she would react. When she didn't turn to face me, I moved ahead of her, blocking the doorway. "I'll give you a ride."

"No, I'm good."

"Wasn't asking you, sugar." I winked. "Just telling you what was about to happen."

She snorted. "Does that work on all of the girls?"

I shrugged as I pulled open the door. "Pretty much." Sage laughed, the sound punching me in the gut and making me want to pull her against me. My reaction was visceral, something deep inside me I could barely control. "Fuck," I murmured, trying to get ahold of myself as she walked past me.

My cell vibrated in my pocket, but I didn't move to take it out because my attention was too focused on the girl in front of me. The girl who had come out of nowhere. The girl who already had me wound so tight. And I'd only met her thirty minutes ago. What the fuck was going on?

She blinked up at me, her mouth moving, but I didn't catch what she was saying. I was too in my own head, not paying enough attention to anything but the way her lips were moving. Sage waved her hand in the air and I shook my head, bringing myself out of the haze.

"Huh?" I frowned and inhaled a deep breath as I pulled my cell out and read the message from Cody, my teammate. "Cody put Thalia in an uber last night. She made it home safely."

"Thank god," Sage sighed. She paused, staring at me as if she was waiting for more, but when I didn't say anything, she continued, "I asked which car yours is."

"Oh." I swallowed and walked toward the black Mercedes sports car my dad had gotten me for my eighteenth birthday two months ago. "This one."

"Holy guacamole," she choked out. "I thought you were a high school student."

"I am." I grinned as I stared at her from the other side of the car. "Captain of the basketball team, if you must know."

Her eyes widened as she spluttered. "You're Storm?" She stumbled back a step. "You're Storm Hartley?"

"That's me." I pulled open the driver's side door and pointed at the passenger one. "Get in. I've got practice in a couple of hours."

"Oh shit, I...yeah...okay." She threw herself into the car and snapped the belt in place. "Sorry." She cringed, holding her hands in her lap tightly, causing her knuckles to turn white. "I just didn't realize who you were, and—"

"You follow sports then, huh?" I turned the engine on then drove around the driveway toward the bottom gates. One flick of a button on my steering wheel was all it took for them to open, then I took a right.

"I know of you." Her voice was softer now, surer of herself. "People at school talk about you all the time." I wasn't surprised one bit by that. If she lived on the other side of town, that meant she went to Lakemere Public, also known as our biggest rivals. They hadn't won a game against us in years, much like last night. Although last night was just a friendly—a warm up until the season started next week.

"You hang with the basketball crew then?" I had no idea where exactly she lived, but I headed toward the other side of town, knowing she'd tell me once we got closer.

"Heck no." She laughed again, but this time it was strained, like she was putting it on rather than it being a natural reaction. "People like that don't hang out with people like me."

"And who are 'people like you'?"

"Nerds."

I glanced at her as we came to the bridge that separated the two sides of town. "You don't look like a nerd," I commented.

"That's because Thalia dressed me." She shrugged then pointed straight ahead. "You can drop me on the corner of tenth and third."

"That where you live?" I asked, taking the turning and knowing I only had two more blocks before she'd be out of my car.

"Yeah." She squirmed in her seat, biting down on her bottom lip again, and fuck, I wished I was the one doing the biting.

Halting to a stop where she told me to, I looked up at the apartment block, making a mental note of the place, knowing this wouldn't be the last time I'd see Sage. Our schools may have been rivals, but there was no way I was letting her get away. Not yet anyway. Not until I knew why the hell I felt such a draw to her.

"Thanks for the ride, Storm," she whispered, opening the passenger door.

"Anytime." I leaned down so she could see me now she was standing on the sidewalk. "See you around, yeah?"

"I...sure." She closed the door gently then ran into the apartment building, leaving me wanting more of her.

WHO IS THIS?
SAGE

Monday came around all too fast for my liking. It was the same as every other day of the week. I made the fifteen-minute walk to school, got there early, and waited for Thalia to meet me next to our lockers.

I'd barely heard from her since I got home on Saturday when she finally answered me and told me she was dying from all of the drinks she'd consumed. I didn't bring up the fact that she left me at the party alone, but that didn't mean I wouldn't.

Damn. I still couldn't believe Storm had given me a ride home. I'd never been in a car like that before, never mind sat in such close proximity to someone like him. He was the best high school basketball player in the state.

"Sage!" The shout was the same one I heard every morning when Thalia spotted me waiting for her, but unlike the other mornings, I didn't have a smile on my face ready to greet her. Instead, I raised a brow and tilted my head to the side. "Uh-oh." She halted a couple of feet in front of me. "You're pissed."

"I see you haven't lost your observation skills," I whipped back at her. "What the heck, Thalia?" I stepped toward her. "Why did you leave me there alone?"

"I'm sorry." Her pale skin reddened, a sure sign she was sincere and feeling bad about it. "I was so drunk that I didn't even realize. Then I woke up at home and I didn't even know how I got there."

"I knew we shouldn't have gone." I shook my head, only half meaning it because if we hadn't have gone, I would never have met Storm.

"You got home okay, though, right?" She darted forward and grasped my arm, panic clear on her features. She gasped. "Oh my god, did something happen?"

"Well..."

"What?" Her eyes widened. "Did someone hurt you?"

"No, no." I shook my head so fast I made myself dizzy. "Nothing like that." I inhaled a breath, not sure how to say what I was about to. "I fell asleep there."

"No way?" She chuckled. "Holy shit."

"It's not funny." I slapped her arm and turned to face my locker, feeling like I needed the barrier between us as the halls filled with students. "I had no idea where I was, and then this guy was there."

"A guy?" Thalia slammed her locker shut and held her books to her chest. "What guy?"

"He gave me a ride home and—"

"What guy?" she asked again, and I knew she wouldn't rest until she found out. Thalia was a gossip—always had been. She never failed to stay up on everything happening at school, even though she wasn't friends with any of the popular kids. She kept her ear to the ground, at least, that was what she always told me. It was the journalist in her. Sometimes I wondered if she realized she was a high school kid running a school paper, and not someone writing for the New York Journal.

"Storm," I whispered, closing my locker softly and turning to face her.

Her expression froze in shock. "Storm?" she repeated.

"Yeah."

"Storm?" Her features melted, the life coming back into her. "As in Storm Hartley?" I nodded. "*The* Storm Hartley?" She said it louder that time, causing some heads to turn. "Storm Hartley gave you a ride home?"

"Yes." I grabbed her arm and dragged her down the hallway as the first bell rang out. "Stop saying his name so loud, Thalia."

"What?" She stared at me, her brown eyes lighting with something mischievous. "I can't help it that you got a ride home from *Storm Hartley*."

"Stop saying his name like that." I let go of her as we walked into the classroom, heading to my usual seat in the front row. Thalia sat behind me, murmuring something, but I stopped paying attention.

I wasn't wrong when I'd told Storm I was a nerd. It was exactly who I was, and I wasn't ashamed of it even a little.

Mr. Sheer clapped his hands twice to gain everyone's attention then proceed to throw a barrage of math information at us, but I'd already studied this chapter in my textbook, so as my cell vibrated in my jeans pocket, I pulled it out, figuring it was Mom getting home from her nightshift at the hospital.

> **Mom:** Just got home. I picked up an extra shift, so I'll be gone by the time you get home. We'll have dinner together tomorrow though, okay, sweetie? <3

> **Sage:** Okay, Mom. Have a nice sleep. <3

I smiled down at my cell, thankful that we were finally getting to have some time together but also sad that it wouldn't be until tomorrow. Mom had been picking up more and more shifts lately. I understood that she was a nurse and had to be on call sometimes, but it meant I hardly got to see her anymore.

Just as I was about to lock my cell and put it back in my pocket, a new message showed up from a number I didn't recognize. I glanced up at the Mr. Sheer, making sure his attention wasn't on me, then opened up the message.

Unknown: I can't stop seeing your face every time I close my eyes.

My eyes widened as my entire body tensed up.

Sage: Who is this?

I stared at the three dots that signaled the person was typing. I waited with bated breath to see who it was.

Unknown: Who do you think it is?

I had no goddamn idea, and I was just about to type that when I scrolled up and saw a picture of me and Thalia sent to the number. I frowned. Why would I have sent that picture to a number not even saved in my contacts?

I rolled my eyes as I saw the timestamp, wanting to facepalm. Of course he sent the picture to his number. He needed it to ask his teammates if they'd seen Thalia at the party.

Sage: Storm?

My stomach rolled as he typed back, butterflies taking flight.

Storm: You got it.

I typed out a message then deleted it. Doing it over and over again, not really sure what to say to him. I was nervous. I only ever got nervous when I was about to take a test. But this was a different kind. A kind of nervous that I'd never felt before.

Sage: Why are you messaging me?

Storm: Read the first message I sent.

I read it again, not sure what he meant by it.

Sage: ...

Storm: I want to take you out.

I felt the smile break out on my face and couldn't help immediately messaging back.

Sage: Is that a question or are you telling me...again.

Storm: It's a question.

Sage: I don't think it's a good idea.

Storm: You won't know unless you try.

I huffed out a breath. I was being real with him. It

wasn't a good idea. We were from completely different worlds. He was rich, and I...wasn't. He was a star athlete and I was a nerd. And then there was the small matter about our schools being intense rivals with everything they were involved in.

Sage: Storm...

Storm: Sage...

I could almost hear his voice in my ear and I shivered.

Sage: This is a bad idea.

Storm: Never said it wasn't.

Storm: Doesn't mean I don't want to do it though.

I blew out a breath and glanced up, seeing the time on the clock above the board at the front of the class. There was only a couple of minutes left until I had AP English.

Sage: I don't know.

Storm: Think about it.

Think about it. I could do that. I could think about it then explain that our worlds didn't mesh. He'd understand, right? He'd get it because of who he was. People like him didn't go out with people like me.

The bell rang and I shot off one last message.

Sage: Okay :)

PATIENCE IS OVERRATED
STORM

I never was good at waiting. When I was a little kid, I wanted what I wanted right away, and I almost always got to have it, no questions asked. But as each day passed and I hadn't heard back from Sage, I was getting antsy—impatient.

It had been three days, and it was only twenty-four hours until gameday. I couldn't wait until after then, so I'd decided enough was enough. I was going to get an answer. Not just that, but the answer I wanted; the answer I needed to hear from her lips.

I took a right turn, entering the other side of town. The streets weren't as clean, the graffiti art on the wall dripping with anger and contempt. Each street I drove down had people turning to look at my car. They couldn't see me through the tinted windows, but I witnessed each and every one of their looks. They were probably wondering what I was doing on their streets, and the simple answer was, I was getting what I wanted, no matter the cost.

The building to the high school came into view, and without a second thought, I peeled into the lot, parked in front of the main doors, then pushed out of my car. The sun beamed down on the black metal, so clean I could see my reflection in it.

It was only a matter of minutes until the school bell would ring out, and I intended to be front and center so Sage couldn't miss me.

I leaned against the side of my car, placed the bottom of my foot on the front tire, then waited. The shades covering my eyes concealed the look on my face, but as the students started to file out of the school, it was harder to keep the mask in place.

I was here alone, without the back up of my team. They didn't even know where I was, but I really didn't give a flying fuck. They wouldn't understand what I was doing, not that I did either. I was taking a risk; I just hoped it panned out.

Gasps and whispers surrounded me as students gathered in pockets around the stairs, then the captain of their basketball team—Troy—made an appearance. I could practically see the steam coming out of his ears as he stared at me. I'd fouled him in the last game and got away with it. Both he and I knew I'd done it. It was yet another time I'd gotten one up on him.

"This ain't your turf, Hartley," he ground out, flanked by several of his team members. I leaned back a little, trying to show him I wasn't bothered by his veiled threat as he moved down the stairs and closer to me.

"Yeah, Hartley," the guy next to him repeated, puffing his chest out. "Get off our grounds."

I rolled my eyes, not that they could see thanks to the Gucci shades I had covering half of my face. "I'm good thanks," I said, speaking just as chilled as I was acting. I wasn't here for them; they just didn't realize that yet.

"You're lookin' for trouble," Troy gritted. "We're not on the court now." He cracked his knuckles, coming to a stop only a couple of feet away from me. The threat was closer now, so I stood to my full height, not prepared to back down. I didn't care if it ended up being the entire school against me, I'd never scurry away.

"Not here for you," I told them easily, keeping my gaze connected to his. *Don't take your eyes off the enemy.* My dad had taught me that a long time ago, and I never forgot the advice.

"Yeah?" Troy laughed, several of his teammates joining in with him. "Who are you here for then?"

I raised my brow, finally taking my gaze off him as I glanced around the growing crowd. I couldn't see her anywhere, and I wondered if she'd seen me and chosen to walk away. Maybe coming here wasn't such a good idea after all?

My body screamed at me to walk away and to give in, but something inside me had me staying put. I couldn't deny the way I'd reacted to Sage when I'd found her in my house Saturday morning.

"None of your business," I told Troy, my voice deeper now. I didn't answer to him, I didn't answer to anybody, especially not a douche who thought he was the best player on the court. He was fooling himself, just like his coaches were.

"I'd say it *is* my business," he growled back, stepping closer to me. "Considering you're on my fuckin' turf."

I pushed my shoulders back, clenching my fists at my sides, and preparing myself to throw down. There was no way I was backing down without a fight. "Step the fuck back," I gritted out. "That's your one and only warning."

"Or what?" he laughed. "What you gonna do, Storm?" He sneered my name as if it would affect me, but it didn't. It rolled right off of me, just like his shit basketball skills did.

"Storm!" someone shouted, the same voice I'd been dying to hear for days. "Excuse me," the voice said again, softer this time. I searched for her in the crowd, seeing her coming from the rear end of my car. I didn't hesitate as I left Troy and his followers.

"Sage," I called out, not quite seeing her, then a flash of blond hair appeared along with a hand in the air. "Move," I ground out at the students piled at the back of my car. Their eyes widened as they parted like the red sea, leaving a clear gap for Sage to make her way through. Her gaze met mine and I knew in that moment I hadn't made a mistake coming here.

"Hey." Her voice was soft and alluring, calling to me like a siren to a sailor. "What are you doing here?" she asked, coming closer to me.

"Came to get your answer." I winked, holding my hand out to her, hoping like hell she didn't turn me down in front everyone. Her soft palm met mine, my long fingers able to wrap entirely around her small hand.

"Really?" A blush flashed on her cheeks, but she didn't move her attention off me for a single second. She was captivated by me, just like I was with her.

"Yeah." I pulled her closer to me, our bodies so close to touching it was almost torture. "So?"

She bit down on her bottom lip, and this time instead of imagining pulling her lip from between her teeth, I placed my thumb on her chin and pulled it away. The tips of my fingers stretched into her silky soft hair, and I wished I could grab it and pull her to me, but it was too soon. Too much all at once.

I had to move one step at a time, and this was the first step of many.

"Yes," she sighed, the word flowing on the air to me. "I'll go out with you."

My lips spread into the biggest grin causing my cheeks to hurt at how wide it was. "Thank fuck for that." I pulled her toward me, closing the distance between us as I dipped down and placed a kiss on her cheek. "I think we should get out of here real quick," I whispered in her ear. My attention moved back to Troy who was watching us with narrowed eyes. I didn't wait for Sage's reply before I pulled her to the passenger side of my car and opened the door for her.

I purposely walked by Troy to rub it in just that little more then slipped into the driver's side. Nobody moved from around my car as I turned the engine back on. "Belt," I growled at Sage, flicking mine on at the same time. "Hold tight," I warned her, then revved the engine so much that smoke came from my tires. An opening appeared right in front of me and I didn't waste another second to get the hell out of there.

GOOSEBUMPS EVERYWHERE
SAGE

My stomach rolled as I heard the telltale sound of his engine coming down the street. Nerves flowed through me, but they weren't the bad kind. These were the good ones. The ones that told me whatever was happening between us would change everything. The ones that told me to take a chance on something.

His tires squealed to a stop and I shook my head with a smile on my face as I opened up the passenger door. "How many tires do you go through each month?" I asked, clicking my belt on like he always told me to.

"Dunno." He shrugged and pulled his sunglasses down his nose, just enough to show me his eyes. "Depends how many people I have to race away from."

I tilted my head to the side, not able to stop the small smile lifting one side of my lips. "And how often do you have to do that?"

"Only when I go to the rivals to get my girl."

I laughed, remembering when he picked me up from school a couple of days ago. We hadn't gone anywhere but him taking me home afterward, but it was enough to show me he wasn't messing around. I hadn't been sure whether he was serious about taking me out on a date, but the five-minute drive to get from my high school to my house proved more than enough.

He'd come to the school alone, knowing he wouldn't go unnoticed. I'd never had anybody do anything like that before. The most attention I'd ever had was from my junior tutor back when I was a freshman, but even then, all he'd wanted to do was get between my legs. I hadn't known better then, but now I did. It had been a lesson well learned; one I wouldn't forget anytime soon.

Storm's hand reached over and landed on my knee as he pulled away from the curb in front of my apartment building. My body wasn't sure how to react. I went hot and cold, not knowing what temperature to finally land on, and in reaction, goosebumps spread everywhere, even behind my ears.

How could one simple touch from him have such an effect on me?

"Where are we going?" I asked as he crossed the bridge back to his side of town. I needed to distract myself from the way I was feeling, but that didn't mean I moved my attention off his hand on my bare skin. Thalia had once again told me what to wear for this date. I hadn't had any choice in it, but luckily, she'd picked from my wardrobe, pairing things I never would have.

I ended up with a flowing wrap around skirt that tied at my hip, and a light green tank top, paired with my faux leather jacket, and of course my trusty combat boots. I grasped the jacket tighter, hearing the crunch of the material, and cringed. I bet Storm had never worn faux leather in his entire life.

"I know a great place," Storm said, and I turned to face him, frowning. It took several seconds for me to remember I'd asked him where we were going.

My nerves were running rampant now, but not because of him. Instead, it was because of me. What if they could smell the poor on me as soon as we walked inside the place? What if we ran into anyone he knew? Would he tell them I was from across the bridge?

My breaths came faster as he pulled up outside what could only be described as a fancy burger joint. It wasn't much different to the one on our side of town, the only difference were the glistening windows, the clean outside, and the sports cars lined up right in front of it.

"Fuck," Storm muttered under his breath. His attention moved out of the window. "I didn't realize they'd be here."

"Who?" I sat up straighter, causing his hand to move higher up my leg as the slit in my skirt opened a little more.

"My teammates." His nostrils flared, his gaze flicking from me to the cars where people were getting out of three of them. All looked nearly as tall as Storm, wealth dripping off the clothes they wore and the way they walked.

"We can go," I whispered, swallowing. "If you don't want them to see me—"

"What?" His head whipped around, his hand tightening on my leg. "Why wouldn't I want them to see you?"

"Because." I raised a brow. "I'm not stupid, Storm." I huffed out a breath, feeling all the insecurity bubbling up. "I'm not like them." I waved my hand at him. "Like you." I snorted, trying to pull back from him. "This was a bad idea." I pulled the passenger door open and pushed out of his sleek car.

"Sage?" his voice called, but I was on a mission. I wasn't going to stick around as he told his friends he was with someone from over the bridge. I wasn't a charity case. I never would be a charity case.

"I'm going home," I told him, not bothering to turn. I was overreacting, deep down I knew that, but I couldn't stop myself. If I walked away now, then I wouldn't get hurt. My logic seemed sound to me in that moment.

I heard footsteps behind me, a couple of deep voices shout Storm's name, then a hand grasped my wrist, halting my escape. "Sage," he ground out, his deep voice hitting me in places I never thought possible. "You're not going home."

"I am." I didn't turn to look at him, too afraid at what I would see in the reflection of his eyes.

"No, you're not." He twirled me and wrapped his arm around my waist to keep me in place. His palm smoothed on the side of my face, bringing my gaze up to meet his. "What was that?" he asked softly.

"What was what?"

"That." He tilted his head toward his car where several people were standing, watching us in fascination. "You ran." His dark blue eyes didn't move their attention off me, probing for answers I wasn't sure he wanted to hear.

"I'm not like them, Storm. I'm not like you." My shoulders drooped as I was honest with him. I'd never been totally honest with anyone about how I was feeling, but there was something about the way he was looking at me that had the words flowing from my mouth without me even realizing. "I'll never be like the girls at your school."

"I don't want the girls from my school." He stepped closer, his chest pressing against mine. "I want *you*."

My breath halted, my eyes glassing over. "I..." I wasn't sure what to say. No one had ever been so open with me before. It was scary, but intriguing all at the same time. My brain didn't know how to react. Should I have continued to walk away and give in before anything really started? Or should I take a leap of faith and dive head first into the unknown.

Storm bent at the knees, bringing his face level with mine as he whispered, "From the second I saw you sleeping on that bed, I haven't been able to stop thinking about you, Sage." He paused, his tongue coming out to swipe at his lips. "I want you, Sage. Just you. No one else."

I bit down on my bottom lip, my stomach churning as he groaned in response to my movement. I wasn't even aware I was doing it until I heard his reaction. And that was all I needed to spur me on and take a chance. "Okay," I whispered, flicking my gaze between his eyes and his lips. "On one condition."

"Anything." He pushed closer, his arm wrapping around my waist and holding me tight against him.

"Kiss me."

He answered me with his lips, but not with his words. His mouth pressed against mine, soft and gentle to start with, but as I wrapped my hand around the back of his neck and pushed my fingers into his light-brown hair, he pressed harder.

His tongue swiped along my bottom lip, demanding entry, and I gave it to him. I gave him all of me. Everything fell away as our tongues danced to a beat only we could create. He branded me with one single kiss, and I knew I'd never be the same.

Not after this.

Not after him.

A PICTURE SPEAKS A THOUSAND WORDS
SAGE

I looked at the picture of me and Storm, the smiles on our faces and intensity in our eyes almost too much to bear. I'd never experienced anything like it, and I wasn't sure I ever would again. Thalia had snapped it when Storm had taken us to one of the Lakemere Prep parties last weekend. She said we looked like we were obsessed with each other, and I had to agree. There was just something about Storm that had me enraptured with everything he did.

It had only been ten days since our first date, but we'd been almost inseparable since then. I'd met most of his teammates, and not one of them cared that I was from the other side of the bridge. Maybe my insecurities were all inside my head?

I shrugged at myself, not caring. It didn't matter what anyone else thought about us. What mattered was what *we* thought.

"Sage?" Mom shouted, and I squealed, scared that

she'd see what I was looking at and ask questions. "Dinner is here."

There was a time when I shared everything with my mom, but over the last couple of years, we'd grown apart. Maybe it was because I was in the midst of high school, or because she was working more and more hours. Either way, we weren't as close as we used to be, and the last thing I wanted was to tell her about Storm on the first night we had together in over a month.

Mom walked into the kitchen, a smile on her face as she held up the white bag full of our food. She'd promised us takeout two weeks ago, but yet again, that had fallen through because she'd had to go in and cover someone else's shift.

"Smells delicious," I said, locking my cell and pushing it into the back pocket of my jeans. It vibrated and my fingers tingled with the need to see if it was Storm, but I managed to stop myself. He knew I was spending some time with my mom, and he had an extra practice at school then a meeting with his coach. But what if something happened? What if he needed me?

"Hello?" Mom waved her hand in front of my face. "Earth to Sage."

I blinked, shaking the thoughts from my brain. "Sorry." I chuckled, trying to act easygoing, but all I wanted to do was check my cell.

"It's okay, sweetie." Mom smiled the same small smile she always did. "You've got a lot going on with school, huh?"

I nodded, deciding blaming schoolwork for my

brain being somewhere else and not here was the best way to go. "Yeah." I opened several of the takeout boxes, chose what I normally ate, then sat at the small table that separated the living room and kitchen. We always had four chairs around it, but we never used more than two.

It had been me and Mom against the world for as long as I could remember.

"I get it." Mom sat next to me, digging into her food. "I remember what it was like to be a high school junior." She placed her hand over mine. "It won't be long until you'll be leaving for college."

"I know." I placed some food in my mouth, trying to keep myself occupied. I didn't want to think about when school would be over. I didn't want to think about in a few months when this year would end and Storm would leave.

He'd already told me about the scholarship offers he'd gotten, and almost all of them would mean he'd leave the state. I may have only met him two weeks ago, but there was something in my gut that told me we were at the start of something special. Something that only happened once in a lifetime.

"Don't look so sad," Mom said, tying her light-brown hair in a messy bun. "You're gonna have an amazing time at college. You'll have adventures you never thought possible."

"I know." I looked down at my food, feeling my cell vibrate again. I shook my shoulders, needing to get out of the frame of mind I found myself in. "I'm excited," I said, putting some pep into my tone as I stared up at her.

The dark circles under her eyes paired with her yawn spoke of how exhausted she was, yet she was still trying to spend time with me. It wasn't easy being a single mom, but she'd tried as hard as she could, and the least I could do was spend some real time with her.

I smiled at her, leaned back in my seat, and asked, "What was it like when you went to college?"

Her lips slowly lifted, her eyes glassing over with memories. "Insane." She laughed, picked her fork up, and side eyed me. "Totally insane."

I NEED YOUR HELP
STORM

I flicked my wrist, feeling the rough material of the basketball scrape against my fingers then bounce from the tips. It flew through the air, but I didn't need to keep looking to know it would make its way into the middle of the basket.

I'd practiced the exact shot thousands and thousands of times. The first time I made it was when I was six years old in my backyard, my dad at my side, cheering me on.

It was different now though. There wasn't a celebration when it whooshed through the basket, instead it was a given, viewed like a person walking down the street. It wasn't the pressure of making the shot that flowed through me every time I lifted my arms to make it, but the pressure to not miss it. My team and coach relied on me to make the shots no one else could, at least not over and over again like I could.

"Storm?" a deep voice called, and I whipped my

head around to Coach who was on the sideline, his clipboard in hand and his red well-worn cap on his head. He'd been wearing it every day for as long as I could remember.

"Coach," I greeted, jogging over to him.

"How's the shoulder?" His gaze flicked to my shoulder that I'd had taped up at the start of the week. It was only a niggle at the moment, but I knew how fast it could become more than that.

"Feels good." I rolled my shoulders back as if to show him I was good.

"Make sure it stays that way." He held the clipboard in the air. "Big game tomorrow." He didn't need to remind me of the game. Lakemere may have been our rivals, but they were nothing compared to the second highest team in the state, Douston Prep. They had the same resources as we did, and some wicked players to boot. Too bad for them that they would stay second.

"I know, Coach." I stood to my full height, taking the pressure on my shoulders yet again. I was used to it, had been since I made my first basketball team when I was a kid. "We'll beat them."

"Good." He raised a brow. "Keep the boys in check. Last thing I need is for one of them not able to play because of their grades."

I knew exactly who he was talking about. Cory hated schoolwork and did everything and anything not to do it. He was the second-best player on the team, and also the guy I relied most on when we were on the court. "On it," I told Coach.

He grumbled something under his breath then blew the whistle to signal the end of practice. Everyone gathered around him, listening as he told us the schedule for the game tomorrow, but my attention was on Cory. I knew he was struggling to keep his grades up, and without the minimum GPA Coach specified, he wouldn't be able to play. He needed help, and luckily for him, I knew the right person for the job.

As soon as Coach finished talking, we all headed back to the locker room. I made a beeline for my locker, pulled my cell out, and shot off a message.

Storm: I need your help.

Sage: Okay. Doing what?

Storm: Do you tutor?

Sage: Yes...

Storm: Good. I'll pick you up Saturday at 2 :)

NOTHING TO STOP US
STORM

I could hear her voice from the other room as she tried to explain to Cory how to work out a math equation. Even talking about a subject that I hated, I couldn't help but be enthralled with her tone and the patience she had with him.

"I don't fuckin' get it," Cory groaned. "I'm gonna fail."

"No, you're not," Sage told him. "You got that one right. You're just stuck inside your own head."

I grabbed three bottles of water from my refrigerator and headed into the living room that looked out onto the pool in the back yard. Sage glanced up at me as soon as I stepped inside the room. Her smile shot across her face, her gaze not moving off me as I came closer to her.

"You've been at it for three hours now," she said to Cory, but she wasn't looking at him. When we were in a room together, there may as well have been no one else with us. I only had eyes for her. "Maybe we should break for the day."

"Thank fuck." Cory cracked his knuckles. "My head is spinning from all this schoolwork."

I laughed and threw a bottle of water at him then sat next to Sage on the sofa. My arm wrapped around her shoulders as I pulled her toward me and handed her a bottle too. "If you actually attended your classes then maybe you wouldn't have to do schoolwork on a Saturday."

"Whatever," Cory grumbled, downing half of the bottle in one. "I'm so over Coach making us keep a high GPA. Who cares what grade I get in Miss Bernard's class? I'm too busy staring at her tight ass body to listen to what she's saying."

I snorted, knowing he wouldn't be saying that if Carter was here with us. "Careful," I warned him, but I only half meant it. The thought of Carter would be enough for him to not say another word about Miss Bernard.

Cory capped the bottle and threw it back at me. "You're no fun, Storm." He raised a brow as if he was trying to goad me, but the fucker knew better than that. I didn't take the bait, no matter who it was from. "I'm headed to Hensley's party." He stretched his arms above his head. "You two coming?"

I turned to face Sage. "You want to go to the party?" I hoped her answer would be no because I wasn't in the mood to share her tonight. It had been four weeks today since we'd first met, and I knew her mom was on a double nightshift tonight which meant she could stay over, only this time she'd sleep in the bed I slept in instead of in the main house.

"Not really," she whispered, shuffling closer to me. "Can we just stay here?"

I dipped my head and placed my lips against the edge of her ear. "We can do anything you want to do."

Her chest heaved with a breath, and her squirm told me my words had the effect I wanted them to. Now all we needed was for Cory to get the hell out of here. I could feel him watching us, but I couldn't resist pressing my lips against the soft patch of skin underneath her ear. I didn't stop there though, I continued on down her neck until her soft moans filled my ears.

"Fuck, man, wait for me to leave at least. Damn."

I chuckled, not stopping even when the door to the guest house slammed shut.

"Storm," Sage groaned out, her tone raspy.

"Sage." I pressed my lips to the underside of her jaw, only stopping when I was a centimeter from her lips. Our eyes connected, something unspoken said without us having to verbalize a single word.

I wanted her. She wanted me. And there was nothing in the way to stop us.

Her hand pressed against the side of my face, her eyes glassing over as she pushed her fingers into my hair. "Baby," she whispered, her chest lifting on a deep breath. "I've never felt anything like this before."

"Me neither," I confessed.

I wasn't sure what we were going to do with the

words we'd just spoken, but the craving to show her how much I meant them was too much to deny.

Our lips joined, but this kiss was so much different to every kiss that came before it. It was more than our mouths connecting, it was a promise, one neither of us would ever break. She was it for me, and I was willing to show her that every single day. Our lives may have been worlds apart, but our souls were as close as two could be.

My hand worked its way over her shoulder and to her hip as my tongue danced against hers. I didn't know if I was going too fast or too slow, but as soon as her legs wrapped around my hips, I knew I couldn't slow down. Not now. Not when we were so close.

I didn't hesitate as I wrapped my arms around her and stood, bringing her with me. She pulled her lips away from mine as I moved us toward my bedroom, but she didn't stop kissing me. She lavished my neck with attention while her hands worked their way under my T-shirt, bringing it up and demanding to take it off over my head.

There was no denial on my part as she threw it on the floor, exposing my chest and abs to her. She dragged her fingertips slowly over my muscles, taking each one of them in.

"You're like a statue of perfection," she sighed out, her gaze meeting mine. I sat on the edge of my bed, holding her to me and needing to see her skin as much as she needed to see mine.

The shirt she wore had buttons all the way up the

front, and although my mind told me to undo each one and slowly reveal her to me, I couldn't wait. I grabbed each side of her shirt, yanking on it, and causing the buttons to pop.

Her red lace bra had me salivating, but it was her nipples peeking through the fabric that had my hips thrusting. My rock-hard cock pressed against her and her moan was enough for me to take charge and take her bra off in the same way I had her shirt.

I didn't wait a single second to dive forward and pull her nipple into my mouth. Her hips gyrated against me, her shorts and my sweats the only thing in the way, so I reached down, undid her zipper, and tried to pull them off.

She leaned to the side, but she couldn't get them fully off while my mouth was still attached to her chest. "Storm," she gasped out. "Storm. Let me take them off. Please."

I didn't want to stop touching her. I wanted to mark every inch of her body with my touch. But to be able to do that, I needed to view all of her body. So reluctantly, I let her go, not moving my gaze off her as she pulled back and stood in front of me.

Her shirt was hanging open, her bra halfway off, and her shorts undone. I placed my hands behind me, leaned back, and watched her with my full attention as she slowly pulled the shirt down her arms, followed by her bra, and finally her shorts.

I salivated at the sight of her curves and the matching red lace panties covering her pussy. My fingers twitched to reach forward and snap them off her body, but I resisted the urge and instead just stared as she pulled them down her thighs and let them drop to the floor.

She took two steps forward and halted when she was between my legs, her naked body in full view.

"Fuck, Sage." My nostrils flared. "You're fuckin' beautiful." The blush that normally appeared on her cheeks flowed down to her chest. She paused her movements, staring at me for a few seconds, and I wondered what she was thinking. Was she second guessing this? Second guessing us. Just as I was about to sit up and hold her to me, she darted forward and yanked my sweats down. My cock sprang free, pulsating at the way she stared down at it. "Wow," she whispered.

Her fingers stroke the head, and that was all it took for me to get back into action. I dove for her, bringing her against me, and lapping at her nipples.

Now wasn't the time for slow and steady. I needed her like I needed my next goddamn breath. "I need you," I told her, not willing to keep my thoughts to myself. My fingers reached between us and I dragged them between her folds, feeling the wetness coat them.

"Me too," Sage moaned out, lifting her hips so that my cock was right at her entrance. We both paused, our gazes connecting. Our chests heaved, our hearts beating like crazy, but neither of us hesitated as she lowered onto me.

I flicked her clit, slowing down as my cock entered her to the hilt. Her pussy tightened around me, but I let her take control of the pace. I let her depict how fast she was going to go. But as soon as she groaned and her pussy clamped around my cock, signaling she was close, I knew I had to take the reins.

I stood, flipped us over, and thrust into her over and over again, and burned the image of her into my brain, promising myself I'd never forget it as long as I lived.

THE LOVE BUBBLE
SAGE

"Mom!" I shouted, for what felt like the thousandth time. I checked my cell, seeing that we were already running late, and got more and more antsy the longer she took to get ready.

"I'm coming, I'm coming!" Several footsteps echoed upstairs and then finally she appeared. "Jeez." She blew her hair out of her face, her cheeks red from her rushing. "It's only a basketball game, sweetie."

I bit my tongue, not prepared to tell her why I was so eager to get to school on time on a Friday evening. This wasn't just *any* game. No. It was Prep vs Public, and this game actually counted toward the championship. I still hadn't told Mom about Storm, but tonight...tonight I had every intention of introducing her to him. I just hoped the spontaneous move wouldn't backfire.

Mom had gotten a rare Friday night off, and of

course it would happen when I had plans to watch Storm play. So, I figured there was nothing I could do but ask her to come with me. I just hadn't expected her to say yes.

Now that we were finally on our way to the school, my nerves were running rampant. I hadn't told Storm I was coming either, and I had no idea how he would react when faced with my mom. Seemed like I was full of surprises tonight.

The lot was jam-packed with cars when we got there, but instead of it being the usual beat up kind, we were joined by high-end expensive ones. I shook my head. Of course they wouldn't ride to a game on a bus like every other high school. These students lived by their own rules, unless their coach demanded they kept a high GPA.

I still couldn't believe they didn't get special treatment when it came to their schoolwork, but the more Storm had explained it to me, the more it made sense. The students at Prep had to get into Ivy League Colleges, and they couldn't do that without being able to actually use at least *some* of their brain.

The roar from the gym got louder the closer me and Mom got, and the sound of the first buzzer to start the game rang out as we made it into the main doors. We both shuffled up the bleachers, trying our hardest to find some seats, but we had to settle with Mom on the end of one of the benches and me on the step next to her. I didn't mind though because from here I had an awesome view of Storm in his navy jersey, the number 7 written on the back underneath the name HARTLEY.

My stomach flipped as he spun around, dribbled the ball, and made a perfect shot from halfway on the court. It looked effortless, just like everything seemed with him. But I knew better. I'd watched him practice his shots over and over again on the court in his backyard. He didn't give up, not until he'd hit a certain number in his mind. Only then was he satisfied.

I wasn't really sure what the whistles sounding out at different stages were, or what position each player was in, all I knew was there was now only thirty seconds left on the clock and Storm's school was up by twelve points. They'd won before the final buzzer even rang, but that didn't mean they stopped. Instead, they played like *they* were twelve points down, right until the last second when Storm made a final basket, just to rub it in that little bit more.

Half of the gym cheered, the players going crazy on the court. Even Mom stood and held her hands in the air, joining in the celebrations, but my attention was too focused on Storm and what he was doing.

He ran his hand through his hair and rolled his left shoulder where he'd been wearing tape for a few weeks. I winced when I thought about the pain that he'd been in the night I'd stayed over. It wasn't until the morning that he let it show on his face, but as soon as he'd taken some painkillers and worked the kinks out, he seemed fine. I could see through it though. He was nursing some kind of injury; I just hoped it didn't make a difference in him playing the rest of his games this season.

I wasn't sure how long I stood there, watching as Storm spoke to his coach then held his hand up to someone on his side of the bleachers, but the gym was starting to empty.

Mom grasped my arm, a look of concern on her face. "Sage? You okay?"

I swallowed, my gaze tracking Storm as he made his way to the locker rooms. *It was now or never.* "I have a boyfriend." My eyes widened. I'd never used that term before, but the more I rolled it around in my head, the more I liked it.

"You do?" Mom tilted her head to the side, her eyes narrowed. "Now it makes sense." She laughed, the soft tinkle echoing around the now nearly empty gym. There were a few people straggling, but no one I knew. "You haven't been distracted by school work." Her lips lifted into a smirk. "You've been in the love bubble."

"Love bubble?" I snorted. "That sounds so...ew."

"What?" Mom pushed her arm through mine and pulled me down the steps. "What's wrong with love bubble?" I screwed my face up, letting my expression do all of the talking. "Fine." She rolled her eyes. "Do I get to meet him then?"

"Hopefully." I swallowed, wiping my sweaty palm on the side of my jeans. "He was playing tonight."

"He's on the school basketball team?" Mom looked

shocked, and I was sure it was because my boyfriend played sports when I detested them.

"He is." I glanced around, seeing some of the players from Prep making their way back through the gym. "He's at Prep."

"Wait." Mom moved back a step, holding her hand in the air. "Your boyfriend is a rich kid?"

I opened my mouth, about to reply when Mom glanced behind me, her face paling. She looked like she'd seen a ghost, and if the small gasp hadn't escaped her lips, I would have been sure she'd stopped breathing. I turned, wondering what had made her have that reaction, but all I was faced with was a guy in a designer suit.

"Lauren?" the guy asked, his voice deep and throaty. "What are you doing here?" He didn't look down at me as he spoke to my mom even though I was stood right between them. There was an air of confidence to him, but he also dripped of wealth.

"Patrick?" Mom's voice was breathy, like she couldn't quite form the single word. "I...I had no idea you'd be—"

"Dad?" My stomach rolled at the sound of Storm's voice. "Who are you talking—" Storm's gaze landed on mine, an instant smile appearing on his face. "Sage?" He boosted his bag up on his shoulder and came right to me. His arms wrapped around me and I pulled in a calming breath, feeling like I was finally home once again. "You didn't tell me you were coming." He planted a kiss on the top of my head then looked down at me. "Did you see the game?"

"I did." I lifted up onto my tiptoes, about to ask how his shoulder felt, but Mom's hand grabbing my bicep and pulling me away from Storm had me smacking my lips together.

"Sage." Her voice was like whiplash, a tone I'd never heard from her before. "What are you doing?" Her chest heaved as if she'd just ran a marathon and I frowned up at her. "Tell me this isn't the boyfriend you were talking about."

"It is..."

I heard Storm and his dad murmuring something, but I wasn't sure what to focus on, not until his dad's eyes met mine. "You promised this would never happen, Lauren," he warned, his attention still on me. If looks could have killed, I would have been bleeding out on the floor in that moment.

"I didn't know you were still in the area," Mom gritted out. "A call would have been nice."

"A call?" He snorted. "We had a fuckin' deal."

"I know we did."

"Dad," Storm interrupted. "What the hell is going on?"

"Nothing." He spun to face Storm. "End the relationship with her, right now."

"What?" Storm laughed at his dad and stood to his full height. "You may be my father, but you haven't been my dad for a long fuckin' time." He took a step toward him, matching him in height. "You don't get to tell me what to do. Not anymore."

"You can't date her."

"Why?" Storm growled.

"Because." His dad turned slowly, his gaze meeting my mom's, then mine, and finally back to Storm. "She's your sister."

SHE'S MY WHAT?
STORM

"What?" My entire body felt like it was floating. Like I wasn't on this earth anymore, but instead heading up into the skies without an ounce of control.

"You heard me," Dad spat, not giving a flying fuck that anyone could hear. I glanced around, real goddamn glad that we were the only people left in the gym. "She's your sister."

"No, she's not." I turned to face Sage, but she looked like she wasn't paying attention, as if she'd gone into a place in her mind where nobody could get to her and I wanted nothing more than to be right there with her.

"She is," Sage's mom whispered, her hand coming up to her neck, a clear signal that she was distressed.

I stumbled back a few steps, realizing that they were both telling the truth. Dad and Sage's mom exchanged a series of looks, both raging from concerned to pissed off.

Good. I was glad they were feeling the same as I was.

"You're lying."

"We're not, son." Dad moved toward me, but I held my hand out to stop him coming any closer. None of this made sense. Not a single word of it. "She's your sister." He paused then pointed at Sage's mom. "And she's your mom."

My chest caved; the breath being knocked out of me. "No," I whispered. "No." My heart begged me to look back at Sage, but my brain told me not to. I was in crisis mode. But it only took seconds for my shock to turn into red hot anger. "Fuck. You," I gritted out, looking at both my dad and Sage's mom. "Fuck the both of you." I didn't waste another second. I spun on my heels and got the fuck out of there before my brain imploded.

GETTING SOME ANSWERS
SAGE

Each moment that passed by seemed to go by at a snail's pace. It had been four days since I saw Storm standing in the gym, his dad and my mom gathered around us, confessing something I still didn't understand.

How could he be my brother? How could my father have been so close all of this time and I never knew? Why didn't I know? Why didn't Storm know? There were a barrage of questions slamming through me, and I hated that I didn't have an answer to any of them. But I also didn't want to face it. I didn't want to confront the reality.

Several times Mom had tried to talk to me since then, but I'd resulted in constantly wearing noise canceling headphones and blasting my music as I barricaded myself in my bedroom.

I didn't want to hear what she had to say. She was a liar, whether that was now or in the past. She'd kept something from me. Something fucking huge. And now...fuck...now I had no idea where I stood. Storm was my brother. My *full* brother. We had the same Mom and Dad.

How did we move on from that? How were we meant to get past what we'd done?

My stomach rolled, only this time it wasn't from seeing Storm, but from the prospect of sitting opposite him later today. Mom had finally had enough of me ignoring her and instructed me to have a shower and to get dressed then I'd be given some answers. Answers I wasn't sure I wanted if I was honest.

I worked on automatic as I did what she'd said, and before I knew it, I was in her car, a baggy T-shirt and a pair of jeans covering my body, my wet hair causing a damp patch on my shoulder. I didn't care though. I couldn't see any light at the end of the tunnel, not after the words they'd spoken and the bomb they'd dropped.

"You're going to be okay, Sage, I promise," Mom said, using her comforting tone, but it did nothing to settle the way the nerves were exploding throughout my body as we pulled into the lot of the café near the bridge that separated the two sides of town.

I spotted Storm's car right away and my hands started to shake. I couldn't do this. I couldn't sit across a table from him, knowing we'd done what we'd done all while he was my brother. *My brother*.

My breath caught in my throat so I grabbed my neck, trying to let it free, but all I could think about were the nights I'd spent at Storm's, our body's pressed against each other's, our lips fused together as one.

Fuck.

What had we done?

"Sage," Mom's voice broke through and I whipped my head around, seeing her face next to me in the open passenger door. "Come on, sweetie. It'll be okay."

I opened my mouth, about to confess to everything me and Storm had done, but I couldn't find the words. Maybe we should keep it secret. What they didn't know wouldn't hurt, right? After all, that was what they'd done to us.

My legs felt like they were going to give way any second as we entered the café. My skin crawled with uneasiness as Mom pulled me toward the back, but as soon as I saw Storm's face, it all washed away.

He was there. Waiting for us.

But he wouldn't look at me, not even when I sat opposite him, our body's so close yet so far apart.

"Lauren," Storm's dad greeted. "Sage."

I didn't turn to face him because the only attention I wanted was from Storm.

"Patrick," Mom replied. "Storm." At the sound of his name, his head snapped up, but still he wouldn't look at me. He didn't say a single word to my mom, and after a couple of minutes silence, Mom continued, "I think you both deserve some answers."

Storm snorted. "You think?" He leaned back, acting like none of this was bothering him, but I saw the tension in his shoulders and the tensing of his jaw. He was pissed.

"Watch your mouth, son," Patrick warned, but his tone was softer, as if he was tired of this conversation already. "We did what was best for both of you." Patrick's gaze met mine. "When Lauren and I split, I wanted to take both of you." My brows raised as he spoke directly to me. "She knew she couldn't afford the both of you, not with that little hospital job she had." His gaze veered over to my mom. "I'm guessing you still work there."

"She does," I answered for my mom, feeling my hackles rise.

"Right." Patrick nodded and took a sip of his black coffee. "Anyway. When she refused me taking both of you, we came up with an agreement." Patrick glanced at Storm, and although my brain screamed at me to look at him too, I couldn't, not while I was trying to sort through what he was saying. "I took Storm, and Lauren took Sage."

I blinked, trying to come to terms with the way he was talking. He was acting as if this was a business deal that had gone bad, and I wondered if he acted like this with Storm too? Was that what Storm meant about him not being a dad to him for a long time?

Storm and I had been seeing each other for nearly two months, and not once had I seen his dad at their house when I was there. In fact, he barely spoke about him.

"So, you thought the best idea was to take a parent

away from each of us?" Storm asked, his voice carefully calm, but I knew it was all a front.

"Yes," Mom answered. "We thought it would be the best thing for you both, and—"

"It wasn't," I cut her off, standing and causing the table to wobble at my movement. My eyes welled up, my throat closing. "I had an entire family out there and had no idea."

"Sage." Mom's hand wrapped around my wrist. "Please understand—"

"No." I ground my teeth together, trying to get myself under control, but I couldn't. Something had snapped. Maybe it was because Storm was sitting opposite me, or the way Patrick spoke so matter of fact, but I couldn't take it anymore. I couldn't sit here and listen to what else they said to justify it. "You fucked up." I narrowed my eyes at Mom and Patrick. "You both fucked up really bad."

"Is this how you raised our daughter?" Patrick asked, one brow raised as he turned to face my mom. "Maybe I should have taken them both after all."

"How dare you," Mom whisper shouted. "You know I didn't want to do it, but yet again, you threw your money around, threatening me with—" I drowned them both out, not caring what they had to say.

Nothing would make better what they'd done.

Nothing would alter what Storm and I had done.

I closed my eyes and gripped onto the edge of the table, trying to just...breathe. But it was too much. Everything was too much. And then a hand grasped my thigh. I snapped my eyes open, my gaze clashing with the blue orbs I'd gotten lost in over and over again.

Everything had changed.

"Sage," Storm whispered, his hand clenching on my thigh, but it broke me. Shattered me into a tiny thousand pieces that would never be able to be put back together again.

I shook my head, feeling the tears finally break through and stream down my cheeks. "I can't," I choked out, stepping away from the table. My heartbreak was clear for them all to see, and I had no idea how to fix it, so I did the only thing I thought would help.

I ran. Ran away from them. Ran away from Storm. Ran away from the reality of the situation.

WHO MATTERED MOST
STORM

My cell rang from my bedroom, but I didn't move a single inch as I stared at my dad standing in the doorway to the guesthouse. He was escaping the turmoil he'd left behind, not giving a shit about the hurt and anger he'd caused.

"I'll be back in ten days," he said, his tone even, as if what had happened this morning hadn't affected him. And maybe it hadn't. Maybe he really didn't give a flying fuck.

"Whatever," I sneered. "Just leave already."

He stood there, his gaze trying to pierce through me, but he hadn't been able to achieve anything with that look since I was a little kid. He'd shown me his true colors over the years, and today had been no different.

Half of his face was illuminated by the lights in the guest house while the other half was covered in darkness from the night. There were two sides of him, I'd learned that a long time ago.

He puffed out a breath, swiped his hand over his face, then left, just like he always did when somebody needed him most. I watched him walk back into the house, and not even a minute later, the roar of his car sped down the driveway, leaving behind the shitstorm he'd created.

"Fuck!" I shouted, clenching my fists at my sides. I didn't want to be here; I didn't want to be anywhere but with her.

Goddamn it.

I ground my teeth together, trying to push her to the back of my mind, but all I could remember was the utter devastation on her face this morning. The way she'd looked at me like she'd lost absolutely everything in one fell swoop.

And maybe she had. Maybe that was it for us, because we couldn't continue, not now we knew the truth. Right?

My cell rang out again, so I barged into my bedroom and snapped it up, not looking at the caller ID before I barked out, "What?"

"Erm...Storm?" a female voice asked.

"Yeah." I stared at myself in the mirror, seeing the anger so clearly written over my entire body.

"It's Thalia." There was a pause and then, "Sage's best friend." I spun around, not able to look at myself any longer. "I think...erm...Sage is drunk and—"

"Where are you?" I ground out, already running out of the guest house and toward the main house. Sage needed me, and my instinct was to go to her. To save her.

"We're at a party on our side of town but she's really upset, and I don't know what to do." Her voice moved away from the cell as she shouted, "No, Sage! Get down from there."

My stomach dropped, my need to get to her taking over. "Text me the address." I hung up, threw myself into my car, and waited for the message to appear. As soon as the text flashed on my screen, I spun out of the driveway, determined to get to the person who mattered most to me.

A MOUNTAIN BETWEEN US
SAGE

My tongue stuck to the roof of my mouth and I groaned at the feeling. I needed water, STAT, and lots of it. My head thumped to the beat of an invisible drum, and as I opened my eyes and sunlight blasted through my retinas, I groaned.

"Oh god." I slapped my hand over my eyes, trying to un-see the light that had tried to blind me.

I rolled over, pulling the covers with me, but it took me a few seconds to realize the light in my bedroom didn't come through my window like that. As soon as recognition slammed into me, my body snapped up into a sitting position, my hands grasping the covers at my chest even though I knew I was still fully clothed.

I blinked over and over again, trying to get the sleepiness out of my eyes as I took everything in. I may not have been in my bedroom, but that didn't mean I didn't know where I was. And as soon as I recognized the colors of the walls and the signed basketball sitting on the dresser, my heart hammered for an entirely different reason.

"Storm," I whispered.

I didn't expect an answer, so when he asked, "Yeah," from behind me, I jumped out of my skin.

I whipped my head around, my gaze landing on him as I backed up on the bed to the edge. He wasn't next to me though, but instead sitting on the chair in the corner, his eyes rounded with dark circles.

"What..." I swallowed and backed up even more, getting out of his bed. The last time I'd been in there we'd been naked and—I shook my head. I couldn't think about that, not right then. "What am I doing here?"

He pushed to the edge of his seat and rested his forearms on his thighs. "You got drunk last night." He paused, his piercing gaze not moving off of me. "Thalia called for me to come and get you."

I nodded, remembering the amount I'd drank at the party. When I'd left the café yesterday, I'd walked for hours then finally ended up at Thalia's. I hadn't told her what had gone on or that my entire world had been shattered. She'd taken one look at my face and declared the only solution was to drown my sorrows.

"So, you brought me back here?" I wrapped my arms around my waist, trying to comfort myself.

"Yeah." Storm blew out a breath then pushed his hand through his hair. "Go shower and then we can talk properly."

Emotion bubbled up into my throat. It was just him

and I here, no one else around. There was a mountain between us, yet I still felt closer to him than ever. I'd thought everything had changed, but had it?

"It hurts to look at you," I confessed, feeling the tears threatening to fall.

Storm nodded, as if he understood, and he was probably the only other person in the world who ever would. He stood, his shoulders pulled back, his strength alluring and begging me to go to him.

"I can't do this." I stepped back, knowing the en suite door was right behind me. "I can't be around you, not when I feel like this."

"When you feel like what?" Storm asked, his voice soft but demanding.

"I can't," I choked out, taking another step back and feeling the cool tile of the bathroom floor on the soles of my feet. "This is wrong."

"What's wrong?" His voice was deeper now. "Tell me, Sage." He moved around the bed, coming closer. "Tell me."

I opened my mouth, my throat closing up, but I managed to rasp out, "I'm in love with you," a second before I closed the bathroom door, shutting him off from my confession.

MY EVERYTHING
STORM

I stared at the door for what felt like hours as I heard the shower turn on, but it didn't mask the sound of her sobs.

I'm in love with you.

Her words echoed over and over again in my head, getting louder and louder each time. She hadn't said that she loves me, no, she said she was *in* love with me. She'd told me how she felt, even after all that we'd found out.

Just because someone told you something, didn't mean it automatically changed the way you felt. And that was exactly what was happening. Our parents had told us who we were to each other—who we were meant to be. But that didn't mean that was what we were.

We may have been brother and sister, but I didn't see her like that, I'd never see her like that.

My foot moved before my brain registered what I

was doing, but as I took another, then another, I knew what I was doing was the right thing. Maybe not to anyone else, maybe not legally, but inside my heart, I knew the truth.

Sage was it for me. She'd been it since the moment I'd laid eyes on her, and nothing or nobody would stand in our way.

My palm grasped the door handle and I slowly turned it, stepped inside, then closed and locked the door behind me. I was separating us from the outside world because they didn't understand, they'd never understand.

Sage froze in the shower, the water thrashing down on her naked body, but I didn't hesitate. She needed to know how I felt too. She needed to see that she wasn't the only one with the feelings she had.

I pulled my T-shirt over my head and slipped my shorts off my hips, then opened the shower door. I reached for her immediately, not able to take another second of not touching her. My arm wrapped around her waist, my hand on the side of her neck, as I whispered, "I'm in love with you too." Her eyes closed, her body relaxing in my hold as soon as she took my words in.

"This is wrong," she murmured, but there was no conviction behind it. "We shouldn't do this, Storm."

I pressed my forehead to hers and held tighter as I lifted her. Her legs wrapped around my waist automatically, her body knowing exactly what it wanted.

"I don't care about right or wrong," I told her as I

leaned her back to the tiled wall. My lips were so close to hers, a temptation I'd never be able to resist. "All I care about is you." Her hand grasped the side of my face, her fingers reaching into my now wet hair. "Tell me, Sage." I pressed my cock to her entrance but didn't thrust forward. "Tell me you want this, and it'll be me and you against the world."

Her breath fanned over my lips, her gaze focused fully on me as she said, "I want this. I want you. More than anything." That was all I needed to push inside her and show her exactly what she meant to me. *Everything. She was everything to me.* "Me and you," she choked out.

"Me and you," I repeated, silently promising her that I'd never give up on us.

ABOUT A. A. DAVIES

A. A. Davies is the darker, alter ego of Abigail Davies.

Abigail Davies grew up with a passion for words, storytelling, maths, and anything pink. Dreaming up characters—quite literally—and talking to them out loud is a daily occurrence for her. She finds it fascinating how a whole world can be built with words alone, and how everyone reads and interprets a story differently.

Now following her dreams of writing, Abigail has found the passion that she always knew was there.

- facebook.com/abigaildaviesauthor
- instagram.com/abigaildaviesauthor
- bookbub.com/authors/abigail-davies

MORE BOOKS BY A. A. DAVIES

Verboten (Inferno World Novella)
Coquette (Carnaval des Ténèbres Series)
Easton Family Saga (Abigail Davies)

Sign up for Abigail's newsletter here

KENJI

BY

YOLANDA OLSON

BLURB

Snow Montgomery walked into my life one day and everything changed.
From the moment that I first saw her, I knew I would never want anyone else.
And when our eyes met and I saw the look of hope in hers, I couldn't help but realize that she felt the same.
Months have been spent beneath the roof of my house.
I provide for her as best as I can because I want to be the man she needs more than the one she deserves.
I teach her discipline and reward her when she's been good. Food, water, the constant knowledge of knowing she'll always have shelter over her head is what I can do best for now.
Always.
A word that holds more meaning to me now than it ever has.
It's what she promised me.

It's what I have to look forward to with Snow.
And I can't wait to spend the rest of our lives together.
Always.

CHAPTER ONE

"Quit being such a pussy and hold still," I tease my client with a playful eye roll.

Virulence and Vanity Body Arts seems to be the place where college girls come and test their pain threshold. The traditional butterfly usually does the trick but this tiny brunette that I'm working on can barely stand the pain of the outline.

I've never heard more whimpers and whines from someone in my life. She's even cried a couple of times.

Today is going to suck.

"I don't know if I can finish," she manages to squeak out and I sit back and sigh. I let my foot off the pedal, then set the gun down on the sterile, metal tray.

"How about we take a break and you go outside and get some air. If you decide you're done, then we'll leave it as is, okay?"

I would hope that she wouldn't want to walk

around with a half-drawn butterfly, though I guess in some circles it could be seen as an abstract piece.

Personally, I see it as unfinished business and it makes me cringe.

The last thing I want is someone walking around with that telling people that it's my work when word of mouth goes far in this business.

But I guess being kind would go further.

The tiny brunette agrees and wipes the sweat from her brow with the palm of her hand. I chuckle and shake my head; if only she knew this was the worst of it, she'd sit still and let me finish.

I take the gloves off my hands and toss them into the trash can under my desk. Reaching for the energy drink I opened before I started working on her, I take a swig before I get to my feet then walk out of the room with the can still in my hand.

I follow the sound of the loud metal music and poke my head into Carter's room. He looks up and gives me a nod, so I take it that it's alright for me to check on the design he's working on.

I head over and stand next to him, tilt my head to the side and lean down slightly.

"That's bad ass, man," I tell him, and I mean it.

He's working on a back piece that's taken him a few sessions to finish and now there's just the color left to do.

It's a massive lily with a koi fish on either side and I clear my throat as he sits back and sets his gun down.

"Alright, go take a breather and we'll finish it up when you come back in," he tells his client. She nods as she reaches for her shirt and holds it against herself on the way out.

I wait for her to get up and leave before I close the door and run a hand over my face.

"Why do you always get the easy ones?" I grumble.

Carter chuckles as he pulls his gloves off and shrugs, "You're a bastard; karma likes to kick you in the balls sometimes."

I grin at him.

I can't respond to that because it's the truth, I just wish that karma would give me a fucking break once in a while is all.

About twenty minutes into energy drinks and bro-chill, Carter's client walks back into the room and gives me a sympathetic smile.

"You okay?" I ask raising an eyebrow.

"Your girl ran off. She said she couldn't take it anymore."

I grit my teeth as I close my eyes for a moment. There's no way in hell she'll get her deposit back now, but it would have been nice to have been paid for the work I did on her.

"Sorry, man," Carter says, his tone echoing his client's sympathy. I open my eyes and look at them both before I shrug.

"Just another day in the life of karma."

I crush the can between my hands in frustration as

I walk out of the room, the sound of the tattoo gun firing up and taunting me.

At least one of us will get paid for a full appointment slot today.

CHAPTER TWO

The shop closed about an hour ago, but instead of going home right away, I decided to take a walk. I need to blow off some steam from the loss of income fiasco or I'll explode when I walk through the doors.

The only thing that I've ever loved in my entire life doesn't deserve the wreckage that my foul mood would cause.

My outbursts of rage have become a point of contention in our relationship and I do my best to be a better man for her because that's what she deserves.

I let out my breath as her favorite trinket shop comes into view. I know it's closed for the night, but I decide to make my way toward it.

I can do some window shopping before Virulence and Vanity opens for business tomorrow. Maybe I can get her a gift that I know will make her smile.

That's something she hasn't done in a long time

and I still have trouble reconciling if it's because of me. I treat her as best as I can and have stopped taking out my frustrations of unfinished pieces and lost wages on her, which I had hoped would have fixed everything.

Verbally, of course.

I've never struck her.

She's had enough of that in her life from people that have claimed they love her, whereas I honestly do.

I catch a hint of my reflection in the large display window when I finally arrive. My reflection stares back at me, a banal expression on his face, yet somehow cautiously optimistic.

My thoughts immediately go to my darling Snow. A name I never did like but because her mother was something of a moron, naming her for the first thing she saw through the hospital window after giving birth.

Snow has always been so proud of her name, though. When she was a child, she would say that the winter flurries were named after her and not the other way around. As a teenager, she took to dying her hair white and maintained the spectacle well into her almost twenties.

Even now, I take special care to keep her hair white as she always had been so fond of doing. Coincidentally, it helps to set off the ice blue color of her eyes and make her seem otherworldly.

Since I've always had a thing for vampire lore, it works out.

But as my eyes focus again, and I still see my reflection slightly, I think about how different we look and wonder what the fuck she ever saw in me.

Kenji Miura.

Heavily tattooed arms and legs, light brown, almond-shaped eyes, straight black hair, and a semi-permanent half-scowl always on my lips.

We look so different yet we're so much alike, that I honestly believe that the only opposite of our attraction is our physical one.

Her skin is pale and flawless; mine is naturally tan and covered with colorful artwork.

Her mother gave birth to her here; mine gave birth to me in Tokyo.

She likes quiet nights in; I like drag racing and having a few beers with the people from work.

And somehow, in a world where things don't make much sense to me anymore, she does.

I reach up and push away a stray strand of hair from my face before I force myself to rebuff my reflection and do what I came here to do—pinpoint something that might brighten her day tomorrow.

Once I've homed in on just the thing that will hopefully bring a smile to Snow's face, I reach into the inside pocket of my denim jacket and pull out my pack of cigarettes.

I retrieve one, set it between my teeth and dig the lighter out of the pack before putting it away, then light it, the fire reflecting in the window.

I look up at my reflection one more time before I

shake my head and decide it's time to turn in for the evening.

"I'm home!" I call out after I've locked the door behind me.

She doesn't respond, though. She hasn't in months and it's all I can do to not lose my mind over it.

Snow has given me the cold shoulder since the last time I let my temper explode all over her and I guess I deserve it.

I said some horrendously unsavory things to her and no matter how much I've begged for forgiveness she's decided to punish me with silence.

The only reason I've decided that it's okay is because I've also decided to punish her in my own way.

I shrug my jacket off as I head into the living room and hang it in the small closet, before I glance around the room and smile when I see her.

In the corner.

On all fours.

Naked with the exception of a pair of white, cotton panties that I allow her to wear.

Face to the wall and waiting for permission to be able to curl up and go to sleep.

Like the good little girl that I've been training her to become, I think with a wistful sigh.

The one that will talk to me again one day. The one

that won't be ashamed of us. The one that will love me as much as I love her.

It all starts with making her smile again.

And tomorrow will be that day.

"Good night, Snow," I whisper as I walk out of the living room and head toward my bedroom.

CHAPTER THREE

After I left the trinket shop and secured Snow's gift under the station in my room, I wandered back into the reception area.

Leaning against the desk, I grin at Carter when he waltzes in and we knuckle bump before he disappears into his station.

I always liked him.

He's the one that turned me onto Snow having a thing for me and he's been helping me with her when I need him to.

Carter gives some of the best advice I've ever gotten from anyone other than myself and he makes sure that shit gets done in the best way possible for both me and her.

As I go back to flipping through the latest copy of *Inked Magazine,* the phone rings. I glance up at the wall clock, pick up the phone, then replace it back down on the receiver without so much as a word.

We aren't open yet and I don't get why people always insist on trying to call for last minute appointments before business hours.

I stifle a yawn with my fist when the doorbells that Carter wrapped around the front handle chime and look up, ready to tell someone that we aren't open for another hour or so but break into a smile instead.

Sariah, the shop's receptionist, walks in and hip bumps me out of the way once she gets behind the desk so she can sit down.

"Morning, Kenji," she greets me distractedly as she attempts to open the desk drawer that my legs are blocking.

"Morning," I echo as I scoot to the side, allowing her to place her purse into the desk. I use my shin to push it back in place, coming dangerously close to catching her fingers inside. She looks up at me with a frazzled expression on her face, but I grin at her and all is forgiven.

I wouldn't have hurt her intentionally but sometimes, I'm not in control of my own thoughts and little close-to-accidents like this tend to happen.

"Sorry, kid," I say as I reach over to ruffle her hair. She swats my hand away and giggles, but immediately reaches into the top drawer for her hand mirror.

Sariah has to be the vainest person that I've ever met, but I guess she kind of has a reason to be.

She's tall—for a girl, anyway, has huge silver-colored eyes, and bright blonde hair that she likes to wear in dreadlocks. Her arms are still half-sleeves, but

Carter and I work on them when time allows. Sariah has her septum pierced, as well as a Medusa and Monroe piercing.

She's definitely something to look at but she's never really been my type—our relationship has always consisted of nothing more than older brother and annoying little sister.

Besides, I've got Snow at home and I've never even thought of being unfaithful to her.

"We have to finish those soon," I say nodding at her arms, and she mumbles in agreement as she leans back in her chair and stretches them high over her head.

"Whenever you say, boss," she replies with a smile.

With a chuckle, I flip the magazine closed then walk around the desk and place it back on the small, wooden desk that displays mine and Carter's portfolios as well.

"Hey, Kenji?" Sariah suddenly asks.

"Yeah?"

"Carter was telling me the other day that the two of you were chatting about maybe hiring another artist ..."

Her voice trails off and I sit on the black, chaise leather couch just in front of her desk as I clasp my hands behind my head.

"Uh huh."

I figure the prod, while menial will probably cause her to finish her thought.

"Well..." Sariah's face turns crimson as she begins to nervously pick at her fingernails. I sit up, now rife with curiosity, and wait.

"Well?" I echo, arching an eyebrow.

She blows out her breath and looks up at me. "My brother gets out of Irongate next week and he's been doing some tattoos on the inside. I was hoping—"

I raise a hand to stop her.

"Just tell him to swing by when he's out," I tell her with a warm smile.

Everyone deserves a second chance no matter how horrid a deed they've done, and I'm hoping that maybe by giving Sariah's brother one, karma will push Snow to give me one too.

I get to my feet and begin to walk back toward my room when I linger for a moment at the front desk. Sariah looks over at me with that damn thankful smile still on her face and I decide it's best not to ask.

Irongate is reserved for the worst bastards alive.

She'll tell me what he did to deserve a stint there when she's ready.

Or maybe he will.

"Hey, Stranger," I greet the tiny brunette as she knocks on my door.

I'm currently in the middle of working on a client, but neither of us seems to mind the intrusion.

"Um, do you have a sec?" she asks in a timid tone.

"I don't know," I say as I remove my foot from the pedal and glance down at my client. "Do I?"

He nods and tells me he'll take the opportunity to

go have a smoke, so I set the tattoo gun down. As soon as he's out of the room, I get to my feet, take my gloves off, then cross my arms over my chest after I've tossed them into the trash can.

Brunette closes the door, lingering with her back to me for a moment before she turns around and begins to wring her hands nervously.

"What's up?"

"I wanted to say that I was sorry for running out the other day…"

"You mean yesterday?" I correct with a chuckle.

She nods, licking her lips nervously as she reaches into her handbag and fiddles around inside, retrieving her wallet.

"I just couldn't take it anymore so I ran, but I wanted to pay you for the full appointment time we had booked," she explains as she holds out a couple of hundred dollar bills in the same timid manner as her tone.

Huh.

"Thanks," I say as I reach forward and take the cash. I put the money into the wooden box I use for safekeeping until the day is over, "I appreciate this honestly."

"Maybe I'll get brave enough to finish this one day," she jokes with a nervous laugh.

"Maybe."

"Okay, well, hopefully you'll be able to fit me in when the time comes."

"Maybe," I state, repeating my prior sentiment.

I'm not entirely sure I want to deal with all of the bucking and crying again but since she was nice enough to come back and pay me, I might set the aggravation aside to help her out.

"What's your name again?" I ask as I reach for another pair of gloves. The door has been opened and my client has reentered the room so it's time to get back to work.

"Hazel," she replies shyly.

"Just like your eyes." She blushes and I have to fight to roll my eyes. It wasn't a flirtation or a compliment—it was merely an observation. "See you around, Hazel."

With a nod, I dismiss her from the room as I prepare to get back to work.

"See you," she replies softly.

Maybe karma is coming around sooner than I had hoped for.

CHAPTER FOUR

It's always a great day when your customers tip well. Not that I ever require it because I think they pay enough, but everyone today added a little something extra to the pot.

As I walk into the front door of my home, I find myself in a good mood knowing that I can get more little keepsakes for Snow because of today's generosity. I also find myself nervous and excited to give her the gift I bought for her.

My darling gal loves animals and I thought that this would be a great way to continue my needing to be forgiven for how I treated her.

I almost always greet her before I walk into the living room to let her know that I'm home, but I think that since I have a surprise for her, maybe she won't mind me not announcing myself.

But when I enter the room, she's not in the corner on all fours like she's supposed to be. She's still curled up in the same ball from the night before and it makes me wonder if that's what she does when I'm out busting my balls to provide a good home for her.

"Snow!" I bark at her.

She gasps, instantly scrambles to her hands and knees, turning to face the wall.

I take as deep a steadying breath as I can and count to ten. I do my best not to throw away her gift. Knowing that I could so easily close my fist around it and crush the bag like the energy drink from yesterday probably wouldn't impress her much.

Not to mention that it would show my obvious frustration and that doesn't work with her since she would know that I'm angry about her disregarding her lessons.

Anger isn't the way to get to her; I should know this by now, but it hurts me that she seems to do whatever the fuck she wants when she knows that I'm not home.

I run a hand over my face before I walk over and sit down behind her. Reaching forward, I grip her by the hips and pull her back against me, then place the giftbag into her hands.

I'll do this as kindly as I can and hope that she doesn't reject the gesture because if she does, I'll be at a complete loss as to what to do with her.

"I got you something," I tell her softly as I nuzzle her neck with my lips. Her body begins to tremble under the weight of my touch, and it fills my heart with joy. It's been so long that Snow's reacted this way to my touching her and maybe it means that we can fix this after all.

My gal nods as she opens the bag as she cautiously slips a hand inside. I'm nervous that she won't like it, but it's not complete yet. Hopefully, she'll see the beauty in the simple base and accept it.

"Do you like it?" I ask shyly as she pulls it out of the bag and holds it up. She uses her other hand to grip one end and the other gives it a firm tug.

"Thank you," she replies in a soft tone.

My heart catches in my throat as, to my surprise, tears start to form. Not of joy, elation, or sadness. It's more my body's reaction to hearing her voice again for the first time in months and it's dripping in gratitude.

For something as small as this.

I clear my throat as I pull her tightly against me and kiss the top of her head. I let my lips linger there for a moment, breathe her in, then pull away and do my best to sound like the sturdy-voiced bastard she knows me as.

"It's about time," I say with a chuckle. A normal person would have replied with *you're welcome,* but I'm tired of pretending to be something I'm not. Snow shimmies slightly in my grip and looks up at me, a small smile on her lips before she turns her attention back to the gift.

It's nothing too major but knowing her love of animals, felines and canines being her favorite, I went into the taxidermy shop a few doors down from Virulence and Vanity and got her a little fox tail.

I'll have to finish it myself and she'll wear it for me like a happy little pup finally accepting of her master.

"If you really like it, I'll go back tomorrow and find some ears to match, okay?" I tell her, rubbing her arms with my hands. Snow nods before she tucks the tail back into the bag, then pulls away from me.

I'm confused at first, angered and hurt, until I see her move back onto her hands and knees, face to the wall.

I'm not overly fond of treating her like an animal, but humans *are* animals too and this one lacks discipline.

I don't know how else to teach her than like this.

"Do you want to sleep in my bed tonight?" I ask as I reach forward and run a finger down the back of her thigh. I follow the line through the curve of her knee, until I stop at the back of her ankle, hoping above all else that she'll say yes.

But Snow goes back to her silence, not answering me with words. Instead she chooses actions as her response and turns to face me.

I smile as my heart starts to beat a little faster inside of my chest.

Even though she keeps her eyes directly ahead, I know she's as happy about this as I am. Especially when I get to my feet and move quickly toward the closet. I hang my jacket inside, then reach on the top shelf for her leash.

Either she'll get to her feet and walk on her own, or she's going to let me lead her.

No matter what happens, this will be the greatest

night of my life—the one I've been waiting for since the first time I laid eyes on her.

I walk back toward Snow and let the leash unravel. It swings lazily in front of her and I wait for her to make her decision.

When she clears her throat and turns her eyes to look up at me, I shake my head fondly and lean down to clip the leash to her collar.

Animal it is then.

CHAPTER FIVE

Snow is settled on the edge of my bed. Her hands are on her knees, her eyes on me, waiting for a command, any command that might tell her what to do next, but I want this to be natural.

I don't want to have to guide her when it comes to being with me—she has to be able to feel it on her own.

Want it.

Need it.

Feed the desire that I know is inside both of us.

I'm on my back, a pillow propped up behind my head, allowing me to watch her next move—if she decides to make one, but when she doesn't, I decide to make it for her.

Reaching down, I pull the zipper of my jeans open and then remove my shirt, tossing it over the side of the bed.

Snow's eyes wander up the bed slowly, deliberately until they meet with mine and I let out a low chuckle.

Maybe it's because she hasn't been touched like this before that she doesn't know what to do. Perhaps, I *should* guide her; isn't that what a normal man would do?

It now dawns on me that I ask myself that question more than I should which only solidifies that I'm far from the norm and I'm quite fine with that.

Grunting, I tug at the leash. Snow lurches forward, losing her balance, and I watch as her hands struggle briefly as she uses them to prop herself up either side of my legs. She looks up at me from underneath the cascade of white hair that's fallen on her face, and I can almost swear that I see the smile curving her lips.

Of course, at this point, it could all be in my head, but I refuse to believe that.

I've had such vivid dreams of this exact moment that it's almost hard to fathom it's actually happening and not another dreamscape that I've wandered into.

The reality of it takes over me like a tidal wave crashing into coastal Japan. I quickly begin to reel her in, wrapping the leash tightly around my fist, until she's hovering above me, panting, and desperate for what's to come.

The pink nipples on her small, supple tits graze my bare chest when I give her leash another tug.

The sheer sensation of it starts to make my dick hard, but I won't let her know. Not just yet. She has to remember her discipline and earn that; no matter how desperately I want her right now.

I raise myself off the bed no more than two inches and brush my lips against hers.

Snow places her hands against my chest and pushes me away. I wrap the leash tighter around my fist and give it a hard jerk. When she yelps and comes dangerously close to crashing against me, I place a hand around the flesh of her minimally exposed neck and look into her eyes.

It takes a moment for them to come into focus, to see me again, but when they do it's almost like she's finally seeing me for the first time.

"Don't do that again," I warn her in a low tone. She nods and I lay back down on the bed, pulling her down against me.

By this point, I could fuck her through the goddamn mattress, but I want to be patient. I have to know that this will all be worth it in the end.

Worth means more to me than love and I've taken a huge risk with Snow being here.

I give her some leeway by letting the leash a little looser in my fist, and when she takes in a deep breath, I smile.

"Do you want this?" I ask her.

I do my best to mask the wheedling in my tone, but I need her to say yes more than anything.

More than the fucking air she breathes.

Which I'm more than willing to cut off again if she doesn't answer me the way I want her to.

"Yes," she whispers after what seems like a torturous century of time.

"This has to be our secret, okay? Just like when you got here," I remind her as I reach up and gently caress the side of her face.

"Our secret," she echoes as she waits.

I can see the innocence in her eyes, in the way she's sitting clumsily on top of me, and the only thing that I have the will for right now is to destroy it.

With a nod, I sit up and unclip the leash from her collar. She places her hands on my shoulders as I pull her against me, slide my hands up her bare skin, then quickly unbutton the collar from around her throat.

It will go back on when we're done because I'm not entirely sure that she's learned every lesson I want her to yet, however, I want this moment to be completely untethered.

After I've placed her collar on the nightstand next to my bed, I shift underneath her so that's she's straddling me properly. Her eyes widen slightly when I allow her to feel how hard she's made me, and I chuckle.

"I'll do my best to be gentle," I promise her before I pick her up off my body and set her on the bed next to me.

Snow looks afraid, excited, and maybe a little lost, but this is what she came for isn't it?

She found me and I can't let her go.

Not now.

Not ever.

I lay next to her and turn on my side, trailing a fingertip from her neck down to her tummy before I grip the inside of her thigh. She lets out a little yelp and I have to bite my grin back. I haven't even had the chance to do anything to her yet and she's already enjoying it or terrified of what's to come.

Either way, she's given herself to me to use by promising to never speak a word of this and what kind of man would I be to her if I let her down?

My fingers ease up on the flesh of her inner thigh as I gently reach over and rub her pussy through her panties. She's already wet with anticipation and that makes me feel good.

It tells me that my hands on her are something that she wants as much as I do, and I won't disappoint her.

I use the tip of my forefinger to push her panties to the side and begin to tease her by running it up and down her slit. She's so goddamn wet that if I'm not careful, I'll slip a finger into her before I mean to.

It would ruin the surprise of what I'm intending, though I know she can't be *that* innocent. She would have to know something about how life works between two people when they love each other.

Snow's legs begin to tremble as I continue the tease, then when she gets to the point where her breathing turns into whimpers, I pull my finger away and take her panties off.

She looks down at me but I'm careful to avoid her eyes. I can feel them on me and that's enough to let me know that she's entirely with me at this moment.

After I've crumpled up her panties and tossed them over the side of the bed, I move quickly, gently prying her legs open, then inhale her scent as deeply as I can.

I would imagine the sensation that comes over me is what high feels like, because I almost become drunk on it.

I use the tip of my tongue to tease her clit. Gently flicking at it, then pulling back each time she whimpers. It sounds almost more like sadness than euphoria which makes me wonder if she's lied to me about wanting to be here.

Taking a deep, intoxicating breath, I bring a finger up and gently press it against her slit. When Snow whimpers again, I begin to push it inside of her, careful not to break her barrier just yet.

That's something that I want my cock to do.

And she does too.

Whether she wants to admit it or not.

I move my tongue away from her clit and begin to push it into her wet, hot core. Again, I'm careful not to break her barrier.

Not when there are more emotions to share, more nerves to bring to life, more ... everything.

Snow reaches down and grips a fistful of my hair and I reach up instantly to twist her wrist.

"Have you earned that?" I ask her in a gruff tone as I glance up at her sharply.

"I'm sorry," she whispers.

I nod and let go of her wrist, then go back to her pussy. The taste is another euphoria all on its own. She tastes like wild blueberries—my favorite.

Snow arches her back slightly, bringing her body off the bed and I use it to my advantage. I reach underneath her and grip her ass cheeks, dig my fingernails into the flesh, as I hold her in place and continue to lap at her.

"Good girl," I whisper against her pussy as she begins to move her hips. Her body is giving her direction that will benefit us both.

Now and when the time comes.

Taking a deep breath, I allow her to lower herself back onto the bed, then push myself up with my fists, giving her a devilish grin.

"Is it still our secret?" I ask her, tilting my head to the side.

"Always," she breathes.

At the moment of her affirmation that this will "always" be ours, I get to my feet and push my jeans down, kicking them to the side, giving her a moment to look at my body.

Snow has never been able to look away from me—even when we first started this relationship.

We both knew that it was something that would eventually come back to haunt us if neither of us was able to keep the secrets I knew we'd share.

That was when I made a pact with her.

For every secret she promised to keep, I would allow her a meal.

She's earned two so far, so tomorrow will be a good day for her.

But tonight, belongs to me.

CHAPTER SIX

I hover over the beautiful, timid girl on my bed and smile when she reaches to put her hands on either side of my face.

The trembling hasn't stopped but neither has the longing in her eyes.

I'll give myself to her tonight because it's the right thing to do.

I take her hand and place it on my throbbing cock. She gently runs her hand down the length taking in every piece of flesh, every vein that's aching to explode for her.

In her.

When she glances over at me again, I tell myself to remain patient. While I don't want to do all of the work for her, I'll have to help get things started.

Reaching down, I wrap a hand around hers while I cross my other arm behind my neck. Snow rips her eyes away from me, completely transfixed by how my stomach is starting to shudder slightly at the sensation of what we're doing together.

She pries my hand away from hers, as she continues the up and down motion. She's gentle at first, the innocence shining through her clumsy movements, but when she gets a better hold of what she's doing, she begins to move her hand a little faster, tug a little harder, and elicits a pained groan from me.

"I'm sorry," she whispers, immediately letting go of my cock.

"It's okay," I reassure her as I push her hand back toward the task at hand. "I don't mind the pain."

And I don't because it's *her* inflicting it on me.

Had it been anyone else, I would have thrown them off my bed and out of my house, but Snow is and always has been different.

There's that word again, I think as I bring my arm around and cover my face with my hands. *Always.* The promise that I wanted—the one she swears she'll keep.

"Kenji?" Snow asks timidly, her hand still moving at a moderate enough pace to get me close to climax.

I use my hands to push my hair from my face as I look at her through lust-hazed eyes, my breathing becoming labored.

"Do you want me to stop?" she asks.

I want to say no, especially since she shows no signs of slowing down, but there's more to what we can have than just this.

"Please," I whisper in a trembling voice and she does.

KENJI

She sits back on the balls of her feet and I sit up, pull her toward me, then lay her on her back.

I want to be inside of her.

I *need* to know what it's like, and the time has finally come.

"I'll try not to hurt you," I say to Snow as I lean down and bite her lower lip. She nods as best as she can, completely unaware of how far I'm willing to go with her. That's when I use my knee to gently spread her legs open.

I reach down and grip my cock, but then have a second thought.

"I want you to do it," I say as I look into her eyes again.

"Do what?" she asks timidly.

"I want you to put me inside of you."

"How?"

I almost chuckle at her question, but this is no time for laughter. It's time to be the man she deserves, and I refuse to be anything less.

"Grab it and guide me," I tell her as I lean down and nip at her bottom lip again.

"What if I don't do it right?" she asks, the tremor returning to her tone.

"Then I will."

My tenor is strong, commanding, reassuring.

All of the things that I know she needs and wants but never knew until now.

Snow does as she's commanded and gets a firm hold

of my cock, spreads her legs a little wider and lets out a sigh as I begin to kiss the flesh of her neck.

One final gesture of kindness before I take what's mine and claim her forever.

When I feel the head of my cock resting against her opening, I push her hand away. I'm gentle in the manner I do it because I don't want her to think that she's done a bad job—I just need the foreplay to fucking end now.

I pull away from Snow, get to my knees, and grip her hips. One hard tug and she's so close to me that I can smell her wild blueberry cunt again. I smack the head of my cock against her clit a few times, watching her as she writhes against the bed, her hands digging into the sheets, and almost pulling them off the mattress.

When I'm sure she can't take being teased anymore, I begin to push inside of her.

Her knuckles turn white.

She tugs the sheets harder.

Her jaw tightens as she begins to grit her teeth.

And when I finally have forced my way into her innocent little hole, she lets out a groan that I'm sure neither of us knew that she was capable of.

"Good girl," I reassure her as I lean back down and hover over her. Snow moves her hands to my shoulders and braces herself damn near ignorant as to what I'm going to do to her.

I begin to roll my hips as gently as I can at first because I promised her that I would be gentle. I'm trying to keep from treating her like the animal that I'm training her to be because then she'll never allow me this moment again.

But when she tightens her core against my next thrust, I lose control. My senses are overcome by her obvious need of me and I begin to fuck her harder than I know I should.

Snow begins to yelp in pain.

She brought this on herself.

I had every intention of being good to her, but she forced me to act like this and now she has to pay the price.

"Kenji," she gasps out, as her fingernails begin to dig into my shoulders. I inhale sharply at the slight sting of her tearing my flesh, while telling myself that she's only claiming her due.

I tore her open and in return, she's attempting to return the favor.

I'm not angry at her for it.

I'd do the same thing if I were in her position, but I'm not and I realize now that it needs to change.

I pull out of Snow and grip her by the arms, roughly moving her on top of me once I lay on my back. She looks scared, nothing like the animal I was hoping she'd be, and I can't fault her for that.

After all, it's her first time and she wants to do as well as she can for me.

At least, that's my hope.

"Climb on," I command her in a gruff tone.

Snow looks down at my cock, sees the blood she's left on it and flits her eyes back toward me.

There's a renewed determination in her gaze now. Almost as if she wants to reclaim what I took from her but doesn't know how.

I grit my teeth and growl as I reach for her and bring her body on top of mine. I smack her thighs apart then settle her onto my cock and thrust up into her cunt.

She lets out a surprised sound—something between a moan and a gasp, and I do it again.

Over and over, until she falls against me unable to keep herself upright.

"Fuck me like you hate me," I grunt into her ear. "Because we both know that you do."

Snow continues her moans and gasps as I keep thrusting up into her. She's so fucking slick that my cock slips out of her momentarily, but I reach down and shove it back in.

I wrap my arms around her and keep thrusting my hips upward. The sound is almost as high inducing as the smell of her cunt.

Our flesh slapping together—the sound of her sloshing pussy as I continue to assault is more than I can bear.

My hips move faster, Snow groans louder, and just when I think I'm able to control myself again, my balls tighten and I come deep into her precious, ruined little hole.

I wrap a hand around her throat to keep her from

falling against me again as I close my eyes and attempt to regain my bearings.

After a few moments of steady breathing, I pull her down toward me and kiss her roughly, taking her lower lip in between my teeth and holding her in place.

She lets out another whimper and this time, I know it's one of pain, but I don't want her to move.

Not until she's been properly secured again.

When I feel a tear roll down her face and land against my cheek, I relent and let go of her lip.

My hand stays firmly gripped around her throat as I lean over to the nightstand and retrieve her collar.

I chuckle when she chokes back a sob.

I guess she thought this half-hearted performance would have been enough to make me see her as a human being, but it was only our first time.

Things in my home have to be worked for, and that's one of them.

I sit up, wrap an arm securely around her waist and hold her close to me as I hold the collar around her neck again and snap the buttons back into place.

As I let go of Snow's throat once the reminder of my ownership of her has been properly fixed, I decide that I want to spend the rest of the night in bed alone.

"Back to the corner, little pup," I tell her, with a tired wave of my hand. "In the morning, you can have breakfast."

Snow's choked sobs come in waves as she slides off the side of the bed and retrieves her panties from the floor. Once she pulls them on, I watch as she wipes her eyes with the back of her hands as she walks out of my room.

Turning onto my stomach, I let out a wide, tired yawn.

Tomorrow she gets to have two meals and we both know that's something that she can be grateful for.

And then the lessons can start again.

CHAPTER SEVEN

Before I leave the house the next morning, I'm sure to serve Snow her breakfast.

I've made her homemade hash browns and a couple of slices of toast with butter. I mixed everything neatly inside of the blender so that it will be easier for her to lick up, then spilled the concoction into her food bowl. I was also kind enough to fill her water one as well even though that's not considered part of her meals.

However, I know that if I want her ready for another night of discipline, she'll have to be strong.

"I'm heading to work now, lunch is in the fridge, okay? The red bowl with the saran wrap around it," I tell her as I watch her crawl toward her breakfast. She looks up at me with her hopeful eyes and I lean down, tilt her chin up toward me, and kiss her gently on the lips.

It's what she always yearns for before I leave, and sometimes, I don't have it in me to do it.

But after last night, I figure she deserves a little affection.

"Thank you," she tells me softly when she reaches her bowl. I nod as I linger long enough to watch her tongue begin to lap the contents out before I turn and walk out of the house.

Today is going to be a better day than yesterday. I can feel it in my bones.

"Hey, you know what I've been dying to ask you?" I say to Sariah as I walk into the shop. She glances up at me with a curious smile on her face.

I get it, though.

I'm usually not so talkative in the mornings so she knows that something's up.

"Hm?"

"Where the hell are you from? Your accent is pretty," I remark as I stop by her desk and rest an elbow against it.

Sariah chuckles as she shakes her head slightly, leans back in her chair and grins at me.

"Wellington."

"Oh. Where is that?"

"New Zealand, Kenji," she replies with a good-natured laugh.

"And what made you end up here?" I press as I glance toward the door when the bells ring. I nod at Carter who breezes by the both of us with a wave.

"To live the American Dream," she says wryly.

I grin at her, then pat her shoulder before I walk into the back of the shop.

I fish around my pocket for my keyring, flip through them until I find the one that unlocks the door to my room, then slip it in and turn until I hear the lock click.

"Hey, man! You got a sec?" I call out to Carter before I walk through my door.

"Yep!"

"Be right there," I call back as I step into my room and flip the lights on. I'll have to ask Sariah how many people I have booked for today.

When she got here and realized how shitty I am at keeping my appointment book maintained, she took it over, and hoards the goddamn thing like it's made of gold.

It's nice to have a helping hand, though, and she's always been nothing but helpful since the day we hired her.

I decide not to set up my room right away since I don't know when my first client of the day will arrive. After I shrug my jacket off and drop it onto my chair, I scratch my neck as I walk out of the room and take the few steps towards Carter's door.

I knock and wait patiently until he looks up at me. He hates being interrupted when he's fiddling with his tattoo gun, but I understand it. They can be fickle machines sometimes and you always want to provide the best for your paying customers.

"What can I do you for so early in the goddamn

day, Kenji?" he asks, after he snaps the final rubber band into place, then looks up at me with a grin.

I return the grin as I lean a hand against his door and cross my legs at the ankles. I wait as I watch his expression go from a playful version of *what the fuck now* to *you're hiding something* before I step in and close the door firmly behind me.

"What's up, Kenj?" he asks curiously as I reach for one of the stools he keeps in the room. Usually the college girls that aren't regulars come with a gaggle of friends and the stools are for them to pile onto while the brave one of the bunch tries to sit under a machine of nonstop needles for a few hours.

"I finally broke her in last night," I tell him, the grin on my face widening.

"No shit," he says with a laugh as he gets to his feet and we slap palms. "I was wondering why you weren't wearing that Miura scowl when I walked in, but it looks like the pussy fairy finally dropped by your place."

I groan and let out a laugh trying to hide the embarrassment. I wasn't sure what I expected him to say, but *pussy fairy* definitely wasn't on the list.

"How was it?" he asks as he goes back to setting up his station and I shrug. I don't know what he's looking for in an answer, but he knows damn well what it feels like.

"Tight," I finally say when I decide on an answer and Carter chuckles.

"And how's the training going?"

"That's actually going pretty good," I say thoughtfully as I slip my hands into my pocket. "Yesterday she slipped, but I don't think she does it often."

"Slipped how?" he presses absentmindedly as he sprays down one of his metal trays.

"I came home, and she wasn't in the corner, but it didn't bother me too much."

Carter looks up at me incredulously and I know that he believes that about as much as I do.

"When do I get to work on her again?" he asks through a yawn as he sets his tray down and picks up another one.

Carter's been eager to get back to the simple, delicate modifications we've been doing on Snow. I watch with a smile as he places his next tray down and reaches for a folder instead. But it's not just any folder; it's a special one.

The one that we use to keep all of the ideas and sketches of how Snow will look when we're finally done with her.

I reach over and swipe it from his grasp. As I flip it over and look at the back of the sketch, I sigh before I had it back.

"What's wrong?" he asks curiously as I hold the paper out to him. I wait until he tucks it away neatly into the folder, then goes back to his obsessive tray washing.

"I don't know. I thought by leaving her topless for a while that her back would start to heal."

"The stitches bust or something?"

I shake my head, "Nah. Those were done tight

enough to hold. I think she's been picking at them when I haven't been home."

"Well, just say when and I'll swing by and redo them. She has to be healed up before I can get back in there and starting putting the implants into place. How else is she going to be able to fly?" he asks slyly.

I rub my chin thoughtfully.

Snow's been doing a lot of things it seems when I've been at work or out trying to clear my head, and it seems that I'm only now starting to realize it.

"Kenji?" Carter presses with a chuckle.

"Whenever you have time," I reply with a shrug.

Carter nods as he wipes down the back of the tray and I know the conversation is over.

He helps me break in Snow when she's disobedient by treating her like more of an animal than I do. We've been modifying her slightly too and I think she secretly likes it.

Nothing too drastic, but just enough to make her look like my dream girl and we always numb her first.

Pain isn't part of the lessons unless I delve them out to her, and last night, we both learned that pain only comes with pleasure.

Snow deserves to be loved and I do it in my own way.

"Hey, New Zealand!" I call out as I walk out of Carter's room, "What's on the menu for today?"

Sariah lets out a high-pitched giggle and I can hear the top desk drawer being opened, then closed. A few

KENJI

moments later, the sounds of her flipflops slapping against the shop door greets my ears.

And when she enters my room, she stays silent—something that Sariah has never done before.

"What's up?" I ask, as I sit in my chair and lean down. I reach for the large case beneath my station and place it on the recliner in front of me. Once I've unclicked the case and pushed the lid open, I look up and give her my full attention.

She's giving me an icy stare and I'm wondering if maybe she eavesdropped on my little catch up with Carter.

Don't be disobedient, I will her silently while I plaster a huge, faux smile on my face. *Disobedient little pups always require training.*

"I don't want her here," she says in an even tone, turning the book toward me and pointing at a name.

I squint at the book, but because she's still by the door, I can't make heads or tails of who the fuck she's pointing at.

"Okay," I reply with a shrug as I go back to setting my machine up. "Who and how come?"

I begin to fiddle with the gun as I snap pieces into place. Sariah stays silent until I glance up at her again, this time with genuine curiosity.

"Hazel Miller. I don't want her in this fucking shop."

I blink rapidly a few times.

I don't recall her paying the rent for this building or writing the paychecks to tell me who is and who isn't allowed inside, however, there's not much that usually bothers her so ...

"Okay, so that's the who, now I need to know the how come," I say as I set the machine down and push my hair behind my ears.

"This bitch is the reason my brother got sent to Irongate," she replies through grit teeth before she spins on her heel and walks out of my room.

CHAPTER EIGHT

My appointments came and went without so much as another peep from Sariah. I called Hazel and canceled, telling her that I had double booked her and to come back in about a week and a half.

Considering Sariah's brother gets out of prison in a week, I think that would be the perfect time for her to take a few days off and get reacquainted with him.

I'll sneak Hazel in and out, and she'll never know. Plus, I'll make damn sure that the butterfly is finished this time before I permanently ban her from the shop.

I haven't decided what excuse I'll give, but more than likely it'll be about her running out on me the first time.

It seems reasonable enough in my opinion, anyway.

"Let me give you a ride home, New Zealand."

She glances up at me as she finishes fixing up the front desk for the evening and nods once to let me know that she accepts my chivalrous offer.

It's so rare to see Sariah in such a bad mood, that I scratch the back of my head nervously. I feel awkward standing there waiting for her to collect her belongings, since I'm used to her sarcastic attitude and witty one-liners.

But Hazel Miller has turned Sariah Taylor into an angry girl—and it's a new experience for me.

"See you guys tomorrow," Carter says as he walks out of the shop quickly. It seems that he's bothered by it too but he's not good at hiding his emotions so he just makes a run for it when he can.

Sariah finally gets to her feet and grabs her shawl off the back of her chair, purse strapped over her shoulder and inches around me so that she can lead the way out of the shop.

There are certain things in life that really aren't the business of others, Snow being mine, yet I'm dying to know what kind of man her brother is and what exactly happened with Hazel to land him at Irongate.

Sariah waits patiently by the front door as I step into the cool, night air and lock up. She's not going to be an easy one to break, but I have every confidence that I can at least put a crack into her tough girl armor.

Even if it's a small one.

All cracks eventually spider into bigger ones, breaking down the foundations they're meant to hold together, and maybe then she'll tell me what the fucking deal is.

We walk across the street to the parking lot that's empty of all cars but mine, and I unlock the passenger side door, holding it open, then closing it behind her once she's comfortably inside.

"Nice car, Kenji," she says after I've slid into the passenger seat and I cast her a grin.

I'm quite proud of my Dodge Charger SXT, and it's nice that someone else seems to be as well. It's got a shine to its black paint, an extremely comfortable leather seat interior, and faster than a most cop cars on the road today.

I don't use this one to drag race, though I do like to show it off when those come together.

"Thanks, kid," I say as I put the key in the ignition and the engine roars to life.

She shakes her head fondly and lets out a sigh as she straps her seatbelt across her body, and I chuckle.

"I'll go slow, Grandma," I tease her as I look both ways then pull out of the parking lot.

Sariah reaches over and swats my arm and I grin at her before I turn my eyes back toward the road.

"Where do you live?" I ask as I roll my window down and reach for a cigarette.

"Crenshaw."

"Cool, I know where that is, just tell me when to stop," I tell her before I slip the smoke between my teeth. I push the lighter button on the console as I ease up at the red light we've rolled up to.

For now, the car is silent and I'm only aware of her again when she nudges me and nods toward the lighter. Apparently, it popped already but I was too lost wherever the hell my mind wandered off to, to notice.

"Thanks," I say as I retrieve it and hold it to the end of my cigarette. I puff a couple of times until it's lit then replace the lighter and rub my forehead with my thumb.

"So, have you talked to your brother about applying at the shop?" I ask. It'll be an easy segue into what I really want to know and I'm sure she'll let her guard down a little if she assumes this is a business discussion as opposed to the interrogation I feel building inside of me.

"Yeah," she replies. I can see her nod out of the corner of my eye and chuckle when she waves away the billow of smoke that's drifted toward her.

"And?" I ask as I use the button on my door console to open her window slightly.

"Thanks, Kenji," she says as she stifles a cough, "He said he's pumped that someone is willing to give him a chance to learn."

I take a drag of my smoke.

I like to teach.

Snow learns discipline from me and...

"What's his name?" I ask Sariah curiously.

"Hudson."

And Hudson will learn how to hone his craft from me, I reason as I blow a stream of smoke out of the corner of my mouth.

"It'll be cool to have another artist at the shop," I say conversationally. "Besides, I don't judge people on what they've done or where they've been. Everyone deserves a fair shake if you ask me."

KENJI

Sariah takes a deep breath, then lets it out slowly. I can't help but wonder if she's caught on to where I'm trying to lead the conversation, but if she does, she refuses to take the bait.

"Thanks, boss," she says softly.

I glance at her again and smile before I shake my head.

She's not going to give it up tonight, and that's okay.

Hudson will have to tell Carter and me what he did on his application anyway.

"Next stop, Crenshaw!" I say as cheerfully as I can to lighten the mood. Sariah clears her throat and then the rest of the way to her house is marred in silence.

And that's okay.

Sometimes, silence can be a person's best friend.

CHAPTER NINE

I didn't go straight home after I dropped off Sariah. Instead, I opted to drive around town for a while.

Los Angeles after dark isn't the best place to wander around, but considering I'm in my car, I know that if any trouble arises, I can either mow it down or make a hasty escape.

I run a hand back through my hair as the night air drifts in and out of the car. A glance into the rear-view mirror tells me that I look like a *Pantene* commercial and it makes me chuckle slightly.

That's the thing about being exotic, though. Something as slight as nature sending a breeze by can make one look like they're meant to be special.

With a sigh, I reach for the pack of smokes I tossed into Sariah's seat after she got out of the car.

I don't know why I didn't press her for more information about Hudson, but I guess I would feel the same way if someone tried to stick their nose into my affairs.

Deep breath and keep driving, Kenji.

I roll up to a stop sign on the corner of Slauson Avenue and Crenshaw Boulevard and light my cigarette. Inhaling deeply, I roll my neck on my shoulders and glance around the otherwise empty street.

In a neighborhood like this, vacant roads are never really a good thing. It could mean that something ominous is about to happen, or more than likely it already has.

I lean my head back against the rest of my seat as I wait for the light to turn green, but another minute goes by and it stays red.

"I'm not in the mood for this shit tonight," I mutter as I sit up. I glance both ways, up and down the intersection, before I press down on the gas pedal and roll through.

There's no possible way that any cops will be out tonight because if they were, the sirens would already be blaring, or the streets would be lined with unmarked cars.

Suffice it to say, I need to get the fuck out of here sooner rather than later.

Gripping my cigarette between my teeth, I glance into the rear-view again to see if anyone is behind me. As soon as I see that no one else is on the road, I turn the steering wheel hard to the left and do a U-turn, speeding all the way back in the direction that I came from, and clear out of supposed gangland territory.

I'll have to poke Sariah again in the morning and

KENJI

figure out why the hell she thought this would be a good place to live in.

———

I've been sitting in the driveway of my home with my eyes closed and the window still open. I haven't cut the engine to the car yet because I don't feel like going inside.

The wonder of why someone like New Zealand would live in a neighborhood where she would clearly be seen as a target bugs the shit out of me.

How many times has she been able to walk down the street and feel safe? Who is she friends with? Does anyone protect her? *Is that really the best place for Hudson to be when he gets out of Irongate?*

I groan as I run a hand irritably over my face.

The only priority I should worry about is the one inside that's waiting for me, but I feel like it's my duty to protect my employees as well.

The problem is that I can't be seen in that neighborhood. Not with the tattoos I have; I'll be mistaken for something I'm not, but secretly would get a rush from.

Do I want to put myself in danger for someone other than Snow?

Not particularly.

I just know that I won't be able to fucking sleep properly if I don't.

A plan begins to formulate in my mind, and I step out of the car, leaving the engine still running. No one in *this* fancy neighborhood would ever dream of stealing a car; especially one that belongs to me.

I'm seen as enigmatic and I revel in the knowledge that most of the people that live on my street are too afraid of me to approach my door, or even wave hello when I step outside.

When I reach the front door, I lean over and pick up a fake stone that holds an extra house key, pry it open, then remove it so I can let myself in.

What I'm planning to do isn't going to sit well with Snow, but she should be grateful that I'm giving her the chance to go outside. It's something she hasn't earned yet, but I have to make sure that my staff are safe at all costs and this is the only way I know how to do it.

I head into the living room quickly and toward the closet where her leash sits on the top shelf. Once I've secured that, I leave her in the corner like the good little pup that she is and walk back to my bedroom.

I don't want her to do this the way I have her dressed in my home because it will just give an excuse to have her taken from me.

Or worse yet; probably raped or killed.

That's not acceptable.

Not when I've been working so hard to keep her in Los Angeles with me.

I pull open the top drawer on my dresser and pull out one of my shirts and a pair of basketball shorts. After that, I go to the closet and drop to my knees to rummage around in the boxes I keep on the floor.

Once I find the box I'm looking for, I shake my head ruefully.

This was supposed to be for a special time. One where she proved to me that she learned every lesson I had wanted to instill in her and that she'd be willing to trounce down a street with me to show off the completion of her lessons.

Instead, I'm breaking my own rules and pushing her to a reward that she still seems miles away from.

I crack my neck as I get to my feet and walk back into the living room. I take the few steps toward Snow and crouch down next to her.

"Get dressed," I say to her softly as I place the items on the floor. "We have somewhere that we need to be."

CHAPTER TEN

I glance over at Snow who's now in the passenger seat, knees pulled up to her chest, arms wrapped around them, watching the world go by outside of her window.

I can't remember the last time she was outside, though I hope she appreciates it even though it's not in the daylight.

Leaning over I place a hand on her kneepads that I had her slip on, to which she lowers her eyes curiously at the gesture, then quickly steals a glance at me. I wait until she looks again before I take my hand away and chuckle.

"Don't be afraid, okay?" I tell her softly. "I promise that I won't let anyone hurt you."

Snow nods as she turns her gaze toward the windshield. She doesn't know Los Angeles because she's not from around here.

She's from somewhere near the Rocky Mountains and she's mostly used to skiing and country life.

Being in a place like this was a shellshock to her when she arrived, but I think she does better with me than she did on her own.

Freedom was something she gained from her parents when her father beat her one too many times and Child Protective Services took her away. I think she was twelve at the time and she aged out six years later. From our first conversation, if I remember correctly, she told me that she got a part-time job at some ski place near the mountains and lived in a tiny, one-bedroom apartment.

Stumbling around on *Facebook* one day, she came across the tattoo shop and messaged the page.

Turns out that Snow was a huge fan of our work after seeing a feature in *Inked Magazine* and was hoping to get some work done by Carter.

I had been on vacation at the time, visiting my mother in Tokyo when Snow arrived, but apparently, she grilled Carter about me.

She told him she thought that I was "cute" and he somehow managed to convince her to stay until I got back a few days later.

I think he gave her a job cleaning up the shop after hours and set her up in a semi-decent motel for a while.

When I arrived back at LAX, he picked me up with Snow and Sariah in the back of his truck.

The introduction, while welcomed, was something I don't even remember because once I set eyes on her, I knew I wanted her for my own.

And when she looked at me the same way, with a

shy smile on her lips, and the gentlest blush to her cheeks, it made it obvious that she felt the same way.

At first, everything was normal.

I took her out sight-seeing around Los Angeles, scooted her around Hollywood, and even took her to a couple of big-time premieres. I think she changed her mind about her Rocky Mountain Life after that because she asked me if it would be possible to continue working at the shop as our cleaning lady.

But I had other plans for Snow, and while we're still working on them, she does her best and gets rewarded when she succeeds.

What I subject her to is always done out of love and never malice like Uncle Abner would do to her, and I think that's why she's a little more trusting with me.

Not that I really knew him, only stories that I heard from my father. He was so angry that his sister Hina, married an American man that we spent the day of their wedding back in Japan.

Hell, I didn't even know that Snow was my cousin until she spilled to me one night about all of the abuse she suffered as a child at the hands of her father.

That's when it all clicked.

And since Dad made damn sure that I never spent time at Hina and Abner's house growing up, I didn't think anything of it when I found out.

To me, Snow is just another perfect, broken girl in the world and she's mine to protect.

Tonight though, that may change on a completely epic level, but Snow knows that no matter what happens, when this is over, she's going to come back home with me.

I've parked the car at the end of Slauson Avenue and cut the engine. My fingers are drumming nervously along the steering wheel wondering if maybe I should get a little closer to Sariah's place.

I run a hand back through my hair then whip my gaze in Snow's direction when I hear the passenger side door open. She smiles at me before she steps out, and I watch as she walks around to the front of my car and waits patiently.

Taking a deep breath, I turn the key in the ignition so that I can brighten up the street with the headlights. I'll help her at first, but the rest she has to do on her own.

Stepping out of my vehicle, I press the alarm button to lock the doors, then walk around to Snow who lifts her neck and waits. The leash in my hand seems heavier than it should, and while I know that this is for the greater good, I'm still having trouble reconciling the potential sacrifice of it all.

"We're going to go for a stroll, pup," I tell her softly as I clip the leash to her collar. "I'll take you to the end of the street, but when we get to Crenshaw Boulevard, you're on your own."

Snow pushes her hair behind her ears and places her hands on her hips. I can see the defiance in her stance, and I hope she isn't planning on giving me any trouble or I'll just end up dragging her the entire way to Sariah's front door.

"Are you ready?" I ask in a stern tone, giving her leash a tug and the defiance disappears almost instantly. Her hands drop to her sides as she reaches down to pull up on the waistband of the obviously too big for her shorts, then drops down to her knees.

"Good girl," I commend her as I give the leash a tug and she follows behind me as closely as she can.

I take a deep breath and keep my eyes forward, though occasionally glance around. I'm not afraid of anyone here or any potential situation I may find myself in, but Snow is another matter entirely.

I fear for *her* safety because she belongs in this neighborhood about as much as Sariah does.

I shake my head as I let out a breath. I hate that some places seem to be subjected to such blatant scrutiny because I know firsthand how it feels to be looked down on for being from somewhere else entirely.

However, tonight, the streets belong to me and if I have to, I'll remove my shirt to gain respect and have a bounty placed on my head.

It's the least I can do for the girl I love that's already suffered so much.

Draw attention away from the pup on the leash and onto me where it would rightfully belong.

A boom of raucous laughter greets us both when we walk by a seemingly vacant house. On the porch and broken stairs sits a group of young men watching us with amusement in their eyes.

I grin at them and nod as I give the leash a tug and we continue on our way.

One of them yells after us that it's the first time he's ever seen something like this. Another claps and asks if walking her like this makes fucking her from behind better.

Both are valid, in statement and inquiry, but neither deserving of any kind of acknowledgement besides the one already given.

I can see the end of the street in sight and the intersection looming under the flickering streetlight.

Snow stops moving for a moment and I give the leash a hard tug, causing her to pitch forward and damn near land on her face. When she looks up at me and sees the stern look in my eyes, she takes a deep breath and keeps moving.

I know she must be tired by now because it's the first time I've ever walked her, however, all lessons are learned with some kind of pain and she's been training for this moment for longer than she knows.

Crenshaw Boulevard.

The sign is above us now and it's time for another test.

"Go to fifteen sixty-seven and knock on the door. Sariah lives there. I want you to bring her back to this intersection. I'll explain when we get back to the house, okay?"

I lean down and unclip the leash and smack Snow on the ass to send her on her way.

Hopefully, she'll make it to Sariah and back again.

And if she doesn't, then I'll find a way to forgive myself for the danger I sent her into for someone that really shouldn't even matter.

CHAPTER ELEVEN

I'm sitting on the porch with the guys from earlier. After thirty minutes had gone by and neither Sariah nor Snow had come back to the intersection, I decided to cut my losses and at least have a somewhat decent night out.

The thing is that I won't just leave Snow here. I'll go retrieve her if I have to, but I want to give her the opportunity to come back to me herself.

"So, what's your name?" one of the guys asks me.

"Kenji," I reply, taking his hand and giving it a quick shake.

"What neighborhood are you from?" another asks, also extending his hand toward me.

"Baldwin Hills," I reply with a sly smile and he chuckles.

It's just outside of the Crenshaw district limits and that's why I know this is a bad place to be, but after World War Two, it became a predominately Japanese-

American neighborhood, so I kind of felt right at home when I settled here.

Granted, it's not that way anymore but I tend to keep to myself, so my neighbors don't seem to mind my presence.

"Why were you walking that girl like that?"

I glance up at the one young kid that's teetering on the railing of the porch and shrug, "How else are you gonna teach 'em?"

That response evokes a round of laughter from all of my newfound pals, and I force a smile onto my face. I don't like talking about Snow this way but I kind of want to keep them in my good graces in the event that I ever find trouble here.

That's not to say that everyone from this side of town is a hoodlum; hell, they're probably some of the most upstanding citizens this side of Los Angeles just having a guys' night out, but I doubt it.

The same way they would doubt me if they ever came to Baldwin Hills.

Not that I have a bad reputation where I live. I just happen to know that there are more whispers and whatnots about who I am and why I've decided to live in their self-proclaimed glorious little neighborhood.

It's a shame too considering that most of the people that live around me are Japanese; born and bred on the island that came here for a better life.

Fuck, I think as I glance down at the time on my phone. Thoughts of the *American Dream* make me think of Sariah and now, time tells me that it's been

KENJI

another ten minutes since I've sat down to shoot the shit.

"It was cool hanging out, but I have to get my girls now," I say to them as I get to my feet.

"You got more than one?" the young kid asks, and I grin at him.

"No. One is just a friend, more like a little sister, and I sent my girl to go get her. But you know how women can be," I state with an eye roll.

The statement elicits another round of laughter as I walk down the sole step below me, then give them a nod as I head toward the intersection.

I shove my hands in my pockets as I cross the street towards Crenshaw Boulevard, and whistle quietly on my way toward Sariah's front door.

Almost instantly, the flash of red and blue lights appears from somewhere behind me and I glance over my shoulder to see about three cop cars racing up the road.

I stop walking for a moment, curiosity taking over me, then turning sour and almost choking me on the stench of it when they stop in front of Sariah's door.

Two of the officers walk out of their cars and jog up the front steps of her home, while the other four that have now exited their vehicles respectively, begin to swing their flashlights up and down the street.

I take a step back and slip behind a hedge before one of the officers has a chance to catch me in his beam of light.

My heart begins to race a little faster in my chest as I watch the scene unfold curiously.

And when I see Sariah step out of the house, her arms wrapped protectively around Snow's shoulders, I get a sick feeling in the pit of my stomach.

The promise of always has been shattered into the fucking lie that I knew it always had been. I know that and accept it when I see a female officer climb the steps and help Snow down.

But I'm sure of it when Sariah glances down the street, and one of the larger officers somehow manages to see me.

The moment she points in my direction, I take a deep breath and a few steps back. When a light suddenly begins to blind me as it begins to lob closer to me, I turn on my heel and run.

I guess Snow wanted a way out of this.

She lied to me and told me that it would be our secret always and as my face slams into the pavement and the officer violently yanks my arms behind my back, I know that I'll never be able to forgive her for this.

"You're under arrest for suspicion of kidnapping," he barks into my ear and I can't help but let out a laugh as I press my forehead against the dirty gravel.

The one thing that never crossed my mind that would happen, finally has.

I guess Carter was right.

Karma *does* love to kick me in the balls.

EPILOGUE

The loud scraping of chairs always makes me grit my teeth. I hate when the new fish arrive because they don't ever know how to behave.

They think that by being the loudest, most raucous motherfuckers they can be, that it will set fear in the rest of us that have been here for a while.

I shake my head as I look down at the cards in my hand, pack them neatly together, and place them face down on the table.

"I fold," I say to Benjiro who smirks and glances at me over the top of his cards.

"Are you ever going to play your fucking cards, Kenji? You fold every goddamn game."

"I don't like to lose," I reply simply with a shrug.

"You must have lost at some point to end up here," Akira says dryly.

I glance to my left at the young man with the bright bodysuit of tattoos peeking through his black jumper.

In any other normal situation, I would have reached over and backhanded him, but Irongate isn't a normal place and some behaviors have to be checked outside the prison walls.

"Touché," I state as aloofly as I can.

Benjiro chuckles as he drops his cards on the table then looks at Akira expectantly who lets out a groan. He shows his hand which I could have honestly beat had I just played to the end, and the head of our little prison gang laughs as he rubs his hands together.

"That's two weeks of laundry. Wanna go for another one?" he asks as he leans his forearms on the table and smirks at Akira.

"I still don't know why the fuck it's all me when he keeps folding," he grumbles as he reaches for the cards and begins to shuffle them.

"Because he's smart enough to know when he's beat."

I run a hand back through my hair as I lean back in my uncomfortable, white plastic chair and look over at the line of society's latest fuckups being escorted to their pods.

If that were true, I would have let Snow go home when she asked me to, but I couldn't. I felt too strongly for her and I had every reason to believe that she felt the same way about me.

I was wrong.

An assumption that I'll be paying for, for the next five years of my life.

"Kenji tell me something," Benjiro begins conversationally as he waits for Akira to deal our cards out.

"Yeah?" I ask, turning my attention back to him.

"Why did you let pussy bring you down? There is a hell of lot more things that could have sent you here; why a girl?"

I shrug, "She was special to me, man."

"Was?" he asks as he arches an eyebrow and a knowing smile creases his lips.

Was.

I repeat the sentiment to myself and come to the realization that I've shaken off the feelings I had for Snow.

It only took six months into my sentence to do so, but it's also six months of my life that I'll never get back with another five years to go.

I can't let her wander around confidently telling her lies to people, making them believe them, as she did with me when I'm the only one bearing the weight of our punishment.

She should be in here with me, or at the very least, a little cage of her own.

One where when bad little pups act up, they're banished to until they're ready to repent and do as their master commands.

"Yeah," I confirm after a thoughtful moment of silence, "Was."

Akira clears his throat loudly as he begins to deal out the cards. I look down at the ones being tossed at me and begin to gather them into my hands, thoughts of revenge burning through my mind.

"Hey," Benjiro says, demanding my attention. I look up at him and see the look in his eyes that he first gave me when I arrived. The same one that they used to scope me out with and try to understand if I was one of them or just another wannabe.

When they realized that I was neither, they decided for me.

"Don't let it go," he tells me wisely. "Five years of a man's life gone based on the lies of a bitch for no other reason than she was tired after going for a little walk is not forgivable."

I nod because he's right.

There's nothing that Snow could say to me now or ever again that would make me forgive her or not seek some kind of recompense.

Sixty-six months is what the court gave me, and that was only because she refused to testify.

But once I explained to Benjiro why I was here and had the absolute bright idea to mention Hudson, he told me to wait. That he would bring him to me.

We had a quick meeting and I told him what needed to be done.

I told him about his fucking sister and about how she gave me up to the cops because of the lying cunt I kept in my house.

The one I provided for, loved like I had never loved anyone before in my life; the one that turned on me when the opportunity presented itself.

And when he left Irongate, he knew that he would have to fulfill his mission. He didn't have a choice. Akira reminded him that there are many like "us" all over Los Angeles and if Snow hadn't been dealt with within the year, he'd have to pay the price for her.

Sariah too.

As I glance at the cards in my hand, I suddenly feel my luck starting to change.

Fuck karma.

I have someone out there ready to get them both for me.

And until the moment comes that I can walk out of the gates and piss on their graves for doing this to me, I'll wait with the fire of vengeance burning in my heart.

"I call," I say to Benjiro with a big smile on my face.

Luck is on my side, even if time isn't.

And if Hudson fails?

Well, I'll have plenty of time with my new brothers here to figure out a way to get those bitches back myself.

ABOUT YOLANDA OLSON

Yolanda Olson is a USA Today Bestselling and award-winning author. Born and raised in Bridgeport, CT where she currently resides, she usually spends her time watching her favorite channel, Investigation Discovery. Occasionally, she takes a break to write books and test the limits of her mind. Also an avid horror movie fan, she likes to incorporate dark elements into the majority of her books.

You can keep in touch with her on:

- facebook.com/yolandasendlesswords
- twitter.com/SymphonyYolanda
- instagram.com/ihateyolandaolson

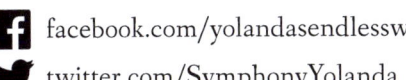

MORE BOOKS BY YOLANDA:

The Lies Between Us
Death Blooms
Scavengers

Sign up for Yolanda's newsletter here.

COTERIE

BY

ALLY VANCE

BLURB

These desires that should tear us apart only draw us closer together. Blood binds, desire unites, and secrecy protects us. But what happens when the secrets become too much and the seams that hold them start to split? Our family is hanging by a thread, and at any moment it could snap. The consequences of my actions weigh heavily on my shoulders. It's not just me who could get hurt, all three of us could suffer for my actions. The snowball is rolling and it's gaining speed, and I've no way to stop it before it collides with our family. We can either adapt, endure, and survive, or be forever crushed by the avalanche.

PROLOGUE
ASTON

There's a wrongness within me, something that can't be cured or erased. It runs deeper than my skin and has spread like poison through my mind. Abandonment threw responsibility on my shoulders at an early age and love became warped with desire.

When I was eighteen, our dad went overseas on holiday and never came back, leaving me with my thirteen year old twin siblings, Sean and Sonea. He isn't dead, he just didn't care enough about his kids and was probably too busy fucking some woman he met over there to come home. I had to get a second job to support them because there was no way in hell I'd let them be taken from me. I was old enough, and I could take care of them. Besides, I love them too much. I couldn't lose them to the system, just because our dad is a waste of fucking space who decided whatever he left behind wasn't worth coming back to.

It's been eight years since he turned his back on us,

and in that time I've watched Sean and Sonea grow up in a way I'd never have seen if I hadn't become their surrogate parent. I didn't get to go to college, and every day I blame him for taking that choice away from me; however, when Sean and Sonea come home from their own schools, I know I wouldn't change who I had to become. I gave up everything for them, but I'll never regret keeping them when our wastrel father decided not to bother.

CHAPTER ONE

SONEA

Walking through the front door to the only place I'll ever call home, the familiar scent of the house washes over me, and I inhale deeply. Aston isn't home. His car is still in the drive but the alarm has been set. I shouldn't be surprised he's not here; I'm home a day earlier than I planned, and I didn't tell him I was coming back today. The semester ended sooner than initially intended. Everyone in our class was ahead of schedule, and there was no point in starting anything new so close to the winter break, so we were allowed home.

Sean won't be arriving for a couple more days, and I'm so excited to see him. It kills me to attend a different school than him, but he got a partial scholarship at one of the best engineering schools, and I was accepted elsewhere. I know it hurts him to be separated, but while we are still two halves of the same whole, we each had our own dreams to chase, and his led him over a thousand miles away from where mine took me.

It's pretty late, and I don't know when I can expect Aston to get home. I could text him, but that would ruin the surprise of me being home early, and it gives me the extra time alone to unpack and get settled. Heading into the kitchen, I grab a can of soda and shoulder my bag again before making my way upstairs. I need to wash off the train ride and freshen up. I let out a yawn and decide to surprise Aston in the morning instead.

As the water eases the long journey from my muscles, I relax and think about the upcoming holiday and how good it will be to have all my family here. I couldn't make it home during the Thanksgiving break, so it's been months since I saw either of them. Soaping up the body puff, I lather my skin, rubbing at every inch of my body. Eventually, I slow my vigorous scrubbing and reflect on the true reason why I didn't make it home, not the excuse about too much schoolwork that I gave to Aston and Sean.

Over the years I've looked up to Aston, admiring him for being everything I ever needed when Sean and I were growing up. He never tried to hide what dad did, telling us the truth instead of lying like most people would. I've watched him work himself half to death to pay the bills and help in any way he could with our schoolwork. When it came to college applications, he supported us through the process, even though I could tell it hurt him to see us accepted, having had to shelve his own dreams to see us accomplish ours.

All I've ever wanted is to make Aston proud and happy. Shame burns in my belly and heat floods south when I think about one of the last times I saw him, shortly before I returned to college after the summer break. My fingers move unbidden to mingle with the juices pooling between my thighs.

Sometimes I wish we had a bigger house, I gripe mentally when I try the bathroom door and find that Sean is using the shower. Great. The only other bathroom with a shower is the en suite in Aston's room, which is the bedroom that used to belong to our dad when he still lived here. Sighing, I make my way along the hallway to his room and walk into the empty bedroom. I dart across to the closed en suite door, and pulling it open, I halt in shock at the sight of Aston. He's standing completely naked in the shower with water running down his bare back and with miles of tanned skin glistening under the ceiling spotlights.

My breath comes out in a soft gasp he doesn't hear, and my heart thuds erratically in my chest when I stand there staring at him instead of turning tail and running. I'm rooted to the spot and unable to move as I stare at his body, drinking in the sight of him. I try to tell myself to stop, to leave and pretend I never saw him, but when he throws his head back and groans with his eyes pinched tightly closed and his teeth gritted as though in pain, I find myself moving closer to him.

This is wrong; I shouldn't be in here. I should leave,

but something's pulling me toward him, and when I notice the hard, angry length of his cock jutting out from the V of his hips and his hand wrapped firmly around it, my mouth waters at what I'm seeing. Water is streaming down his body, and my eyes track the paths of the droplets as they move over the dips, ridges, and curves of his muscular back and toned ass. My mind has blanked, and all sane thought has left my body. I've seen a naked man before, and I've had sex and loved every moment, but nothing has incited as much desire in me as the man standing in front of me right now.

Absently, I press my finger to my clit through my jeans, attempting to alleviate some of the ache that's building there. Aston lets out a long, low moan, fisting the base of his cock, and as he rhythmically moves his hand again, swiping his thumb over the head with every pass, I rub faster. I'm lost in the moment, forgetting that I shouldn't be in here, forgetting that the man in front of me isn't a stranger, and forgetting that at any moment he could turn around and catch me.

A tingle of pleasure ripples through me at the sounds leaving his mouth, pairing with the sensations my fingers are creating at my own touch. Frustration builds the longer I stand there, trapped by a crushing need I can't seem to snap out of; impatience drives my desire. I've been possessed by something far stronger than my own will, and I've become a slave to it. I one-handedly undo my jeans while maintaining my rhythm until I'm able to touch my own bare skin.

Licking my lips, my mouth feels dry, but as I slide

my fingers into my panties, I feel the wetness that has gathered there. Now with slick fingers, I resume my ministrations until a buzzing sensation floods through me and I let out a soft moan.

I must be louder than I thought because Aston's eyes fly open as he lets out a guttural shout, "Sonea!"

Thick ribbons of cum spurt from the end of his cock, coating the water splattered glass between us, and I shudder through my own orgasm at the sight. Still floating in the post orgasmic haze, I barely realize Aston has switched the shower off and wrapped a towel around his waist until he's standing directly in front of me, his furious expression telling me I've really fucked up. But as I withdraw my hand from my jeans, I feel his shallow breaths on my face and see the warring emotions in his eyes. Love, anger, confusion...and fear.

I look away but I'm still frozen in place, this time too scared to move, to face him and see the raging conflict on his face. The juices from my pussy are drying on my fingers, and I quickly wipe my hands on my jeans, embarrassment heating my cheeks at what I've done; Aston's my brother, and I've just got myself off to the sight of him masturbating in the shower!

Surprise fills my chest and warmth spreads through me when I feel his large, damp hand under my chin, tilting my head back, so I'm facing him.

I close my eyes, too terrified to do anything else, and whisper, "I'm sorry. I don't know what came over me."

Soft, warm lips press against my forehead, and when his husky voice washes over me in the familiar blanket of comfort I've come to rely on, I feel the tears I was holding back slip free.

"Don't do that again, Sonea. I'm not meant for you, sweetheart. Wash up. Dinner will be here soon."

Confusion spreads through me at the calm tenor of his voice. I expected him to shout, to yell that I was disgusting, and a part of me wonders exactly what he's thinking right now. But he doesn't linger, instead he leaves me alone in his bathroom with my shame and the remains of his cum still soaking the glass wall of his shower.

I've thought a lot about that day, far more than I should, and I'm stuck in a tortuous purgatory where I want more but know I shouldn't. Every fantasy I've masturbated to since then, Aston's starred in, and each time, I've finished with his name on my lips, juices soaking my hand, and thinking of him. I'm disgusted at myself, yet I can't bring myself to stop this terrible need plaguing my fantasies.

I skipped Thanksgiving, but I can't miss sharing another holiday with my family. I don't know how to face either of my brothers, though, when I have this sickness in my mind, spreading through me like poison. I'm wanting things I should never desire and will never have, and I'm feeding it with every new fantasy and every single touch.

CHAPTER TWO

ASTON

Sonea should be home tomorrow, and Sean will be here a few days after. His semester finishes after Sonea's, and he also has farther to travel. I sip at the same drink I've been nursing since I got here over an hour ago. Downing it, I grit my teeth and order a shot. I was restless and needed something to do, but in this town not much is open late at night apart from the local rock bar and a few restaurants. I'd already eaten at home, so I opted for the bar.

Nerves are attacking my gut at the thought of seeing the twins again. I saw Sean at Thanksgiving, but I haven't seen Sonea since the summer, and I'm still not sure how to handle what occurred that day in my room. I was too stunned to do anything other than speak a few words to her; not while the aftershocks of my orgasm were still vibrating through my body and the scent of her arousal surrounded me when I approached her. I almost gave in to the desperation that was written across her flushed features, but someone has to be the responsible one, and even with my thoughts swirling in an endorphin-ridden blur, I wasn't about to completely ruin the relationship we have and destroy everything I've worked so hard to build for my family.

I left, and ever since, I've tried to obliterate from my mind the image of my little sister with her hand down her pants, her eyes dilated with lust, and cheeks flushed from her orgasm. But, the damage has been done and I don't know how to repair it. I can't fix what I've seen or erase what she did. I can't remove the memory of how I came with Sonea's name on my lips as I shouted in surprise at the sight of her standing there. No matter what I do now, her name and her face flit into my mind every time I shower, and I can't hide from what she's initiated.

I knock back the shot and this time ask for a double. I don't know what's gotten into me, usually I'm not much of a drinker. I realize I do know, though, when the memory of Sonea's face twisted with rapture seeps into my brain, and I dig my nails into my palms. A part of me hates her for wrecking my peace of mind and setting the relationship I have with her on a precarious ledge. The real test is about to come, but I'm going to do my damnedest not to let what I'm sure was an isolated incident ruin the holidays. I'm going to pretend it never happened and hope she does the same. I won't be able to cope with losing the closeness I share with my little sister if she persists in chasing something so elusive and impossible.

I'm hoping that the few days we'll spend together before Sean gets home won't be awkward or filled with tension, and we can either act as though nothing happened or find a way to get past it and keep the truth buried. In spite of the conflict that wages inside me when I think of Sonea, I *have* missed her, and I'm still looking forward to seeing her again. Why did she have to make a mess of everything, and what am I going to do if we *can't* move past this?

Shaking off the thoughts niggling at my conscience, I finish off my third drink and get to my feet. I'm not drunk, I'm barely even tipsy. The strong flavor from the shots tastes like regret on my tongue and letting out a heavy sigh, I leave the empty glass sitting on the bar and head for the exit. I don't know what to do about this, but sitting in a noisy bar surrounded by the thump of heavy music isn't the place to think things through.

Making my way out onto the quiet street, I leave the sound of fast riffs and heavy drumbeat behind me. Normally I love the music and the feeling of getting lost in the pounding rhythm, but tonight I'm just not feeling it.

It's getting colder, and at this time of year it's not unusual to get a sharp frost or even snow, although according to the weather report it won't hit for at least another week. I left my gloves at home, and the cold is biting at my fingertips even though I've buried my hands deep in my jacket pockets.

I've got to figure this out, and I've got to do it soon. That niggling little thought I'm keeping buried is trying to unearth itself, and I'd sooner smother it than uncover it. I'm not going to entertain the ridiculous notions that have been sprouting little seedlings ever since I witnessed Sonea getting off to the sight of me...

As my blood rushes downward and my cock thickens in my pants at the vivid memory, I exhale sharply. Maybe I'm more drunk than I thought, because right now, I'm wishing I'd licked her fingers clean, and I'm wondering if they'd have tasted like the erotic scent surrounding her. *No, I can't go down that road.* It's wrong, and it's fucking disgusting to think of my little sister in such a way.

I'm grateful the bar isn't too far from home, but the brisk walk is long enough to have cleared my head and sobered me up. Tonight I'm going to do whatever I can to get these urges and thoughts out of my system, so tomorrow when dawn shines on my mistakes, I can shut them away and pretend nothing ever happened.

When I finally get through my front door and have locked it behind me, I clumsily hang the keys on the hook and head for the kitchen. *Definitely not as sober as I thought.* Pouring myself a drink of water, I down it and refill my glass before grabbing some painkillers and going to my room. I fumble with the buttons on my jeans and slide them and my boxers down my legs, discarding them together with my t-shirt onto the floor. The house is already too warm, and with my forbidden thoughts sending extra waves of heat roaring through my blood, I lie down on my bed on top of the bedclothes and palm my aching cock.

Rubbing the precum down my length with my thumb, I let loose the worst fantasies I've ever dreamed up. With no preamble, I proceed to fuck my tightly fisted hand as though it's Sonea's pussy. Imagining how it would feel if she were wrapped around my cock, I squeeze my rigid length, wishing she was riding me with bliss written all over her face as I pump into her. I come with a growl, and my body jerks from the force of the orgasm tearing through me as cum coats my hand and stomach. I lie on my bed, breathless, boneless and shaking hard through the residual sensations still wreaking havoc on my body.

A soft voice cuts through the lusty fog like a beam of sunlight, and I blink in the sudden brightness that illuminates my room and the chaotic mess on my skin and in my mind.

"Aston, are you okay?"

As I stare groggily at the shocked expression on Sonea's face, I feel a prickle of confusion sweep over me. *Why is she here?* An awareness of the compromising state I'm in hits me, swiftly followed by a heavy dose of shame.

What the fuck did I just do?

CHAPTER THREE

SEAN

It's been hell spending so much time away from Sonea, and I'm not sure if I'll ever get used to the heaviness in my chest with her absence. As we grew older, our looks weren't so closely mirrored anymore, and where her features softened and her body began to curve gracefully, mine hardened and filled out in a different way to Sonea's. Hell, these days I look more like my big brother Aston than my own twin. I miss them both, and I'm a little peeved that Sonea has already finished up for the holidays and I still have to sit through another two days of lectures before the end of my semester.

I'll be flying home, and I'm hoping Sonea will come to meet me at the airport with Aston, who has already offered to pick me up. Sometimes I miss Dad, but I'd never trade in the memories and relationship I share with Aston for more time with him. Even though I know in my heart that Aston did a better job than Dad ever could have, I do wonder how we'd have turned out if he hadn't bailed on us. Aston has always looked out of us. We'd always been close, and what happened with Dad just made our bond even stronger.

When I walk through the door to my room in the dorms, my roommate is sprawled on his bed, mashing the buttons on his Xbox controller so rigorously I'm surprised they haven't caved in. He's a hardcore gamer and while I play too, I'm not as intense a player as he is. The sounds of his video game and the rapid-fire click-click-click of the buttons fill the room.

"Hey, Robin. You gonna be heading home for the holidays or camping out here?" I ask him, dropping onto my bed.

"Home. My parents have set up this big family get-together with all my siblings and little nieces and nephews. I'm dreading it. Those kids are fucking loud," he grumbles, but I can hear the affection in his voice when he talks about his family, and I wonder if I have the same inflection to mine when I mention Sonea and Aston. "What about you?" he asks.

"Home as well. I'm gonna spend the holidays with my brother and sister," I respond lazily, trying not to contemplate how the next few days are going to drag by.

Robin knows it's just the three of us, and after I gave him the very short and not so sweet version about my dad being a child abandoning asshole, he's not brought him up again. We're both studying the same major and a lot of the same electives.

The next few days pass uneventfully, and as I

predicted, they drag by agonizingly slowly. I swear, even during the run up to holidays the professors still expect us to get a shitload of schoolwork done along with drilling us on what we've learned this semester. One of them is a complete demon and sprung a difficult quiz on the very last day when all our brains had already switched into vacation mode.

I'm packed, ready to leave, waiting for the cab to arrive to take me to the airport to catch my flight home. Robin left late last night as he has a long drive to get to his parents' place, so I had the place to myself for a change. It was odd without his presence there, filling the room. The silence was almost unsettling, but I was too focused on making sure I had everything ready for this morning.

It's still dark, and even though the nights here stretch on for longer this time of year, it's barely even the butt crack of dawn. I decided to book an early flight rather than grabbing a few more hours sleep and a later one home. My excitement at the prospect of seeing my family is greater than my desire for a lie in; I can always do that tomorrow when I'm at home with them, back with the people I love the most.

CHAPTER FOUR

ASTON

Breakfast the following morning has to be the most awkward fucking meal I've ever shared with Sonea, and I can feel her eyes tracking me as I move around the kitchen, preparing drinks and food. Every time I glance at her, she averts her gaze, and it's getting on my fucking nerves. She's the one who created this damn mess, so she needs to face what she's done. We've got to straighten things out between us before Sean comes home. He absolutely mustn't find out about this, and if we can't act like a normal fucking family around each other, then he's bound to ask questions I won't know how to answer.

"Sonea, we need to talk about what happened in the summer." I broach the subject, speaking slowly and clearly, scrutinizing her for some kind of response.

When she finally looks at me, her cheeks are flushed and her pupils dilated. I'm left wondering exactly what she's thinking, and a dull sense of foreboding settles over me when I consider the fact that, for her at least anyway, this may not be a one-time incident. My stomach jolts at the thinly veiled longing hidden in her eyes, and I have to fight not to break the connection of our gazes.

I'm not going down this route with her, and I'm going to do everything in my power to ensure nothing like this happens again. I'm thankful it never went any further, but as the memories intertwine with the vividness of the previous night's fantasy, I'm afraid I'm going to sink under the weight of the thoughts that are burying themselves within my mind. I do my best to ignore the way my body responds to them and focus instead on the fact she's not some random woman I've taken an interest in. *She's my sister*.

"We never spoke about it then, but it can never happen. You're my sister, and I love you. You're my family, and I cherish our bond, Sonea, but we must never cross that boundary. It's not just illegal, it's wrong. If I catch you in my room again, there'll be consequences."

"I'm not a kid anymore, Aston. You don't need to treat me like one, and your threats don't scare me. You're assuming I've thought about you in that way after that one time, but the reality is I got caught up in the moment," she snaps, defiance giving her tone a sharp edge.

"Can you honestly tell me you haven't thought about me like that since?" I narrow my eyes, not buying her excuse for one second. "You didn't just suddenly forget I'm your brother, and it hasn't escaped my notice how flushed your face is right now or how you haven't met my eyes almost all morning."

"Maybe because I'm embarrassed I walked in on my big brother jerking off again last night!"

"Embarrassment doesn't change the fact that you got yourself off in my bathroom while watching me in the shower, Sonea. We need to not be acting this way around each other, sweetheart. Stay out of my room from now on, and then maybe you won't see anything that will cause those cheeks of yours to turn such a pretty shade of pink," I finish, and she sits silently, staring at me with her face sullen, and all lingering embarrassment, or whatever the fuck it was, is gone.

"Fine," she huffs the solitary word and focuses intently on the coffee and food I've just set down in front of her.

"Hey, look at me," I prompt.

When she glances back at me, I see a familiar defiance glowing in her eyes, and my gut twists at the sudden thought she may not let this go. I know all too well how powerful the call is of something forbidden. It creates the kind of yearning that only grows the more it's denied. I'm afraid of what such a terrible secret could do to our family. I will not see us torn apart over it, and I will not risk Sean being caught in the crossfire.

"I love you, Sonea. I don't want to hurt you, and I don't want to hurt Sean. Regardless of whether it was an accident or not, this cannot happen between us, and I need you to tell me you understand."

"I understand, *Dad*," she drawls, and I bristle at the term she only uses when she's upset I've berated her.

"I'm not him, and you know it," I fire back defensively, and she has the good grace to look sheepish at my tone.

She lets out a sigh, and her sad, hazel eyes, which so closely mirror mine and Sean's, strike me down. I realize that she does get it, and not just the fact I'm not Dad but also the severity of what happened, and how it could affect our whole family if it gets out. I close my mouth, the rest of my ire fading, and I decide to drop it. It won't happen again. *But why does that thought make my heart clench with disappointment rather than relief?*

CHAPTER FIVE

SONEA

Sean is coming home today, and I've been buzzing around the house with excitement all morning, waiting anxiously until we need to leave to collect him from the airport. The past couple of days have been strange, and there's been a weight of tension hanging over Aston and me, but nothing as bad as I'd have expected. I've been careful about keeping my thoughts shielded, so Aston can't see how much this is torturing me.

Since the first time I caught him in the shower with his hand around his dick, I've been losing myself piece by piece to a consuming desire that's slowly eating me alive. I've succumbed more than once to my incandescent need in the time I've been away, and I've bitten my lips each night I've been home to muffle the sounds of every forbidden orgasm I've given myself.

Aston's told me this can never happen, but words can't erase the intense longing that's built up in the months we've been apart. I may never be able to have my brother as anything other than my family, but it doesn't stop me from chasing the delicious dreams he fills as surely as he fills me within them.

He was right about one thing, though. We can't ever tell Sean about this. The thought of hurting my twin cuts me deeper than Aston's rejection. Shoving all thoughts of Aston aside, I decide to concentrate on Sean and how much I've missed him. I can't wait to wrap my arms around him and sink into the feeling of being complete.

I never imagined when we applied and went off to separate colleges that it would be this painful. It's not just that we've never been truly apart before, but the pull of my twin stretched over so many miles rips into my heart. The distance between us wrecks me more than I'd like to admit to anyone, and more than once, I've considered transferring to a different college so I can be closer to Sean.

Time ticks on, and after what seems like forever, it's time to leave. Sean will be landing soon, and we need to get going or he'll have to wait for us to get there.

"Aston!" I call out, and he comes barreling into my room wearing nothing but a towel and a harried expression on his face.

Aston's messy hair is soaking wet and dripping down the sides of his face from where it clings to his cheeks. Tendrils of water trickle down his chest and toned abs before seeping into the fluffy material of the towel wrapped tightly around his waist. The sight of him standing there like that is mouthwatering, and I'm unable to keep the groan I intended to keep internalized from slipping out.

"What?" he asks, and as his eyes track where mine just traveled, his own flash with heat at the sound.

His reaction fills me with surprise. I'm guessing I'm not the only one being tormented by what I can't have. It doesn't make me feel any better, and we don't have time for me to confront him about it right now. Maybe I can catch him off guard one day soon, and we can really talk about what's going on, only minus the lecture. I know I shouldn't be pursuing this, but my heart refuses to be contained by the restrictions he's trying to chain me with.

"Umm, we need to leave. Sean's flight will be here in less than an hour, and we've still got to get to the airport."

Aston rolls his eyes. "I'm aware of that. If you'd given me five more minutes instead of shouting like you're being attacked, I'd have been dried and dressed by now. I'll be right back...and wipe that look off your face, Sonea."

"I will if you will," I shoot back, and he scowls as he walks back out of the room, mumbling about bratty sisters.

It's a small victory, but I'll take it. It seems he knows just as well as I do this isn't going to go away with a lecture and a persistent refusal to acknowledge it. I'm not sure how we'll be able to keep Sean in the dark with us constantly at each other's throats like this. Knowing the lengths that Aston has gone to over the years to keep us safe and protect us, pure will and stubbornness will probably be the best tactic he can use. However, subtlety has never been my strong suit, so if anyone fails to conceal it from Sean, it'll probably be me.

I let out a heavy sigh and quickly pull on my shoes and a jacket before heading downstairs to wait for Aston to finally show his face.

It's windy out. The bitter air nips at my exposed face and fingertips, and it blows loose strands of hair across my face. Prying the hair from my mouth, I attempt to tuck it behind my ears but another strong gust whips it back. I huff in irritation and make my way over to the car, closely followed by Aston. I slip on a wet patch of pavement just as I reach the front passenger door and fall backward, but Aston catches me before I can hit the ground.

Where his large hands make contact with my body, it sends electricity zapping through me, and I wonder if he feels it too. It's in that moment I realize this is the first time he's touched or held me since I've been back, and sadness at that fact tugs at my heart. One foolish moment has already ruined what we used to share.

"Thanks," I mumble, and when he finally sets me upright, I avoid his gaze and brush a tear from my cheek when I know he's not looking.

I'm not as stealthy as I thought, because when I turn to open the door, Aston is staring at me with an unfathomable expression on his face. Before I can open my mouth to ask him what's wrong, he closes the distance between us and pulls me into his arms, enveloping me in his warm embrace.

"I'm sorry," he whispers into my hair, and I let him hold me while I fight back the emotions threatening to break through.

After a moment I lift my own arms and wrap them around his waist. I don't say anything. Instead, I just stand there and savor the feeling of being held tightly by my big brother. The longer we stay the more my tension and pain dissipate until I feel a lightness inside me, and I think maybe, just maybe, we'll be okay after all. Eventually, he releases me, and I don't miss the way he inhales deeply, breathing in the scent of my hair.

"Come on, we better get going," he says, and his husky voice bathes me in the warmth I hadn't noticed was missing until now.

Nodding my acknowledgement, I slide into the car and watch as he moves around to the driver's side and follows suit. Within the confines of the car, the lack of tension between us is more visceral, and I feel like I can finally breathe.

"I love you too," I tell him, finally responding to his earlier declaration, and when I smile over at him, his own lips curve into the familiar grin I love seeing on him.

It's not better, not by a long shot, and I'm not sure what to do about the emotions and needs that continue to linger, but even with the vast impossibility of our situation, maybe there's some hope for us after all.

CHAPTER SIX

SEAN

I hate flying, and as the plane judders to a stop after hitting the asphalt I heave out a sigh of relief. If it wasn't so much quicker to catch a flight than to drive, I would take the slower route, but it's a long way to travel alone. This is more convenient, even if it does make me nervous as hell. Listening to music throughout the journey helps calm my anxiety, and the heavier the band the more relaxed I feel.

When the seatbelt sign dims, I flick open the clasp and get to my feet as quickly as I can, and after grabbing my bag from the overhead compartment, I head toward the exit. The stewardess is just opening the door, and as soon as she sees me, she gives me a broad smile and the standard spiel thanking me for flying with them. I acknowledge her words with a nod of my head before finally setting foot on the jet bridge that will take me to the terminal. I speed up, eager to get to where I'm hoping my brother and sister will be waiting for me.

Exiting the bridge, I make my way toward baggage claim, scanning the crowd for any sign of my family. Disappointment curdles in my stomach when I don't spot them, but I remind myself they'll be here and they're probably stuck in traffic. After I grab my small case from the conveyer, I hear a voice that makes my heart jump.

"Sean!"

I've barely had time to turn in the direction the shout came from when I spy the figure I know as well as my own reflection. Sonea shoves her way through the crowd, flying across the packed terminal toward me. Letting go of my case, I open my arms and catch my favorite person in the world before she can crash into me and take us both to the ground. Squeezing her form to me, I smile against her shoulder as the scent of home wafts from her clothes and the last of my anxiety from the flight fades away. No matter where I am or who I'm with, Sonea is my home.

"I've missed you so much, I wish you didn't live so far away," she admits, an edge of desperation in her voice, and I tighten my arms around her in response.

"I've missed you too, I'm here now, though," I chuckle, and she leans back to roll her eyes at me, but I can already see the smile teasing the corners of her mouth. I glance over her shoulder. "Where's Aston?"

Sonea twists her head to look behind her, and

confusion pulls her eyebrows closer together and her lips downward. "I left him by the car, I would've thought he'd have caught up by now. There he is!" she exclaims, just as I spot him myself.

Setting her down, I take her hand in one of mine and my suitcase in the other and drag them both toward the approaching figure of the man I look up to the most in the world, and my second favorite person after Sonea. I let go of my sister and the case to pull him into a quick embrace, and he gives me a friendly clap on my shoulder and grabs the luggage from beside me as Sonea slips her hand back into mine.

"Welcome home, Sean."

Aston grins at me, but as his eyes flutter down to where mine and Sonea's are entwined, something flickers so briefly in his expression I'm not certain I saw anything at all. After he gives me another quick one-armed hug, he turns to lead us out of the airport terminal to wherever he's parked the car. As we draw closer, he pulls out the key and unlocks it. Popping the trunk, he swings my suitcase in, and I drop my backpack beside it before we all get into the car and start the final leg of the journey back to our home.

Sonea slides into the back seat with me, and taking her hand again, I lean my head back on the headrest and close my eyes. The heat from the radiator fills the car with warmth, chasing away the wintry chill that blasted us the moment we left the airport, and I'm finally able to stop shivering. The long journey combined with the comfort of being with my family and heading back to the one place in the world I never want to leave lulls me into a light sleep.

CHAPTER SEVEN

ASTON

I keep finding myself looking in the rearview mirror to the backseat where Sean has just fallen asleep and Sonea is sitting beside him. A fleeting glance over my shoulder tells me that they're still holding hands. They're twins and have always been very close, so why is it bothering me so much now? Sonea and Sean share a bond I'll never understand, and even after years of watching them grow up from babies into the adults they are now, it's always confounded me. Truthfully, I've always envied them that closeness.

Maybe the reason it stings so much now is because I can't seem to figure out a way to repair the broken tethers between Sonea and myself. Every touch we share, no matter how innocent, feels weighted with hidden meaning. I want back what we used to have, but I can't deny the thought of touching her with complete abandon and without consideration of the implications sends a bolt of frenzied desire through me.

As the errant thought flits into my mind, I forcibly swipe it away by attempting to remind myself of all the reasons it can't happen: she's my sister, she's off limits, and if anyone were to discover such an immoral physical union had taken place between us, we'd be severely punished by the law. Glancing up into the mirror again, my heart freezes momentarily in my chest when my eyes meet Sonea's. The conflicted desperation and heat in her gaze warms my blood. But, my heart stutters back to life when I look over my shoulder and see the locked hands in the center seat and our brother sleeping peacefully next to her.

It hits me like a ten ton weight in that moment that if he weren't there, I'd be strongly tempted to pull over and say fuck it to everything holding me back. As it is, I'm left feeling like I'm losing control. The pull between us shouldn't be this strong or this intense. Her unwavering stare is proving to be my undoing, and for some unknown reason, the sheer lack of intent within it is feeding into my growing hunger.

After what feels like an age, I slowly pull into our driveway, set the car in neutral, and engage the handbrake. I leave the engine idling for a moment and swivel around in my seat to look at Sonea. Her eyebrows furrow, and an expression of deep thought passes across her features. I'm not entirely sure what she's seeing on my face right now, but the intense moment is shattered when Sean stirs in his seat and slowly wakes up. Opening his eyes, he blinks blearily and stretches, lifting up Sonea's hand and arm with his.

I spin back around and switch off the car.

"We're home. Let's get inside before the cold gets to us."

Getting out of the car, I head to the rear and open the trunk. I loop Sean's backpack over my shoulder and haul out his case, setting it on the ground while I shut the lid with a thunk. The sound of two doors shutting in perfect unison makes me smile as I'm reminded of the way the twins fall into near perfect sync when they're around each other. It's not always exact, with one occasionally a second behind the other, but it's so close that unless you pay careful attention or have lived with them, like I have, you would never notice. It's not intentional, just a strange occurrence between the two of them.

They head up the pathway to the house just ahead of me, and I notice that Sonea is lagging a little behind. Hurrying to catch up, I fall into step with her, and we walk the last few feet to the house together. She moves aside and lets me into the house first, so I can set Sean's bags down while she follows me in and shuts the door behind us. I can already hear the sound of the coffee maker humming from the kitchen and I smile. *Sean's home*, I laugh silently to myself.

Sonea disappears into the kitchen in search of her brother, and I stare after her for a moment trying to straighten out the chaos building inside my head. Five months this has festered, and I've been frantically denying the truth about the onslaught of desire that's been growing ever since. Sonea awoke something that day in my bathroom, and not just within herself. Blood shouldn't want blood, but instead of killing the desire it's feeding it.

Hopefully, Sean's presence will provide the shield of control I'm scrambling to hold onto, but I'm not sure I can outlast the siege warring on my mind. Gritting my teeth, I leave the bag and suitcase at the bottom of the stairs for later and head through the house to seek out the rest of my family. Maybe seeing them together will help reinforce the wrongness of this whole fucked up situation.

Laughter seeps out through the open kitchen door, and I walk in to see the two of them talking and joking like the past five months of separation haven't happened. Seeing Sonea so vibrant and happy with Sean sets my heart alight, and like the moment we shared earlier before we went to collect Sean, it serves to reinforce the fact things aren't the same between us. Fierce longing to reclaim the easy relationship we used to share burgeons in my chest, and the spark of jealousy I've always harbored flares up painfully.

Taking a deep breath, I urge my body to relax. I can't let either of them see me losing control or view me as anything other than their older brother, the responsible and controlled one who always put them first. I squash the treacherous thoughts whispering to me about how I need to put myself first sometimes. *No, my little brother and sister must always come first.*

CHAPTER EIGHT

SONEA

Aston's acting strangely, but Sean doesn't seem to have noticed anything's amiss. I would've thought of the two of us it would be me failing to keep my thoughts and feelings obscured. I'm worried because it looks like Aston's carefully maintained control is slipping, and I'm not entirely sure what he's thinking right now. His eyes have hardly strayed from me since we left the airport, and I sense that something in him is about to be unleashed.

I inch closer to Sean, not just for the comforting aura his calm presence offers me, but also to put a little distance between me and Aston. I want what we should never share, and I want it so badly I'm afraid of what might happen if I surrender to it. I don't think he'd do anything with Sean around, which provides me with a small amount of solace. I don't know what to do. I'm so confused by all of this, and up until now, I believed Aston would continue to reject me. Something has shifted in him, exacerbated by Sean's arrival, and now I'm left uncertain as to what's going on with him.

The rest of the day passes with an almost palpable tension hanging over us that I'm sure doesn't go unnoticed by Sean. I'll have to talk to him later, and even though Aston was adamant about keeping it from our brother and I agreed, this is eating me up. How could I have believed I'd be able keep anything from my twin, especially a secret as insane as this one?

Sean excuses himself early, and I let him go without even attempting to stop him. He's just traveled over a thousand miles in the span of a day, and he's exhausted. He doesn't need me laying a weight like this on him his first day home. Maybe I can wait it out a day or two and give myself time to think and find clarity. I could potentially discuss it properly with Aston, but I'm not sure how to approach him with the way things are between us right now.

I curl up on the couch, watching the rerun of an old sitcom on the TV when Aston takes a seat next to me. The air in the room charges the longer we sit there silently, and when I feel like I'm about to scream I get to my feet.

"Be back in a minute," I tell him with a smile, and he nods but doesn't speak.

I dart from the living room and into the small bathroom on the first floor. I take my time, trying to catch my breath and calm my racing heart. Splashing water on my face, I let the cool liquid sap the heat from my flushed cheeks and refresh me so I can go back out there. When I finally feel ready, I open the door and damn near jump out of my skin when I see a shadowed figure waiting on the other side...for me.

The shadow steps forward, and I see it's Aston as he quickly muffles my noise of surprise with his hand. "Shhh, you don't want to wake up Sean and bring him running down to see what the commotion is."

I'm breathing fast, waiting for him to release my mouth or explain what the hell he's doing right now. Quite frankly, he's scaring the hell out of me. The lack of lighting in the hallway has cast eerie shadows over everything, and even in the poor light, his obscured expression is hungry. I'm not sure what he's thinking or planning, and some sick part of me wants to find out, but the part that doesn't want my twin to be hurt by this makes me struggle in his grip.

"I've tried so hard to be a good brother, Sonea. All I've ever wanted is to protect you, keep you safe, love you, but somewhere along the line, it's all gone wrong. That brotherly love has morphed into something much more base and carnal. Why can't I keep my eyes off you?"

His voice is pained, and my heart twists and my body heats at the words leaving his mouth. Here in the darkness where we can barely see each other, it's harder to recognize what's really holding us back. Aston's other hand crosses the darkness to settle on my hip and the warmth from it seems to melt through my clothes to my bare skin beneath. A surprised gasp leaves my lips, vibrating against the hand still covering my mouth, and he flexes his fingers in response before squeezing the flesh of my hip, eliciting yet another gasp from me.

Sure fingers dip beneath the waistband of my leggings, teasing the sensitive skin before delving lower without hesitation. My heart's thumping like a jackhammer inside my chest, threatening to break out with the speed and force of its beat. Aston moves closer, narrowing the gap between our bodies until there's barely anything between us. A moan works its way up my throat when he brushes my clit with the pad of his forefinger, stroking the tiny nub with tantalizingly light strokes.

"I think you like that," he whispers, circling it with his fingertip.

My breaths are hot against the palm of his hand, and though my hands are free and hanging loosely by my sides, I'm too stunned to move or do anything other than fall victim to the zinging sensations he's creating.

The teasing is driving me mad, his touch still feather light on my body. Frustration sends my hips rolling toward him, chasing more, but it makes him stop. I fail to hold back the whine at his cruel maneuver, and finally unfrozen, I reach out to grasp his wrist to encourage him to continue; only instead, he removes his hand completely.

I stare up at him, squinting to decipher what he's thinking, to read his expression. He lets go of my mouth, and sliding both hands under my thighs, he lifts my body to straddle his waist. I let out a small sound of surprise that he quickly smothers with his lips, and without further ado, he carries me up the stairs, bypassing his bedroom and opening the door to mine. Setting me down, he flicks on the light and the look in his eyes causes my heart to skitter. Instinctually I step away, increasing the space between us until the backs of my knees hit the bed, and I slip into a seated position. Aston tracks my movements with his eyes before trailing after me. His gait is slow, purposeful...predatory as he draws closer.

At this moment, I feel less like the pesky younger sister he's always had to take care of and more like a woman he looks set on devouring whole, and I find myself trembling with anticipation, waiting for him to capture and claim what I'm freely offering to him. I'm still fully clothed, but I feel naked beneath his gaze. As he moves nearer to me, Aston's eyes never leave mine, and with each step, he sheds a piece of his clothing until he's almost completely naked in front of me. The material of his boxers is stretched taut from the stiffness of his erection tenting the fabric, and my mouth waters at the sight of his naked skin and clear desire.

My sharp intake of breath makes my chest heave, and he lowers his head slightly to watch as my breasts rise and fall with each rapid breath continuing to escape me. Before he reaches me, he stops, and a smirk lifts his full lips and his hazel eyes darken until the brown encompasses the small amount of green in them. I'm practically salivating at the sight of him so exposed to me. A few days ago, I'd never have imagined we could move beyond the anger and frustration of what we were both fighting against, and now he's standing in my room like this. I know I'm not going to get out of here unscathed, and all my senses are tingling with anticipation while I wait for his next move.

"Strip, I want to see you, Sonea...all of you," he orders, and the husky command has me swiftly rushing to obey.

My fingers grip the hem of my shirt, and lifting it over my head, I discard it on the floor before I lower my leggings and pull them off over my feet. Rising again, I stare defiantly at Aston. Like him, I'm now wearing nothing but my underwear. A groan of satisfaction rumbles in his chest, and he runs a hand through his hair, almost tearing at the strands before he strides across the room, and shoving me back on the bed, he crawls between my thighs. The friction of his hard cock against my sensitized clit through the material of my panties makes me squirm, and I whimper.

Aston pauses, and his expression is so tortured it stabs my heart.

"We shouldn't be doing this, but damn I don't think I can stop. Tell me you want me to stop, Sonea," he begs.

My throat clogs with emotion, yet somehow I manage to choke out a response. "I'm sorry I can't. I don't want you to stop. Please don't make me lie to you, Aston."

At my words, he lowers his head and catches my lips in a kiss. His hands grip me in a touch so searing I feel it burn through my flesh to my bones. Sliding one hand up my body to cup my breast, he pinches my nipple through the fabric of my bra before pulling the cup down to expose it. He quickly covers the rosy bud with his mouth while his other hand yanks my panties down my thighs, and I scrabble to remove his boxers. His mouth is everywhere, his tongue driving me to distraction as I lift each of my legs in turn to help him divest me of my underwear.

"Last chance to stop me," he offers, and his hot breath on the damp skin of my nipple makes me shiver.

My silence gives him my answer, and when he slides his large cock into my pussy, I gasp at the fullness as he stretches me wide to accommodate him. I'm not a virgin, but he's just claimed what I know now should have always been his. He's always been in my blood, and as he sinks his cock deeply into my body, I know I'll never be able to remove his brand from within me.

CHAPTER NINE

SEAN

The soft sounds of feminine moans filter through the walls, waking me up. When masculine grunts punctuate the air in response, I frown in confusion because the only other people in the house are my family, or at least, that's what I thought. They never mentioned anyone else, and unless someone arrived after I went to bed, something strange is going on.

Grabbing my phone from the nightstand and seeing it charged, I tug the cable from the socket and use the screen light to guide me, not wanting to alert anyone to my presence. I get out of bed onto the soft carpet that molds beneath my bare feet, muffling my steps as I edge out of the room.

I can see a light on in Sonea's bedroom, seeping out into the hallway through the door that I notice is slightly ajar. I'm already beginning to doubt my reason for sneaking down here to see what she's doing, but curiosity drives me onward. Still using my phone to light my way so I'm able to mind where I step and avoid the two creaky floorboards, I move toward her door. Peering through the crack, I spot her bed and the two naked figures moving on top of it. I can only watch in disbelief as the powerful body of a man with his back to me drives into her body.

Something unexpected comes over me, and with shaking fingers, I hurriedly press a few buttons on my phone and hit record. After checking the angle of the screen, I lift my eyes to watch the scene unfolding in front of me, and shame fills me when my dick thickens in response to the sight. I close my eyes in pain, and open them again before sliding my free hand down the front of my boxers to rub my dick in time to the movements of the man fucking my sister to within an inch of her life.

I don't know how long I stand there completely enraptured by what I'm seeing. Eventually, Sonea lets out a high keening sound that morphs into a long pleasure filled moan, and the man between her thighs lets out one last grunt and stills just as I find my own release, coating my hand and my underwear. As he lowers his head to kiss her he turns slightly, and I nearly drop my phone in shock when I see my brother kissing Sonea fully and deeply on the lips, tangling his hand in her hair at the same time.

I stop recording and dart silently back to my room, my breath coming in ragged gasps, and my mind rebelling while simultaneously replaying every moment. Glancing down at the phone still clutched in my hand, I see the word 'saved' flash across the screen.

CHAPTER TEN

SONEA

Waking up, I feel a heavy, warm arm draped across my waist and a large body cocooning me. I twist slightly to see Aston sleeping behind me and smile at his peaceful face. Gone are the lines of worry that occasionally pull his eyebrows together and the almost perpetual frown that mars his features when he's stressed. He's done so much for me and Sean, and last night he took care of me in a way I'd never expected to be cared for by him.

Stretching as best I can without waking him, I groan at the ache of my straining muscles and the dull burn between my legs. Aston surprised me last night; his power and the way he moved his body with mine to create something that felt almost otherworldly was overwhelming. I was completely swept up in him.

As much as I want to continue to lie here in the shelter of his arms, I know we can't do that. Sean will no doubt be waking up soon, and he can't catch us like this. We took a risk as it was, and thankfully didn't disturb my sleeping twin in the process. Aston should've gone back to his room last night, but exhaustion and the hazy bliss of sex whisked us both away before he could.

Rolling over to face Aston, I trace the line of his jaw with my fingertips and brush my lips over his. As he stirs, he lets out a sleepy groan and tugs me closer to him, slipping his leg between mine so I'm straddling his thigh. A blush heats my cheeks when I feel his morning wood digging into my hip, and when I try to wiggle away, he grinds against me.

"Unless you want to take care of that or be fucked and possibly wake up Sean, I suggest you stop moving about like that," he mumbles, his voice husky and thick with sleep.

Feeling bold, I kiss his lips and slide lower beneath the bedcovers until my face is level with his cock that's standing proudly. Kissing the head softly, I trail my tongue over the ridges, down to the base and back up.

"Fuck, Sonea. You're trying to get in trouble now. Don't make me ground you or something," he threatens, rolling onto his back and lifting the sheet to watch me with tired eyes and a little smirk tilting the corner of his mouth.

Giving him a wicked grin of my own, I lower my mouth over his length until I feel it kissing the back of my throat. Inhaling deeply through my nose, I swallow past my gag reflex, and he instinctively jerks his hips up to fill my throat. I can't breathe enough to gag, and I can just about manage to move my tongue to lick around his shaft. A strained grunt passes from his lips, and his palm finds the back of my head to guide me off him before he thrusts back in again.

I gag this time, and the way his eyes flash and his fingers tighten in my hair tells me he's enjoying what I'm doing.

"Fuck, keep doing that with your tongue," he groans, dropping his head back and letting me take over while still fisting my hair and using it like a leash.

It doesn't take much longer before his whole body stills with his cock buried deep inside my mouth and my nose pressed to his pelvis. He suffocates me as he comes, spilling his cum down my throat. Aston releases his grip on my hair and I pull back, gasping down a huge lungful of air. I can still taste him on my tongue, and I swallow again before grabbing my bottle of water from the nightstand and taking a drink to clear it.

"That was a nice way to wake up," he smirks, rubbing his thumb along the seam of my mouth and wiping small droplets of water from my lips.

I smile and kiss his thumb before I throw back the covers, and getting out of bed, I turn to look at him more seriously. "You need to get back to your room before Sean notices or hears that you're in here with me. He may ask questions."

"I can't come and speak to my little sister?" Aston says testily, and I bristle at his condescending tone.

"You can, but you shouldn't have stayed last night. It was too risky. Besides, it's far too early in the day to be coming by my room for a chat," I respond just as snippily, gesturing in annoyance at my clock with its glowing red numbers that read 8:30am.

"You want me to do the walk of shame, when you're the one that started this, Sonea? You wouldn't let it drop even when I told you to, and now it's gotten this far, suddenly you're worried about perception. You and Sean have always been close, but right now flaunting that closeness when we're fighting isn't helping." Aston's voice is getting louder, and I can see the hurt and anger simmering in his eyes, all the contentment from our moment having faded.

"I'm not the only one at fault here, Aston. Last night it was you who touched me first *and* kissed me first. It was you who led me up here. You could've left after, and you should've." Shaking my head, I let my annoyance show. "I may have started this months ago, but you chose to finish it. I'm going to the bathroom to shower. I'll see you at breakfast."

As I reach over to grab my phone from the nightstand, Aston lunges out and grabs my wrist. I look up at him and he pulls me into his arms, squeezing me tightly and kissing the top of my head.

"I'm sorry, Sonea. This isn't a normal situation, and with yesterday and then this morning, can you blame me for feeling a bit rejected?"

"No, but you should remember that you rejected me first before you start throwing around blame. You may be the 'parent' in our little family, but you're not the only adult anymore. I may not have been thinking clearly before, but I am now, and all I want to do is to shower and spend some time with Sean today." I pull back to look at him, and when I see the understanding and acceptance in his eyes, I relax a little.

Aston leans forward and kisses me chastely. It's such a light brush of his lips over mine, and I shiver at the faint tingle he leaves behind when he pulls back. Without another word, he lets me go, and spinning on my heel, I leave my room and my big brother lying naked in my bed.

CHAPTER ELEVEN

SEAN

The sound of the bathroom door slamming jars me from my dreams, and when I open my eyes and see the familiar walls with old band posters covering the dark blue paper, I remember I'm home. I roll over to check the time and groan when I see how early it is, but now I'm awake I won't be able to get back to sleep. As the rest of the previous day slowly comes back to me, my stomach twists with an unrecognizable emotion, and I recall the saved video.

My fingers twitch to pick my phone up and look at the recording, to see if what I remember is different from what actually happened. I was exhausted, and in the morning light, I'm wondering if maybe I imagined seeing my brother in the room with my twin sister. The more I think about it, the more implausible and impossible it seems. Plus, it's sick to have even thought about filming my sister having sex, let alone actually doing it.

I don't understand what possessed me to record it in the first place.

Deciding to leave the conundrum and put off watching it until I'm thinking more clearly, I swing my legs out of bed and get up. All the while my phone sits on the nightstand, hiding the video within its confines and taunting me with its secret, begging me to unveil it. Shaking my head, I leave my bedroom, nearly bumping into Sonea who's just leaving the bathroom, a towel wrapped around her hair and another fixed tightly around her body.

She smiles brightly when she sees me and throws her arms around me, letting out a happy sigh. "I'm so glad you're home, I missed you."

Bringing my arms around her, I tug her close and hug her. I try not to think about the curves I saw last night and how they're pressed against me right now, only hidden by the thick material of her towel. I'm sure my cheeks are fire-red, and I hope she won't see my embarrassment and ask me what's wrong. I'm not sure I could admit to the sickness that swept over me last night and how the memory of her soft moans and cries is now embedded in my brain. I let her go before she notices the semi I'm sporting due to her closeness and near nudity.

"I missed you too. Now move your ass, Sis, I need to have a shower. You better not have used all the hot water," I tease, and she lets out an indignant huff, but her amused expression saps all the power from it.

"See you downstairs, Sean."

I dash past her and into the bathroom, shutting the door behind me. I exhale heavily, and attempt to slow my racing thoughts and heart. Sonea didn't seem to realize anything was amiss with me, and if she did notice the feel of my semi-hard dick, then I'm hoping she'll put it down to morning wood, and not what it really was...the evidence of a wrong kind of love.

Smothering all those feelings, I distract myself by mentally playing music in my head. I concentrate on the shower and let my mind go blank of all the confusing and shame-inducing thoughts. By the time I finish, I'm feeling refreshed and calmer than I was when I came in here. Leaving the bathroom, I head down to the kitchen to find Sonea and Aston. I'm drawn to the room by the scent of fresh coffee and toasted bagels.

Something is different this morning, and I'm not sure if it's my imagination playing tricks on me, or whether the previous night wasn't just a fucked up dream conjured by my tired subconscious. Aston seems more at ease, but Sonea seems distant, a faraway look in her eyes as though deep in thought, and she's only half paying attention to the food on her plate.

"Earth to Sonea," I sing-song and she blinks, focusing on me.

"Huh?" she asks.

"Well, your coffee is probably cold by now, and you've shredded that poor bagel of yours. What's wrong?"

She breathes out a laugh, and shrugs. "Nothing. Just tired, I guess."

I let her lie slide. She must be tired if she thinks she can pull the wool over my eyes. We've always been able to tell when the other is hiding something; that's partly why we've never kept any secrets from each other. I suspect that whatever she's lying about is the reason she didn't come home for Thanksgiving. It stings that Sonea feels she can't trust me with what's bothering her, because of all the people in the world, she's the only one I'd trust unconditionally with my life. I love my brother, but the bond I share with Sonea runs deeper than family, and deeper than the blood we all have running through our veins. Besides, she's not the only one with something to hide right now.

Breakfast curdles in my stomach when I think of the secret I'm keeping. Sonea would be disgusted to know what I did last night, even though I suspect what's bothering her has to do with what I saw. I don't even know how to ask her about it. We talk about almost everything, but there are some things we've unanimously agreed not to share. Sex isn't something we discuss, and although Sonea and Aston both know I'm bisexual as I came out to them a couple of years ago, I've never divulged anything more about my sex life than that to her. Even if we did share those kinds of things, I'm not sure I'd be able to.

After breakfast, I make an excuse and disappear up to my room. I can't put this off any longer. I need to know what's on my phone, and I have to see the truth so I can hopefully put a stop to the chaos whirring around my brain. Maybe I'll find the courage to confront my sister if my suspicions are confirmed, even if it means admitting how I found out. Shutting my door, I pick up my phone and unlock it.

Digging through it, I locate the camera app and load the album. The last saved item is the video, and my thumb hovers hesitantly over the play button. Swallowing the nervous lump in my throat, I take a deep breath and hit it. The video starts up, and my mouth goes dry as I watch the scene from the previous night unfolding in front of me. There's no doubting it; there on the screen is my older brother and twin sister fucking each other like their lives depended on it. The intensity of their movements and the pleasure on their faces has been captured with clarity by the tiny camera, and now their brother is watching it on replay.

The video ends when they do, and by time I'm done watching, my hand is shaking, my body is covered in a thin sheet of sweat, and my dick is throbbing painfully. Before I can stop to consider the madness of what I'm doing, I swipe back to the beginning, press play and grab my dick in my hand. I grunt at the almost instantaneous relief that follows my touch.

At first I start slowly, and eventually I'm moving my hand in time with their thrusts. I'm so close to coming. I can feel it building as my balls tighten, but just as Sonea lets out a high moan and rapture crosses her face, my bedroom door opens and I jump in shock. I try to cover myself up, and the phone flies from my hand and hits the floor. As I glance up to see who it is, I watch frozen as Sonea bends to pick it up. Fear douses the heat within me like a bucket of cold water when she looks at the screen and her face goes as white as a sheet.

Accusation and a shock that mirrors my own fills her tone when she says, "Sean, what's this?"

CHAPTER TWELVE

SONEA

Sean stares back at me, his cheeks crimson and expression horrified. The video he was watching stopped playing when it hit the floor at my feet, but I can see on the pause screen mine and Aston's naked and entwined bodies. *He saw us having sex, and he recorded it!*

I don't even know what to say right now, and it seems he doesn't either. Turning, I slowly force my feet to move, and I leave his room, heading for my own. I need to think, and I want to discover exactly what Sean observed. I can barely process the fact he recorded me and Aston, and when I walked in his room, the way he jumped as though he'd been shot makes me wonder what he was doing with the video. *Was he touching himself?*

Closing the door to my room, I move on autopilot toward my bed and sit down. Looking at the screen, I can see the video's nearly finished, so I carefully take it back to the beginning, and after hitting mute, I press play. My hand flies up to my mouth as I watch my body moving in tandem with Aston's as he slowly fucks me, getting faster and more rigorous. My own cheeks begin to flush as I watch the two of us together and the way Aston's muscles flex and my breasts jiggle with every thrust.

I can still feel where Aston's hands were on me, the press of his skin against mine, and I wonder how Sean felt when he saw us. *Did he enjoy watching us?* Sean and I shared so much together growing up, and a sudden thought crosses my mind. It occurs to me he might like the wrong things too…just like I do. I know Sean almost as well he knows himself, and there's no way he'd ever be able to talk to me about this. Sex is the one topic he's always been private about. He's the shy one of the two of us when it comes down to it.

I give Sean space for the rest of the day. Both of us are quiet at dinner, and I know Aston notices, but I shoot him a look to leave it alone when he goes to ask what's wrong. He doesn't press it, and I'm guessing he thinks Sean and I argued, and for now I'm happy to let him think that. At the moment my focus is on my twin and how to talk to him and fix this gaping chasm that just fractured our relationship. I won't lose him. I refuse to let us fall apart. We're stronger than this, but I know that out of the two of us it needs to be me who approaches him. This never would've happened if not for me, and I need to somehow make this right with him.

Aston seems to sense I need space, and even though

I'm sure it pains him to do so after our argument this morning, I'm grateful he gives it to me. Sean disappears off to his room following dinner, and I let him. He's embarrassed that I know what he saw and that I caught him with the video, so I'm giving him the chance to calm down. Hell, I need it too if I'm being honest with myself.

After I've gotten ready for bed, I grab Sean's phone from my room and walk down the hallway toward his bedroom. I don't knock, I just walk in and quietly shut the door behind me. His room is dark, but I can make out the shape of his form in the darkness, lying on his bed, and I move toward him. Setting his phone down on his desk, I lie down next to him with my back to his front. He doesn't say anything and neither do I, but after a few minutes of us lying there side by side, I feel his hand on my stomach, tugging me closer to him.

His warmth wraps around me, and the feeling of home comforts the ache in my soul that's been throbbing since this morning.

"I love you, Sean...and I know what you saw. I'm sorry you had to find out that way. Aston tried to stop it, to stop *me*, but somehow neither of us could keep apart from each other. Do you hate me now?" I ask, my voice small.

Sean groans and squeezes me. "How could you think I'd hate you? I could never hate you, Sonea. You're the other part of me. I'll always love you."

I find his hands in the dark and grip them tightly in mine. "So, when I walked in here this morning...were you masturbating to that video? Did you like what you saw?"

Silence follows my question, but I feel him bury his face in my hair, and after a few minutes pass, he answers, "Yes."

My heart thumps, and my breath escapes in a small whoosh. I lick my lips, and using my grip on his hand, I slide one of his up my body to my breast, leaving the other where it is, pressed flat against my stomach. Sean groans, and I feel his cock stiffening against my ass. With no prompting, he massages my flesh in his palm. His fingers search out and locate my nipple, and I let out a soft whimper as it sends a rush of heat surging downward. Sean's lips find my neck and he kisses the soft skin there, running the tip of his tongue across it and making me shiver. Feeling bold, I nudge his other hand downward and he follows my hint, sliding his fingers beneath the waistband of my pajama pants to rub my clit.

"Sean," I murmur, closing my eyes at the myriad of sensations he's creating within me, gasping out loud when he slides his fingers through the wetness of my pussy before delving in to it. "Fuck, don't stop."

His cock is rock hard and digging into me, and I reach around to rub it, his grunts start mixing with my moans that are getting louder the longer he touches me until I come with a soft scream. The door flies open and the light switches on, but Sean doesn't stop, even as I shudder through another orgasm with his hands on my body and Aston's eyes blazing with heat as he watches us.

"Don't stop touching her," Aston orders, and Sean's hands still for a moment before he continues. "Take her pants off, and kiss her pussy."

My jaw drops open in shock at his words, and Sean leans over to look at me and I nod. He swallows hard, glancing nervously between Aston and me, but when he grips the top of my pants, his hands are steady and his eyes are dilated with desire. I lift my ass to help him as he peels them agonizingly slowly down my legs.

"Don't tease me," I scold in a breathy voice, and he grins at me before tossing them aside and lowering his head between my legs.

The first lick of his tongue is tentative, almost shy, but as soon as the whimper escapes my lips he sucks on my clit with fervor, sending a short scream bursting from me.

"Oh, God. Oh, God," I chant as he flicks it confidently with his tongue, and I cry out when an orgasm rips through me.

I'm quickly silenced by the invasion of Aston's cock in my mouth, and I gag around his length. Sean kisses his way slowly up my body, sucking and biting the skin, and paying close attention to my nipples before he reaches my widely stretched mouth. He licks my lips, circling around the base of Aston's cock, garnering a hiss from him and a moan from me. I can feel his cock through his boxers, and I reach between us, gently snapping the elastic at the top to indicate I want them off while my words are being choked from me by Aston thrusting into my mouth.

I don't even have time to process what's happening before I'm moaning at the delicious stretch of Sean filling my pussy with his thick cock while Aston fills my throat. Before he can come, Aston pulls away, and a thin string of saliva trails from my mouth to the head of his cock.

Sean fucks me slowly, and as his confidence builds and his pounding becomes more rigorous, my body becomes coated in sweat, and when he starts ramming my G-spot, I can feel another orgasm building. *He may not be as long or thick as Aston, but he sure knows how to fucking use it.*

I just about notice Aston moving behind Sean, but when Sean stiffens, pausing while buried to the hilt inside my body, I wonder what my older brother's up to. Sean lets out a soft grunt of pleasure, and though I can't see what Aston's doing, I feel Sean's cock twitching in response to whatever it is. Aston climbs on the bed, and it dips beneath the weight of three of us as Sean leans down to run his tongue over my nipples, and when his finger finds my clit, I let out a string of whimpers

"Oh, fuck, Aston. That hurts, but don't fucking stop," Sean grits out, face twisting with pleasure and pain.

My twin hisses against my nipples, but it swiftly turns into a long, low groan vibrating through me when Aston moves and Sean's body is pushed toward mine.

When it happens again, I realize Aston is fucking Sean as my twin fucks me. The thought of it combined with Sean's cock hitting my g-spot, over and over, as he impales me at Aston's behest has me screaming and convulsing with one of the most powerful orgasms I've ever had.

They don't stop, and I'm a weak and crying mess as my over-sensitized body is pushed to its limits and beyond. Their heavy grunts and our combined panting fills the air, and the erotic scent of sex surrounds us until I feel Sean thickening even more inside me.

"Oh, fuck, I'm coming, Sonea."

He moves out of time with Aston and jerks until he comes to a stop, finishing deep inside me, while Aston continues to drive into his ass in a near frenzy until his strangled grunt rends the air and he reaches his own finale.

EPILOGUE
ASTON

Every day the twins are away at college, I miss them furiously, even though I know one day they'll come home to me forever. Every night I remind myself that no matter what happens, they're still *mine*. It's the same thing I've been telling myself for years, only now the word holds more meaning than it ever did before. In every way, they're mine, but in just the same way, I'm also theirs.

I never intended or expected the bond between us to explode and create something new and beautiful, but one moment set off a chain reaction and a cascade of events that's changed everything between us. I love my little brother and sister in a way that's terribly wrong, yet it's also terribly perfect.

I love my family, and I'll always take care of them, and even though I occasionally listen to the nagging little voice telling me to put myself first, I'll always put them above myself. These illicit desires that should tear us apart only draw us closer together.

Our blood connects us, our desire unites us, and the secret we guard binds us.

THE END

ABOUT ALLY VANCE

Ally is an International Bestselling Author who writes in the Dark Romance & Horror genres. Ally also co-writes with her close friend Michelle under the pen name Ally Michelle. Ally lives in Kent, in the United Kingdom with her husband, stepson, and two cats.

You can keep in touch with her on:

facebook.com/AuthorAllyVance
amazon.com/author/allyvance

OTHER BOOKS BY ALLY VANCE

Flower in the Dark

Fractured Darkness

Delinquent: Cavalieri Della Morte

TAKE A
Chance

BY

JM WALKER

BLURB

She's young, perfect, and just what I need...
When I meet Rina at the bar after friends invite me out, it takes everything in my power not to consume her from the first moment.
A few drinks later when we are still nothing more than just a name to each other, we take it to the next level anyway.
After spending the night wrapped up in each other, a family obligation comes up and we part ways.
But I never expected to see her again and so soon.
Especially at my brother's place.

CHAPTER ONE

RINA

It was my birthday. Twenty-first to be exact and I wasn't having fun. At all. I should have been excited. I got to get dressed up, go out, spend time with my best friend, maybe see some cute guys and have a few drinks. But in all honesty, I would much rather be at home in sweatpants with a tub of ice cream and a corny movie.

As a little girl, I would start counting down months before. I would run to the calendar on the fridge and count each day leading up to my birthday. It had been my favorite day until my parents got too busy to celebrate with me and I no longer cared. We used to celebrate my day by spending the mornings having breakfast followed by me opening up my presents. When I got older, my parents started giving me money and that was it. Not that I didn't appreciate it but I still liked the idea of opening presents and spending the day with them. Most times, we didn't even celebrate my birthday on my actual birthday anymore. And today of all days, neither of them were home, so I was stuck celebrating it by myself. Until my best friend called me up anyway.

Happy Birthday, Rina.

"Rina, smile."

I took a sip of my fruity drink and ignored Jessa Andrews. She meant well by taking me out, but my best friend and I were very different when it came to things we liked doing. She was a partier, while I was a homebody. Most people would wonder how we were even friends, but we just were. She was the salt to my pepper. The peanut butter to my jelly. She was the sister I never had. And I would never replace her for anything. It wasn't fair to her, but I just wasn't feeling it tonight. I knew that she meant well but I still couldn't help my mood.

"Rina."

I sighed, finally looking at her. "What?"

"You've been grumpy ever since I picked you up." She pointed a manicured finger at me. "You need to get laid."

I rolled my eyes. "I'm good." I had two hands and B.O.B. I didn't need a man to make myself feel good.

"Come on." She swiped an arm out in front of her. "There are a lot of guys here who would love to dive between your legs."

I laughed, shaking my head. "Not happening." Not that I was opposed to one-night stands, it just wasn't for me. Or maybe it would be if I found the right guy. But the guys my own age were either too immature or taken. And guys my own age didn't overly do it for me anyway. I wanted a man who was set in life. Who knew what he wanted. A man's man. A hard worker. I wanted to feel his rough calloused hands on my skin as he forced pleasure out of me. I squirmed in my seat, shifting and clenched my thighs together. God, had it really been that long?

But a one-night stand with the guys at this club wasn't happening. They all looked younger than me. With their baby faces and unmarked hands, they wouldn't know a hard day's work if it bit them in the ass.

"You need something, Rina." Jessa batted her long lashes that were done up by fake lashes on top of her natural ones and mascara. She was beautiful. Why she added on the extra shit was beyond me. Her lashes looked like little butterflies trying to escape her face.

"I'm good," I repeated, taking another sip of my drink when I realized it was empty.

"Fine. Will you dance with me at least?" She pouted.

"You go. I'm going to get another drink." I needed something stronger and none of this fruity crap.

"Are you sure?" Jessa looked longingly at the dance floor.

I laughed, pulling her into a hug. "Go." I kissed her cheek. "Have fun and I'll have a drink waiting for you when you come back."

"Okay!" she exclaimed, heading out onto the dance floor.

I grabbed another Cosmo for her and a scotch on the rocks with a lemon twist for me. My heart fell a bit, remembering how I used to sit with my grandpa while he drank his scotch and puffed on his cigar.

"You shouldn't smoke around her," my father would say.

Grandpa would put out his cigar and light it up again once my parents were no longer around. He would also let me sneak a puff and a sip here and there. He had told me it would leave an impression with the guys. I never understood what he meant then. I would also join him for his Poker game. Until my parents found out and no longer let him babysit me.

"Ma'am?"

I jumped, finding the bartender staring at me. "Sorry. Thank you." I paid for the drinks and brought them over to the table Jessa and I were standing at.

I scanned the crowd.

She was dancing between two men. I envied her. I wasn't overly shy, but I wasn't outgoing either. She had been the complete opposite of me. She took life by the horns and tackled it to the ground while I stayed back and watched. She loved being in the spotlight. Especially when men were watching her. I noticed the two guys who were dancing with her were older. Maybe late thirties. Early forties. She had never mentioned a preference when it came to age but clearly them being older didn't bother her.

The tiny hairs on my body tingled suddenly. I looked past the throngs of people, my gaze landing on a couple other guys sitting in one of the half-circle booths against the far wall. They were watching Jessa with the two guys. It made me wonder if they knew them or not.

My gaze went back to Jessa. She would laugh every so often, grinding between them and letting their hands roam her body. It bordered on inappropriate. I was almost jealous of her. She just didn't care. It was a trait most didn't have. Maybe I should be the same way. At least for the night. It wasn't like my parents cared to spend my birthday with me anyway. Jessa had been the only one. She reminded me that I didn't have to be alone and there I was, being a party-pooper.

I took a large sip of my drink. The burn of the scotch simmered deep in the pits of my belly. It warmed every inch of me, giving me the strength I needed to get through the rest of the night.

Once the next song ended, Jessa left the two guys and came toward me.

"Have fun?" I asked, taking another swig of my drink.

She nodded, wiping her brow with the back of her hand. "It's hot out there." She laughed.

I handed her the Cosmo I ordered for her.

"Thank you." She took a long sip. "The guys invited us to their table. They got bottle service and said we can have as much as we want." Which usually meant that they wanted sex as payment.

"Are you sure that's a good idea?"

"Why not?" She hooked her arm in mine. "You need to live a little."

I planned on it, but it still didn't mean I wanted to spend the night with random men. Especially when I was sure they would expect some sort of payment in return.

"I can live a little and not spend my time with creepy old men."

She snorted. "Come. They aren't creepy." She dragged me to the other side of the club. "They're nice."

It was my turn to snort. "They were nice because they had a hot little thing shaking her ass for them."

"Aww." Jessa batted her lashes. "You think I'm hot?"

I rolled my eyes.

She laughed.

And I couldn't help but laugh with her.

Once we reached the group of guys, Jessa sat between the two she had danced with earlier while I had stood off to the side.

"Is Nick on his way?" one of the men asked.

"Yeah. He said he was caught up at work," another answered.

"Good. Lord knows he needs a night out," the first man told his friend, scowling.

While Jessa conversed with the two guys she danced with, I tried not to listen to the others talking about this Nick guy, but I couldn't help but be curious to know more.

"He needs to find a young thing, someone without baggage, and just fuck her brains out," another guy with light blond hair and the greenest eyes I had ever seen, said.

"Truth."

"I agree."

Several more grunts of agreement sounded around the group.

"I'm sorry." Green eyes came up to me. "We never introduced ourselves. I'm Jonah." He stuck his hand out. "That's Reed and Issac. The two with your friend are Shep and Patrick."

"I'm Rina and she's Jessa," I said, returning the handshake. The hairs on the back of my neck suddenly tingled.

Jonah glanced over my head. "It's about time you showed up."

"I would have been here sooner," a deep voice said from behind me. It was so deep, it rumbled through every inch of me. "I need to hire new staff."

"Well come have a drink." Jonah walked away. "We got bottle service."

"Good." The new guy who I could only assume was Nick, stepped past me. When his shoulder brushed mine, a tingle shot through me.

I gasped.

Nick glanced over his shoulder, his bright blue eyes locking with mine. His eyebrow rose in question.

I lifted my chin. I wasn't sure why I was defying him. But something told me to do it. He was older. I was younger. And I bet his hands would feel good smacking across my ass.

My cheeks burned at that thought.

His lips pulled up into a smirk.

"Nick, sit." Reed patted the spot beside him.

Nick sat, crossing his ankle over his opposite knee. He carried on a conversation with his friends, but I couldn't focus on anything that was being said. He was beautiful in a rugged way. With dark hair that fell in a wave on top of his head, it sat just above the top of his ears. Dark scruff with a hint of gray, covered his chiseled jaw in a thin layer. I had never been one for older men, but Jessa did tell me to live a little. Maybe tonight would hold many firsts for me.

I took a sip of my drink, enjoying the warmth the scotch provided.

"Rina."

My gaze snapped to Jessa. "Yeah?"

"You good?"

My cheeks heated even more when I realized all sets of eyes were on me. "Yup."

Much to my surprise, Nick stood and came toward me.

"What are you drinking?" he asked, standing close. So close, I could smell the scent of his spicy cologne.

"Scotch on the rocks with a lemon twist."

"Scotch?" His brows shot up. "Really?"

"Why?" I asked, which came out a little more abrupt than I expected.

He chuckled. "Just asking, babe."

"I like scotch because it reminds me of my grandpa and another thing, I am not your babe." I walked away and headed back to the bar. My blood burned through me at the cocky asshole who assumed that someone like me couldn't drink scotch. I hated people and their stereotypes. Pissed me off every damn time. I should have been a cat.

Once I reached the bar, I ordered a shot and a drink. Slamming back the shot, I sat on a nearby empty stool and spun around until I faced the group of guys Jessa was still mingling with. A part of me expected her to follow me. But when I saw that she was still focused on the two men sitting on either side of her, I knew I would have to go this one alone.

I looked around the group and noticed that Nick was no longer with them.

"Looking for me?"

My heart jumped to my throat.

Spinning around in the chair slowly, I found Nick sitting beside me. He had moved his stool close enough to mine that his knee brushed up against mine. The shadow from his big body loomed over me.

"What do you want?" I took a sip of my drink, trying to ignore the fluttering of my heart at how close he was.

"To apologize for being a dick."

I looked at him then. "Really?"

He pulled back a swig of his beer. "Why not?" he asked, licking his lips.

The back of my neck burned. I wasn't a flirt. That

was all Jessa. I wished I had at least half of her confidence.

"Shouldn't you be with your friends?" I made a point of looking back at the group. Jessa was laughing at something one of the guys said.

"She's safe," Nick pointed out, following my line of sight.

"She told me to live a little tonight." I snapped my mouth shut, unsure as to why I blurted that out.

"Oh?" Nick brushed his thumb along my knee. "So, have you lived a little yet tonight?"

"Depends on what you consider living a little?" I threw back at him, ignoring the way his touch made me feel. It was like his thumb burned into the deepest part of me. A part no one has ever been able to reach.

Nick's lips twitched, his eyes searing into me. Several beats passed between us where nothing was said and we just sat there, staring and wondering about the other.

"Maybe an extra drink. One more than you usually have. Or you hook up with a random stranger." He winked. "Something you normally wouldn't do."

I laughed. "Are you hinting?"

He gave me a cocky grin. "I have no idea what you're talking about."

My laugh turned into giggles, surprising myself. I shook my head. "Right," I said slowly. "I'm sure there's someone here who you could hook up with if that's what you're wanting." Hook up with. Did people even say that anymore?

A sly grin spread on his face. "I'm sure there is." He paused. "So, I never did catch your name."

I held out my hand. My parents drove me crazy half the time but they did teach me to use my manners. "Rina."

He slid his fingers into mine before bringing my hand up to meet his mouth. "Nice to meet you, Rina." His lips brushed the back of my knuckles, the scruff from his beard, tickling them.

A wave of heat rushed through me.

My breath caught. "Nice to meet you too."

"Nick," he added, giving me a wink.

"Oh." I pulled my hand from his. "I know."

He sat back, not taking his eyes off of me.

"What?" When he didn't answer, I huffed. "*What?*"

"You're beautiful," he said, taking a sip of his beer.

I followed suit and sipped at my scotch. The liquid heated me from within. I wasn't used to this attention from the opposite sex. I almost thought there had been something wrong with me half the time. No guys ever showed interest. Even the men my parents tried setting me up with because it looked good for them. When really, the men weren't even men. They were guys my age who wanted one thing. Maybe that was what Nick also wanted but for whatever reason, it didn't bother me like it usually did.

When I finished my drink, I placed the empty tumbler on top of the bar. "Well, Nick. It's been fun." I slid off the stool and went to walk away when his gentle but firm hand grabbed my arm.

"Where are you going?"

"To the bathroom, if you must know." I pulled from his grip and rushed away from him, disappearing into the throngs of people. Truth was. I just needed to get away. Before I did something stupid. But I had a feeling that no matter how hard I tried; I would still do something stupid tonight. And a part of me looked forward to it.

CHAPTER TWO

NICK

She was beautiful and I let her leave like the fool that I was. But I wouldn't press her. Not yet. There had been a connection between us. One that I had never felt before. Not with any of the women I had ever been with. Not with my ex. Not with the woman who tore out my heart and ate it like the viper she was.

I wanted Rina.

She had said that her friend suggested her having some fun tonight, so I would make it a mission to give her that. Even if I never saw her again, I wouldn't let Rina end the night without feeling me against her. My touch. My kiss. My cock that was now pressing up against my fly.

I palmed my crotch, looking around the vast expanse of the club but Rina was no where to be found.

She was young. Much younger than I ever went for. But maybe that was what I needed. What we both needed.

Swallowing the last of my drink, I jumped off the stool and headed in the direction of the women's washroom. There weren't many dark corners in the club that Rina and I could hide in. I didn't want anyone seeing or hearing what I was doing to her anyway.

Once I neared a long hall that had signs pointing to the bathrooms, my cock jerked. In my forty years of existence, I had never fucked in a bathroom stall. The women I had been with weren't exactly the adventurous type but somehow, I had a feeling that Rina would be.

The closer I got to the women's washroom, the harder my dick became. My bones vibrated beneath my skin. The need to consume her, controlled my actions until all I could think about was slipping my cock inside her hot flesh.

It had been a long time since I had been with a woman. Especially one as carefree as Rina. She looked to be out of place with her jeans and t-shirt, but she also gave off the appearance that she just didn't care. It was refreshing to say the least.

When I neared the women's washroom, I waited a few minutes to see if anyone went in or out. Rina must have still been inside and like the creeper I was, I slowly pushed the door open.

She was standing at the sink, washing her hands. Her head snapped up, her gaze landing on mine in the reflection of the mirror.

I half expected her to demand that I leave the bathroom. That it was women only. That I was in the wrong place. But when she turned off the water and pulled a paper towel from the dispenser hanging on the wall, keeping her eyes locked on mine the whole time, I knew I was in the right place.

When female voices sounded from the other side of the door, Rina gave me a wink and made her way into a bathroom stall.

I followed her, shutting the door behind me as the voices became louder. Locking the stall, I shivered at how close Rina was now that we were locked in together.

She looked up at me, licking her lips and placed her hands on my chest.

Grabbing her hands, I spun her around and slammed her up against the door.

The fact that we weren't alone only made things more intense.

The girls were talking about who they planned on going home with tonight and other shit that I didn't care about. I was too focused on Rina to pay attention to what they were saying.

Leaning down toward her, I kissed her cheek, brushing my lips down the length of her jaw. "I wonder how long it'll take for them to realize that there are two people in this stall," I murmured in Rina's ear.

A breathless laugh left her. "I don't think they'd care."

"No?" I pinched her chin, turning her head toward me. "Too bad. I think they'd be jealous."

"Oh?" Rina's eyes twinkled. "And why's that?"

In a quick move, I shoved a hand between her legs, cupping her center. "Because you're about to get fucked within an inch of your life."

Her laugh deepened. "Is that so, old man?"

Her sass burned through me. Fisting her hair, I tugged her head back and sunk my teeth into the spot beneath her ear. "I'm going to fuck you until you forget your damn name."

"Geezus." Rina shook against me.

I smirked. "Unzip my pants and take out my cock."

Like a good little girl, she did as she was told. When her fingers wrapped around my length, I bit back a groan.

"Nick." Her wide eyes dropped to my waist.

"Yeah, baby. This is all for you. It's going to fill you up. Make you come and have you screaming my name in a matter of seconds."

She swallowed. "Is that even a thing?"

I chuckled. "Oh, it's a thing. Now stroke it. I want you to get acquainted with it before it disappears inside your body."

Her hand gripped me tight, stroking from base to tip. Her thumb ran over the head, swiping up the pre-cum leaking from my body.

My balls tightened, a hard tingle racing down my spine at the contact I hadn't felt in so damn long I almost forgot what it was like to be with a woman.

"Nick?"

My eyes popped open, not realizing I had closed them.

"Kiss me."

Rina

When his mouth crushed against mine, I realized that this was the thing I had been missing. Jessa told me to live a little tonight and I was. Nick felt so damn good against me, I couldn't control the need for more. My center ached, throbbing with need to be filled by him. His cock was hot, swollen, so damn hard for me.

Running my thumb along the bottom of the veiny ridge, I smiled when he growled into my mouth.

"Fuck." He slapped a hand against the door beside my head, his big body shaking.

Releasing him, I undid the button of my jeans and lowered the zipper.

His dark eyes became even darker as he watched me.

Turning around, I pushed my jeans off of my hips.

Nick cupped the back of my head, pushing it against the door and ran his other hand over the seat of my ass. His fingers slid beneath the string of my thong, pulling it to the side and dipped lower and lower. He grunted when he felt how I wet I was for him. Pulling the string toward him, he inserted a finger into me in one smooth thrust.

I whimpered, chewing my bottom lip.

Releasing my head, he pushed the tip of his cock between the crack of my ass.

My breathing picked up, the ache deep in the pit of my center becoming more pronounced as time went on where he wasn't inside me. "Please."

A tin foil wrapper sounded a moment later.

I braced myself, knowing that this would most likely hurt but in a delicious erotic way. It was exciting. I didn't know this guy. Just his name. Jessa was going to lose her shit when I told her about this.

Nick pulled the string of my thong again, bending me at the waist. Before I knew what was happening, he thrust every inch of him inside me in one powerful move.

My eyes widened, my body clenching down around him.

"Fuck," he growled, sinking his teeth into the back of my neck. He pulled back, leaving only the tip of him in me when he pushed forward. He kept up the movement. It was slow, deliberate but powerful thrusts. Pleasure consumed me. It was something I had never felt before. Not even when I spent hours touching myself.

My body shook, my thighs trembling. My knees quaked the longer time went on with him fucking me. Nick took everything he wanted from my body. He made it his, showing me for just a moment exactly who he was.

I pushed back into him, slamming my ass against his pelvis.

"That's it." He fisted my hair, holding my face

against the door and powered into me. "You're a little slut for my cock, aren't you?"

"Yes," I heard myself say.

"That's right. I'm only giving you a taste, baby. Imagine all the things I could do to you if we were in a bed."

I moaned.

He chuckled.

And I fell.

CHAPTER THREE

RINA

"Well..." Nick gave me a cocky grin. "I wasn't expecting to do that tonight."

I laughed, my cheeks heating. "Neither was I."

"Can I see you again?"

I winked, leaving the bathroom stall.

Nick followed me, gave me a quick kiss on the back of the neck and started walking to the door. "I'll meet you at the bar. Oh and Rina?"

"Yeah?"

"I don't suggest standing me up."

I shivered at the threat hidden beneath his deep voice.

Once I washed up, I made sure I didn't look like I just had my guts rearranged and went out to join Jessa.

When I neared the bar, I found Nick sitting at it with a beer in front of him and another drink off to the side.

I joined him, sitting on the stool beside him.

"For you." He pushed the tumbler with amber liquid swimming in the bottom, closer to me.

"Thank you." Crossing my knee over the other, I turned to him. "Shouldn't you be with your friends?" I asked, nodding toward the group of guys who Jessa was still currently hanging out with.

"Nah. It does seem like your friend is getting acquainted with them though."

I snorted. "She likes her men." She was leaning against one of the guys with her legs resting on another's lap. "She really likes her men."

Nick chuckled. "It's one thing I've never been able to do."

"Oh? What's that?"

"Share my women." He jutted his chin. "Shep and Patrick love sharing women. I wouldn't be surprised if they both ended up with the same one, one day. But it's not my thing."

"I don't know. Two of you seems pretty delicious." I waggled my eyebrows.

Nick's laugh deepened.

"Not my thing, babe."

It wasn't my thing either, but it didn't mean that I couldn't fantasize about it. While Nick and I continued drinking our drinks in silence, I watched the crowd of people move with the deep bass of the music. Sex was in the air, literally, and I couldn't help but wonder how many others were getting their brains fucked out in a bathroom stall tonight.

"Rina." Nick's deep voice pulled me back around.

I turned in the stool toward him, taking another sip of my scotch. "What?"

"I want to see you again."

He had said that already. Truth was, a man like him could break me. He was older. More experienced. Clearly. And while we certainly had a connection, it didn't mean that I was ready to take this to the next step and have a relationship with the guy. I just wanted some fun tonight. Jessa told me to. Happy Birthday to me.

"Today's my birthday," I told him.

Nick tilted his head, his eyes twinkling. "Is that so."

"Yup. I turned twenty-one." I waited to see if the fact that I was young grossed him out, but it only seemed to make that delicious tick in his jaw beat more. "Does that bother you?" I asked anyway.

In a quick move, Nick pulled my stool closer to his. He leaned toward me, his hand gripping the seat of the stool that I was currently sitting on. There was hardly any room on it for me, let alone his hand. But when his thumb brushed back and forth over my hip, that touch burned into me. I had jeans on and yet I could still feel him everywhere. Was this normal? Did my parents ever experience this? Jessa?

"You're thinking." Nick pinched my chin. "You need to stop thinking and live a little. Isn't that why we did what we did tonight?"

"I was bored." I wasn't sure why I said that but a part of me wanted to poke the bear and see how long it would take for him to snap and maul me.

A wicked grin spread on his face. "Careful, little girl." He leaned down to my ear, his hot breath scorching the side of my face. "Now that I know what you feel like, I won't stop until I know what you taste like as well."

I swallowed hard, my body heating at what he was suggesting. "Take me out of here," I heard myself say.

His body stiffened.

Ha. Looked like the guy wasn't expecting me to say that.

I shoved my head out of his grip and jumped off the stool before stepping between his knees. "You want me again?" I cupped his inner thigh, giving his ear a gentle nip. "Then take me out of here, Nick."

In a quick move, he shoved to his feet and grabbed my hand. Leading me out of the club, we quickly walked to what I could only assume was his car. He seemed like the type to have a sports car or a large SUV.

When we hit the parking lot across the street, Nick quickened his steps, keeping a firm grip on my hand.

I rushed to keep up with him, the muscles in my legs burning from the excessive use. "Nick."

He suddenly stopped in front of a red truck, pulling me in front of him and slammed me up against the side of it.

All breath escaped me at the rough move. "Nick."

"Shut the fuck up." His hands roamed down my sides before digging into my ass and lifting me into his arms.

"Make me," I threw at him.

He smirked, crushing his mouth to mine.

The kiss was frantic, fast and all consuming. I had never felt anything like it. Not even earlier that evening in the bathroom stall. I felt this kiss down to my toes. The pleasure tingled over my skin. Even though we were fully clothed, my body burned for him.

With rough hands, Nick unbuttoned my jeans, pushing the fabric below my ass. His fingers massaged and kneaded my flesh, igniting the raging inferno inside of me.

Breaking the kiss, he gave me a soft peck before spinning me around.

My heart raced, my chest rose and fell with ragged breath. I couldn't believe this was happening. Outside. Late at night. In the damn public no less.

"Stick your ass out." His deep voice slid over every inch of me.

I tilted my hips, waiting, wanting, silently begging for him to do what he did best.

Nick brushed the hair off the back of my neck and pushed the tip of his cock between my legs. "I'm going to spend the night using your body." Before I could comment, he thrust inside of me.

I whimpered, chewing my bottom lip to keep from crying out.

"You feel how hard I am for you?" His thrusts deepened, his cock hardening even more. "You feel what you do to me?"

"Yes," I moaned.

He chuckled. "Good." His hips powered back and forth, lifting me onto the tips of my toes with each hard thrust.

My body tingled, my pussy aching at the rough but delicious use. An electric current rushed through me, the release hitting me fast and sudden.

Nick grunted, his own orgasm spilling into me.

My eyes widened, realizing then that he hadn't used a condom.

Pulling out of me, he brushed the tip of his cock over my center, his cream coating me.

I shivered, pushing back into him.

In his own way, he was marking me, claiming me as his. And I guess I was. For the night anyway.

NICK

I had no intention of fucking Rina outside and against my truck for that matter. But there was something about her that I needed. I became addicted and fast. She felt good. So damn good wrapped around me. But stupid me, slipped my dick inside her without covering up first. Once I helped her with her jeans, she told me she was on birth control. Thank God for that.

When I drove us to my little house just outside the city, I didn't learn much more about her. Just that she had a sex drive that could bring me to my knees.

"Fuck." I cupped the back of her head and forced her mouth further down my throbbing cock.

She gagged, a low moan escaping her.

I held her head, liking the feel of her throat working over my dick. She widened her mouth, taking me even deeper. That single action shot through my balls and made me come hard and fast. "Fucking hell."

Rina swallowed every drop, gave the tip of my cock a final kiss before sitting back in her seat. She wiped her mouth, her dark eyes meeting mine. "You need to drive faster."

I chuckled and like a good little boy, I listened.

CHAPTER FOUR

RINA

Making my way into my parents' house, I tried to be as quiet as I possibly could. It was only nine in the morning. I was exhausted, sore but absolutely satisfied. I had never felt pleasure like I had last night. Nick did things to my body that I never even knew were possible.

"You like that, baby?" Nick murmured against my ear. *"You like when I choke you?"*

My neck tingled from the way he had kept a firm hold on my throat. He had been gentle in the bathroom stall compared to how rough he had been later on. But I never complained. I never told him no. I never told him that it was too much. I could still see his dark eyes staring down at me. I could still feel his powerful cock inside every inch of my body. I could still feel him dominating me in ways I never thought I would enjoy.

Making it to my bedroom, I breathed a sigh of relief that my parents weren't up yet to catch me sneaking in. I had told them that I was spending the night at Jessa's.

After texting her once we got to Nick's place, I had found out that she was going home with two of the guys she spent the night dancing with. I wasn't surprised in the least. Men loved her. Especially older ones.

A soft knock on my door, startled me. "Rina? I heard you come in."

I rushed to my dresser and quickly got changed into pajamas before answering the door.

My mother stared back at me, giving me a small smile. "I wasn't expecting you home so soon."

"Yeah, Jessa had some things to do today and I couldn't sleep, so I figured I'd come home and maybe sleeping in my own bed would help." Luckily it wasn't overly a lie. I always had an issue sleeping in someone else's bed. Until last night that is when I passed out in Nick's bed.

Mom closed the distance between us and pulled me into a hug. "Happy belated birthday. I hope you had fun."

I did. More than I could ever tell her. "Thank you, Mom."

"Listen, your uncle's back in town and he's coming over this evening for dinner. It's been awhile since we've seen him."

"Uncle?" I frowned.

"Yeah." Mom released me and stepped back out into the hall. "Your dad and his brother had a falling out when you were born. Long story short, their egos got in the way and Nick left."

My heart stuttered at the name. "Funny, I met a guy last night at the club, named Nick."

"Oh yes. I heard he had gone out for drinks with the guys." Mom laughed, shaking her head. "I miss those days."

Something odd nudged at me but I couldn't quite place what it was.

"How come I never met him or even seen pictures?" I asked, following her downstairs.

"Because my brother is an ass," Dad said, coming out of the kitchen with a mug in each hand. "Did you have a good birthday?"

Eventually. "I did."

"Good." He gave Mom a kiss on the cheek. "Nick will probably be here early. Trying to make up for lost time I guess."

While they talked about my uncle, I couldn't help but wonder exactly who my uncle was. It still didn't make sense why I never met him or even seen a picture of him. After all of this time.

Excusing myself, I took a shower and got dressed when my phone dinged with an incoming text. As I was slipping the dress over my head, I glanced at my cell, my stomach flipping.

Nick: I want to see you later.

Me: How much later?

Nick: I have a family thing and then I'm free. I'm itching for a taste of that juicy cunt.

I shivered at his vulgar words.

Me: I'm sure I can slip away. I have a family thing too.

Nick: Family comes first.

Why did I sense a bit of sarcasm in that text?

Me: It does. Most times anyway.

Nick: What are you wearing?

I laughed.

Me: A dress.

Nick: Good. Don't wear any panties.

I smirked.

Me: Wasn't planning on it.

Nick: Good girl.

Me: Have a good day, Nick. See you later tonight.

Nick: You too, Rina.

I spent the day doing nothing. It was nice actually. I listened to Nick and didn't put on any panties but as the hours went on, I found the anticipation getting worse. I was wet for him and he hadn't even done anything. He made promises and I knew he intended to keep them.

Later that afternoon, I was sitting outside when I heard voices coming from the kitchen. I put my book down as my parents stepped out into the backyard.

"Rina, I'd like you to meet your Uncle Nick." Dad moved to the side as a large man came out of the house.

When those dark eyes landed on me, my heart fell to the ground beneath me.

CHAPTER FIVE

NICK

As I stared back at my niece, I realized then just how cruel life was. Not only was she my niece, but she was also who I had spent the previous night with. We did things. We did unspeakable things. And now I came to learn that Rina was actually my niece.

She stood from the patio couch she was sitting on and came toward me. "It's nice to finally meet you. I've heard a lot."

How she could be so calm was beyond me. "It's nice to finally meet you too."

"Good. Now that introductions are done, I'll grab us a beer." Jason headed back into the house.

"I really wish you two would have met sooner," Liz said. "But better late than never, right?"

Rina only nodded, crossing her arms under her chest.

"Well, I'll let you two get acquainted, while I

continue working on dinner." Before either of us could say anything, Liz headed back into the house.

Rina and I only stared at each other. As much as this wasn't right, what we did, what we shared the night before, I couldn't help but want to go to her. To pull her into my arms. To hold her. Touch her. Be there for her. But that couldn't happen. What we did. What we shared. It could never happen again. As much as I found myself wanting it to, it wasn't right. This was all sorts of fucked up.

"Did you know about this?" Rina finally asked.

I grunted. "Yeah, because fucking my niece is my kink."

Rina's jaw clenched, her cheeks turning red. "What we did..."

"It wasn't our fault. I had no idea who you were."

She looked away. "It was fun," she murmured, her voice soft.

"It was more than fun, Rina." I took a step toward her. "It was the best night of my life."

She looked at me then, a slow smile spreading on her face. "It was mine too."

Before we could elaborate more on the subject, Liz and Jason took that moment to join us.

Jason tried playing nice, when in all reality, I really wanted nothing to do with my brother. Or half-brother technically. We shared the same father, but our mothers were different. Which still made Rina my niece by blood. My stomach twisted. Fucking hell.

Jason and I used to be close but after he got the girl,

I left. It had been too hard seeing him with Liz. Even though it had been years ago, being near them again made me uneasy.

"Nick."

My head whipped around as Liz came toward me while Jason stood off to the side, talking to his daughter.

"I know this is...well...weird." Liz gave me a small smile.

She had no idea. "It's fine."

"Is it?" She placed her hand on my arm. "I am sorry. For everything. I never meant to cause a rift between you and your brother."

"I know." I pulled her into my arms, giving her a hug. "It's fine. I promise."

"Okay." Liz returned the embrace, giving me a gentle squeeze.

Releasing her, I pulled back the rest of my beer, wishing it was something harder.

"What's going on?" Jason asked, joining our little duo.

"Nothing." Liz stood on tip toes and placed a soft peck on his cheek. "Dinner will be ready in about ten minutes." She left us and went back into the house.

I caught Rina's gaze.

Her brow was raised, probably wondering what the hell was going on between me and her parents.

"Nick."

"Yup," I said, staring at my niece.

"We never should have let a woman come between us."

I looked at my brother then. I searched his face for a sign that he was lying but when I couldn't find anything, I clapped his shoulder. "I'm glad we're talking again."

"Me too, brother." He grinned. "Me too."

RINA

I slept with my uncle. No. Correction. I fucked my uncle. Or he fucked me for the most part. I couldn't believe this was happening. After all this time, I finally found a man who made me feel things I never thought I could feel before only to find out that I was related to him. It didn't matter that they were half-brothers. We were still blood related.

While I sat at the dining room table, waiting for my mother to dish out dinner, I took a sip of my wine.

The back of my neck tingled as someone sat beside me. I knew who it was but there was no way I could look at him. I was embarrassed. Memories of the things we had done the night before came rushing back.

"You're a little slut, aren't you? Swallowing my big cock like a fucking whore."

My throat burned. I could still feel him sliding along my tongue.

My core ached, throbbing with need for the man I could never have.

"Rina, I promise I didn't know," Nick's deep voice slid over every inch of me. "I swear I didn't."

Sitting back in the chair, I placed my ankle on the opposite knee. My dress rode up to my thighs.

Nick's dark eyes glanced down at my lap before meeting my gaze. "You can't do this shit."

"I'm not doing anything." I suddenly remembered that I wasn't wearing any panties. Because he had been the one to tell me not to since we were meeting up later. But now that he was there, I suddenly felt exposed.

When I went to lower my foot, he stopped me. His hand cupped my knee, his fingers digging into the bone.

My skin burned, knowing this wasn't right but craving his touch just the same.

While my parents were in the kitchen getting dinner ready, Nick slid his fingers up my inner thigh. His gaze dropped to his hand, his jaw clenching.

My heart raced at how dangerous this was but exciting just the same. Getting a hint of bravery, I moved my foot from my ankle and placed it on the edge of his seat, opening my body up to him even more.

As much as I knew we shouldn't be doing this, I couldn't help it when he was looking at me like he wanted to damn near rip me apart.

When his fingers hit my center, I let out a soft whimper.

"Shhh..." In a quick move, he thrust his middle finger into my body. The movements were slow and deliberate, almost like he was damn near teasing me. As he kept fingering me, Mom and Dad joined us at the table.

I lowered my knee, pushed the chair further under the table and grabbed onto Nick's hand that was currently between my legs. God, I was going to hell but I would sure have a hell of a good time before doing so.

While my parents and Nick caught up, I looked between both my dad and him. Side by side, you could see the resemblance they shared. They looked like brothers but meeting Nick the night before, I had no idea that he was related to me in any way. Life wasn't fair.

CHAPTER SIX

RINA

By the time supper was done, I was damn near vibrating out of my skin. Nick had kept his hand between my legs the whole time. He teased and touched, massaged and tickled, but never let me have that orgasm I craved.

The fact that he was my uncle should have stopped me, but it didn't. I wanted him. Maybe I always would. This wasn't right. No matter how much he made me feel good, this couldn't happen again. But God, he felt so good at the same time. I was confused. I almost wished my dad and him never reconciled, then I never would have known that he was my uncle. It was selfish of me to think that way but at that point, it was all I had.

After dinner, I needed to step away and gather my thoughts. Also maybe rub one out so I wouldn't be tempted to have Nick or Uncle Nick rather, do it for me.

As I was able to lift my dress to my hips and slip my fingers between my legs, the door to the bathroom opened.

Nick stood there.

My eyes widened, my cheeks burning at being caught.

"Well don't stop on my account," he said, closing the door behind him and leaning against it.

"What are you doing?" I lowered my dress.

"What does it look like I'm doing?" He pushed away from the door and came toward me.

Holding my hands up, I backed up until I hit the wall. When I couldn't go anywhere, I dropped my arms at my sides and just waited.

Nick placed his hands against the wall on either side of my head. "You were going to rub this sweet little pussy, weren't you, Rina?"

"I have no idea what you're talking about," I said, my voice not as confident as I would like.

"No?" He grabbed my hand, bringing it up to his mouth and nipped the tips of my fingers. "These fingers were going to rub that little clit. Were you hoping to come?"

"You teased me. I need...I need something," I confessed.

"Then let me give that to you." When he dropped to his knees in front of me, all breath escaped me. "You want to ride my face, baby?"

"Yes," I heard myself say.

He winked, sliding his hand up the back of my

thigh before hooking my leg over his shoulder. "Let me have a taste." When he covered my core with his mouth, I bit my bottom lip to keep from crying out.

I wasn't sure what changed besides the revelations that had come to light in the past few hours, but his mouth had me coming in a matter of seconds. He growled against me, the scruff of his jaw scratching at my inner thighs. He seemed almost desperate for me.

"I..." My body shook, my knees almost giving out at the pleasure rushing through me.

He cupped my ass, lifting me against the wall and ate at me hard. He sucked my clit between his lips, giving it gentle nips until my body was gushing as another release slammed into me.

Once I calmed down, he released me and wiped his mouth.

In a quick move, he had me on the floor beneath him. With my dress up and over my ass, he shoved every single inch of his cock, deep into my body.

It was brutal in the way he took control of me. Never letting me get used to the size of him, the thrusts turned violent. They were painful but at the same time, had another orgasm screaming through me.

He grunted his satisfaction, knowing I liked it rough. "Is your ass still sore?" he asked, brushing his lips along the shell of my ear.

"Yes," I whispered.

"Good." He pulled out of me, lining the tip of him against the tight rim between my ass cheeks.

Before I could brace myself, he pushed into a part

of my body that had never been used for pleasure before.

His hips slammed against me, his balls slapping my pussy after every powerful thrust. "You're a dirty little slut, aren't you? My niece likes being used up."

My skin tingled, my pussy clenching at the dirty words.

He chuckled, wrapping his arm around my shoulders. "Ride me, Rina. Show your uncle how much you like his cock in your ass."

"God." I whimpered, pushing back against him and took his dick even deeper into my body.

"That's it. Such a good little girl." Nick fisted my hair, pulling my head back. "Spread your legs."

I did as I was told when his other hand landed against my center. The move had been so quick, it took me a second to realize what he had just done.

He did it again. And again.

Slap. Slap. Slap.

I cried out, not caring in the least that my parents could possibly hear me.

Nick growled, sinking his teeth into the side of my throat and continued slapping my pussy all while fucking my ass.

Another slap and I gasped, swallowing a scream as a powerful orgasm exploded through me.

"Such a good little girl." He bit my neck, the sharp sting sending a flush of heat throughout every inch of me.

"You need to stop." But as I said the words, I knew

that I didn't want him to actually stop. It didn't matter that we were blood related. He made me feel things I had never experienced before. I couldn't help it. I was damn near addicted to the man currently inside of me.

"Are you sure you want me to stop?" he growled, running his hand back and forth over my pussy.

I whimpered, my thighs trembling.

"That's it. Come again for me. Let your uncle hear how good he's making you feel."

"This..." I moaned. "This isn't right."

"Are you sure?" Nick wrapped his hand around my throat, gripping it tight and held me back against him. "Come. Again. Now."

No matter how much I didn't want to listen to him, my body broke, earning me a satisfied grunt of approval.

When he was done, he stuffed his cock away, leaving me on the floor. He stepped over me. "I'll see you out in the backyard. Your parents are having a bonfire and have invited me to stay for a drink."

Before I could respond, he left the bathroom.

I pushed up on shaky limbs and stood in front of the mirror. I was a mess, but I had a glow nonetheless. Even though Nick was my uncle, he felt good. Too damn good. And I wasn't sure I would ever be able to curb this new addiction. Or that I even wanted to.

CHAPTER SEVEN

NICK

I shouldn't have taken out my anger on Rina. It wasn't her fault that we were in this mess. But even after finding out that we were related, even if it was just by being half brothers with her father, the same blood was still rushing through us. It wasn't right. I found since finding out that she was my niece, that I wanted her even more. It was sick the things I wanted to do to her. The more I couldn't have her, the more I wanted her. I craved her. Needed her. I wanted to fucking rip her open and make her beg like she did the night before. She was a dirty little thing and gave just as good as she got.

It wasn't right.

But if it wasn't right, then why the hell did it feel so damn good all at the same time?

This didn't make sense.

Should I tell Rina's parents? No. It would just cause more issues for us. Especially Rina. It wouldn't matter that we didn't know each other at first. I fucked her in the bathroom after I found out.

I was going to hell.

While I was outside with Liz and Jason, I couldn't help myself and kept glancing at the patio door.

"What's wrong with you?" Jason asked, a deep frown settling between his brows.

"Nothing." I glanced at the door again. "I bumped into Rina on the way to the bathroom and she said she wasn't feeling well. Just wondering if she's okay." I was a little shocked at how easy the lie rolled off of my tongue.

Rina took that moment to join us in the backyard.

"How are you feeling?" Liz asked her daughter.

Rina faltered in her steps, her gaze shooting to mine.

"You told me you weren't feeling well. Must have been something you ate," I told her, mentally begging her to play along with the lie.

"Oh." She smiled at her parents, sitting beside me on the patio couch. "I'm feeling much better. Thank you."

"Good, I'm glad," her mom said, smiling at her daughter. She wouldn't be smiling if she knew what her daughter was doing only a few minutes ago.

My cock twitched, lengthening against the fly of my pants. Fucking hell.

"Nick," Rina said gently. "This is weird."

"Yup."

Of all the women in the whole entire world, I had

to spend the night with my niece. It wasn't even like our town was a small one. A town somewhere in the middle of nowhere, I could see people ending up with someone they were related to but in our city? It was damn near impossible to run into someone you already knew. Life was fucked.

"You know we can't do this again."

"Do what?" I asked her, keeping my voice low.

Even though her parents were talking amongst themselves, I didn't need them hearing anything they shouldn't have been hearing.

"Fuck," Rina said, the dirty word leaving her full lips sending a shiver down my spine.

"I know." But even though I knew that we couldn't have sex again, it didn't mean that I didn't want to. It was messed up because the more I couldn't have her, the more I wanted her just the same.

RINA

While my parents chatted with Nick or Uncle Nick rather, I quietly excused myself and went to my bedroom. This wasn't right but being close to him did funny things to my belly. The only way I would be able to control myself was by putting distance between us. As much as I didn't want to, I couldn't be near him. I was happy for my father that he had his brother back but I wanted nothing to do with him.

Oh who the hell was I kidding? I wanted everything to do with Nick.

With his hand pressing firmly against the back of my neck, he fucked the very air from my lungs. He took everything that made up me and made it his own. His hips powered back and forth, owning me with each deliberate thrust.

I shivered, remembering the night before. I had lost count of how many times we had sex. I needed to call Jessa. Maybe she would know what to do.

Shutting the door behind me, I went to my bag sitting on my bed. Fishing for my phone, I dialed Jessa's number and waited.

"Hey girl," she answered after the first ring.

"Hi."

"What's wrong?"

I frowned. "Why would you think something's wrong?"

"Because you never call me. You only text."

My stomach twisted that she knew me so damn well. "Uh...I have a situation and I really don't know what to do."

"What's going on?"

"So you remember those guys we met last night?" I swallowed hard, trying to ease the anxiety rushing through me. "And you remember the guy I was sitting at the bar with?"

"Yes. He was hot."

"Well..." I cleared my throat. "I went home with him."

She squealed. "That's fucking amazing. It's about damn time. You know the guys I was dancing with? I didn't go home with them but I got their numbers and I gave them mine and we're meeting up next weekend. You should come."

"Well, that's the thing," I said when she finally took a breath.

"What? What's the thing? Oh God. Don't tell me he has like a small dick or something."

"No. Not that." Definitely not that.

"Then what's the problem?"

I took a deep breath and let it all out. "I didn't know this until last night. He's my father's brother. God, Jessa. It's so awful. I had no idea. It's such a small fucking world that this would happen. The first guy I like, hell, the first guy I go home with and he's my..."

"Uncle," she whispered. "Holy shit. Are you fucking kidding me right now?"

"I swear I didn't know." My eyes burned, my chest tightening. "Please don't judge me." It was funny. As much as I was worried that my parents would lose their shit over this if they ever found out, it was Jessa's opinion of me that I cared about the most.

"I don't judge you. Wow, Rina. He's your uncle. Really? And you had no idea?"

"Not at all. They don't even look related until you put them side by side."

"Well, if you didn't know. That's not your fault."

"It wasn't until we...uh..."

"You had sex. Again. After you found out, didn't you?"

"God." I laid back on my bed. "I'm going to hell."

Jessa laughed. "Girl, if you're going to hell, then I'm driving the damn bus."

"Really?" I sat up, leaning against the headboard.

"Yes. Listen, let me tell you a story. I can't believe I've never told you this. But your dirty little confession made me think of it."

I sat forward, curious as to what my best friend was about to tell me when I thought I had known everything about her.

"So a few years ago, my cousin Geoff came home from college. Do you remember meeting him?"

"I do. He was hot." And he really was. With dark shaggy hair and dimples, he had looked like he walked right off a fashion magazine.

"Well, we had gone out for dinner to catch up and had a little too much wine. Later that night while my parents were in bed, Geoff came into my room."

My heart jumped. "What happened?"

She laughed. "He fucked me, Rina," she confessed like it was no big deal and that she didn't just tell me she had sex with her cousin.

"Really?"

"Yup. It only happened the once, but it's been our dirty little secret ever since. Now he has a girlfriend and he's happy. But I'll never forget that night."

"This is wrong on so many levels."

"Maybe but at least for you, you didn't know that

you were fucking your uncle. I knew Geoff was my cousin. When he crawled onto my bed, I never pushed him away. Sure, it's fucked up but girl, it was the best sex I ever had. It makes me sad that we couldn't keep doing it, but it is what it is. At the time, he didn't want to settle down and neither did I."

I let out a slow breath. "Thank you. This makes me feel a little better I guess."

She laughed. "Anytime. Now go have fun and be a good little girl for your uncle."

"Oh God."

Her laugh hardened. "I love you, Rina, and remember, you have no judgement from me."

"Thank you and I love you too." We said our goodbyes.

When I placed my phone on the nightstand, the door to my bedroom opened.

Pretending to play on my phone, I ignored the way the tiny hairs on my body tingled. I ignored the way my heart jumped when the door shut, and the lock was clicked into place. I ignored the way my stomach did a somersault, knowing I was now alone once again with Nick.

I continued to play on my phone as he neared the bed.

His large shadow loomed over me, the scent of his cologne invading every ounce of me. He reached a hand out, cupping my face.

My stomach fluttered.

Nick brushed his thumb along my bottom lip. "I know we can't do this again," he said, his voice low.

"But?" I looked up at him then.

"Rina." His eyes darkened.

"I know." A shuddered breath left me.

"I'm sorry." He tilted my head back. "For how I treated you in the bathroom. It's not your fault. None of this is your fault."

"I wasn't complaining."

He smirked, sitting on the bed in front of me. "Who were you talking to?"

"Jessa." I placed my phone on the nightstand and leaned against the headboard.

"Did you tell her?"

"Yeah, I did. She did something worse than what we did." I explained how she fucked her cousin.

Nick's eyes were wide. "Seriously?"

I laughed lightly, giving my shoulders a small shrug. "Yeah."

"Holy shit." He ran a hand through his dark hair. "I know I'm finally talking to my brother again, but I can leave. You'll never have to see me again."

"No. I don't want that. I..." I grabbed his hand and held it in mine. "In another life."

He sighed. "Yeah, in another life, Rina." He stood from the bed, releasing my hand and towered over me. Placing a soft peck on top of my head, he let his lips linger. "You take care of yourself."

My breathing wavered, my heart clenching.

When Nick went to the door, he stopped and turned back to me. "Another life."

I nodded, my eyes welling. "Another life."

He slipped out of my bedroom, shutting the door behind him gently.

It took everything in me not to run after him. Not to beg for him to be with me. But I knew we couldn't be together. And I wouldn't do that to his relationship with my father, not when they only found each other again.

Knowing what I would have to do, I rubbed the tears from my cheeks. It was the only thing I could do to get through this. To help Nick get through this as well.

I would have to leave.

For good.

EPILOGUE
RINA

Sometime later

It had been awhile since I had seen my Uncle Nick. I hadn't even thought of him until I ended back at the bar I had met him at quite some time ago. I wasn't sure what made me even come to this bar. Maybe I was thinking of him without even knowing it and just ended up there.

It felt like just yesterday where we met, flirted and ended up fucking in the bathroom stall.

I wasn't sure if he would be there tonight but a part of me hoped he would be. Not to start anything up again but just to see him. To see how he's doing and if he was happy.

"Rina."

The deep voice coming from behind me sent a

flutter of hope dancing down my spine. I turned as Nick sat on the stool beside me. "Nick."

"It's been awhile," he said, signaling the bartender. After ordering a drink, he nodded toward me. "Still drinking scotch, I see."

I laughed lightly. "Yeah. How are you?" And that was when I saw it. A single gold wedding band sat on his ring finger on his left hand. I expected my heart to drop or my stomach to sink but when it didn't, I realized then that I was truly happy for him.

"I'm not too bad. How are you?"

I shrugged. "Not too bad as well."

"How long has it been?"

"Eight years." And I was still as single as the day I had met him. I dated but none of the guys had ever compared to Nick. My uncle. And that thought alone left a sour taste in my mouth, so I could never open up my heart to anything more than just a random fuck.

"Long time, Rina. Too damn long." Nick brought the beer up to his lips, taking a long swig before turning back to me. "Seeing anyone?"

"Nope." I jutted my chin forward. "But I see you are."

He grunted, fingering the wedding band. "Nah. Divorced with no kids. I just wear this shit to remind me of what could have been I guess."

My chest tightened. "I'm sorry."

Nick shrugged, giving me a small smirk. "Not a big deal. We were never right for each other anyway. After you, I just fucked any random hole I could find. Makes me sound like a dick but it's the truth."

"I get it." And I did. We met and were attracted to each other almost instantly. The fact that we were related changed everything. I knew for myself, it made me believe that I didn't deserve anymore than just random sex here and there. I didn't deserve happiness or a family of my own because in all reality, I had wanted my uncle. My stomach twisted with unease.

"Listen, did you want to grab dinner sometime? Just as friends. Nothing more."

I looked up at him. "I think I'd like that."

We spent the next couple hours having a few more drinks and getting to know each other. I had already learned from my parents that they had become closer with Nick. Which I was happy for. But after he left my bedroom that night so many years ago, I applied to a college out of our city and moved, never to look back. Until now.

I was a little surprised that my parents never told me Nick had gotten married. Maybe they didn't even know. It didn't seem like he had been married for long. Or if he had, he definitely wasn't happy. I felt sorry for the woman, knowing that I had something to do with their failed marriage.

When last call was called, Nick paid for our drinks and walked me out of the bar. We exchanged information and promised to meet up for dinner.

As I was slipping into the back of the taxi, he

leaned on the edge of the door. "It was good to see you again, Rina."

I smiled up at him. "It was good to see you too."

He shut the door, giving me a wave.

The taxi started driving away, the image of Nick only getting smaller and smaller. I lifted my hand, giving him a small wave back anyway. It was probably the last time I would ever see him. I almost expected a sense of sadness to come over me but when it didn't, I turned around in my seat and let out a small sigh.

Seeing Nick again, spending the evening with him, gave us both a sort of closure I never realized we needed.

Even though he was my uncle, whatever we had that one and only night together, felt right. It was wrong on every level to want to do it again.

Pulling my phone out of my bag, I opened up my messages and sent Nick a text, letting him know what hotel I was staying at.

Me: I'm in room 1604.

Nick: I'm on my way.

Stuffing my phone away, I smiled.

ABOUT THE AUTHOR

J.M. Walker is an Amazon bestselling author who hit USA Today with Wanted: An Outlaw Anthology. She loves all things books, pigs and lip gloss. She is happily married to the man who inspires all of her Heroes and continues to make her weak in the knees every single day.

"Above all, be the HEROINE of your own life..." ~ Nora Ephron

Website:
http://www.aboutjmwalker.com/

Facebook:
https://www.facebook.com/jm.walker.author

Reader Group:
https://www.facebook.com/groups/JMsJems/

HARLEY'S
Aero

BY

C. L. MATTHEWS

BLURB

Blood.
Family.
Loyalty.
It was what my brother and I always lived by.
Somewhere along the lines, it got tainted.
Blood became our pact.
Family became our burden.
Loyalty became our livelihood.
It was only us.
Him and I.
Aero and Harley.
My devil, his trouble, our sickness.

CHAPTER ONE

HARLEY

The bond between brothers is unbreakable.

It precedes friends and succeeds changes.

It outlives fights and conquers every loss.

No matter how twisted and split we get, the blood and the bonds created between us are forever tethered. It's probably why I risk so much for my insanity, knowing he'll always come back and never leave me behind. Not forever, at least.

At least, that's what I tell myself as Aero's fists fly into the face of the guy in my bed.

What have I done now?

I guess I should explain how we got here.

For that, we have to discuss some troubling facts. The first, me being my position of desperation. The second, me being cornered and forced to give in my hand. Not always, but I'm sixteen and weak, and I'm done feeling left out when my brother discusses his sex life while I'm a virgin in nearly every sense of the word.

Stupid or not, it's a big motivator. Lastly, it should be said that this is exactly how I *wanted* this to go. Well, not in the case of Uly, but the reaction from my brother.

Red, red, red.

It splatters.

The color rains over my gray sheets, sprinkling like the water on our lawn in the summer. It marks the bedspread like an artistic tool, streaking it with strokes of anger, resentment, and *jealousy*.

He loves me.

He loathes me.

He *can* have me.

My brother's fists hiss against Uly's skin, striking him like a viper and bringing more damage than necessary. It's deranged hit after hit, and neither Uly or me is able to stop the assault. Uly doesn't fight back. I'm not sure why he easily takes the beating, being that he's nearly the size of my big brother, but it's as if he allows it to happen. Does he think he deserves this kind of treatment? We only kissed and fondled a little. There wasn't even penetration.

Aero's face gathers sweat from the back and forth motion of his arm. Exhaustion flickers in his eyes, but it doesn't stop him. He barely falters as his skin splits unnaturally. If he keeps this up, he'll knock Uly out or, worse, kill him. He's close enough to eighteen. They wouldn't bat an eye to sentencing him as an adult. I've got to stop him, to tell him it's my fault, to do anything to force his wrath on me instead of the first guy I've touched. Why does he care? It was just fooling around.

Ulysses Dobric, like me, is gay. He's open about it. It's why I decided to pick him to take my virginity. Maybe picking the one guy at Oasis High my brother can't stand wasn't my best choice, but as I said, I'm *desperate*. It makes no sense why Aero hates Uly. I've never seen them interact.

"Aero," I struggle to say steadily.

My brother pauses, his blond hair wet and dripping. Is it from blood? From exertion? Both? A mistake, that's what this is. His eyes are so dark right now, black and lethal. Usually, one is sky blue, bright and lively. The other is green, dark, and troubled like the other, more depraved part of him. Right now, though, they appear obscure, deadly, and ready to end everything.

"Why him, *Trouble*? Why Dobric?" It's a snarl. He spits with disgust and apprehension, making sure to attack every sense of mine easily. "Fucking Christ."

He shakes his head, not expecting an answer, but the question burns in his expression along with disappointment. They never warn you how debilitating it is to have your favorite person in the world stare at you like you're a failure. It's like being punch in the nuts, where you lose your balance from a crippling ache that reaches the inside of your body.

My eyes scan Uly. His face, red and purple, is bloody, bruised, and so goddamn swollen it's slackened. His naked torso that only minutes ago hovered over my body, kissing, touching, and making me groan with anticipation, now seems wrong.

He's passed out, more than likely from the pain my brother has put him through. Despite Aero kneeling above an unconscious Uly, my brother is the one I'm worried about. His chest heaves uncontrollably, sporadic, almost unable to decipher which speed it's supposed to beat at and drained from lack of breathing. Rage does that to a person. It blinds you, seals your fate, and takes all conscience away.

"I'm sorry," I try. My voice cracks. Out of the two of us, he's the careful one. He's the good child while I'm the troubled one. He'll go places, and I'll be lucky to graduate. It's why he calls me *Trouble*.

We're opposites.

He's loved. I'm hated.

He's coveted. I've avoided.

He's popular. I'm a basket case.

"When did you know?" he questions.

"K-Know what?"

He couldn't possibly understand or know that I'm sick in the head, heart, and soul, but I should know better than to underestimate Aero. Nothing gets passed him, not even my attraction. It's an easy answer. *Him. He's when I knew.*

"That you were attracted to men," he states dumbly, like I'm an idiot.

Oh. That.

When I watched you tongue fuck that quarterback from Valley West. I don't say that, though, especially since he's not out in the open or even to me. That game, I snuck off to see where he left to, and boy, did I get an eyeful of them and a lungful of bitter rage.

What are the odds he's not only attracted to the same types of guys as me?

"Last year. You?"

"Not sure," he snips, but the curl of his lip speaks volumes. The way he grimaces makes me believe he doesn't want to say the truth. That's us. Lies. Secrets. Hatred. When did it change? Why does he hate everything about me to the point that he runs away from my bedroom?

"You've got to go. If he decides to freak out, the cops will come," I try and explain.

He smiles evilly. It's disarming the way he almost sees through me.

"Nothing will happen, Trouble. He's too fucking stupid to ever go against me."

As he says the words, he's stalking toward me with purpose. I'm naked, my junk only covered by a sheet as I lean against the wall of my room. The crimson streaks on Aero's shirt stare at me, a blatant reminder of my spoiled plan. When my gaze reconnects with his darkened one, I'm struck stupid.

"O-Okay," I mutter dumbly.

His calloused thumb digs into my skin as he tips my chin roughly, glaring.

"Next time you decide to *fuck*," he hisses, his statement slapping me with its ferocity, "do it with someone who has a *good* dick, Harley. Pencil penis over there doesn't know how to use it on *willing* boys. He likes when they fight. With your luck, it'd go limp halfway through the first breach."

I swallow the lump forming in my throat, hoping he doesn't notice the way my body trembles at his proximity.

"I-I wasn't—"

He smacks the wall with both hands, my head goes to where his hands connected with the drywall, streaking it red, effectively boxing me in with his built body. A war rages in me, one that's been battling for the better half of a year, one that's lost at every turn. It's a no-man's land, a desolate existence waging on pain.

"Don't lie to me! Yes, you fucking were. He was going to stick his nasty shit in your ass and give you all sorts of diseases. When you'd beg him to stop, that's when he'd get excited and hurt you so badly you'd be useless to the ones who actually *deserve* you."

His cruel words strike me again, and though they're menacing and harsh, they turn me on. Not the actions he believed Uly would have taken. No, the last half, where he insinuates someone else is more worthy.

In my mind, it's *him* he's talking about wanting me. It's *him* who wants to defile me and bring me to my knees to choke on his cum as it spills down my gullet. It's *his* body that worships and bruises me and makes me bleed, He would lick the wounds thereafter, his own kind of stitching to the madness he would inflict on me.

My dick hardens at the imagery, tenting the sheet,

warming my flesh and sealing my fate as the fucked-up brother in lust with his own flesh and blood.

It takes Aero all but two seconds to notice. His arms that closed me in flex under the tensing of his shoulders. His palms that were flattened are now digging into the drywall. A low growl emanates from him. It's harsh like him. Animalistic. Unhinged.

A ceaseless urge presses me forward.

My mouth touches his softly.

So softly I almost believe it's in my head until his teeth bite into the plump lower swell of my lip, bringing forth a groan and whimper simultaneously. My body aches from the defectiveness of my cravings. It's no longer festering. It's suffocating me, putting its fingers around my esophagus, closing, closing, closing.

He lashes out at my mouth with his tongue, sliding it between my lips like a battle of its own, one neither of us will win. His body aggressively presses against mine. Beneath the softness of the sheet, there's a sword pressing against mine. It's a warning of demise, a silent promise of the end.

Our end.

But then he's pushing back. His face looks almost inhuman with his distaste and repugnance. It's true. I'm repulsive. He should run far the fuck away and never come back or end me now and save us both from my ill intentions, ones bound to kill us both by their severity and unnaturalness.

"Fuck, Harley. *Fuck!*" The morphing from disgust to abhorrence is swift and brutal. His fist collides with the wall behind my head. "You can't fucking do that, Trouble. Fuck! You're my fucking *brother*."

He pulls at his hair, drywall dust coating the locks like powder truths and making my lies impossible to hide ever again. Now, he knows. I'm obsessed, enamored, in love with my own brother.

"Brother," I repeat and shake my head. "I don't know what I was thinking."

Lies. Lies. Lies. All I do is lie.

"It won't happen again, Aero. I promise."

That's the thing about lies.

They're only true in the moment.

Later, all is fair game.

CHAPTER TWO

HARLEY

ONE YEAR LATER

My brother hates me. This much is true. It's my fault, really. How can he not despise me when I'm constantly ruining his life? No, it's not intentional. It's from being young and dumb, but it's also from the need for attention.

His attention.

And then there's the *kiss*, the stolen one that made him cut ties with me entirely.

My brother walked out of my room and hasn't been back since. Not there, his room, or the house except for the forced Sunday dinners to appease our drug-addled mother. Guess my plan backfired that night.

Instead of bringing him back to me, it completely pushed him off the cliff of dis-ownership. He moved into his own place when he turned eighteen eight months ago. School is only four more months, and then he'll graduate. He'll be completely gone and probably won't come for Sunday dinners anymore either.

I'm nearly eighteen, but where will I go? He's all I've got left.

We don't talk when we're in the same room. I try, but his eyes narrow, his jaw ticks, and then he excuses himself. Mom and Dad don't notice a thing, not that they could. Dad's busy fucking randoms from his office, and Mom is high on Valium and vodka, the only two loves of her life.

My best friend tries to keep my mind off my broken relationship with Aero, but it's no help. She doesn't understand. Of course she doesn't know about the kiss Aero and I shared or the fact that every time I try to kiss someone, I can't. It's like I get whiskey dick but not as a result of whiskey.

"There you are!" Char yells, crossing the commons area.

Charlotte Ellis. My best friend, all of four-foot eleven-inches, runs toward me. Her bright fuchsia hair, straight and hella long, sways as she tries moving too quickly in her six-inch platform boots.

Did I mention Char dresses like a Suicide Girl? Tattoos litter her skin like it's their job, and the pin-up-esque daily attire solidifies the entire getup. If I were into pussies, she would be one I would ram into, but alas, I like dicks, and she digs pussies. Two of the same yet opposites through and through.

We're so similar, in fact, that I dyed my hair this summer to black with hot pink and teal patches to give it a variation. I look like Hot Topic puked me up and said, "Voila, your goth dick has arrived."

My brother didn't say anything when he saw my hair for the first time, but he noticed if the fists he made when he made eye contact with my change were anything to say.

I wait for Charlotte to catch up, seeing her septum piercing for once. She usually tucks it up like me. The principal likes to give us both a hassle for our body modifications, but she'll just have to remember her dress code doesn't refute it. Fair game and all.

"What's up, SG?" I ask when she finally hooks her arm into mine.

She smiles at me. I remember the first time I called her that. She did not think I meant Suicide Girl. *She thought I meant Stupid Girl.*

"I'm thinking of ditching Social Studies and getting high behind the bleachers."

Weed does sound enticing.

She raises her eyebrow, giving me the silent question. *Coming or not, loser?*

"I guess," I mutter.

It's not like I want to go to Hessler's anyway. It's the only class I have with my brother—gym, where he's half-naked, sweaty, and making my dick grow and hanker for something it isn't allowed to seek. Gym insinuates physical activity.

While I'm fit and work out daily, listening to the other assholes call me fairy and princess doesn't really appeal to me. My brother lets it happen. Guess it helps that he's in the closet about his sexuality.

He even dates Serenity Danielle. She's the head of the Drill Team, a glorified cheer squad if I'm being honest. I would say she's my worst enemy, but it would be a lie. She seems nice even if she talks about his dick too much.

I hate it, but I listen every fucking time.

I'm jealous, but I refuse to hate someone who has a claim to his heart and body when I don't. Maybe he's bisexual and digs pussy as much as dick. It's not my place to label him. I can barely label myself.

"*I guess,*" she mocks, trying to imitate my voice. "Don't give me that bullshit line, HarHar."

"That's still the dumbest fucking joking to date," I complain.

"Harley HarHar," she teases and then bursts out guffawing, tipping her head back loudly and obnoxiously.

Not giving her the satisfaction of a laugh at her dumb impression, I flick her nose and walk away from her.

"Come on, Harley! I was just joking. Don't be such a pussy!"

"Why not? Maybe you'd be nice to me then?"

"Okay, now who's the one bad at jokes? That was lame, even for you."

I chuckle and wait as she flops her boots like they're fifty pounds per step.

"Smoke a joint with me," she says. "Let's not deal

with people we don't like, and then we can fool around if we get high enough."

Grimacing, I think of the one time we tried that, testing our tastes. I like dick. She definitely likes pussy, but hands are okay*ish*. Okay, not really, but we've attempted.

"Fine, but if your tits get close to me again, I'll cry." I'm not lying. They freak me out.

She's covering her laugh but can't stop the snort that slips out. Her visualization game is on point. I have the same.

"Yeah, I remember how that went last time," she says. "Maybe we need two joints?"

"Nothing is going to stop me from being gay. Same goes for you. We can't change what our bodies crave because we're lonely."

She nods and frowns a little. "It's just lonely. Not many girls are gay here. Or if they are, they hide it. The ones who are open aren't into me and same for me to them."

"I still cart around a dick, dude. That's not magically going to turn into a cunt, and at least there *are* lesbians here, Char. As far as gay goes, only Uly is out in the open. We both know how that went."

We keep heading south toward the football field. Under the bleachers is where we get high. I've heard it's a hot spot for fucking, but I haven't witnessed a single couple. Maybe Uly only told me because he expected me to mess around.

After Aero practically beat him to death, we didn't

speak a word. He doesn't even look in my direction anymore, which makes me feel even lonelier. The one dude who can possibly get me off won't even acknowledge my existence.

Being different in any sense is so fucking isolating. People don't warn you that coming out will make you an outcast. Imagine if they knew the only dick I wanted is related to me. Bet Maury wouldn't have a facial expression for that clusterfuck.

We take the long trip across the field. It would be faster if Char didn't wear huge ass boots that make her wobbly. She's a klutz on her best days in ballet flats or Converse. On her bad days? It's like she's tanked on a fifth of gin.

"What are you going to do this summer?"

Her question comes out of nowhere and has me stopping to gawk at her. She has this expression, almost curiosity mixed with knowledge. Does she know something I don't?

"Well, if Mom is getting high and Dad is fucking broads, I'm sure I'll be getting high and finally losing my virginity," I answer honestly.

Sometimes, people make big ass deals about innocence and whatthefuckever, but not me. Being me is a disease, I swear, being stuck with a reminder that no one has taken interested in me. It taunts me, telling me I'm useless, just like Dad always says.

"You know, I feel that."

"Is that so? You're hot. I'm sure some chick will stick

her fingers up in that cave and do whatever you chicks do," I badly explain, nearly gagging at the thought. Why does a woman's parts make me so squeamish? And how the hell does my brother fuck Serenity when I couldn't even finger my best friend when she wanted to get off?

Yeah, we probably shouldn't do stupid shit when we're high and drunk, but when you're two losers unable to find love, you do what you can with who you can. Or at least, that's what we tell each other. It hasn't ruined us.

Yet.

The saddest part? Neither of us really enjoy it. I mean, we both always come, but it's to our own twisted fantasies of other people. It has nothing to do with each other. We don't communicate or look at each other. It's honestly really fucking awkward. I've always wondered if that's how hookers got off with Johns. Do they pretend they are somewhere else with someone else? Do they enjoy the sex? It's nothing against what they do. They're just fulfilling the needs of others, but how do they deal with it?

"You're thinking awfully hard, HarHar," she comments, staring at my face.

What? Is my forehead wrinkly? Do I look like I can't read? Because that's how I feel like I look.

"Yeah, let's light up," I say, diverting her attention from me.

"Right now?"

I peer around us, seeing nothing but open field.

Gym starts in fifteen minutes. Then we'll be more at risk.

"Yeah, may as well. No one's out here."

She nods at me and pulls out her joint. It's fucking huge. She's never made it this big. I find myself smiling at the relief we're both about to get. We might even be high enough to get off.

The problem with her hands on my dick is that they're too small and dainty. My brother's hands are huge, veiny, and calloused. I've imagined what that texture would feel like against the soft flesh of my shaft.

My body heats as I picture it. *Fuck.*

She takes a long drag, holding it for longer than usual. Grabbing my arm, she brings our lips close, and I know what she's about to do. I open a little for her as she blows the smoke into my mouth. It rises, and I sense the hiss of it through me immediately. Finally letting it out, I feel the tightness in my chest ease. Fuck yeah. This is exactly what I needed.

We only get two puffs in before rounding the back gate behind the bleachers. She and I both stare at each other before we wedge inside the huge hole.

One would think the school would patch this up, especially if they don't want to risk delinquents like us getting out, but they're not very bright. They don't lock the locker rooms or classrooms that aren't being used for free periods. The library is the only thing with detectors, and that's only because books are apparently expensive.

When we creep past the metal fencing, we hear

noises. My ears perk up, recognizing that sound. If the years of porn didn't educate me, Netflix's lack of censorship—which is dope by the way—definitely taught me a thing or two. First, vaginas aren't cute. Next, women's moans are prettier than men, but something about it grates on my ears. It doesn't make me hard.

The skin slapping, though? Whether a dude is slipping in an ass, mouth, or cunt, that did it for me. It harmonized with each connection, making a sloppy noise that I enjoyed. Besides the high-pitched moans, I can hear that familiar clap resounding.

We exchange open-mouthed expressions.

Guess it's time for me to see what the hype is about.

We sneak quietly around the base of the bleachers, past the biggest metal beam in the cement brace. I see the two people, one bent over grabbing her ankles.

I wish I hadn't decided to miss class.

My eyes connect with my brother's. His one green and one soulless blue orbs meet mine. A smirk curves his lips as he sneers at me. It's a mixture of evil and sensual. I hate it.

I assume the girl is Serenity. She hasn't spotted us yet, but my brother's gaze hasn't veered off. It's connected with mine.

His thrusts pick up as he glowers as me, his body hitting hers harder. Her moans get louder and more annoying. I close my eyes, and as if hearing his silent command to not be a little bitch, I open them again in time to see him release inside her with a gravelly grunt.

Not realizing it sooner, I notice Char isn't looking at them. She's squeezing my arm hard, her nails biting into my flesh, but my dick is so hard and disgusted at what it just witnessed that her pain doesn't register on my mind.

"You okay?" I whisper, leaning in so only she'll hear.

"Fuck no. God. Goddammit."

Her words are fast and annoyed, sad maybe? That doesn't make sense unless... Is she into Serenity?

"Ohmygod!" Serenity squeals. There she goes with that inane high voice of hers. "D-Did you?"

"Shut the fuck up, Ren," my brother barks harshly.

That's when Char lets her grip of me go and rushes him. "Don't you talk to her that way, you piece of shit!"

She's up in his space, but he has over a foot on her, even in her big shoes.

"What, is Suicide Barbie jealous? Can't get your own pussy, so you pine after mine?" he taunts.

"Stop!" I roar, stomping toward my brother and pushing him backward.

The initial touch of our skins causes mine to burn in return. His forehead is all sweaty. The normally blond locks look nearly brown, soaked in his sex-filled labor. He glares at me, his two different eyes sending shivers down my spine while also making me hate myself for enjoying his attention. It's been so fucking long. I'm starved for it. *Ravenous.*

His hand grips my bicep hard, indenting my skin in a way that should hurt but has my dick pulsing in tempo of my heartbeat instead. He leads me away, his face pinched in an unreadable way. It could be frustration, aggravation, or something I want.

Lust.

"Did you enjoy the little show, *Trouble*?" he mocks.

Hearing my nickname on his lips does something to me. It makes my heart run rampant and my palms sweaty. God, the inability to breathe correctly flusters me.

"You like seeing me sink my cock in girls? Turn you on—"

"Fuck. Be quiet," I hiss, peering around us. We're far enough away from the two chicks that they can't hear us, but still, it's not exactly world knowledge that I'm sick. The risk is too high. He hasn't spoken two words to me in a year, yet he's turning me on with his callouness. For what? For fucking what?

"Scared your little bitch will hear what your tastes are like?"

I meet his eyes at that. For a millisecond, they soften and then, like a camera flash it's gone.

"Don't call her that," I say. My voice is too calm, almost detached. If I sink into him again, fall for his abyss-inducing thrall, I'll break. I'll do something he won't like and fuck us up for good.

"Why? Does it make your little dick hard?" he derides, his top lip curved up, showing his teeth.

Will he gnash at me next? Bark? Jump me like a goddamn animal? It wouldn't be a reach, not with him. Never with him.

"Aero," I beg, my voice a mere whisper. I don't want to set him off when there are people watching, people who could ruin our lives, more than I've already done for us. "Why are you doing this?"

He turns us so his back is to them. With his height four inches on mine, he towers me. After a breath, he grips my throat, squeezing the sides loosely but harshly enough to make me shake.

My dick jumps.

Goddammit.

My response to him isn't nature versus nurture. It's bad and wrong and wrong and wrong.

"I'm doing this because I've spent the worst year of my existence avoiding my own flesh and blood," he growls, flaring his nostrils as if they've betrayed him for existing. "I've had to fuck some stupid bitch while thinking of dicks and sticking it in their asses while they cry from both pain and pleasure."

He leans forward. The crisp air bites at me almost as harshly as he does with his existence. It's like he wants to kiss me, eat my horror for a midday snack, and make me his slave once again.

"I'm beyond pissed that I can only get off with one memory in mind, Harley. Every goddamn moment I'm in her cunt and its silkiness grips me, I die inside because the one person I want—the one I'd fuck until he cries—isn't someone I can have."

Who is he talking about? Who drives him insane?

My breathing has gone shallow, and my skin prickles. My dick? God, it throbs. It's in tandem with my heartbeat, and I swear I lean into him. Or is it a hump? I'm not sure, but I whimper. It's loud and clear as day. His grip tightens, and a hiss escapes me at the pleasure riding me.

"I want you to bleed, Trouble. I want to slice your skin with my blade and bend you over my car and drive into you. My cock craves that ass of yours, but not until after I'm done making it red and raised from my palm," he growls, his voice lower and heated.

It's me he's talking about?

"It's your mouth I wish I could choke with my rod, Harley. It's you I want to hurt so fucking bad it feels just as good. And your tears as they leave your face? I want those too."

"Fuck," I hiss. My orgasm literally skirts my shaft, and he hasn't even touched me.

As if he knows, he reaches down, slips inside my skinny jeans and flexes his fist around me.

"You see, little brother, you've woken the monster that lays awake at night haunting you under your bed, waiting for the perfect moment to steal your blood and fuck you dead. That's all I've wanted since we've kissed. That's all I crave. It's all I fucking think about."

He pumps me three times and leans in, licking my ear.

"Now come like the little freak you are, thinking of your big brother sinking inside those tight virgin walls of yours."

And I do.

I fucking explode in the tight confine of my black denim jeans and all over his ruthless hate- filled palm.

He lifts it out with a hateful smirk and licks two fingers as he stares at me blatantly. My knees grow weak as he lets go of my throat and rubs his cum-covered palm across my face, chuckling darkly.

"Watch yourself, Harley. Next time, I won't be so kind."

When he struts away as if he didn't just make his brother nut, I noticed both Serenity and Char are gone.

I sit flat on my ass with soaked jeans, my own seed on my cheek, and more shame than I've ever felt.

That tiny high I had has long past subsided, and my dick weeps with its first taste of man.

Correction. It weeps for my goddamn brother.

CHAPTER THREE

AERO

One year. Three-hundred and sixty-five days. Give or take.

It might even be possibly longer since I've avoided my baby brother. When you're supposed to protect your younger sibling since your parents abandoned you both, lines blur really quickly. Well, they aren't supposed to, but for us, they had.

As soon as he turned sixteen, I noticed his eye stray to *guys*. Even now, I haven't come out to other than him. I'm the captain of the baseball team. Of course I'm not going to tell anyone.

Do you know what happens in Odessa when you decide to come out? You're a spotlight. We're not as small Valley West, but we're just as primitive, which means alienation on the best days and a hospital bed on the worst. No thanks.

Sweat still lines my spine from Trouble's fascination with me.

My mind jumps to earlier, from the lead-up of ramming into Serenity and hating the smell of her and the wetness of her slick heat to visualizing my little twink brother just to get hard.

She begged me for it, literally got on her knees in attempt to suck me off. By the way, like most chicks, she sucks at it.

Pun intended.

In the year we've been seeing each other, she's barely learned to wrap her lips around it. It's a feat in and of itself to get my dick hard.

Even then, she's as clueless and untalented as Alan Fredrickson on the Thespian team. He may be the leader and head of all plays, but he doesn't have a talented bone in his flimsy body. Fuck. That's the exact description of my girlfriend. She's talentless but looks pretty.

As sad as it sounds, that defines you in this shit hole.

Holding up the standard of golden boy of Odessa bores me, but someone has to do it. It's the only thing that keeps me above the drivel of loserdom like my brother and eighty percent of this school, and it gives me options for when I get the fuck out of this town. Maybe that makes me heartless or soulless. Don't care either way.

My life wasn't promised, but my future sure as hell will be. How else would I escape? Especially if I have any chance of taking Harley with me. There's no chance in hell I'll leave him behind. Whether he likes me or not right now, abandoning him isn't in the cards.

"Did you really let your brother watch us fuck?" Serenity snipes, bringing my mind back to the moment. It's nearly time for practice, but she doesn't care. All she wants is attention and *love*.

Gag me, please.

Love shouldn't be forced or driven by how amazing you are at everything you try. Ren doesn't get that. She thinks that since we're both socialites, which isn't true for me, we should be together and happy. Does that make a lick of sense anywhere on this horrible shit place we call earth?

"What? Did you want me to stop? You seemed to be enjoying my dick enough," I mutter boringly

She scowls, hiking her bag strap higher, as if that brings an ounce of confidence forward.

Serenity oozes that shit when people are around, but inside, we both know she is a sad, broken girl who doesn't know what the fuck daddy problems hide beneath her skin.

"Shut up!" she hisses, smacking her dainty palm over my mouth.

If it were Harley, what I would do to such a disrespectful move... His ass would be red, and his blood would be mine. Ren isn't Trouble. She's stupid, but she's not yelling for reaction.

"My reputation can't handle that kind of confirmation," she says.

Her words only add more water to my oil fire, making it burn and spark stronger.

Gripping her wrist, I wrench her palm away. She stares at me in shock, but she fixes it for a fake smile. Ever the actress.

"If you really cared about your reputation, you would date a sweet guy who gives a fuck about you. However, you don't care. It's a cross between wanting to be some stupid gossip girl and being popular. Why go with me, the meanest prick on campus, unless the point is to be *noticed*?"

It's cruel, the words twisting around her like rose thorns, pricking her skin. Wonder if the Barbie bleeds. Is she too dead from selling herself out for clout, or are there vital organs under that faux-pas tough skin she has?

"You're such a dick," she whispers, noticing the people enter the locker room for a clothing change before heading to practice.

Her body is nearly flush with mine when she leans in, her breath low but too loud from her closeness.

"Don't think we don't both realize we're using each other, Aero Austin. You can fuck like a porn star in some cheap ass home video that gets us both off, but it's not *me* you're thinking about."

I'm unmoved, unwilling to admit anything. Hiding for so long doesn't put me in a panic. It puts me in a numb heart-shaped box.

"You're right, Ren. It's definitely not your pussy I'm thinking about. If you think I'll admit to who I'm thinking about, you're in for a rude awakening. Better yet? Enlighten me."

She steps back. That plastic smile is back as coach and Darby walk by. Then it melts as her rage explodes. "You better not fuck anyone else. I don't care if your tastes are as insane as you are, Austin, but if you stick that thing in anyone other than me, we're done."

Placing my palms in front of my eyes, I rotate them, mocking her and her crybaby tendencies. "Boo hoo," I say derisively. "Poor princess doesn't like that she's not the queen of my cock. If my dick wants to dip elsewhere, don't worry. You won't know."

She lets out this loud angry squawk that nearly makes me laugh. She's such a spoiled child, needing to be the best, desperate for the top tier, and obsessed with being seen. It's disgusting but makes so much sense. I'm not the only one with peculiar tastes. If she didn't come on my shaft every time we fucked, I would think she pined after pussy. After all, there's something about the way she looks at that other freak—Charizard or someshit—the one who dresses like Gothic Weekly birthed her. Maybe she's like me and wants someone she can't have. This stupid relationship is nothing other than a play-by-play.

"You're a pig, Aero Austin. A disgusting—"

"Put a cork in it, Ren. Talk to you tomorrow. I've got shit to do."

Her little hissy fit as I turn and head toward my locker has me wanting to punch walls until skin splits, leaving my blood as a message that states *Don't pretend anymore.*

This anger inside me needs to go. It's a driving force many days, and while it won't make me hurt people, restraint will definitely damage me.

The first time I realized my attraction to guys, I told my dad. Bad idea. He called me a faggot. Not that the word bothered me. His fists did. He beat me until my words changed.

That's why I became the school's golden boy, why my parents act like I'm the best child, and why I've always kept my distance from Trouble.

Gayness isn't contagious regardless of what my father told me. I knew. Harley knows it. Dad is just too fucking daft to see it.

Either way, I listened.

Kept my distance.

Became what he envisioned so he kept off Trouble's case.

It was hard. Harley and I were close in secret. Dad being gone all the time and Mom being high or wasted on repeat helped us be together too.

Harley was alone. I could see his misery. Like Serenity, he craved love and needed affirmation that he's worth it. Unlike her, though, I want to give it to him. I want to hold him tighter and tell him he's perfect. There are far more things I'm not allowed to want but I do.

That wasn't always a curse, our craving for one another. What started as a comfort, a way to reassure him and make him feel better became an urge I believed was one-sided. It helped me move away. It's my fault. He may only be a year younger than me, but he's my baby brother. It's my fault he got twisted.

It happened before our kiss. Before lines were crossed entirely. Before everything changed.

"Dad told me not to hang out with you," Trouble *muses from the doorway to my room. "Is there a reason he thinks you have a disease?"*

He doesn't laugh or smile, just hones in on my face, watching everything. That's Harley, though. He dissects, studies, and pays too much attention to detail. Whether large or minute, he doesn't miss a thing.

"Maybe. Can you keep a secret?" I ask, curving my finger to tell him to come in. "Close the door behind you, and lock it."

His brows raise, wrinkling in the center, but he has half a mind to keep his mouth closed. Smart kid.

He shuts the heavy wood, putting the tiny lock into place. The air feels tighter, suffocating, and irritable, almost like a balloon waiting to pop from excessive helium.

As he travels to my bed, standing and staring at me the entire way, I keep my face passive. If I don't, I'll crumble.

The past year, we've spent secret time together—movies, comic books, you name it—but it's always done away from home, in the quiet and safety in one of our rooms, or at the park a mile away.

Dad watches me when he actually pays attention.

He gives me a scathing look, one that strips me of any fantasy of having a friend in my brother. It ruins my idea of happy, hardening my heart and scraping my soul clean from my body.

"What is it?" Trouble asks after a moment of silence. He bites his lip with nerves.

My palms sweat as I try to form words. The scrape of my jeans as I wipe my damp flesh burns me. It's like sandpaper abrasions. The rawness from sports wears the skin thinner with each passing season. Now, it's showing the outcome.

"You know how when you notice a pretty girl," I start, "and you—"

"I don't find girls pretty," he mutters almost angrily.

His face reddens with fear and almost trepidation, and he sucks in a shaky breath. I watch it wheeze out of him a moment later as he tucks his knees under his chin.

"They're pretty, I guess," he mumbles.

The correction causes me to crunch my nose. Does he think they're hot? Is he into guys like me? I'm really confused, and it has nothing to do with my own sexuality.

"What are you saying, Harley?"

His eyes shoot to me at the use of his name. I guess it could come off weirdly. He's been Trouble to me for a long while. It's just how it is.

"I..." He pauses and almost tucks his head deeper. "Girls are beautiful... but, Aero... it's guys who are hot."

He explains it simply but barely. On the crux of sixteen could do that, I guess.

"It's okay, Trouble. I'm gay, too."

That was the first night he stayed in my room and cuddled me. When Dad came home belligerent and drunk, probably after screwing someone, he scared Harley so much that he slipped in my room and begged me to keep him safe.

When Dad found Trouble dressing differently, dyeing his hair, and getting tattoos and that fucking tongue and septum piercing, he flipped. So did I, but it wasn't because he looked like he wanted to be fucked. No, it was from knowing he would be using that tongue ring on some lucky sonofabitch who wasn't me.

That night, when he cuddled me, it was the first time my body and flesh both warmed and hardened for my brother. As unnatural as my feelings are, they haven't abated. It was also six months before he kissed me, which means I ruined him. I've fucked him up. Badly.

CHAPTER FOUR

AERO

Practice doesn't last as long as usual. Coach has some plans for his wife and cuts our drills off early. I would be more frustrated, but honestly, my body aches from emotional strain. As much as I would like to blame Serenity, it's not her who's constantly taking residence in my thoughts. It's Harley.

The anger, disappointment, and sadness in his eyes while I finished inside my girlfriend hurt me, but it also made me cum harder than ever before. His gaze locked with mine like that was the hottest I've ever been. What's stuck on my mind is the taste of him and the way he soaked my palm with his stolen pleasure. I wanted to lick every drop so it didn't go to waste.

All of this is why I find myself driving to my parents' house and not to my apartment.

The roads blur while my car travels down the remembered paths home. It all seems the same. Trees, boulders, cliffs, and the gravel lead me to the house that holds as many happy moments as terrors.

Harley's car sits in the long drive, Mom's too. Dad isn't here.

Of course not.

It's been a few weeks since I've been here for the Sunday dinners. Mom hasn't called. Dad avoids me as much as possible, and Harley sets me off.

It's better to keep my distance, for Dad's sake and mine.

After today, though, I need a fix, just enough to hold me off until I'm in college and he's eighteen. Then I can tell him all the meanness and detachment was for a good reason. I'm protecting us still, keeping us safe. It's what I've always done.

Harley is six months from eighteen. Half a year and he's mine. Half a year until he can run with me, not from me. Six months until we're okay.

Our being related is one of the largest obstacles, but I'm willing to try for him. If I get accepted into Valley West, we'll move. We'll change our names if we have to.

My friend Texas used to live out there. Maybe he has someone who can save me. He knows how hard it is to live in a small town, to be stuck, suffocating, dying from the inside out.

That's why he left. He married his best friend's dad, and now he's in Vegas, living his best life.

I want that.

Harley.

Us.

Marriage.

After sticking my car in park down the street, I head over to my old house. I make sure Dad didn't park behind the house or in the garage. When the coast is finally clear, I open the back sliding-glass, sneaking in and avoiding the front doorbell camera.

The kitchen's empty as I step inside. Noise trickles in from a TV. Must be Mom. She usually zones out while watching soap operas and Maury. She's a zombie who does nothing except mope and slowly kill Harley, eating his soul to live.

Her room is on the top floor. Trouble's room is in the basement, mine too. Dad did that purposefully. He didn't want us hearing when he beat Mom or fucked her brutally as she cried. He's a freak, and when she stopped condoning his behavior, he took himself out of the equation. Now, he hardly comes home.

Silently stepping down the staircase to the basement, I avoid the spots that creak. They're how Dad knew we were sneaking out for food late at night.

After safely making it to the bottom, I look around. It's dark. There are three rooms down here besides our joint bathroom and bedrooms. The last is a second living room Dad donned his *Man Cave*. He spends next to no time down here. Hell, he doesn't come here most nights? Why would he have time to waste in his designated room?

Light shines from under Harley's door, but instead of knocking, I slip through my old room. Since moving out, I haven't stepped foot in here. It's nearly the same.

The bed's stripped of everything, and the single dresser, lamp, and random shit I didn't want to bring with me is still here.

My fingers trail the hollow walls, memories filtering in with each stroke.

When my palm resides on the door to our connecting bathroom, my heart pumps for the first time in a year. The blood rushes in, telling me my heart's alive and needs sustenance. It needs Harley. My body warms with the new thrum in my veins. It's heating, blistering, and tingling. It's ready to explode.

That's what this house does to me.

As I turn the knob, my favorite memory of Trouble hits me like a fresh wave of weed.

"Fuck me harder," he hisses, and that's when I rush to see who's touching my Harley. Who dare think they get to have him, taste him, fuck him?

When I round the clear glass of the shower, I see his shut eyes. He's leaning against the wall, his throat exposed, water droplets trailing lasciviously down his flesh, inviting me to touch, to taste, to take, take, take.

I peer downward, seeing if someone is somewhere hiding, but there's no one, only my brother fisting his cock like he's angry.

"Please fuck me..."

His moan is so desperate that my own shaft is pushing against my zipper. My heart aches as I wonder who has him all knotted up like this, so twisted that he's envisioning them inside him, delving into the sweet tightness between his cheeks.

"Aero, fuck."

My eyes go upward, wondering if he caught me watching, ogling, desiring.

No. It's me he's lusting after. It's me he's wanting inside him.

"Why can't I stop, Aero?"

"Because I don't want you to," I whisper to myself.

Before he can see me, I rush out.

That night, I jerked so many times my hand was raw. I couldn't see straight the next day. The fog of what sickness we have held me under water, rushing through my nose and mouth, and made me die a little.

He feels it too.

Even now.

I can't hide anymore. Avoiding him and staying away are impossible now. My dick aches as the memory leaves me. I wait in our bathroom, trying to calm it down before I rush in there and fuck him like I've fantasized about for ages.

The brass of the doorknob cools my skin as I finger the roundness in hope of strength. One would say my brother makes me weak, but they don't know Harley. He offers strength in a way no one else can.

Whether he realizes it or not, he pushes me to be better, to work harder, and to keep my soul intact. Without him, I would have drowned in my darkness.

My body hums with a scary kind of peace. It's like I've been fighting a war inside my mind for so long, and now that I'm accepting it, it finally relaxes.

As soon as the door pushes open, the scent of

Trouble fills me, infiltrating my nose with intense manliness. In the center of the room on his bed, my brother fists his cock, watching his phone. The sounds of two men fucking echoes in my ears. It's quiet enough that silence would bleed from this room, but it's so fucking loud to me, knowing he's getting off to two men instead of me.

Darkness pervades me. A cloud of envy as red and black as can be mixes in my system, swirling like a fog of recklessness, urging me forward.

Swallow me whole, demon. Bring me to my kingdom.

He doesn't notice me as he thrusts his hips and groans, but fuck, I see him. Creeping toward him, I beg my body to calm, but it beats erratically, drumming like an *Escape the Fate* song. He lets out this whimper, and I'm done for.

"Stop," I command.

His phone falls, and his bright green eyes connect with mine. The black part of his pupil is dilated, hiding the pretty effervescent shade that looks nothing like mine. It's almost feral. Vicious.

"Why?" It comes out as a whimper, and he drags his teeth over his lip, digging in deeply all while thumbing the head of his cock.

I approach him cautiously, my fists tight with infernal cravings, each step more nefarious than the next.

My knees connect with the plush comforter on his

bed. It dips from my weight, hiding under me, like it knows my intentions.

Trouble's gaze doesn't deter from mine. He knows... He feels it.

When I'm practically on top of him, I close his naked thighs, feeling the hot flesh beneath my hands covered in goosebumps.

Taking his phone next, I lock the screen and toss it on the pile of dirty clothes by his closet.

"Because if you're going to jerk to something—give your orgasm to *someone*—it's going to be *me*," I bark, feeling my skin prickle with our closeness.

His mouth drops open, showing those taunting pieces of metal.

"You and I both know, Trouble, your body, blood, and life are all *mine*." My palm shoots out to grab his chin, feeling the force of it before he does. "If you don't close this mouth, I'll make good use of it and those piercings."

He closes it slightly, only opening it to bite on his tongue ring. It unfurls me. Leaning in, the room around us is hushed. We both groan when I bite down, tugging gently as his sweet flavor erupts my taste buds. Fuck me. He twists it in my mouth, the little ball teasing me in the best way.

Release.

Let go.

Give in.

My mind chants for me, and I listen.

"Do you still have that knife I bought you for your

seventeenth?" The question comes out before I can stop it resulting in a tilt of his lips.

"The one you shipped to me since you refused to see me after Uly?" He rolls his eyes with amusement. "Yeah, it's in the drawer."

His gaze goes to the dresser against the wall, and my blood pumps fiercer, ready to do something that is as wrong as it is right.

CHAPTER FIVE

HARLEY

If you told me ten minutes ago that my brother would have showed up and flirted with me as I opened my favorite porn download to get relief from school earlier, I would have laughed at your stupidity. Guess I'm the dumb one.

Aero searches my dresser, touching everything, not missing an item, all while I watch from my bed.

My dick is out, still hard, and my balls kind of ache.

If I touch while watching him, will he print my skin with bruises?

The thought alone has me testing the theory. Instead of waiting for his direction, I grip my stiff flesh and stroke harder than before. Now, there's an uninhibited need for pain as he rifles through my stuff.

When the pleasing resonant of metal against metal echoes in the stagnant room, my dick jumps in my palm. Aero turns, his eyes darker than before, headier, unhinged.

"Uh, uh, uh," he reprimands, twisting the blade in his fingers, mocking it as if it wouldn't slice right through us both. The blade skims my skin, sending a fresh wave of goosebumps over my flesh. "Don't make any jerky movements, brother."

His face heats as a red mark becomes visible on my skin. He's in too many clothes. I haven't seen anything. Even growing up together, not once had I witnessed his junk. Now, I wish I had. It would give me something to think about and dream about later.

"What are we doing, Aero?"

It's a simple question, but why does it feel more complex than the hardest algorithm I've ever done?

That makes his movements stop. He leans in close, so close that I can barely breathe.

"What I've been dreaming about doing since you kissed me," he utters slowly before taking my mouth in the hottest kiss I've ever had.

Like the blood I would willingly give to him, light seeps from my veins, and darkness takes its place. A titilating chill of wonder tears at my skin for more touches, more lust, more, more, more.

He groans when I slip my tongue inside his mouth, tasting his Mountain Dew-coated flavor. Aero plays with my venom piercing, exploring every metallic space.

When he pops out, I let out the air I'd been salvaging, feeling lightheaded and airy, decadently ravenous and parched all in one. He sets the blade down then reaches for my shirt. Aero hasn't seen me without a shirt since that night. Which means he hasn't seen—

"What the fuck are these?" he hisses, the pain surrounding his tone almost makes me sad.

Did he want to be there for them? Is he jealous someone has touched me so intimately? Or is it deeper —a missing moment of being able to touch every inked inch, the forever pebbled dusky nipples, losing time to experience how good all would feel against him?

"Tattoos?" I mutter lamely.

His fingers ghost the ink, driving me fucking mad with the softness he's offering.

"Not those, dick." He flicks my nipples and then touches the scars near my heart.

Oh, those.

"Not sure what you mean."

He looks pointedly at me, pulling on my barbel. "Scars, Harley, the fucking scars. Where did they come from? D-Did Dad?" He stumbles on the second question. Pain and understanding settles in his expression, making me wonder what the fuck he's talking about.

"No, not Dad," I say, shocked.

Dad hurt him this badly? Other than a backhand or two, he never touched me. Calling me a fairy was an often occurrence, but he acted like being gay is spreadable, so he refused to show any affection or hatred by skin contact.

"Then who?" He grips my chin, and his thumb digs in a delicious way. "Tell me," he demands.

"Me, okay!" I yell softly. He's startled, dropping his

hand immediately. "I like the pain." It's all I can say. It's the only explanation I've got. "Sometimes when I jerk, I smoke weed and burn myself on purpose. It feels good."

Almost understanding, he nods a few times. "I like pain too," he answers a question I didn't plan on asking. "Like giving it more."

"Fuck," I respond, liking the idea of him marking me up as he touches me. Would he fuck me? It's something I've craved for almost two years. "Touch me, Aero. Please."

The implications float through my mind. They're there, but I'm not grasping them. No matter what we do, no matter how wrong it is, I don't care.

All I can imagine is his skin and mine, us together, and if that's wrong on every level, then the levels should change.

He doesn't say anything else, just pushes my naked body backward and hovers me. Smacking my palm away from my dick, he replaces it with his own. It's bigger, rougher, knowledgeable.

His first stroke of me has a commending sigh wheezing from us both. It's tension-filled. The bubble of us can be severed with a knife.

"I've wanted this for so long, Trouble." His words are reverent, a soft caress across my heart, tattooing it with his name.

"Me too." His next draw has me weak, nearly coming. "You've got to stop," I implore breathily, losing my grip on reality with the way his touch fucks with me. "I-It's too much."

"This is nothing," he promises, gripping me fiercely. "Wait until I'm deep inside you. Then you'll feel too much and beg for so much more. When you cry and I eat your tears, you'll still want more, and I promise I'll never stop giving everything you need."

My balls pulse and tense up with his words, and without him moving across my shaft again, I'm exploding against my stomach and all over his hand.

"You've got to stop wasting this," he chides me, bending down. His tongue glides against my abs, licking each dip and swallowing every droplet of cum, making sure to lick my belly button slowly. "So delicious, Trouble. So fucking mine."

"Yes," I agree, high off the rush of Aero. He barely touches me and drives me mad, imagining purposeful brushes of his fingertips.

"My turn," he hums, finishing his cleanup by teasing my sensitive nipples. My dick already jumps again, ready for more. Whatever he wants, I want it too.

He gets off the bed to free himself from the burden of clothing. As soon as his shirt is gone, I stiffen. I've always said my brother doubled me in muscles, but seeing him without a top that hides the planes and valleys of his chest and abdomen, I'm lost. His skin is bare of ink, not one drop beneath that perfect skin.

"If you keep staring at me like that, I'm going to be too unstable to do anything safely," he admits, emitting a groan when I start stroking myself.

I'm solid beneath my palm again, hot and unrestrained as he starts at his jeans.

The fact that he's not even naked and I'm salivating should feel like an issue, but it's not. I'm enamored. I'm fucking gone for my own brother.

"We have to take it slow." His words are too quiet, fearful even. "I've never done this before, Trouble. And no matter how much I've dreamed and craved it, I want to be safe. Savoring you—being safe—it's important to me."

I nod, unable to form words while my fist rotates erotically. He's barely able to keep my gaze as his travels down my body agonizingly slowly.

The path of his light brown hair trailing his abdomen and the veins that lead to where my body wants to lick most has me sweating profusely. It's no hotter than it was moments ago, but fuck, my body doesn't get the memo.

His fingers hook his boxer briefs and jeans at the same time, sliding his pants down as he watches me watch him. His massive cock bobs up like an elastic band on the brink of snapping, making my mouth drop open obnoxiously wide.

It's angry and huge. So goddamn huge. He's as big as my favorite porn star, possibly bigger. How? My eyes widen a bit, wondering if it'll even fit in me, especially when I see metal pierced through the head.

"A Prince Albert," he explains, touching it and the beads of precum slicking him. "Don't worry. I'll take it out our first time. Don't need to permanently damage you... yet."

My blood burns with anticipation and the utmost requirement.

He stalks me, crawling the bed with purpose and no nerves, unlike me. He's more practiced. Even with him being with a chick, he at least knows what to do without the uncertainty of not knowing where to start.

As if noticing my nerves, he invades my space and kisses me with force and fierce strokes of his tongue. When he tongues my piercings again, surer this time, I'm humping into him.

Our flesh connects, our dicks rubbing against each other in a punishing torment, bringing us both to part with heavy breathing.

"Fuck," he lets out, fisting himself as if to slow the beating he has to be experiencing. "Try not to stress. I can see your fear, baby brother. It's unnecessary. None of it's like this. None. It's like this is my first time, too."

His reassuring words have me closing my eyes in attempt to relax. He's right. This is different. This is us.

Wrong.

Forbidden.

Us.

He grabs the knife he discarded earlier and brings it to my hips. The blade is turned toward him, not penetrating my skin as he slides it across the veins and muscles there. They ache, flexing in anticipation of the pain. They want it, his pinch of dolor, something he's saved only for me.

"Please."

My one-worded plea has him flipping the knife, my dick practically jumps at the first bite of metal.

The slice is as narrow as a paper cut, but it has me groaning.

His eyes flick to mine. The adoration and hunger there isn't to be questioned. He needs this as much as I do.

His gaze goes back down to where the blade connects him to me. He slides it deeper, and the sizzle under my skin from the ruth of his ministrations has me whimpering. When I peer down, the line he traced prickles with blood. The little bubbles of near-black are absolutely beautiful.

"Harley," he husks, his face morphed into reverence, pride. It's almost like he's worshiping me. "You're killing me."

If I didn't know exactly how he felt in this moment, I would wonder what he means, since the only moving I've done has been breathing. While erratic and shuddering, it's not enough to disrupt his tortuously slow movements.

Leaning down, cresting over his work, his tongue slicks against me.

"Aero."

No more words escape my lips. It's unnecessary, but I'm unnerved by each new sensation between us.

He lifts up, his lips smeared with our shared DNA. *Perfect.*

I draw him to me, and we connect again.

Chest to chest.

Heart to heart.

Blood to blood.

We rut together, grinding our hips, our cocks swollen and destitute as he holds the knife and himself above me. I'm entranced at the way he's so powerful above me while staying soft and threatening in an ameliorate-blended mess.

His piercing, his cum, his everything glides against me methodically. The jerkiness from me doesn't deter him or hinder his precise thrusts. He's always in control, perpetually sure and perfunctory.

"I'm scared to hurt you, Trouble," he whispers across my skin like a sin or proverb, thorny, absolute, yet truthful. "But fuck me for wanting nothing more than to hurt you and ease your pain in the same breath."

"Hurt me, Aero. I'm yours to unleash on."

He rises off me silently, his pouty lips still freshly smeared with my spilled blood. His retreating form should scare me, but I know he's not leaving permanently.

When he's coming back into view with a bottle of lube, I sit up straighter. Everything I've begged for comes to fruition as he fluidly saunters to me.

His face is heated, and his teeth are slightly bared. He's coming apart like me. In this moment, it doesn't matter that we're brothers, that our mom is twenty feet away, or that the illegality of what we share is very real.

The only thing that exists is him and me.

Harley and his Aero.

The dark demon himself and his troubled angel.

Two brothers.

Two souls.

A bond everlasting.

"Spread your thighs for me, Harley. This is going to be messy."

CHAPTER SIX

AERO

He's inarguably the most beautiful human I've laid eyes on.

Our familial connection doesn't defer those feelings or marginalize them. It almost separates, reforms, and subsidizes them into something new, unbreakable, sacred.

As soon as I uttered the command, his thighs separated sublimely, spreading him open to me entirely.

With the lube bottle in one hand and his knife in the other, I find myself between his thighs again. As I lick the soft flesh of his inner legs, he croons for me, and I suck, leaving every possible proof that this isn't a maddening dream, and we're finally together. No matter how long, no matter how little, just us.

He bows his hips when my tongue trails to his sac. Pulling and tugging with my teeth a moment later, he has to bite his pillow to silence the noises escaping him.

I trail the blade across his balls, making sure not to

slice deep, needing the raised skin but not the rush of blood. It's beautiful, the way it peaks, reddens, and elevates as if it's acknowledging my work.

The silver glints over the underside of his shaft that weeps at the tip for me. His parted thighs flex when I nick his head.

He cries out softly as I kiss the mark, taking every prick of blood. It's taunting me, slicing him this way, marking him permanently in reverence for only us. Because in this moment, Harley Austin is entirely mine. Not the world's, not our parents. Fucking *mine*.

I take him deep in my mouth, salivating over his taste, coming undone at his splendor. When I pop off, his eyes are shut. He's sedated, and soon, with the medicine only my brother can offer me, I will be too.

"What do you want, Harley?"

It isn't something I care to ask anyone, but this is special. Our first time. Possibly the only shared moment we'll ever have, and fuck if that doesn't make me want to make it perfect.

"You. I want you inside me, Aero."

I growl as his admission leaves his lips. The words brand my soul, changing me forever. Dropping the knife on the nightstand next to the bed, I lower myself to his throat.

"Want you so badly, Trouble, the taste of you, your blood, my fucking brand across every single each. Need that," I barely hiss as his skin becomes my canvas.

Teeth, tongue, lips, they press against him as he

writhes. I lick every inch, making sure my markings paint his skin.

"Shit," he groans deeply, rocking against me, requiring friction.

I drag my palms down his body as snake my way between his legs. He shakes while I make purchase between his cheeks with my tongue. I dip, rimming him slow and surely, knowing he'll either love or hate this.

With how he shudders and moans loudly, I'm sure it's a positive response. Lifting his thighs over my shoulders, I draw him closer, dividing his cheeks and eating the feast he's offered.

"Aero, Aero, Aero," he praises throatily, grinding against me.

I grab the lube. Earlier, when collecting it from my drawer, I removed my piercing. I've done research after getting it pierced, in hopes of this moment. It can hurt really fucking bad to a bottom, especially if they're not used to taking.

My baby brother hasn't fucked anyone, and unlike Uly, I'm going to worship him from top to bottom and make sure it's the only thing he'll ever think about. If I'm going to take his body, it'll be the only body I'll please, the only one I'll keep, secure, and love.

That's what I'm doing, isn't it? Loving every part of my flesh and blood, reveling in its purity, succumbing to the demon inside me, begging for its fill.

Lubricating my fingers, I reach for his exposed asshole, rubbing my thumb against it. His chest rises and falls more, making him vocalize his pleasure louder.

"Quiet, Trouble. Can't have mommy dearest hearing her eldest son fucking her baby to completion, now, can we?"

Sweat lines his face as he shakes his head.

"Think she'd beat me if she saw me eating your ass? What about these fingers pressing that little button of yours?" I tease and press a single digit in, watching his eyes roll backward as his eyelashes flutter. "Think she'd be pissed that I'm about to take your virginity and make you mine? Fuck my little brother like he's mine to fuck?"

I groan against his balls as I grind into the bed. My cock throbs with temptation. The sudden urge to slam into him, fuck him with abandon, and drink his blood as I thrust into him it rushes me, poking me like a cattle prod.

"Do it," he commands on a whispery hiss. He presses down on my finger, fucking himself as I barely hold onto the desperation firing my body from top to bottom. He stares at me, the plea there, the same desperation mirrored in his eyes.

I rise, stroking lube on my cock, tingling all the way to my toes with how much I need this. How much we both do. It started as a kiss, a fucking simple kiss. Guess the truth in that lie. It was never simple.

It was our undoing.

Slathering more lube on his ass and some on his stiffened rod, I bring our bodies together.

"Just do it, Aero. Fuck—"

I shove inside him. He yelps as I wheeze in relief. Then he's wiggling beneath me, a crazed expression on his face. His body cants off the bed as I grind, rotating, making sure the pinch of pain from adjustment leaves him before I claim every whimper from him.

"H-How's your ass?" I mumble, suddenly nervous.

"It'd be better if you fucked me like you promised. Scared, brother?" he taunts me then bites his lip harshly.

It unravels me, seeing him angry from delayed gratification. I lean down and take his mouth, pulling almost all the way out just to ram back home, securing my way between his cheeks where I belong.

"Like this, Trouble?" Repeating the action several times, I mock his words. "Need my cock to fill you with seed? We both know your ass is mine now. No one will ever sink inside you again."

The idea of someone touching my Trouble has a rage building in me. My speed picks up at the imagery.

"I'll kill anyone." The words bleed from me harshly. "Any motherfucker who dares touch what's mine, I'll slice him open and watch the blood leak from his body."

I rut and rut and rut as he moans louder and louder and louder. We're a mess of thrusts, sweat, and blood. He reaches for the knife and brings it to my chest. I stop to watch him. The tip digs into me, bringing a sweet hiss of pleasure-pain I never knew I wanted. It kisses me like a long-lost lover as he slides it across my chest. It's purposeful, each glide of silver against my skin. The wet life seeps from each strike. It tingles and burns, sliding down my chest in a promise.

"Mine," he barks, his voice throaty, commanding, and hot as fuck. "Mine, Aero. Fucking mine."

"Yes," I confirm.

He takes the knife, crimson coating the blade, brings it to his mouth, and licks it while keeping his gaze connected with mine. It's such a heady look, biding us together. After its clean of our shared blood, he sets it down and bares down on me.

"Now fuck me like you fake-fucked Serenity earlier," he grunts harshly. "And if I ever see you fuck her again, I'll carve your heart out and eat it."

I laugh at that. He's such a jealous fuck. Who knew?

"I mean it, Aero. Just like your chest now bleeds the word, you're *mine*. Branded irrevocably. Now *fuck me*."

Looking down at his handiwork, I can see the words bright as the sun. *Mine*. Scrawled. Inscribed. Forever engraved.

In return, I fuck him.

My hips smack the backs of his thighs as I ram into him. He clenches, and I lift his thighs for more control, watching my bare cock fill him repeatedly.

Pouring more lube all over, making a mess, I angle him more. The orgasm builds and builds, suffocating me, all while exorcising a loud growl I've never heard before.

He grips his dick harshly, his knuckles turning

white from the pure pressure he's using. We both groan as we release. His seed sprays everywhere. So much cum squirts out of him like it has been stored his entire life for this.

As I pump continuously, my cum coats the inside of his ass, leaking out all over his bed. My balls are so tight and pained from the exhausting hour-long tease we've had. They're soaked from my cream and coated in lube and blood like a crime scene.

Harley stares at me as I soften, slowing my movements inside him. We both let out sated sighs. Our lips connect again, our labored breathing loud and heated.

"Mine," I mutter, exhausted.

"Mine," he argues.

We kiss and kiss, our bodies disgustingly caked in everything. It's beautiful in its disaster.

"Let's shower," I offer. "Together."

"Will you fuck me again?" he asks, his eyes alight with yearning.

"Pretty sure my cock is spent, Trouble, but don't worry. Once you move in with me, I'll hardly leave your tight ass. Best I've ever had."

His face lights up, and I kiss him again, unable to hide the way his happiness mirrors my own.

He bleeds my darkness and infuses it with light.

"I love you, Aero, more than my brother. You're my fucking everything."

The words take the air from my lungs, stealing my life and promising me something more valuable than death.

His love.

He loves me.

My heart hammers in tandem of the pulse heading back to my spent dick. It's a primal feeling. Even knowing I've claimed him entirely, taking his body for my own, acknowledging I have his heart fills me with even more pride.

"I love you too, Trouble. You're my soul." The words have tears pricking my eyes, and when his connect with mine, they're trailing with the same emotion.

Completion.

EPILOGUE
HARLEY

We ran.

After our shower that night, we packed everything, stole the fifty-grand in Dad's safe, and left. An old friend from Valley West named Texas and his husband helped us get new identities and a place to stay in a small town in Nevada. They understood our love for one another. They witnessed our passion firsthand, and they've kept us safe since.

Both Aero and I work at their bar, Loveless. We're going to help them grow it, and eventually, after we both graduate college, we're going to get married.

Married.

My brother and I.

My heart swells at that realization. It's the last brand we owe each other. It's been over a year since we left. Since then, Aero has put his name across my chest, matching his almost entirely. We fuck more than necessary, but it's like we're in heat, unable to keep apart for long.

We haven't kept tabs on Mom or Dad. Dad never came after us. I'm sure he knows from the mess we left all over my bed we've crossed a path we never want to return from.

"Trouble!" Aero yells from outside our house. Our home is on a five-acre piece of land. The nearest house is five football fields away.

I turn off the video game I'm playing and make my way to my brother.

My lover.

My demon.

He's leaning against his new Corvette Stingray. It's all he talks about. He's so proud of being able to buy it. Between what we make at Loveless and now being a part of Atlas' and Kenji's marijuana dispensary, we have more money than we could ever wish for.

I hardly leave the house for more than work now. Aero likes to keep me home to map my body with his mouth. If I didn't know any better, he planned on locking me here forever to raise the kids he's been begging me to adopt.

Maybe we will.

I'm only nineteen, but raising kids with my best friend and our friends is better than I could have wished for. Before we gave in, my life felt hopeless, like there wasn't a reason to continue. He gave me life again, feeding me his love, fulfilling every craving I have.

"Get the fuck over here," he barks. It's not cruelly. The glint in his eyes proves it. Closing the distance between us, he grips my throat and hauls me over to his car. "I've wanted to do this for years, Trouble. Pull down your pants, and let me see that ass of yours."

I whimper at his commands, feeling my dick nearly break from its need to escape. In one move, I'm bottomless, waiting for his next order. He turns me toward the hood of his car, pressing his thick erection against the crease of my ass. Forcing me to bend at the knee, he lowers me over the car. The Nevada heat on his hood burns my dick. Pain slices through me, but like the freak I am, I moan in response.

"Spread those pretty thick thighs. Let me see you."

I adjust and widen as much as I can. The feel of the blade doesn't surprise me as it kisses my ass cheek. There's not a part of me this blade hasn't bit. Aero traces it across both cheeks before he sides it to my balls. I'm rubbing my dick all over the hood of his precious toy in response.

"You don't know how long I've fantasized fucking you against the hood of my car, Trouble. We're missing one vital piece, though."

"What's that?" I ask breathily, humming at the palm tracing my hips.

"Those raised hand marks," he coos, his voice low and heady with lust.

Before I can respond, his palm connects with my skin. and I hiss. It doesn't take long for the pleasure to consume me after. Aero hits both cheeks several times, and the flame that stirs in my stomach for his cock is inarguable.

"Going to fuck me, Demon, or just cocktease me to death?"

It's a jab. He likes long spouts of torture before he sinks into me, but now, I can handle all of him, his hot-as-fuck piercing and all. We still make each other bleed every chance we get, and not a day goes by that I'm without a mark from his mouth, teeth, or hand.

I hear the hiss of his zipper as he releases himself. He smacks my ass with his cock, teasing me. "You've been a bad little boy, Harley. Now I've got to fuck you and teach you a lesson."

"Please, please, please," I beg unabashedly.

He rifles around I'm sure for the spare lube packets in his wallet, but then his mouth is between my ass, and I'm pushing against him greedily. He's ruthless as he tongue-fucks me and leaves slobber for his cock to use.

Lube coats me as he squeezes it. Without stretching or warning, he pushes into me. I cry out. The pain isn't anything I don't crave. I wouldn't be surprised if my ass is forever scarred from how brutal we are to it.

He fills me to the hilt before pumping impulsively. The clink of his knife makes my balls tighten. My favorite place for his torture is against my back, my spine, and when I'm beyond bloody from his elongated lack of mercy. The raised skin from his brand of scars gets me hard every time I see it in the mirror.

We're dangerous together, but we're miserable apart even for mere hours.

Whether toxic, dark, or unhealthy, I couldn't imagine my life without my lover.

My brother.

My everything.

"You're slacking, Aero. Thought you fantasized for a long—" I begin taunting before he's holding me down, forcing my face flush with the car as he fucks me harshly.

The metal burns my face, building pressure and pleasure all at once. He rocks into me, and we're both groaning so loudly I'm sure the neighbors a mile away can hear our restless fucking.

"Your mouth makes me fucking mad, Trouble. Makes my cock swell and groan with the need to shut it up."

"Missed your chance with that, brother."

"Fuck," he grunts, spilling into my ass as he thrusts harder and harder. "I love filling this ass," he says finally after pulling out. His seed seeps from me, leaking down my cheeks and thighs. It's so fucking hot. He flips me over, staring at me with so much love it's painful. "Lean back, baby. Let me ease that ache."

I do.

His release paints his car as I spread wide for him. He sinks to his knees and swallows me back, massaging my swollen balls. Reaching behind them, he teases my sore hole, sinking two fingers in.

The sigh of relief coming from me makes him chuckle around my cock. Pressing down on my prostate, he pops off, making me whimper in complaint.

"Such a slut for me, aren't you, Trouble?"

"Yes, yes, yes," I repeat as he strokes my pleasure spot.

"Be a good little boy and cum for me then." He deep-throats me, biting my shaft as he bobs his head all while fingering my ass. I explode in his mouth, and the fucker swallows it all. He doesn't like to waste it.

"Fuck!" I yell as soon as he sucks off every drop.

"Good little slut, now clean my car, or I'll make you lick it off."

I smile at that because we both know I would. As humiliating and shameful it sounds, I would be so fucking hot for him after.

He gives me a look of understanding and a smack on the ass. "Knew you'd like it."

Then he takes my mouth, kissing every sassy rebuttal he had coming his way. When we break apart, I put on my pants.

As I turn around, I notice my brother on one knee. His eyes—one blue, one green—stare back at me in reverence. It's the same look of worship he gives me every day.

"Trouble," he enunciates, his voice low and emotional, "you're the light to my soul, the cure to my darkness. You're my best friend, my brother, and my lover. You make me fucking happy and proud every fucking day I'm alive." A tear leaves his eye, trailing his face perfectly. "I've loved you since your birth, and we share the last name in secret, but I'd like for us to get married and be bound in the only way we have left. Will you marry me?"

Tears spill down my cheeks, making me choke up. He smiles sadly, almost like I'm not going to accept, but I bend down, taking the slim black band and putting it on my finger.

"I've been waiting," I muse. "I'd love to marry you and have you in every way."

He smiles and takes my mouth, stealing my breath away. He lifts me, and I wrap my legs around him. We don't stop to breathe.

We just kiss.

And kiss.

Endlessly.

Forever.

Harley and his Aero.

Demon and his soul.

Brother and his brother.

The End

ABOUT C.L. MATTHEWS

C.L. Matthews lives in lala-landia with her husband and invisible friends. She wants to riot the lack thereof authentic Mexican food in her state, but she's an introvert at heart. She enjoys tacos, Red Bull, and warm water because she's crazy. She's an oddball, and realizes it's been mentioned before, just go with it. Her joys in life consist of writing unconventional romances, making book covers, causing havoc to her reader's hearts, and genre-hopping when she needs a change of scenery. She's a special kind of weird and enjoys every moment of it.

www.clmatthewbooks.com

BURIED
Truths

BY

FAITH RYAN

BLURB

GIDEON

I've lived a fairly sheltered life, but I knew it was for the best. My mother's illness controlled our lives and now that she's gone, I'm afraid my father will bury himself alongside her. Then he shows up. A connection to my father's past and my mother's only remaining family.
He may just be the saving grace we need.

BISHOP

My wife and son have been my world for so long, I don't know how I'll make it through now that she's gone. Being strong for Gideon is the only thing I can do. Until my past shows up with an offer I can't refuse. Feelings I buried long ago threaten to take up residence in my heart once again and shatter the illusion of myself I've created.

ORLANDO

It's taken my sister's death for me to face Bishop after so many years. I've never forgotten or given up hope that we'd see each other again. Their son radiates love and innocence that, like a magnet, pulls me in just the same as he does Bishop. Past mistakes tore us apart, but he is the key to bring us all together. All we need to do is unbury the truths of who we really are.

CHAPTER ONE

GIDEON

It's cold and wet. Even the skies wept at the loss of Ophelia Josephine Merrick-Cartwright. The ground beneath my feet is muddy and soft; it sucks at my feet with every step toward the gravesite. My father, Bishop Wayne Cartwright, walks with his shoulders slumped. I'd never seen the man as devastated as he is now. My mother had fought a long battle with cancer and it even surprised the doctors she'd lived as long as she had, but my father had been in denial that the sands in her hourglass were running out.

I wipe at the tears that haven't stopped since her death. I feel as though I've never known a minute without her or her illness. I know I must have had memories from before, but they've been obscured by the many doctor's visits and chemotherapy sessions.

The pastor is chatting with a man when we arrive at the tombstone that marks my mother's life and death vividly. I've never met the man before, but the way my father's back visibly stiffens and his hands fist at his sides, tells me he has. The pastor excuses himself when he sees us approach.

"Orlando. What are you doing here?"

"She was my sister Bishop; you can't change that even if you want to. I'm here to pay my respects to her and give you my condolences." Orlando blows out a breath. "Come stay with me at the cabin. I know you hate me, but I think Phee would've liked for us to reconcile after so long, don't you?"

"This is my wife's funeral. For God's sake, Lando, why are you asking me to come home with you now?"

Orlando looks around the desolate cemetery. "Bish, she told me."

"She told you what? And when?"

"She called me about a month ago, told me she was worried about you and Gideon. She knew she didn't have long left." Orlando looks at me for a moment before turning his attention back to my father. "Bish, she told me about the bank foreclosing and asked me to help. This is me helping. You and Gideon can say with me until you can get back on your feet, no matter how long it takes. It's what Phee wanted, and honestly, I wouldn't mind having my best friend back after all this time."

"I don't need your help."

My father stomps away, leaving me and Orlando to stare between each other and our feet. He looks like her. The sorrow from missing her eases a bit at that thought.

"I'm Gideon Michael Cartwright," I announce and offer him my hand.

Orlando's lips twitch in a half smile as he takes my hand and shakes it. "Orlando Nathaniel Merrick. Do you always introduce yourself by your full name?"

"Mom said we were given our names for a reason. Why wouldn't I use my full name? If I weren't meant to use it, why do I have it?"

"You're Opehlia's son all right," Orlando laughs. "But you can call me Lando. Just because you know my full name doesn't mean you need to spit out that mouthful every time."

He winks at me and I find myself smiling despite the reason we are here.

"Gid. I mean, you can call me Gid, if you want."

"Gideon! Get over here!" my father calls for me as if I'm a child.

I sigh and leave Lando to go to my father. Lando is my mother's brother and I wish I had known about him before. I'm curious about why neither of my parents have mentioned him before. What could've happened to cause a rift that deep? Whatever it was couldn't be too bad if my mother had reached out to Lando.

"Is he telling the truth? Is the bank foreclosing?" I ask my father as I take my place by his side and he puts an arm around my shoulders in a semi-hug.

"Not now, Gideon."

I take that as a yes, but don't confront him about it. I listen to the pastor read his scriptures and prayers. Lando stands on one side of the freshly dug grave while my father and I stand on the other. We make eye contact a few times and I can see the grief in his is easily as strong as mine and my father's. Tear tracks are visible on his cheeks and I can feel the matching trails on my own face.

Whatever had happened between my father and Lando led him to miss out on his sister's life. It's also kept me from knowing any other family outside of my parents. Dad's parents died in a car accident before I was born, and Mom never talked about her family. I want to know the only family I have left. He's been kept from me, but I won't allow him to stay that way. All I've ever known was my mother and father's presence. Being their only child, combined with Mom's illness, made them overprotective. I was homeschooled and never made any friends, though I tried. I'd just rather spend the time with my father, and my mother when she was feeling well enough. A part of me hopes that I can find the same closeness I have with my father with Orlando.

After we toss our roses on the casket and the first shovel of dirt falls, I head back to the car with my father. My mother is gone, and I'll grieve her for a long time, but Orlando is very much alive. He's reaching out to us and I want to meet him halfway. Maybe it will make this transition into a life without Mom easier.

"I think we should go stay with Orlando," I tell him as we walk.

"What? Why? You don't even know that man, Gideon."

"And why is that?" He doesn't answer, just glares down at his feet as he crunches over the gravel drive. "Right. Well. I think I'll go stay with him... with or without you. He's family and I'd like to get to know him."

"Gideon," he says my name as a reprimand, but I've made up my mind and no amount of scolding will change it.

"No. I'm going. Mom is gone, and he's a connection to her I never knew existed. I don't want to sit around mourning her for the rest of my life. I want to learn about her life before I was born. Before she was sick. Memories Orlando can share with me. I'm nineteen, Dad, I can make my own decisions. I have nothing keeping me here, and neither do you. I want you to come with me, but I can't make you."

"You don't know him, Gideon."

"I know, but I want to."

I turn on my heel and run to where Orlando is climbing into his car.

"Everything okay?" he asks when I stop beside him to catch my breath.

"Yes. I need your address."

"Has he agreed to come stay with me?"

I shake my head. "No. He's not coming. He's stubborn and a fool. Give him time and I think he'll come around, but for now you just get me."

"And me."

I turn at my father's voice to find him standing behind me. Determination has him standing tall and

I'm hopeful he'll see that this decision is for the best. Mom would have wanted it this way.

"Are you sure, Bish? You don't have to. Phee suggested it and I want to rebuild what we've lost, but I don't want to force you into it," Orlando tells him.

"Gideon is right, I'm a fool. If Phee thought it was time to move forward, and Gideon wants to as well, then I can at least try. Besides, like he said, I have nothing left here. Ophelia is gone. If I stay I'll only end up pushing myself into the open grave beside her."

Orlando nods and pulls out his phone. I wait patiently as he exchanges numbers with my father, then texts him the address. Today is the end of one chapter in my life, one I'll never forget. Tomorrow is the beginning of the next, one where new memories await.

CHAPTER TWO

BISHOP

Gideon and I spend the week moving the furniture and other items from the house into storage. We're bringing only what's necessary with us to Orlando's cabin. *The Merrick family cabin.* I throw the last of my bags into the trunk of the car, dismissing the memories that threaten to resurface. There'll be plenty of them ready to assault me once we arrive later tonight.

"You ready?" Gideon asks me as he tosses a duffle into the backseat.

"Yeah." *No.* "Is that everything?"

"That's it. Nothing left in that house to hold us here. I know it's hard, Dad, but Mom wouldn't want us to live in a place where almost all of our memories are of her illness. Even if Uncle Orlando hadn't shown up offering us a place to stay, moving was the only option we had. The bank foreclosing just made it easier to make the choice now instead of later."

He's right, but I wish Orlando wasn't our only option. I've just lost Ophelia. I'm not sure I'm ready to face the past with him so soon after. Phee must have really wanted us to reconcile or she wouldn't have contacted him, and Gideon wants to know him too, so for them I'll try.

"I know, Gid. I just... there's a lot that happened between us and I'm not sure I can face it yet." I slam the trunk closed, then climb in the driver's seat. Once Gideon is seated and has his belt done up, I insert the key and start the ignition. Before I put the car in gear, I turn to Gideon. "I'm going to try, Gid. I really am."

"I know, Dad. That's all I ask."

Gideon reaches over and squeezes my hand before he puts his ear buds in. I pull out of the drive and can't stop from taking a glance in the rearview mirror. Gideon has a point, all the memories in that house are tinged with Ophelia's cancer. But as I continue to steal peeks until I turn the corner and the house disappears from sight, my heart breaks. It feels as if I boxed up Ophelia and our life together and left it behind in storage with the rest of our memories.

Orlando's cabin is a five hour drive away, and Gideon falls asleep halfway through the journey. It's dark when we arrive, and my headlights illuminate Orlando where he's sitting on the porch waiting. Gideon must have texted him to let him know we were on our way. They've sent messages back and forth all week while Gideon and I packed our things. A connection is already forming between them and I know I should encourage it, but the past won't let me.

I park the car and quietly open and close the door, not wanting to wake Gideon just yet. I need a moment alone with Orlando to let him know where he and I stand. Orlando moves to stand at the edge of the wraparound porch and I stop below the first step. I stare at him, unable to voice the warning I had carefully worded in my head over and over on the drive. He's older, as am I, but Orlando still looks like a man used to getting what, and who, he wants. It's one reason I've fought to keep the distance between us all these years. Ophelia had tried several times to get me and Orlando in the same room in hopes of reconciliation. I regret that it took her death for it to happen, and that Orlando was the one to cede to her wishes.

"You look good, Bish. I know you don't want to hear that, especially from me, but it's true."

"Fuck you, Lando. I'm still mourning my wife, *your* sister. I'm not in the mood for your advances."

"For fuck's sake, Bish. I'm not hitting on you. I'm stating a fact. You look good. I know life hasn't been good to you, what with Phee's illness and her death, but you've still grown into a handsome man. And Gideon is following in your footsteps. That boy will be beating them off with a stick soon, if he isn't already."

"Keep your hands off my son."

"Whatever, Bish. I'm just trying to be friendly. There was a time when you would return my banter.

We were friends once, remember? I'm sorry I ruined that."

Fuck. This is harder than I thought it would be. *Maybe because you don't blame him for what happened.* I curse the voice in my head for reminding me that I never considered any of it to be Orlando's fault. It's easier to let him think so, though. Truthfully, I blame myself for letting it happen and for enjoying it as much as I did. Afterwards, I was scared about what it meant for all of us, so I asked Ophelia to marry me and ran as far from Orlando as I could get. It's not every day that you realize you're in love with your girlfriend *and* her brother.

"I remember," I whisper and turn away, unable to look at him anymore, and I use the excuse of waking Gideon to end our conversation.

"Hey, Gid, we're here," I gently shake him awake. I ruffle his hair and place a kiss to his temple before moving around to the back of the car to start unloading our bags. I keep an eye on both Gideon and Orlando as I pretend to busy myself with our luggage. When Orlando wraps his arms around Gideon in welcome, a surge of jealousy shoots through me. I shake it off. Am I jealous because Orlando is becoming close with Gideon, who has been the center of my world since before Ophelia's passing? Or is it that I want to be close to Orlando again without compromising my relationship with my son? Is it possible to move beyond our past and have them both in my life?

No. I can't allow myself to give in to the emotions

and the wants being around Orlando brings out. The man makes me crave things that are forbidden and unnatural. He'd convinced me I could have anything I wanted as long as I was in his arms. But that was a lie I won't let him fool me into believing again.

CHAPTER THREE

ORLANDO

In the week that Gideon and Bishop have been staying with me, Bishop has avoided me as much as possible. Gideon tries to get him to see reason, but I know it will take time before Bishop is ready to face our past and what that means for the future of all of us.

I've always blamed myself for ruining our friendship and the closeness I had with Ophelia. I think if it had just been me and Bishop, things would've turned out different. But Ophelia was the anchor point for both of us. Without her there would never have been an us. And that's where I went wrong. I believed that because he wanted it and gave in to what all three of us desired, everything would end with a happy ever after. I thought Bishop, Ophelia, and I could be a true family together. Then the morning came and he ran, taking my sister with him.

I gather my dirty laundry. Bishop and Gideon left for the grocer a little while ago and catching up on chores seems to be a good way to occupy my time until they get back. I toss a pair of boxers into the basket, then check that I haven't missed any stray socks before making my way down to the basement.

I notice an empty laundry basket and after loading my laundry into the washing machine and setting the cycle, I grab the basket and begin to empty the contents from the dryer into it. Gideon did his wash yesterday and must have left it.

An item falls out during the transfer from the dryer to the basket. I reach to pick it up and the silky feel to the material piques my curiosity. Holding the black garment up for closer inspection I realize it's a garter belt. There's probably a rational explanation for the lingerie being in with Gideon's things, but my mind conjures up a vision of him in nothing but the belt and a pair of matching thigh highs. Gideon is lean and his body would be perfectly fit for wearing such an article of clothing.

A car door slams and I am jerked from my immoral thoughts. I place the garter belt back in the basket and cover it with a shirt, so it's not obvious that I saw it. I head back up the stairs and meet Gideon and Bishop in the kitchen where they are unloading the groceries they purchased.

"Gideon, you left your laundry downstairs. I brought it up for you."

A blush tinges Gideon's cheeks and he mutters a thanks before taking the basket from me and rushing off to his room. Bishop continues to unload the groceries, but I see the longing in his gaze as he surreptitiously watches Gideon leave the room. I don't call him on it as he's not ready. Instead, I grab the sack of canned goods and place them in their proper spots within the pantry.

Once I've finished, I watch Bishop and admire the way the muscles of his back flex beneath his tight t-shirt. Gideon is much smaller in comparison to his father. Bish has always been a big man, and though time has lessened his size a bit, he is still the same in many ways, including his looks.

"Quit staring at me. How many times do I have to tell you that it's never going to happen?"

"I think you're obsessed with me, Bish. One glance in your direction and you have me trying to get into your pants. Is that what's on your mind whenever you think about me? If that's a yes, then maybe you need to stop denying what you want."

I walk away from him and down the hall to my bedroom. If I stay in his presence any longer I'll do something I'll regret, though not likely while I'm doing it.

Gideon exits his room as I'm passing and we collide with each other. I grab him by the shoulders to keep him upright and he shakes me off once he's steady on his feet.

"You okay?" I ask him and he nods, then backs away until his back is against the wall.

"Those weren't mine," he blurts out.

"Umm, okay. What wasn't yours?"

Gideon looks incredulous at my question, and

honestly, I would be too. We both know what he's talking about.

"You know," Gideon gestures to his room, alluding to his laundry and more specifically the garter belt. "It's my girlfriend's. Well, ex-girlfriend. She left it at the house and I must have grabbed it by accident."

"Okay."

I don't call him out on his obvious lie or ask how it ended up in his dirty laundry. If he wants to pretend it's not his I'll let him... for now.

"Yeah. Okay. I'm going to go help Dad."

Gideon walks off and my gaze snags on the way his ass fills out his jeans. I wonder if he is wearing a belt and hose now. My cock throbs at the thought and I mentally strip him down to nothing but the garter and thigh highs from my earlier fantasy.

Fuck. I press my palm against my cock and the pressure adds to the lust filling me. With a groan I hurry into my bedroom, slam the door closed, quickly undo my pants and shove them down my thighs. I'm swimming in a sea of lust and can't be bothered to move farther than where I'm standing, so I lean my back on the hard wood of the door as I take my cock in hand. I'm still imagining Gideon and my fantasy from earlier, but somehow Bishop intrudes into my mind, taking control of me and Gideon.

I jack myself hard and fast to the images filling my mind, spreading precum over my hard length. If I thought picturing Gideon was hot, it's nothing compared to adding Bishop into the mix. It doesn't take long before I'm coming all over my hand with a moan.

As I come down from the lust-fueled high of my orgasm, I slam my head against the door. I thought I was doing the right thing by fulfilling Opehlia's last wish, but I don't know if I can take being around Bishop and Gideon much longer before I give in to my want for one, or both of them.

CHAPTER FOUR

GIDEON

I run away from Orlando. Well, technically I just walk very fast, but it feels like I'm running. My mother was the only one who knew about my love of lingerie. *It was our secret.* Not because she didn't approve or thought my father wouldn't, but because it was ours, our thing. I want to keep it as ours alone for as long as I can. I'm not naïve enough to think I can keep it to myself forever, just for now. I even kept some of her hose and garters, and I really don't want my father to know I've been wearing his dead wife's lingerie.

It's super weird and fucked up, I know it is, but it's not the only weird and fucked up thing about me. If anyone ever found out my thoughts, I'd be institutionalized. When I realized I was gay, it was no big deal. Both my mother and father were supportive and happy to let me be who I am. I don't know if that would have still been true if they knew how I came to that realization.

My father is such an uptight and strict man, I know he would've flipped.

I was thirteen when I saw another man's cock in a sexual way for the first time. The sight drew my full attention and I couldn't help but stare. And when he started to stroke himself, I couldn't look away. I watched until he climaxed and spurts of cum decorated his chest, hand, and dick. I immediately ran off to do the same with the mental image of him in my mind. I came hard that day. And every day since, all my fantasies have starred my father. Lately, Orlando has been added into the scenes my mind conjures. The two of them together while I watch. All of us together, fucking and sucking. In my mind, we're just three men who want and love each other. It's wrong. I know it's wrong, but I can't stop fantasizing about what it would be like.

I shake away those thoughts as I enter the kitchen. My father is finished putting away the groceries and when he sees me a bright smile lights up his face.

"Want to help me with dinner?"

"Sure. What are we having?"

"Roast with vegetables," he says as he sets the potatoes in front of me. "You chop while I season the roast and get it ready."

I dice the potatoes, then I slice some carrots and an onion, mindlessly watching as my father prepares the meat. The way his hands massage the spices and oils into the meat for flavor has me salivating and wishing he was rubbing his hands over my body instead of a slab of beef. I'm so entranced with watching the way his hands manipulate the meat that I miss Orlando coming into the room.

"Mmm. That smells good, Bish."

"It's not even in the oven yet." My father grunts at Orlando like he does after any interaction they have and pointedly ignores him as he asks me to bring the vegetables over.

"Well, whatever spices you're using smells amazing. I can't wait to eat. Maybe we can watch a movie together while we wait."

Orlando looks at me with a smile, then turns back to my father. It's been like this every day since we moved in. Orlando tries to get us to do something together, then waits patiently for my father to deny him and his suggestions with a flimsy excuse.

"I need to..."

"Dad, come on. You can't make excuses forever. It's just a movie. What do you think is going to happen?"

He flicks a nervous gaze toward Orlando. They have a stare down and I let out an exasperated sigh. Dad will never give up this grudge or whatever he's holding onto from their past. It seems pointless to even try to coerce him into letting it go.

"Come on, I'll watch with you, and then Dad can do whatever it is he finds more interesting than spending time with us."

I grab Orlando by the arm and walk him to the family room. He has a nice set up with a theater-like atmosphere that makes watching films and gaming comfortable and fun. I push him to go sit on the sofa while I choose a Blu-ray to watch. I just want to zone out and relax, to forget about earlier and the tension between my father and Orlando, so I pick some action movie I won't have to think through to enjoy.

I take my seat at the opposite end of the sofa and prop my feet on Orlando's lap. He instantly picks up a foot and begins to massage my instep. It feels amazing and I close my eyes to enjoy the way his fingers press into my skin.

"I'm sorry," he says after a few minutes.

"Huh?" I open my eyes to better gauge what he's talking about, but I don't see anything that would require an apology.

"For earlier in the hall, and for not trying harder with your father. I want to reconnect with him and make this work, but I can't help my reaction when he acts as though I am the reason for every bad thing to ever happen to him."

I ignore the comment on our run-in and focus on the part regarding my father. It's true that he has been trying harder than my father, which isn't difficult considering the man isn't trying at all, but he's just as guilty of letting whatever their past contains control his reactions.

"I don't know what happened between the two of you, but if you let it go and live in the now, you might get somewhere. Whatever it was, my father is holding a grudge and every time you let it surface, he falls deeper into his dislike for you."

Orlando lets out a deep sigh. "I wish it was that easy, Gid. I really do."

I study the defeat on his face, the sadness in his eyes and I know that I need to help them get over whatever hold the past has on them.

"Okay. New plan. We make him confront the past. But to do that, you'll need me to help you. Which means you need to tell me what happened."

Orlando gives me a nod. "Just... try not to judge us until the story is over."

CHAPTER FIVE

BISHOP

I hover in the hall contemplating the stupidity of me spending time with Orlando. It's not that I don't want to move on, it's just hard to do. The guilt of betraying Ophelia has festered inside me all these years, and I put all the blame on Orlando so I could ease my conscience. It worked too, until he showed up at Phee's funeral.

I can hear Gid talking to Orlando, the words are too low to hear but he's making an effort to have the man in his life. I should do the same, if only so he can know the only family he has left. I push the thoughts back that are insisting this is a bad idea and step through the entranceway toward the family room.

Neither Gid nor Orlando notice me, and I take a moment to let myself really look at them. I'm attracted to them both. It's wrong for so many reasons, reasons that were easier to remember before Orlando barged his way back into my life. When I hear what Orlando's saying, I'm glad I'm halfway hidden by the wall separating us.

"Bishop was dating Phee for a while before I met him. They were perfect for each other. Phee was happy in a way I hadn't seen in a long time and I wanted that to last forever for her. Then I met Bish, and I knew why she was so happy. He has this way of making you feel special, well, when he wants to anyway. I think at first it started as a way to show Phee how much he cared about her. We became friends. We spent almost all our time together, with and without Phee. One day we became more, and it seemed like a natural progression of our friendship."

As Orlando continues the story, I relive those days when we were closer than friends tend to be.

I can feel the pleasure building and I thrust harder into Lando causing him to let out a groan and clench around me.

"Shh. We can't be too loud. Someone might hear us."

I place my hand over his mouth to muffle any sounds that may escape. Honestly, having sex in a park wasn't the wisest of ideas, but the plan had been to shoot some hoops and have a nice lunch before heading back to Lando's place. We've been sneaking around for a few weeks now, and while I love the time we spend together, guilt always inundates me when we get back and I see the smile on Phee's face.

Lando tries to say something, but I can't understand

him with my hand covering his lips. I remove my hand from his face and use it to grip his shoulder.

"What?" *I gasp out between thrusts.*

"I said, stop thinking or we'll be here all day trying to get you off."

He's right. It's happened before, I get too caught up on what Phee would think of our betrayal. I shake all thoughts of Phee away and focus on the here and now, on Lando and the way he makes me feel.

"Fuck. Yes, Bish. That's it. No thinking, only feeling."

Lando clenches around me again and my orgasm barrels out of me and into him. I continue moving in and out until he finds his own release and my dick becomes too soft and sensitive to keep going. I want to collapse on top of him and relax into his hold as we bask in the pleasure of our lovemaking, but we can't. Instead, we hurry to right ourselves before gathering our things and heading back to reality. The one where I'm dating his sister, the girl I love and want to marry. But I love Lando, too. He knows this, but he says I need to stay with Phee so she can be happy. I wish there was a way for all of us to be happy together.

"Hey." *Lando grabs my hand and pulls me to a stop just before we get to the parking lot and his truck.* "Don't, Bish. It's better this way. You don't know how much I wish things could be different, but Phee deserves to be happy more than anything. Don't ruin what little time we have together, it'll be over soon enough."

Lando pulls me in for a quick kiss, then squeezes my hand before letting go.

"You're right. I just can't help wanting things to work out for all of us. If only there was a way."

Lando looks at me quizzically for a moment. He opens his mouth as if to say something but closes it without speaking. When he begins walking to the truck, I follow silently. We toss our things in the back and climb into the cab. Lando turns the key and revs the engine.

"I'm going to figure out a way to give you what you want, Bish. You deserve to be happy just like Phee does."

I didn't know that would be the beginning of the end for us and our friendship. If I had I might have found a way to stop what happened next. At the time it seemed like the perfect solution. In hindsight there was only one way it was bound to turn out. I'm just lucky that Phee still wanted me after. She was the only thing that kept me going in the months and years that I mourned Lando as if he was dead and not just hours away.

I can't forget what we did, what I did. I'm the reason he did it, and I've had to live with that burden for years. I can't stop carrying it now. If I do, I may fall into old habits and who knows what relationship I'll destroy this time.

I step back into the hall and head toward the kitchen as Orlando continues to lay out my shame for my son. I can only hope that once he knows the truth, he'll understand why I can't be around Orlando. I'll have to leave soon, but until I know that Orlando and Gid will be happy, I have to stay. Their happiness trumps all, and I will make sure that they get it. I had my stint of happiness, however brief it may have been, and now it's their turn.

CHAPTER SIX

ORLANDO

Gideon looks shocked and intrigued at the revelation of my past relationship with Bishop. I couldn't tell him all of it. I didn't tell him the part where I ruined everything for all of us, that's a secret for another day. It would be better coming from Bishop rather than me anyway. My emotions still run high at the catastrophe that followed my actions.

"So, my dad hates you because you guys dated when you were younger?"

Gideon scrunches his brows together and the look of concentration on his face is adorable.

"In the simplest of answers; yes. But in reality, it's much more complicated. There's more to our story, but it's not my place to tell you. Especially since Phee is no longer here to tell her part of it. If you want to know what happened, you need to ask Bishop."

"Why can't you two just tell me? I'm not some kid. I can understand more than either of you think I can.

Keeping things from me isn't helping anyone. Not me. And definitely not you or my father."

"It's not easy to tell your secrets to someone, Gid. Family or not."

"I'll tell you a secret too."

"I already know that the garter is yours."

Gideon rolls his eyes. "I figured as much. I meant I'll tell you a different secret."

"I'm listening."

"If I tell you, then you have to reciprocate."

I nod and motion for him to go on.

"I'm gay."

"Not a secret."

Gideon glares at me. "I'm gay, and the reason I know for sure is because I—I saw my father."

It's my turn to stare at him inquisitively. Is he saying what I think he is?

"I can tell by the look on your face you know exactly what I saw. I know it's wrong to lust after him, but I do it anyway." Gideon swallows and I watch the movement of his Adam's apple. "Just the same way I lust after you. My predilection for lingerie is the least of my secrets. I lust after my own blood. If I was given even a chance with either of you, I wouldn't turn it down. No matter how perverted it makes me."

"Gideon, I—"

"It's okay. You don't have to say anything. I know how messed up it is. Now it's your turn. Tell me this secret that drove my father to hate you."

"I love Bishop, and I loved Phee with everything I

am. She was my sister and the only one who was always there for me. I need you to understand that."

"I do. I can see it in your eyes. When you look at him and when you think of her."

"I thought that since we all loved each other that it would be enough. I loved Bish and Phee, they loved each other and also me. In my mind the next step was for us all to be together. So I convinced them to give it a try. It was wonderful... at first. Then we decided that we should also be together intimately as well. It was the best day of my life. I'll spare you the details, but I'd never felt loved like I did that night. Not before, and definitely not after."

"What happened?" Gideon asks, but I can see he already knows.

"Bishop freaked. Convinced Phee we were sinners and going to hell if we continued our relationship. I didn't want to lose them, so I agreed with him. I thought we would go back to the way it was before, but he had other ideas. They married and moved away less than a month later. The last thing he said to me was how I was a mistake and that he didn't want me near him or Phee. He was afraid I would corrupt them to sin again. He told me he hated me and that I had ruined everything. I didn't see him again until Phee's funeral. She called me often, though he didn't know. She wished that it could have been different, and it could've been if Bishop wasn't so stubborn."

"Stubborn," Gideon huffs out the word. "That's one word for him."

"Yeah. I wish I could break down the walls he's put up between me and him. We could be happy together. Not just me and him, but the three of us. I'm just as perverted as you, Gid, maybe worse seeing as how I actually gave in to my desire for my own blood. And I'd do it again, because as much as I want Bishop, I want you just the same."

I leave Gideon sitting on the sofa. I need to get away from him before I do something to ruin things again. Maybe not between us after our confessions, but it will most definitely push Bishop farther away than he already is.

I run into the man overtaking my thoughts in the hall and instinct has me pushing him against the wall.

"Why won't you let me in Bish? Why are you still punishing the both of us? What happened all those years ago between you, me, and Phee wasn't wrong. It was love. Pure and undiluted love. I loved you, Bish. I still do. I probably always will. Why is that so wrong? Why was loving Phee so wrong? Tell me, because I can't understand how love can ever be something so immoral regardless of who that love is for."

"It was incest, Lando. It was a sin. If Phee hadn't been your sister..." he lets his words trail off.

"But you know as well as I do, it was because she was my sister that our love was as intense as it was. You may have refused to see the beauty in what we were, and what we could have been, but I didn't. Not then and not now."

I press my lips to Bishop's in a quick, hard kiss.

"I let you and Phee go because I thought it was what you needed to see the truth of our love, but all you've done is use the distance and Phee's illness to solidify the wall between us. I won't let you do the same thing with Gideon. He deserves love, and I'm going to give him all I have. I think you should think about doing the same. That boy wants you in the same ways I do. In the same ways you want me and him. I saw it from the beginning. Don't let your stubbornness deny you what you want again."

I push away from him, leaving him standing there to process my words.

CHAPTER SEVEN

BISHOP

I follow after Lando, not stopping when he enters his bedroom. When he stops in front of his bed, I grab him by the arm and spin him around to face me. Being this close to him is bringing back memories I've tried so hard to forget, but I need to know what he meant about Gideon.

"What do you mean Gideon deserves love and wants me? I do love him. I'm his fucking father!"

"That's not what I meant, and you know it, Bish. You can deny it and pretend you have no idea what I'm talking about if you think it'll make you feel better about yourself, but that boy wants you. I want you. Why can't you give me a chance?"

"Because it's fucking wrong, Orlando. You shouldn't have those desires for your own sibling or nephew."

"Why is it so wrong, Bish? Because society says so?

It's not wrong to love someone. I refuse to believe that. I loved Phee and I love you, and now I'm growing to love Gideon. It's not wrong, it's beautiful."

"I can't love my son that way."

"But you already do. I'm not blind, Bish. I see the way you look at him. He doesn't see it, but your lust for him is strong. Hell, the way you look at him gets me hard. I've fucked my hand several times imagining the heat in your gaze was directed at me instead."

I shake my head. I can't be with Gideon. I could probably make it work with Lando, sure I'd feel guilty because he's Phee's brother, but he's not my own flesh and blood like Gideon. I open my mouth to tell Lando just that, but he puts a finger to my lips to keep me from talking.

"Shh. Don't. Get out of your own way. I'm going to ask you something, and I want you to answer truthfully. No overthinking and rationalizing it according to society's made up rules. Do you want Gideon?

"I—"

"Stop. Yes or no, Bishop. Do you want Gideon?"

I meet Lando's unwavering stare and swallow down the urge to say what has been drilled into my head for decades and blurt out the truth for the first time. "Yes. I want Gideon. Just like I want you and how I wanted you and Phee all those years ago. I want him, okay, but that doesn't make it right."

"Why do you have to be so fucking stubborn?"

Lando grips my shoulders and pushes me to take a few steps backward until my back meets the wall. He follows with his body, only stopping when there's only a breath of space left between us. His forehead touches mine and he licks his lips. God, how I want to taste him. I wonder if he still has the flavor of cinnamon I remember, or if it's changed as he's grown into the man standing before me.

"Tell me you don't want me and I'll leave you alone. I can't keep chasing a man that doesn't want me. That doesn't mean I'll back off Gideon. He's already let me know my feelings are reciprocated. I'd like it to be the three of us, but I'm tired of fighting your warped morals. I love you Bish, I always will, but I can't do this with you anymore."

"Lando, I—"

Fuck it.

I close the last bit of space between us. My lips move along his, my tongue licking along their seam and begging for entrance. My body is flush against his, my hard cock pressing into his thigh as he grinds himself against my stomach.

"God, Bish. I've missed you."

I grunt, but don't stop my assault on him. The want, the need for him I've spent so many years repressing has taken over and I can't fight it any longer. I walk us to the bed without breaking the kiss. My hands grip Lando's hips to keep him from moving his body except to make small thrusts against me. My hands roam over his body, impeded by his clothing, but before I can remove them and get my hands on his warm skin, a noise at the door makes me jump away.

Gideon stands in the open doorway, his face reflecting his surprise at the sight of me and Orlando together. My instincts tell me to defend myself and what I was doing.

"Gideon, it's not what it looks like."

"For fuck's sake, Bishop. You just can't help yourself, can you?" Orlando's words have bite and I flinch.

"Dad, it's fine. You can do whatever you want, with whoever you want. I just didn't expect to find you in here is all."

I shake my head. "No. There is nothing going on. Just a lapse in judgement."

"Fuck you, Bishop."

Orlando's words are like a slap to the face and I have to admit that I deserve it and more. I want to forget all the ingrained prejudices and societal expectations. I want to go back to the way we were all those years ago and choose us. I want to be happy again. Not that I wasn't happy with Phee, and later Gideon, but it was a happiness tinged with sadness for the man I'd left behind.

I regretted my decision as soon as I'd made it. Orlando's right. I let my stubbornness combined with other's expectations direct my life. Thinking back, I realize I lost more than my friend and lover. In a way I lost Phee; not completely, but enough for me to realize that she was happier before. I lost them both that day in different ways, but I also lost myself. And if I'm honest, I'm still lost.

"Lando," I try to apologize, but he doesn't let me.

"Don't, Bishop. I can't do this with you anymore."

The longing and hurt etched onto his face threaten to eviscerate my already broken heart. I have to make a choice; Orlando and Gideon, or my morals. And I need to decide soon.

CHAPTER EIGHT

GIDEON

I can feel the tension between them and I want to snap it. So I do the one thing guaranteed to get their focus on me and maybe move beyond whatever standoff they're having. I strip off my shirt followed by my jeans. Both men turn to see what I'm doing and immediately I have their attention as they both pause to stare at me, neither of them moving. I shift from foot to foot, the silky rub of the hose ramping up my arousal. My cock hardens behind the lace, letting them know how much just the thought turns me on. I hear a sharp intake of breath; I can't tell who it came from, both men are open mouthed, and their gazes fixated on my body.

My father stares at me and I'm not sure what he's thinking, but I hope he likes what he sees. Uncle Lando clears his throat, bringing my focus back to him. "Gid, what are you doing?"

His question brings doubts to my mind. He'd said he wanted this just as much as me, right? The doubt must be plain on my face because he rushes to me, threads his fingers through my hair, and forces me to look into his eyes.

"No. Don't think that, Gid. I do want you, but I want you to be sure. Once we cross that line there's no going back. I know you want this but wanting it and having it are two different things."

I see the look Orlando gives my father, and I turn toward him hesitantly, afraid of what I'll see. When I take in his lust filled eyes, a sigh of relief escapes and I turn to Lando again. My mouth is dry, making it hard to get any words out. I wet my lips. Lando stares, following the movement, and I nod as much as his grip will allow.

"I want it. I want you. And I want Daddy. I want the both of you." I flush when I say the word 'Daddy', knowing I've never called my father by that term of endearment before now. But that's who I want him to be. Not my father, but my Daddy.

Lando squeezes his eyes closed, and for a moment I think he's pained by my words, but when he opens them, the blue is only a thin strip surrounding his blown pupils. The lust and love looking back at me is staggering, but I don't get a chance to find relief in his acceptance before his lips crash down onto my own.

Lando's tongue strokes across my lips, forcing me to open to his intrusion. He licks into my mouth and tangles our tongues together. He uses his grip to tilt my head slightly, deepening the kiss. The euphoria rushing through me doesn't cancel out my fear that he'll change his mind.

I tentatively reach out a hand and run it down his chest, over his abs until I reach the hem of his shirt. I stroke the tips of my fingers under the fabric, slowly bunching the cotton upward. I can feel his stomach muscles tightening and releasing under my caress.

His kiss moves from my mouth, across my jaw, down my throat and up again, ending below my ear where he sucks and bites, likely leaving a bruise. He pulls back and his breath is heavy in my ear.

"Touch me, Gid." He whispers the words, but lust makes them incomprehensible. I am touching him; can't he feel me?

Another set of hands land on my body from behind. Another set of lips kiss my neck. Another voice whispers in my ear, "Gideon, my sweet, sweet boy. How have I never seen this side of you until now? You're gorgeous. Do you have any idea what the sight of the two of you together is doing to me?" His words are strained, and I know he is still fighting the sense of wrongness ingrained in him from so many years ago. But he's trying, and that's what matters. Tomorrow he might have regrets, but for now he's mine. Well, mine and Orlando's.

My father—no, I can't think of him that way any longer—*Bishop* grinds his pelvis into my ass, his hardness easy to feel through his thin slacks as he rubs against the bare skin of my ass which has been left exposed by the lacy jockstrap.

I've dreamt about this since the night I met Lando and my fantasies grew to include him. Maybe this is another dream. If it is, I don't want to wake.

Bishop's hands smoothe from my hips to my chest. When he reaches my nipples he pinches the stiff peaks, causing me to jerk between him and Lando. My ass brushes his cock, then my own collides with Lando's on the forward motion.

"Fuck. Bishop, do that again," Lando growls before attacking my mouth. Bishop alternates between pinching my nipples and teasingly tracing circles around them, overwhelming me with sensation. My body pushes back into him and rebounds against Lando; over and over. They're playing a sexually charged game of ping pong and I'm the ball neither wants to miss.

"I can't wait any longer, Lando. I know I have so much to apologize to you for, but for now, strip and let's show our boy what it really means to be loved by family."

Lando gently breaks our kiss and takes my hand, leading me to the bed. Bishop follows, unbuttoning his shirt and tossing it aside. Bishop quickly undoes his slacks and pushes them down his legs, along with his briefs. He kicks the pants to one side and takes his cock in hand, slowly stroking from the base to the tip.

I use the bed for support as my knees go weak. I want to fall to the floor and worship him with my tongue. I lick my lips imagining the musky flavor of his skin and take a step toward Bishop.

A rustle at my side jerks my attention toward Lando. He has lost his T-shirt and his jeans are open at the fly, his hand inside fondling himself as he watches Bishop. Again, I doubt how much they want me here with them.

"Gideon. Lay on the bed," Bishop commands and I hurry to comply.

Once I'm on the bed he adjusts me the way he wants, my body stretched across the bed sideways with my head hanging off the edge. The room is upside down, and when Bishop stands in front of me his cock is level with my mouth. I can't help but stick my tongue out to lap up a taste. The flavor is musky and bitterly sweet, making me hum in appreciation, and I distantly hear Lando chuckle, "Like father, like son it seems."

They go back and forth, but I tune them out, choosing instead to suck the head of Bishop's cock into my mouth. I swipe my tongue around the ridge, then dip into the slit to lap at the precum leaking steadily.

"Jesus. Damn, Gideon." Bishop's words spur me on and I try to take more of him into my mouth. The angle of my head, however, doesn't allow me the freedom I need to accomplish this, and I let out a whine. "Shh, it's okay. Let me do the work."

Bishop bends his knees, lowering his body a fraction, and pushes his cock into my throat. He pulls out, resting the head on my tongue and I slurp at him before he pushes back in again, fucking my mouth at a pace that pleases him.

I'd forgotten about Lando until he begins a light

caress up my legs, massaging circles over the hose I'm still wearing, getting closer and closer to where I'm desperate for touch. He bypasses my cock and places his hands at my hips. His lips follow the path he made with his hands as he inserts his body between my legs after he removes my jock.

Lando blows light breaths over my cock and watches it twitch with each puff of air. I can't tell him how much I want his touch with my mouth full, so I reach for him with my hands. He entangles our fingers and rests our combined fists by my hips. Using his shoulders, he pushes my legs up and folds my body in half, lifting my ass off the mattress.

Lando's licks at my hole at the same moment Bishop pushes deep into my throat. Bishop thrusts and Lando licks, again and again. I suck and moan around Bishop's cock, tonguing the vein on the underside with every thrust he makes.

Suddenly Bishop pulls away and I let out a whiny "Daddy" at the loss. He leans over, kisses my lips, then tells me, "I'm not ready to come, yet. I think I'll watch you and Lando for a bit." He makes himself comfortable at the head of the bed, his gaze riveted to where Lando is eating at me.

Lando pulls me up on the bed so my head is no longer dangling and adjusts his position, forcing my ass higher into the air. This time when his tongue licks the puckered skin around my hole, I let out a moan that echoes around the bedroom.

CHAPTER NINE

ORLANDO

I can't get enough of Gideon's taste. I'm not sure how experienced he is, but something tells me he is more innocent than his lingerie and impure thoughts imply. Pressing a finger to his hole, I continue to lick and suck at him. My awareness of Bishop is acute and causing Gideon to lose himself to the pleasure of my mouth is as much for him as it is for Gideon. I need him to see how much we want this, want him. Sure, he was a willing participant a few moments ago, but Bish's mind works overtime and I refuse to let him just accept those thoughts.

I lift my head from Gideon's ass as I add another finger and let my eyes travel up Bishop's body. His thigh muscles flex with restraint as he jerks himself. His abs quiver and I want to dip my tongue into the contours to taste how close he is to release. When I reach his face I expect to see his gaze on where my fingers disappear into Gideon's body, instead I find him looking at me with his mouth open and pupils dilated as his stare burns into mine.

"Bish," I moan his name as a shiver wracks my body and I throw my head back.

The bed dips causing Gideon to bounce on my hand and a whine of need to escape the boy. My eyes open and zero in on the empty spot where Bishop had been. Disappointment fills me and I blink back the tears that threaten to fall. I direct all my focus onto Gideon and resolve to make this an enjoyable experience even without Bishop.

I add another finger and feel him stretched tight around me. The mewling sounds and the way he is writhing on my hand are almost enough to have my orgasm spilling from my body without any direct stimulation. But I want to be inside Gideon when I find my release.

I remove my fingers from his ass and grip my cock tight in my fist to keep from coming before I can feel the tight heat of his hole. I grab the lube I'd pulled from the nightstand and set beside Gideon when I still had my senses about me. Gideon's hose-clad legs move against my skin as I position myself between his thighs and cover my length with lube. I slide my cock along the crease of his ass until the head of my dick presses against his hole.

"Please. Do it, Lando. Fuck me." Gideon's words are fueled by lust, the same lust that is beginning to fog my mind. I let out a groan and hold myself still, not daring to enter him just yet. If I do things will be over too soon and I want it to last.

"What are you waiting for? I think the boy told you to fuck him." Bishop's voice is a throaty whisper in my ear and another shiver runs through me jerking my body into Gideon's enough to feel him clenching at my cock.

"I thought you'd left," I tell him and turn my head enough for me to see his face from where he stands behind me. He winces at my words.

"I'm sorry, Lando. I'm so fucking sorry for how I've treated you all these years. It might take me some time, but I'm going to try to be the man you and Gideon need. Promise me you won't give up on me."

"Oh, Bish, I could never give up on you. No matter what I say I'll always be here for you."

Bishop leans in and we kiss, it's awkward and sloppy because of our positions but it's one of the best kisses I've ever had.

"As sweet as this is, can you fuck me now and be romantic later?" Gideon whines.

I smile against Bishop's lips at Gideon's impatience.

"Don't keep the boy waiting, Lando."

Bishop pulls away with a chuckle and slaps my ass. I miss the heat of him so close, but I slowly push into Gideon until his ass is nestled against my groin and I am fully buried inside. I take a moment to relish the feel of Gideon surrounding me and Bishop takes advantage of my stillness, using it to push his body into mine. The hairs on his chest prickle against my back and his hard cock notches into the crack of my ass. Bishop kisses the back of my neck before pressing his dick to my hole.

"I'm going to fuck you Lando and as I do, I'm going to use your body to fuck Gideon."

I nearly come at the promise in his voice as he thrusts until he is as deep inside me as I am in Gideon. Then he grips my hips and uses the hold to pull me back, forcing me to mirror his movements. Retreat and advance. In and out. Over and over Bishop fucks me and Gideon to the pace he sets. And when he climaxes, the warm stickiness inside my ass causes me to release into Gideon, who erupts all over his own chest.

My dick slips from Gideon's body and I fall to my elbows above him. Bishop follows me down, laying heavily on my back for a moment before rolling to his side in the bed. He props his head on one hand and caresses my jaw with the other.

"I love you. Both of you."

My heart feels overly full at his words, words I've waited years to hear again. I can't help the smile that stretches my lips until they ache.

"I love you too, Bish. I always have. Even when you hated me."

"I love you too, Daddy. You and Lando are my world. I know I don't have much real life experience, but I don't need it. I have everything I could want or need right here."

Gideon lets out a yawn after his declaration. His

eyes drift closed, the small satisfied smile on his face is innocently adorable.

"I couldn't agree more," Bishop says, reaching a hand to the back of my neck and pulling me in for a quick kiss. When he pulls back, I see the tears in his eyes.

"Bish?"

"I'm okay. I'm just so happy. For the first time in a really long time, I'm happy."

I nod in understanding and we adjust our positions so we are in bed correctly with Gideon between us. I fall asleep with my arm around Gideon and my hand on Bishop's hip.

EPILOGUE
BISHOP

I stare at my men as they sleep. It's been a month since that night we were all together for the first time and I have times when I struggle with the immorality of it all. But I'm trying to forget society and just live for me. It's easier to do out here in the woods. Gideon has adjusted better than me, and I'm glad my stubborn convictions didn't rub off on him.

Quietly, I leave them in our bed and make my way to the bench swing Orlando recently installed on the porch. I rock back and forth gently as I take in the changing colors of the trees. Leaves have already begun to fall and the ground has a sparse covering of orange and yellow. Fall was always Phee's favorite season. Watching nature take its course to the next stage of a never-ending cycle, I wonder if she would approve of the life I'm making here with Orlando and Gideon. I'd like to believe she would.

In a way I have her to thank for the life I have now.

Even on her deathbed she knew the long-buried truths of our past would be the key to a future where Gideon, Orlando, and I were all able to love and live in the way we were always meant to. Although, I don't think she realized how big of a part Gideon would play in our contentment.

I smile up at the crisp blue sky and feel the heat of the sun on my face. The warmth and brightness remind me of Phee's smile, and I feel like she is surrounding me with her blessing.

"Thank you," I whisper.

ORLANDO

I wake with Gideon in my arms. The sheets where Bishop slept are cool to the touch, but I've grown used to it. The first week whenever I woke and he was gone, I'd have a moment of panic. I'd rush from the bed and search the house. I'd find him in the same place every time, on the porch staring into the tree line. I'd installed the swing so he would have a place to sit.

I hate that he still has demons to fight every day in order to be with me and Gideon, but since he hasn't once tried to run as he did all those years ago, I don't say anything. I'm here for him and he assures me that's enough.

I extract myself from Gideon and after a stop in the bathroom to take care of morning necessities, I head out to sit with Bish. I'm wary of intruding on his private time, but Bishop always welcomes me to sit with him.

"Good morning," I say as I plop down in the space next to him.

"Morning." Bishop wraps an arm around me and presses a kiss to my forehead.

"Phee would have loved this view. Especially today, with the season changing." I comment on the deliciously crisp air and the bright sunshine before snuggling into Bishop's neck.

"I was thinking about her too. It's funny, but I swear this day is a gift from her. Like a blessing for me to live my life with you and Gideon. That's crazy, isn't it?"

"Not really. Ophelia Josephine Merrick-Cartwright would definitely use the seasons as a quirky way to let you know she approves of you being happy."

"Is that so, Orlando Nathaniel Merrick?"

"Why, yes, it is, Bishop Wayne Cartwright."

I fall into a fit of giggles at the way we are using Phee's preferred use of full names. Bishop's right. It feels like she is here with us today and giving us her approval.

"I love you, Phee," I whisper. Bish hears me and he hugs me closer, but otherwise ignores my words. He lets me have this moment with my sister and I love him all the more for it.

GIDEON

I stretch my arms across the bed but sit up once I realize there is no one here with me. I hate waking alone. Sure, I've spent most of my life waking up alone, but now that I have Daddy and Lando I don't want to. I know Daddy has issues of his own to work through though, so I'm trying to be patient.

I roll out of bed, take care of business in the bathroom, then pull on my favorite thigh highs and garter. They're a sheer pink set that Lando ordered online and surprised me with a few weeks ago. One of Daddy's button up shirts lays at the foot of the bed where Lando stripped it off him last night, so I pick it up and slide it on, leaving the buttons undone.

A glance in the mirror assures me my outfit has the desired look I'm aiming for. My cock hardens at the reactions I hope to elicit, and I hurry to find Daddy and Lando.

They're cuddled together on the swing Lando had installed for Daddy and I don't hesitate to climb on with them. I sit sideways on Daddy's lap with my legs stretched out across Lando's. My ass is in the perfect position for me to wiggle over Daddy's cock, so I do.

"What are you doing?" Daddy asks with a spark of laughter dancing in his eyes.

"Getting comfortable."

Lando's hand grips my cock and gives one stroke before just holding me tightly in his palm. His other hand comes to rest on my thigh to hold me in place as

Daddy wraps an arm around me. They effectively have me locked in place.

"We're trying to enjoy the morning, Gideon Michael Cartwright." Lando gives me a smile as he says my full name, and I remember how I introduced myself to him.

It feels like such a long time ago that we stood in the rain to bury my mother. Rain has a way of unearthing what lies beneath the surface, and I guess it's fitting that my mother's stormy burial did the same for us. The truth of the past shapes our future. A future that I fully believe Ophelia Josephine Merrick-Cartwright would approve of.

As a gentle breeze moves over my skin it reminds me of my mother's comforting caress. She's giving us her blessing to live and love for as long as we have, in whatever way we choose. I relax into Daddy and Lando, then close my eyes to feel the sun's warmth against my face and enjoy my family. Sex can wait, but not too long, I hope.

The End

ABOUT FAITH RYAN

Faith Ryan is wife to a handsome bearded man and mother to three, yes three, teenage girls. She lives in a small town in Ohio and is a weirdo to the max. She is in love with love of all kinds, especially the dark, dirty, and forbidden. She enjoys torturing her characters, sometimes figuratively and other times literally. Faith's writing leans to the weird, dark, and unconventional. If you like your stories with a bit of blood and taboo, you're looking in the right place. But don't worry, Faith also has a sweet side she lets out on occasion.

FB Page: https://bit.ly/FaithRyanFB
Reader Group: https://bit.ly/Fiendom
NL: https://bit.ly/FaithRyanNL

DECIET

BY

CHARITY B.

BLURB

Adam

The last thing I ever wanted to do was hurt her.
I've always done what I thought was best for her.
But this could destroy us, and that terrifies me.
I love her more than anything, but that love has become muddled with things I shouldn't feel.

Isobela

I don't know if I'll ever be able to see him the way I used to.
I feel like I'm losing my mind.
Everything is different now, yet my feelings haven't faded.
It was a mistake that neither of us expected.
There has to be way to undo this and get back to how things used to be.

I: BLACK SHEEP
ISABELA

I had to have those last few shots of tequila, didn't I? Maybe if I would've stopped when my vision began to blur, I wouldn't be stumbling up my driveway missing a flip-flop.

Billy Brewster *revs* the engine of his stupid Mustang, swerving down my street without kissing me goodbye. I don't really care, but I did suck his unimpressive dick tonight, so it would have been a nice gesture.

At least he drove me home. Even if it was dangerous, seeing as he's even more wasted than I am. Although not quite as dangerous as getting a DUI and my parents finding out I was partying all night.

My parents, Carol and Jack Hinkley, are your run of the mill, conservative, God-fearing Americans. Getting drunk, high, and blowing dudes doesn't exactly fit into their idea of who they think I should be. I don't feel like I'm doing anything out of the ordinary for being nineteen. Besides, I already chose marketing and communications over fine arts to appease them.

"Doodling isn't a career, Isabela. Stop dreaming and grow up. Either declare a real major or find your own way to pay for college."

This from the man who's pounded student loan debt horror stories into my head for years.

I was doomed to disappoint them from the beginning. They already had their cliché golden boy, and I was far from planned. Nevertheless, having an abortion is a no-no to my parents, so here I am: The official black sheep of the Hinkley family.

My purse refuses to stay on my shoulder. Slipping from my grip, it falls to the concrete, spilling its contents across the front porch.

"Shit!"

Oops, that was loud. I cover my mouth as if it will quiet the noise I've already made. It takes longer than it should to shove everything back into my bag, though, in my defense, I'm seeing two of everything.

The yellow glare of the porch light being turned on signals how screwed I am. I mumble under my breath, attempting to stand up straight without swaying.

Think sober. Think sober.

My dad opens the door, glaring at me. "Are you aware of what time it is?"

"I know ith's late—" Crap. I hang my head and sigh because there's no way I'm getting out of this.

"What's going on, Jack?" My mother rushes behind him, tying her blue bathrobe closed.

"Our daughter just came home. Drunk. Again."

"I only cad a houple."

Shut up, Isabela. Shut. The. Fuck. Up.

"Get in the house. Now."

My dad grips my arm, yanking me inside, only to have me trip over myself and fall on my face in the entryway. Imagining how ridiculous I surely look has me laughing uncontrollably. Every time I try to stop, I only laugh harder. Why is this so damn funny?

A scoff accompanied by a disgraced shake of the head is Dad's only response while Mom covers her mouth, holding back her sobs.

Guilt is the cure for my fit of hilarity. I don't want to hurt them. Their reaction just seems dramatic to me. I'm in college, for God's sake. It's absurd to expect me not to party.

Dad sneers in disgust. "You never fail to disappoint me. If you can manage to pull yourself together enough to get to your room, I suggest you do it. Or sleep on the floor. I don't care either way."

He takes my mom's hand, leading her down the hall before *slamming* their bedroom door. I sigh, dropping my head on the tile when Bucky, our giant mastiff puppy, barrels out of the kitchen to meet me, slobbering kisses all over my face.

"At least you still love me." I scratch his ears before attempting to stand. "Come on, goofball."

Halfway down the stairs to my room, I miss a step and fall on my ass. Bucky barks when I scoot myself the rest of the way. "Shhh. I'm fine, buddy."

Flipping on my cloud shaped string lights illuminates the space enough to see as I pull my striped narwhal tee over my head. My jean shorts, which my dad constantly bitches about being too short, are shimmied down my legs, leaving me in my skull bra and panty set. Bucky jumps on the bed as I fall backward onto my fluffy narwhal comforter.

Taking my phone out of my purse, I rest my head against Bucky. A blinking notification alerts me that I have a text from my big brother.

Adam: I'm coming over for dinner on Sunday. Will you be there?

He sent the message over four hours ago. Maybe he's still up? Considering he's the poster boy for the perfect child, he's actually pretty chill. Having him here always makes being around my parents more bearable. Since he moved out when I was eight, I don't have much memory of us living together, yet somehow, we've remained close. I text him more than I do my own best friend, Jessie.

Me: Don't have a choice. You up?

Bucky, the big dork, snores in my ear, sprawling across my bed. I shift to the small amount of available space as my phone *pings*.

DECIET

Adam: Yeah. Why are you? Don't you have class in the morning?

Reversing the camera on my phone, I take a selfie.

Me: Not till 10:00. I got drunk at a party, but Mom and Dad caught me sneaking in, so they're pissed.

Rolling off my bed, I grab the joint and lighter I stashed in my narwhal statue. I've had a thing for the sea creatures since I was a little kid, and anything described as a 'Unicorn of Death' is something I can get on board with.

Adam: Just tell me you were safe.

I grin. He's always been overprotective, which I suppose is an unavoidable side effect of having a big brother.

Me: Are you asking me if I got laid?

I blow three hits out the window before he responds.

Adam: I don't need to hear that shit. Nice bra btw. Does Dad know you have that?

My dad connects skulls with the devil, the occult, and generally all things evil. He would shit if he knew how much stuff I wore with them on it.

Me: I don't generally make a habit of showing Dad my lingerie.

The smoke floats out my open window as he responds, clearly trying to end the conversation.

Adam: Good to know… Listen, I have company. Call me tomorrow if Mom and Dad don't kill you first.

'Company' obviously means he has a date at his house. Irrational jealousy at him choosing to spend time with her rather than talk to me makes my veins itchy. I've always hated thinking about him with girls. Maybe I'm a little overprotective too.

Me: K. Love you.

He doesn't respond until I'm back in bed next to Bucky.

Adam: Love you too, sis.

That's the last thing I see before I close my eyes and let sleep overtake me.

II: DEVIANT
ADAM

The ice *clinks* against my glass as I finish my drink. I don't really know why I continue to use these sites. More often than not, the profile pictures are at least ten years old, and the accounts are mostly full of bullshit. I don't understand the point in lying. It makes it harder on everyone. My profile is completely straight forward about looking for someone to fuck on a regular basis. I don't even need to necessarily like them as long as they're fun in bed.

I'm not interested in a relationship right now, but I also don't want to keep hooking up with random people. It shouldn't be so hard to find someone willing to sleep together recurrently without any other expectations.

The *knock* on my door has me blowing a large breath through my lips. It's probably Moonshine, my date. Even though her name is painfully stupid, she claims to not be interested in anything more than a physical relationship.

It's a pleasant surprise to open the door and find she's actually much hotter in person. That literally never happens, so we're off to a great start.

She bites her lip as her syrupy gaze assesses me. "Adam?"

I step aside to let her in. "Yes, Moonshine, is it?" I'm really hoping it turns out to be a nickname with a clever backstory.

"Yep." She combs her fingers through her long, curly hair as she looks out my apartment window. "Wow. This view is gorgeous."

Standing in front of her, I trail my finger down the pale skin of her arm. "It's even better in the sunlight. The palm trees frame the ocean perfectly." I'm much taller than she is, so I have to lean forward to reach beneath her fringed hippie dress and touch over her panties. "It's like paradise." Though her posture momentarily goes rigid, she knows what she's here for. There's no reason we shouldn't just get to it.

"What do you do?" she asks, dropping her giant purse on the floor.

"I write and illustrate comic books. Have you ever heard of *The Horrifying Tales of a Zombie Princess*?"

Seeing the unamused quirk of her eyebrow, I'm guessing not. "I'm not really into comics."

Removing my hand from inside her dress, I gesture for her to follow me with a nod of my head. "That's fine. You don't need to be to suck my cock." The offended gape on her face makes me laugh, yet I apologize so I don't ruin this before it gets started. "Sorry—bad joke." After tonight, I'll refuse to censor myself with her, however, I'd prefer this evening not be a complete waste of time.

She stays silent on the way to my room, and as soon as we're inside, my lips are on her slender neck as my fingers find the waistband of her panties. Flattening my palm, I slide my hand beneath the fabric. Trimmed hairs brush against my fingers before the slickness between her thighs guides me inside.

My teeth nip at the shell of her pierced ear. "Get undressed."

She immediately sheds her clothes, and I admire the perfect size of her tits. Gently holding her throat, I kiss her while guiding her to my bed.

Her chest heaves as she scoots back on the mattress, watching me kneel in front of her. Her pussy is bald aside from the short, brown patch of hair right at the top. I spread her legs apart to lick along her glimmering slit. Her toes dig into the comforter as she moans my name like she won't remember it otherwise.

My phone vibrates in my pocket, and I groan. The last thing I want to do is check my texts while I have a mouthful of pussy, but it might be Isabela.

"Shit. Give me a second."

Moonshine lifts her head to glare at me. "Are you fucking serious?"

All it takes is shoving three fingers into her hole to replace her bitching with gasping. My lungs expand when I swipe open my phone to see the message. I worry about my Bella Boop a lot more now that she's in college. I'm constantly afraid that she'll get hurt or into trouble.

The time on my phone reads two-fucking-thirty. I had no idea it was that late. It's a school night, for Christ's sake. Why isn't she asleep? She's going to be exhausted tomorrow. Texting her back with my left hand is tricky seeing as my right hand is knuckle deep in Moonshine.

Isabela's response has me pounding my fingers harder when she confirms that my worries are valid. I know she's not doing anything I didn't do, it's just different because… well, because it's her.

Removing my fingers, I stand. "Come over here and get on your knees."

"Are you gonna be on that thing all night?" Moonshine whines while lowering to the floor.

"It's my goddamn sister. Now open your mouth."

Her eyes narrow before she obeys. I unzip my heathered shorts, stroking myself a few times before tapping the tip of my cock against her tongue. Typing my response to Isabela, I thrust between Moonshine's lips. While she may have an idiotic name, she gives great head.

Isabela's response has me clenching my jaw for two reasons. The idea of any hormone-fueled douchebag touching her makes me sick. Even though I know she's growing up and is bound to have these experiences, it doesn't make me despise it any less. When her photo comes through, I grip Moonshine's hair and shove down her throat so hard she tries to pull away.

The image is so jarring, I barely hear Moonshine gagging and choking as I force myself deeper. Seeing Isabela in only a bra has my cock twitching inside the girl's throat. I'm disgusted with myself as I stare at the little skull broach between her adorable tits. Her strawberry hair lays in waves over her shoulders as her glossy teal eyes stare at me through the screen.

I answer with the most appropriate thing I can think of without taking my eyes off the image of her. Desperate to end this conversation, I send one last message before tossing the phone on the bed and pulling out of Moonshine's mouth.

She gasps for breath, wheezing as drool drips down her chin. "What the fuck, Adam?"

Nodding toward the bed, I pull my shirt over my head and drop my shorts to the floor. "Get back on the bed."

"You're kind of a dick, aren't ya?"

I grin on my way to get a condom. "It'll be worth it. Face down, ass up."

She rolls her eyes, but once again, does what I tell her. I've made my intentions clear, so if she gets her thong in a twist, it's on her.

Kneeling on the bed behind her, I rub my sheathed erection against her entrance, pushing into her with as much force as I can.

"Fuck!" she yells over her shoulder.

I smack my palm against her ass cheek, leaving a

red handprint when she pushes her hips back to meet me. Despite her previous attitude, her moans and the way she's rocking her body against mine suggests she's enjoying herself.

My phone blinks with a notification, making me inwardly cringe at how badly I want to see if Isabela sent me another photo.

I'm able to resist looking at my cell for an entire two minutes before I slide out of Moonshine, rolling her onto her back.

"Hold on, I'm going to blindfold you."

Lifting her arms above her head, she grins. "Ooh, okay. That's kinda kinky."

If she only knew why I want to. I yank the case off a pillow, lowering it over her head and tightening it with a knot just above her nose.

I can't believe I'm actually going to do this.

There's no reasonable explanation as to why that picture is affecting me so much. Sexually thinking about Isabela has not only never happened before, it's also incredibly gross. Or at least, it should be. Regardless of every other thought screaming at me not to cross this line, I reach for the phone and lay it next to Moonshine's arm. My finger swipes across the screen as I re-insert myself into her body, anticipation crawling up my spine.

I'm definitely going to despise myself for this later.

Isabela didn't send another picture, only an 'I Love You' text. I quickly respond before clicking on her photo so it fills the screen. My eyes scan over her full lips, wondering who they were on tonight. As dirty and deviant as this is, my cock jumps at the vision, making me pivot faster, feeling too good in this moment to give a shit.

Sliding my fingers into Moonshine's mouth, I assault her body while staring at Isabela's face. I bite my lip to keep from saying her name.

Fantasizing that I'm inside of Isabela instead of Moonshine while her ocean eyes stare at me from my phone has me filling the condom. As soon as my balls are empty, self-disgust consumes me.

Did I really just do that?

III: FAMILY DINNER
ISABELA

"Shit, I gotta go. Adam's coming over for dinner in thirty minutes." I sniff my shirt as Jessie puts her hand on her chest with a swoony sigh. She's had a crush on him for a while. It's super fucking annoying. "Do I smell like weed to you?"

Sniffing me, she shrugs, "I dunno."

"Can I borrow something to wear?"

She rolls her eyes while walking to her closet. "You know it's super lame that you don't live in the dorms, right?"

When she hands me a sundress, I yank it from her hand. It's not exactly my style, but at least I won't reek like a 'rap concert' as my dad would say. "Not all of us can have chill, rich parents."

With a smirk, she falls back on the couch as I tug on the floral ensemble. Her dorm door swings open to reveal Jessie's bitch roommate, Lin, and one of her minions who I haven't yet had the unfortunate pleasure of meeting.

Lin waves her hand in our direction, barely looking at us. "That's my roommate and her trashy friend."

The girl, who's apparently too good to tell us her name, giggles while pointing to Jessie. "Is that her? The fake Asian?"

Lin nods with a grin, leading her across the room. Being adopted by white parents doesn't make Jessie any less Vietnamese, and it pisses me off every time Lin says that shit.

Jessie laughs. "I'd rather be a fake Asian than a real cunt."

I snort as I toss my phone in my purse. Jessie doesn't need anyone to protect her besides Jessie. Leaving them to offend each other in peace, I make my exit.

"I'll text you later."

Rushing down the stairs, I shove open the glass doors of Parkview Hall. The warm Florida air heats my face as I walk to my piece of shit Yaris sitting in the guest parking area.

My mom's pissed off that I wasn't home to help with dinner if her passive aggressive texts are any indication, so hopefully Route 41 isn't backed up, and I'll at least beat Adam there.

The Glenvar Heights suburb comes into sight at six fifty-three p.m. Seven whole minutes to spare. Unfortunately, my brother's white Lamborghini, which he refuses to shut the fuck up about, is sitting in our driveway.

The moment I walk inside, my mother crosses her arms. "Oh, I wasn't sure if we'd be lucky enough to have you join us. I'm glad you could make it."

I groan and Adam winks at me as he scratches Bucky's ears. "I was at Jessie's and lost track of time. Sorry." Leaning down, I kiss Bucky's big, furry head, whispering, "Go lay down, buddy."

"It's fine, Mom." Adam chuckles. "She's in college now, give her a break." With a grateful smile, I stand to wrap my arms around my big brother. "Hey, Bella Boop."

I keep thinking he'll knock it off with that nickname. I'm not freaking five anymore.

My dad walks in, patting Adam on the back. "Good to see you, son. How's work?"

Adam oddly bristles at the question, rubbing the back of his neck like he does when he's nervous. "It's uh...good. Busy as usual."

The smell of brisket wafts into the living room as my mom clasps her hands together. "Since we're all finally here, let's eat."

Adam drapes his arm over my shoulder, kissing my temple on the way to the kitchen. "How's school?"

"Boring." Every day I regret giving in to my parent's desires instead of pursuing my own. I literally give zero shits about marketing anything, but it was better than nursing.

As usual, the conversation revolves around Adam.

Even the food is his favorite. I push around my vegetable medley as my dad asks, "When did you get back from Orlando?"

My ears perk up as I watch Adam's reaction. He specifically told me he just got back from *Jacksonville* on Wednesday, and I know he doesn't travel that much for his job. He's a cloud engineer, or something like that, for a big energy corporation.

He shoves a bite of brisket into his mouth as soon as he says, "Tuesday afternoon."

My mouth drops open. That big lying liar. He's lucky I've matured because eight years ago, I would have ratted his ass out. What the hell is going on?

Smiling at me, Adam asks, "What have you been up to these days, Bella Boop?"

My dad scoffs. "Besides being a disappointment?"

While I'm used to my parent's snide comments, I still flinch. "Nothing special."

Quickly shifting the conversation to Mom, Adam asks her about the ladies' group at the church and other stuff I know he doesn't care about.

I hate broccoli, but Mom will literally not let me get out of this chair if I don't eat everything on my plate. When I finally swallow the last bite, I cut in the moment my mom's mouth stops moving for five seconds.

"May I be excused? I have a paper due."

"It's Sunday night. It should be finished already." Dad scolds.

"I'm almost done."

Adam winks at me when I stand up, defending me as I leave the kitchen. "She's an adult now, guys. You could cut her some slack."

"She isn't acting like it. And as long as she's still living beneath my roof, she'll respect our rules," Dad predictably responds.

Back in my room, my laptop glares at me from my bed. Regardless of what I told my dad, I'm nowhere close to being done with my paper. Bucky's sprawled across my pillows when I plop down to get it over with.

Just as my eyes are about to crawl out of my head from boredom, there's a light tap on my door. I sit up as Adam's dark blond head pokes into my bedroom.

"Hey, have a sec?"

I grin, setting down my laptop to pat the space next to me. "Sure." He hesitates before finally sitting down. "What is up with you? You've been acting kind of weird today. And what's this about Orlando? I thought you went to Jacksonville?"

His hand rubs the back of his neck as he releases a nervous chuckle. "I got my lies mixed up. There's something I haven't told you." Embarrassment bleeds into his laugh when he says, "I don't work at Earth Fuel anymore. I quit over a year ago when my comic books got popular."

My mouth falls open. He's always liked to mess with that nerdy crap, but Mom and Dad will lose their shit if they find out he gave up the career they paid to educate him for to 'doodle'.

"How the hell do you afford your fancy apartment?"

He shrugs with a smug smirk. "Like I said, the comics have gotten a lot of traction."

I'm proud yet simultaneously jealous of my brother for following his dreams. It obviously paid off. While I completely understand why he lied to our parents, I'm a little hurt he wasn't honest with me.

"Why are you just now telling me?"

He falls back on my bed and reaches over to pet Bucky. "Because I have a proposition for you."

I lie down next to him, resting my head in my palm. "Oh, yeah?"

His fingers comb through his hair before he presses a kiss to my forehead. "I hate seeing Mom and Dad on your case like they were at dinner. I remember how that felt, and it seems even worse for you."

"Okay, so?"

"How would you like to move in with me?"

Whoa. Is he serious?! Excitement sends vibrations across my skin. "You really want me living at your house? What about all your 'guests'?" I smile to soften the unintentional snark in my comment.

"I do have doors. And it's not like I'd smash in front of you."

"Ewe!" I grimace even though the mental image angers me more than sickens me.

He laughs one of his deep laughs. "So? What do you say?"

I squeeze him tight with my hug. All I want to do is start packing. "Mom and Dad are going to freak."

"Let me talk to them. When do you want to move in?"

"Tomorrow?"

Leaning up on his elbow, he smiles. "You have school, I don't want to mess with that. How about this weekend?"

I hug him again because this is probably the nicest thing he's ever done for me. "Thank you, Adam."

IV: ROOMMATE
ADAM

The conversation with my parents could have gone better, though, ultimately, they knew it was Isabela's choice. I didn't go to dinner last week with the intention of asking her to move in, it's just always broken my heart, the way they treat her. They were strict with me, too, but no matter what she does, they scrutinize it. I saw the way her face fell when Dad called her a 'disappointment', and it took everything in me not to go off.

Sitting on the now stripped bed, I stare at the bare walls of what will be her room. I'm excited to have her here with me. Even if the guilt from using her photo to masturbate multiple times sits heavy in my stomach. I'm hoping her being here will make it too weird for that to continue. It's not as if I intend on using her picture. I'll start watching regular porn, then the hornier I get, I move on to incest porn, until finally I just want to see her face so I can come. Afterwards, I always feel like a scumbag, yet I continue to repeat the cycle.

The doorbell rings, and I nearly run to answer it. Isabela's standing in the hall next to her friend, wearing a grin and skimpy shorts.

"Hey, Bella Boop. Hey, Jessie."

Jessie flutters her lashes and bites her lip. "Hi, Adam,"

Isabela rolls her eyes, walking inside without an invitation. "Hey, bro."

I lead them down the hall, and Jessie whistles when I open the bedroom door. "This place is nice, Bells. Imagine how much more narwhal stuff you could fit in here."

Isabela laughs, falling back on the bed as I leave them to discuss the decorating possibilities.

It's another hour and a half before the movers arrive, giving me some time to get a head start on my newest *Zombie Princess* issue.

When Isabela's things finally get here and everything is unloaded into her new room, I order her favorite takeout for dinner.

Once it's delivered, I set up the food on the coffee table and make my way back to her room.

Her things are partially unpacked, strung haphazardly all over the space with empty boxes stacked in the corner. "I ordered Golden Shenzhen, you guys hungry?"

Isabela pumps her fist as Jessie stands up, stretching

with a groan. "Actually, I have a date tonight, I need to go get ready."

After Jessie leaves, Isabela meets me in the kitchen. "Thank you for this, Adam. It's going to be amazing living without Mom and Dad breathing down my neck every day."

I pick up our plates, handing her one as I shrug. "At least you're less annoying than you used to be."

With a playful gape, she shoves my arm. "You dick. I've never been annoying."

Chuckling, I grab the chopsticks and walk to the living room, pointing toward the TV as I sit on the couch. "I have most streaming services. Pick whatever."

"I have most streaming services," she mimics, piling food onto her plate. "God, you're so old." My eyes narrow as I grab a pot sticker off her plate and shove it into my mouth. "Hey! Asshole."

"You aren't allowed to cuss," I say around the dumpling. She almost makes me choke the way she glares at me. Swallowing it down, I laugh. "I'm just giving you shit."

She picks a show about a guy who stalks and kills people all because he's obsessed with some girl.

"It's kind of romantic, though, right?" she swoons.

I shake my head. 'Romantic' isn't the adjective that comes to mind. "Twenty bucks says this bitch is dead by the end of the season."

She kicks me with a laugh. "I'll take that bet. There's no way. He's in love with her."

Once the food is gone, Isabela takes a shower as I clean up the food and grab the bottle of tequila. When she returns, she raises an eyebrow at me pouring our shots.

"We need to get you unpacked. The best way to do that is drunk. Bottoms up, Bella Boop."

V: OLD PHOTOGRAPH
ISABELA

I had no idea I owned so much stuff.

"What the hell is this?" Adam asks as he removes my collagen lip mask from a box.

I snatch it out of his hand. "It makes my lips soft and kissable." I give him a smoochy face and snort at his glare.

"We should probably set some ground rules. No boys is the first one that comes to mind."

Well, that's bullshit. "So, then you can't bring dates here either?"

He scowls as he unpacks my birth control, staring at the pills like he's trying to set them on fire with his eyes. "Oh, no. I'll definitely have women over. I'm the adult, and this is my apartment."

Asshole. I shove him, but he ignores it as he stands up to leave my room. Crossing my arms, I follow right behind him. "I'm an adult too. And I thought we were going to be like roommates. Roommates don't have double standards. Parents do."

His steps falter for a moment, which I hope means my words are sinking in. We're equals. Him being older shouldn't matter. "We'll see, okay? How about neither of us bring home friends of the opposite sex for a while."

As soon as we reach the kitchen, he pours yet more shots, and I roll my eyes. He's going to learn quickly that I won't let him control me like I let Mom and Dad. I reach for the shot glass and throw it back. The room around me is already a little wobbly, however, I'm not about to let my ancient big brother outdrink me.

I go back to my new room and pick up the box of beauty products Adam was going through. There's not enough space to fit the box next to the nightstand, so I scoot the table over. When I do, something peeks out, stuck between the wall and the nightstand. Reaching out, I grab it to see it's an old photograph. I run my fingers over the glossy image.

It's a picture of a blonde girl, maybe middle school age, with hideous fashion sense. She's wearing a fishnet crop top, smiling beneath the rim of a Von Dutch trucker hat. Even though I don't remember ever seeing her before, there's definitely a familiarity about her.

Adam walks in, and I immediately wave the photo next to his face. "Who's this?"

He scrunches his eyebrows, yanking it from my hand. For a second, all expression is wiped from his face, then he shrugs and gives it back to me. "She's an old friend from school." Looking over his shoulder, he nods toward the hall. "Another shot?"

We literally just got done taking one. "Sure."

He nearly sprints from my room, and the glasses are already poured when I meet him back in the kitchen. I toss the photo on the counter as he throws back his shot.

"Is there any way we can finish this tomorrow?" I ask. "I'm over it for tonight."

He chuckles as he picks up the bottle and shot glasses. "No complaint on my end."

Following him into the living room, I sit on the couch when I realize issues of his comics are displayed beneath the glass of the coffee table. I didn't notice them earlier because of the Chinese food.

"So these are why you quit your fancy job?"

He plops down next to me. "Yep."

"And you're the illustrator?"

He's always had this embarrassed laugh that I think is so cute. "Yeah. I write the dialogue too…you want to look at one?"

I think the alcohol is fucking with me, because for some reason, my stomach tingles, giving me the desire to giggle. I suddenly want to touch him, and I can't explain why. Scooting closer, I comb my fingers through his dark blond hair. "I'd love to."

With the way he's looking at me and his hesitancy to move, I feel like I've made him uncomfortable, so I pull my hand away. He eventually stands and walks across the room to a cabinet, taking a box from the very top shelf.

"This is the first issue." Sitting next to me, he hands me the comic. The color scheme consists mostly of vibrant pastels. The main character, Zibby, has lilac patchwork skin and very pale pink hair. He won't hear this from me because he's already way too conceited, but his take on surrealism is adorable and impressively well done. "She's supposed to become the Zombie Queen, but she doesn't want the crown, so she does everything in her power to piss off her parents in hopes they'll strip her of her title."

As I read through the story, I realize I can relate to her a lot. She even has an older brother. "Gotta say, I like this Zibby girl's style."

"Well that's good because she's you. Or rather, inspired by you."

It's as if a bubble forms in my heart and explodes little emotion crystals everywhere.

His beautiful smile makes my skin burn with hot little pricks. I have no idea what I'm feeling. I can't decide if I want to laugh, cry, or...

Suddenly, the urge to kiss him overtakes me, and before I even question it, I grab his face and press my lips to his. I don't know if it's the alcohol or what's going on with me, so I ignore every thought telling me I'm losing my mind.

His hands wrap around my arms as he pushes me away. Without speaking, his blue eyes scan mine with... I can't place it. It's not sadness exactly, however it's definitely not happiness. Abruptly, he cups the back of my neck and kisses me. Hard.

The second his tongue licks at mine, it's as if his mind snaps him back to reality. He jumps off the couch, jabbing his finger toward the hall. "Go to your room."

His command leaves no space for argument which pisses me off because he's acting exactly like Dad.

"Are you fucking seri—"

"Now, Isabela." His fists are balled up at his sides, and even though he orders through clenched teeth, there's something more than anger in his tone.

I do as he says, but not without giving him the finger on the way to my room. In a huff, I rip off my clothes, crawling into bed wearing nothing more than my underwear.

Even though half my brain is grateful he stopped me before things went too far, the other half is pissed because the way he kissed me proved that he wanted it as much as I did. I toss and turn for at least half an hour before the guilt sets in.

Getting out of bed, I throw on a shirt to go apologize. I'd put him in an extremely uncomfortable situation, and that wasn't fair. His room is on the opposite end of the hall, and when I reach his door, I softly knock.

"Adam? Look, I'm really sorry, okay? I'm just drunk. Can't we forget about it?" He doesn't answer, so I sigh and drop my head against the door. "Come on, bro. Don't make me feel worse than I already do."

When he still doesn't respond, I swing open his door in frustration. "Adam! I'm trying to apolo—"

The sight of him stops me in my tracks. He's sitting at his desk, headphones covering his ears as he thrusts his very hard, very *large* erection into his palm. It's not just the fact that the panties I left in the bathroom hamper are pressed against his nose that shocks me. It's that I can clearly see the selfie I sent him last week on his computer. I inch closer, allowing me to barely hear his faint whispers. "Isabela."

All he would have to do is turn around to see me, and honestly, that sets my skin ablaze even more.

"Fuck yes, take my cock," he murmurs into the fabric.

I don't know when my point of view of him changed, yet as I stare at the muscles in his arms flexing with each stroke, I find my own hands lowering inside my panties. All I want is to watch him come knowing I'm who he's fantasizing about.

Even without his awareness of my presence, it's as if our bodies sense each other when he moans out my name, his come squirting across his chest right before my own orgasm crashes through me. I bite my lip to be quiet even though he can't hear me with his headphones on.

When he leans back against his chair, he covers his face in his hands and groans, "Fuck."

The amount of pain in his voice makes my stomach tumble to my knees. I back down the hall before he notices me, quietly crawling into my bed.

I hate that he feels so guilty for his desire even though I understand it. These emotions are clearly perverse. No normal, healthy person would have them, but no matter how hard I try to erase the mental image of my brother touching himself in the sexiest of fucking ways, it plays on repeat in my brain.

Succumbing to the ache between my thighs, I reach down, giving in and letting my darkest thoughts consume me until they once again bring me to climax.

VI: WEAKNESS
ADAM

Isabela still isn't awake. It's Sunday, though, so she won't need to be in class, and to be honest, after what went down last night, I'm glad for the time to clear my head.

I can't believe she kissed me.

I can't believe I kissed her back.

It was probably half stupidity and half denial that led me to convince myself her living here would in any way eliminate my deplorable desires.

The tequila didn't help the situation, so it's unfortunate I happen to be somewhat of an alcoholic. As I fill up the coffee pot with water, I assure myself that when the newness of our situation wears off, this unexpected craving will too.

"Morning, roomie."

My lips lift at the sound of her voice, and I turn to her, nearly dropping the coffee pot when I see what she's wearing. Her long legs are bare, her panties covering at least as much as a swimsuit would. Her white tank top, however, is nearly sheer, allowing me a clear view of not only her nipples but the ample shape of her breasts.

"What the hell do you have on? Put on some goddamn clothes. Jesus Christ."

Ignoring me, she makes her way across the kitchen to reach into the cabinet for a mug, giving me an eyeful of her round ass peeking out from beneath her panties. My dick grows in my boxers no matter how much I mentally beg it not to.

"If I'm going to live here, then I get to walk around in my underwear like you do," she retorts.

I refuse to let her see how hard I am. We're obviously going to ignore the horny elephant in the room, so I grind out, "Fine. We'll both get dressed. You first."

She rolls her eyes yet thankfully leaves the kitchen. I can't help but watch her ass as she heads toward the hall. Once I hear her bedroom door close, I let out a heavy sigh and go to my own room. I stare at my reflection in the mirror as I pull on my sweatpants, reminding myself that this is Isabela, not some random hookup.

She's already back in the kitchen when I return, and though she technically has clothes on, they don't cover much...especially those shorts.

"How do you want it?"

My eyes spring up to hers, worried she caught me staring. "I'm sorry?"

"Your coffee?"

"Oh...uh a cube of sugar and some milk."

I make a one-eighty turn to the bathroom when she bends over to dig through the silverware drawer. As soon as the door is closed behind me, I splash cold water on my face. I'm being too hard on myself. She's growing up into a stunning woman. Maybe what I'm feeling is more normal than I realize. What really matters is I don't act on it.

When I feel as composed as I can make myself, I return to find Isabela in the living room with our coffees, flipping through the comics I left out last night. Without looking up from the pages, she asks, "What are we doing today?"

I assumed she would have her own plans. I was hoping to get more work done on the new issue that needs to be sent out for production next week, but spending the day with her sounds more appealing than expected and waiting until tomorrow to work won't hurt anything.

I take a seat next to her on the couch and turn on the TV. "We can do some more unpacking and then pick somewhere to go for lunch."

"Come on," she whines. "We have forever to unpack my shit. Let's do something fun."

I rest my head against the couch. "Like what?"

She jumps up to her feet. "Don't worry about it. Go shower. I'll make the plans." Spinning on her heel, she runs down the hall before hollering, "And put on a swimsuit!"

I take a few more sips of coffee and return to the kitchen to add something stronger.

With my mug empty, I head to my room to do what she asked. After I'm dressed in my swim trunks and a tee, I find her in the kitchen wearing those tiny shorts and a bikini top, adding food along with a tequila bottle to a basket.

"What's all this?"

She grins as I force my eyes to meet hers instead of trailing down her exposed legs. "We're going on a picnic!"

Her excitement for something so basic makes me grin. "A picnic? That's your big plan?"

Tapping the tequila bottle, she grins. "It's more of a drink-nic. Let's go before all the good spots are taken."

I'm not sure day drinking is the smartest idea right now. Before I can say anything, she totes the picnic basket and a beach bag out of the apartment. "Are you at least going to tell me where we're going?"

"South Beach...obviously."

She sings off-key the entire way to the beach, exactly like she has since she was a kid, and although I've always thought it was cute, somehow, it's sexy now. I shake my head because 'sexy' is the last word that should describe anything about Isabela.

I park the car, and she grabs the bag, making her way to the beach as I follow behind her with the picnic basket. She smooths out our towels and lathers herself with tanning lotion while I lay back, closing my eyes so I'm not tempted to offer applying her lotion myself.

A few minutes later she asks, "Wanna take a shot?"

Cracking my eyes open has me jolting upright. She's completely bare for everyone on the fucking beach to see. South Beach may be open about its topless policy, but that rule doesn't apply to Isabela.

"What the hell are you doing?!" God, it's impossible to keep my eyes off her perfectly perky breasts bouncing right in front of me.

"Not getting tan lines...obviously."

This makes me extremely uncomfortable. I just don't know if it's because of the new light I've been seeing her in lately, or because I'll never be okay with her showing her boobs to anyone able to look.

"Are you wanting to piss me off?" My jaw hurts from how hard I'm clenching it.

"If my tits piss you off, that's on you, bro."

She's trying to get under my skin, and fuck, it's working. "Seriously, Isabela, put on a goddamn top."

She rolls her eyes, relieving me when she covers herself. "Whatever. Are we drinking this tequila or what?"

I shake my head as she throws back a swig from the bottle then follow her lead. Fuck me, I do need a shot.

———

Luckily, she keeps her clothes on as we spend the day making fun of people on the beach. I don't remember the last time we've hung out like this. I've missed it.

My stomach growls reminding me how hungry I am. "Are we going to actually eat at this picnic?"

"Ooh, yes. I made chicken wraps." She sets out the plastic plates, tossing a wrap and a bag of chips on mine.

My teeth barely sink into the sandwich when a male voice speaks behind me.

"Isabela?"

Her eyes widen as she drops her food onto her plate, quickly wiping her mouth. "Chad?!" She jumps to her feet to meet the bleach blond with a smile that belongs on a toothpaste commercial.

All my muscles tense when she hugs him, and he rests his hands above her ass. *Chad.* I remember this motherfucker. He cheated on Isabela their junior year in high school, completely obliterating her heart. So why the hell is she hugging him like that?

Tossing his hair out of his eyes, he asks, "Hey, what are you doing tonight? A friend of mine is having a party. You down?"

Sorry, Chad, there's no way she'll bail on me to hang out with a piece of shit like you.

"Um..." Isabela looks at me as if asking my permission. Seriously? I'm sure my eyebrows shoot up in disbelief. Her gaze narrows on me for a moment before she straightens with a big smile and hands him her phone. "Sure, put in your number."

I don't stop my scoff when he enters his contact information into her cell. The bastard nods at me as he walks away, and Isabela sits back down with that smug smile she used to wear when she won at Candy Land.

"You're actually going to a party with that prick?"

Crossing her arms, she tilts her head with a smirk. "Is there a reason you don't want me to go? Aside from the fact that you're obviously not a Chad fan?"

I grab the tequila bottle and throw back a big swig. "Nope."

VII: LITTLE VOYEUR
ISABELA

Chad Evanston is a cheating fuckboy who can kiss my ass. I'll admit, seeing him for the first time since graduation was a bit of a shock, but the look on Adam's face was worth it.

The idea of catching him jerking off again springs into my brain, and I can't get the image out of my head. I thought day drinking would have loosened him up enough to at least kiss me again, but other than the occasional boner he attempted to hide, it was a normal day.

He's been in a mood since we got home from the beach, and it's really hard not to smile when I know it's because of Chad and the party. When he finally gets in the shower, I knock on his bathroom door. "I'm going to head out. I want to meet up with Jessie first."

"Bye," he bites out.

I grin, sneaking back to my room to watch for him through the crack in the door. My heart pounds loud in my chest when he leaves his room completely naked. How have I never noticed how cute his ass is?

As I wait for him to return, my common sense rears its head. I slump my shoulders with a silent groan. This is completely insane. What am I even doing? Being here with him has made me completely crazy. I sigh, about to give up on this ridiculous plan when he walks back into the hall to return to his room.

The increase in my heart rate has my stomach twisting itself into a kink. What exactly am I expecting to happen if I do find him like I did last night?

As I pass his room, I tell myself to keep moving. To walk out the front door and to my car. I'll go to Jessie's and admit my fantasies. She'll be my voice of reason.

Regardless of my good intentions, I find my hand on his door handle, turning it slowly.

His heavy breathing can be heard as soon as I walk in. Nearly in the exact same position as last night, he's wearing headphones with my panties against his nose and my picture on the computer.

A huge knot is stuck in my throat as I tiptoe closer. If he looks up and sees me, I have no idea how he'll react.

"Yes, suck it."

His fist pumps rapidly as he thrusts up to meet the motion. The curiosity of how he would feel in my own hand has me inching forward. The moment he closes his eyes to take a deep inhale of my lingerie, I fall to my knees between his legs. Before he opens his eyes to stop me or I change my mind, I wrap my lips around his tip and suck.

He instantly lurches beneath me, ripping off the headphones as I look up to see his eyes wide in horror. "No, no, no." His voice begins as a whisper yet gets louder with every word he speaks. The panic in his tone has me taking him out of my mouth, not sure what to say. "Fuck, why did you do that?!"

The disgust in his blue eyes chokes me with shame as I nod toward the computer. "I...I saw you last night." His cock jerks as his chest heaves harder with each intake of breath. "You've clearly thought about this too."

Slowly, I reach up, wrapping my fingers around his length, gently stroking. He squeezes my wrist, and just when I think he's going to yell at me, he uses his grip to guide my hand up and down. Never taking his eyes off mine, he grinds out, "This is very fucking bad."

Honestly, I think that's part of why it's so hot. The wrongness of it has me soaking through my underwear when he pushes down on my head with a groan, shoving himself between my lips.

"You came in here and watched me last night?" I nod since my mouth is full of my brother. A half laugh releases when he clutches a chunk of my hair to move my head up and down faster. "You little voyeur."

Drool drips down my chin as I gag around his girth. Jolts of arousal pulse their way between my legs and I wonder if I could come from this alone. Reaching inside my panties, I rub at my swollen clit.

He thrusts his hips to fuck my face so hard I'm scared he'll make me throw up. Suddenly, with a frustrated growl, he holds my arms, pushing me off him. I gasp for breath as he lifts me to my feet and grabs my throat, kissing me with even more aggression than he did last night. He walks me backward to the bed, his quick strides twice as long as mine, nearly making me trip.

Releasing my neck, he pushes me back onto the bed, not even waiting until I've landed to start ripping off my shorts and panties. It's as if he thinks that if we don't do this quickly then we'll come to our senses and stop.

His hands claw down my thighs, his gaze fixed between my legs. "This is beyond fucked up." He pants heavily, pushing my legs, as far apart as they will go, and I moan at the stretch. His tongue explores my folds before he sucks my throbbing clit between his lips. "I'm going to hell for how much I love your taste."

As his tongue dips into my hole and flicks at my clit, my mind fabricates fantasies of what could have been if we'd understood this desire sooner. I find myself pretending we're back at our parents' house, giving in to the deviance of it all. "Yes, eat my pussy, big brother."

Those words have him digging his fingers into my thighs as he devours me. Every inch of my flesh comes alive as I explode my pleasure into his mouth. My heart's still pounding from my orgasm when he climbs up my body. He hovers above me, his cock, which I'm aching to feel, rests on my clit as I shamelessly thrust against the side of his shaft.

Touching his forehead to mine, he groans. "Fuck." He lifts my shirt, pulling down the cup of my bra to rub his thumb over my hardened nipple. "We're gonna hate ourselves for this..."

I kiss him and squeeze his hips, pressing myself harder against him. "Just put in the tip for a second," I whisper.

"Shit." His head dips down to suckle at my breast. "You're so fucking hot." When his eyes meet mine, I see regret, tearing my heart in half. "And you shouldn't be." He taps himself against my clit, rubbing the head along my entrance. In one movement, he raises his ass and shoves into me, ripping a gasp from my throat. "Fuck that's a tight fit." So much for only 'putting in the tip'. His movements become faster before he leans back to rub his thumb over my hard nub. "I can't believe we're doing this."

I touch his face to make him look at me as I meet each of his thrusts. "It's okay, I promise. It's our secret."

He fucks me so hard, it's almost as if he's trying to hurt me.

Flipping me to my stomach, his fingers squeeze my waist as he lifts my ass in the air. Without warning, he impales me again. The longer he goes, the faster he pumps. "You look so gorgeous around my cock."

I don't think he's slowed his pace once, and I'm beginning to get sore. He fists my hair as another orgasm inches toward the brink. Kissing up my back, he whispers, "Roll over. I want to see your face when you come."

Once I obey, he throws my legs over his arms and hammers back into me. His thumb circles my clit, and before long, I'm coming with such ferocity that I arch my back and cry out. When I open my eyes, he's watching himself going in and out of my pussy.

Lifting his gaze to mine, he pleads, "I love you. Please don't hate me for this."

He jolts, moaning his pleasure with obscenities as he empties himself into my body. I've never had someone come inside me before, and I love how warm it feels. As soon as he breaks our connection, he shakes his head, and I can tell he's about to freak out.

Taking his hand, I tug on his arm so he'll lie next to me. I kiss the worried creases on his forehead before touching my lips to his. "I could never hate you, bro." His eyes squeeze shut, making me wonder if those words were somehow the wrong ones.

VIII: LIAR
ADAM

Fuck, fuck, fucking fuck.

How did I let that happen? I've always known I was a dick, but a sicko? A legitimately disgusting human being? I'd never thought that's who I was before now.

Prying myself from her touch, I jump off the bed to yank on my shorts. How did I screw this up so epically? The moment I felt her mouth, I lost all my resolve, but why the hell do I want her in the first place? What am I supposed to do now? Kick her out? Send her back to Mom and Dad's? How would we even explain that?

"Adam?"

Isabela calls after me as I storm to the kitchen and pour myself a double shot. My gaze lands on the photo of Amaya still sitting on the counter before I down my drink. Isabela walks into the kitchen in her underwear and a tank. Even now, after I've destroyed everything, I'm still admiring her body.

Resting her hands on her hips, she frowns. "Do you drink constantly?"

How is she so calm about this? "Oh, I'm just fucking getting started."

I pour another shot and drink it as she sighs, walking toward me. She rests her hand on my arm, and I try not to flinch at the burn of her touch, reminding me that I've ruined both of our lives because she makes my dick hard. "Look, we might have made a mistake, I'll admit that."

"*Might* have? We definitely fucking did."

She ignores me and continues trying to comfort me. Shouldn't it be me comforting her? "Adam, I wanted it, okay? It's not like you raped me, and we won't ever do it again. We'll keep it between us and forget about it." She waves her hand, trying so hard to be nonchalant. "So you dicked down your sister... It's not like you killed anyone." With a shrug, she adds, "Perspective."

Fury at my mistake and exhaustion from years of lies pour from my lips as I grab her arms, screaming at her, "You're not my goddamn sister!"

I push her away, and she shakes her head in confusion. "What are you talking about?"

Grabbing Amaya's picture off the counter, I shove it at her chest. "This isn't just a friend from school. She's your mom." Her eyes widen as she takes a step back, eyes flipping to the photo. "I got her pregnant when we were thirteen."

The anger I've been waiting for overtakes her face.

Her voice sounds like I've never heard it before when she asks, "What the fuck are you saying, Adam?"

"Mom and Dad are your grandparents. They adopted you. You were never supposed to know..." As much as I want to hold her, tell her I'm sorry, she looks like she'd sooner stab me than hug me.

"Say it," she grates out. "I want to hear you say the words. Who are you to me?"

My shoulders fall, and I slump against the counter. This is so hard to say. I hold my face in my hands because I can't bear to look at her. "I'm your biological father."

Tears drip down her cheeks as she shakes her head. "I don't believe you." Suddenly she lurches at me, shoving my chest. "You lied to me my entire life! All of you!" I don't know what to do. How to make this better. She sobs while she rips her hands through her hair. "Please tell me this is a really horrible joke."

I reach out to her, silently pleading that she'll let me hold her. "I'm so sorry."

The moment my hand lands on her arm, she spins away from me. "Don't fucking touch me!" Her eyes travel down my body in repulsion. "I don't even know who the fuck you are."

She stomps out of the kitchen, and a few minutes later, the front door slams. I release a huge breath that feels like I've been holding for nineteen years.

Amaya's photo stares up at me. I wonder if she's ever thought about us. Mom and Dad basically paid her parents for her not to have an abortion. She probably still hates me. When she was pregnant, I cheated on her with a girl in the ninth grade. I knew she was in love with me, and we'd taken each other's virginity, but she had this whole life planned out. She talked about me getting a job and raising Isabela together. As an eighth grader, that freaked me the hell out. During my fourteenth birthday party, she caught Kirsty Jenner giving me head in the party room at Laser Games. She refused to speak to me after that and wouldn't even let me in the delivery room when Isabela was born. We haven't seen each other since.

I bring the photo to Isabela's room, putting it on the nightstand. She has to come back eventually. I need to fix this...somehow.

———

Since Isabela is all I can think about, I put it to good use by working on the new *Zombie Princess* comic. It's perfect, really. About four issues ago, Zibby's brother, Prince Alek, accidently killed the human boy Zibby's in love with, and of course, ate his brain. In this issue, I think she should find out. As I try to mimic the way Isabela looked at me earlier and translate it to Zibby's face, my cell goes off. I don't even have to check to know who it is because her ringtone is a recording of her saying, *Adam, it's your mother*, over and over.

I answer, putting it on speaker so I can continue working. "Hey Mom, what's up?"

"Is Isabela there? Every time I call her, I get sent straight to voicemail," she shrieks in my ear.

Shit. They're going to find out she knows sooner or later. "I told her, Mom...she's furious at all of us."

Her voice drops about five octaves. "You told her what?"

"She found Amaya's picture, and... I ended up blurting it out." Not a complete lie.

"Adam Jacob Hinkley! Why on earth would you do that?! Wait until your father finds out. The very second Isabela walks in that door, you have her call me. Am I clear?"

"Yeah, I'll tell her."

"I love you," she bites out before hanging up on me.

I love my mother unconditionally, but God, she can be a passive aggressive bitch. I spend a few hours adding shading and finishing the rest of the dialogue before my phone rings with Isabela's ringtone. My heart pounds hard against my chest as I answer.

"Bella Boop." I breathe out heavily

"It's not Bells." The voice is panicked and familiar, taking me a minute to realize it's her friend.

I'm a little thrown and worried as to why she's calling me from Isabela's phone. "Jessie? What's up?"

Loud music blares in the background, making me strain to hear her, which doesn't help when she's speaking a mile a minute. "She's been freaking out all night. As soon as we got here, she went crazy taking shots. Now she's passed out in the bathroom, and I can't get her to wake up. I don't know what to do."

Jumping up from my stool, I sprint into the hall, barely remembering to lock my apartment. "Is she breathing?"

"I-I think so..."

"You *think* so? Where the hell are you?"

"A house in Coral Gables," she slurs.

"An address, Jessie, I need a fucking address." Drunk girls are the absolute worst. "And call an ambulance."

"Okay, hold on." I cringe at the he sounds of *chug, chug, chug!* chanting in the background until finally, she reads me the numbers and street name.

"I'm on my way. If the ambulance gets there before I do, call me."

"You know she's like this because of you, right? How could you have lied to her about that?"

I'm not having this discussion with her. Hanging up, I climb into my car. She's right, though. For more than half of my life, I've had to push back my parental wishes and just be Isabela's sibling. There was so much shit that my parents put her through that I didn't want for her. I was never able to be her dad and honestly, I became accustomed to my brotherly role. Most of the time, I don't see her as my child. I'm sure I feel differently about her than the average brother feels about his sister or fathers feel about their daughters. It's just a weird limbo.

One thing that's been consistent, though, is the need to protect her. Something terrible happening to her is what I've constantly feared since the day she was born, yet it's never been a real risk until tonight.

The ambulance lights flash in front of me as I turn onto the street of the address Jessie gave me. The home is a two-story townhouse overflowing with Gen Z idiots. I'm barely out of my car before seeing the EMTs pushing Isabela away from the house on a gurney. My entire body turns cold. It feels like my soul is clawing its way out of my chest when I see her unmoving form.

I scream her name as one of the med techs stops me. "You need to get back."

"She's my sister!"

"We're taking her to Dade Memorial. Do you know where that is?" He speaks so calmly while Isabela lies unconscious behind him.

I can't respond with words, so I nod, watching as he returns to help the other medics secure her in the back of the ambulance.

Jessie is talking to a police officer when I find her. "I told you, I have no idea who bought the alcohol."

The policeman looks at me with a stern look, asking, "And you are?"

"My sister's being taken to the hospital. Is there anything more you need from Jessie?"

He grunts, shaking his head before walking away. I turn to Jessie as I try to rein in my anger. This isn't exactly her fault, however, she was with her when it happened.

"How the hell could you let her drink so much?"

Her eyebrows raise, and she crosses her arms.

"Because I'm not her parent...which is more than I can say for *you*." I narrow my eyes, and she adds, "Besides, you try stopping her when she's on a mission to get shit-faced." Her voice softens as she turns to where the ambulance was moments ago. "Is she going to be okay?"

Inhaling deeply, I lead her to my car. "She has to be."

I wait until Jessie climbs into the passenger side before I peel out onto the street. Isabela said that us sleeping together would stay between us, although that was before she got wasted.

"What did she tell you, anyway?"

Jessie scoffs. "That you're liar McLying face."

I give her a sarcastic smile. "Mature." At least I'm pretty sure that means Isabela kept our other secret.

"Come on, man. You have to admit that's fucked up. Why didn't you just tell her?"

Huffing, I turn from the neighborhood onto the main street. "You can't even begin to understand the situation."

"Okay, boomer," she mocks.

"That's not even accurate. I'm like twenty years away from being a b— you know what? How about we stop talking so I can think?"

She fiddles with the radio and thankfully doesn't speak again until we reach the hospital.

I know for a fact that I'm Isabela's emergency contact, so at least Mom and Dad won't ever have to know about this. I can hear my mother now: *Less than forty-eight hours in your care, and she ends up in the hospital?!*

Jessie's right behind me as I rush up to the front desk in the ER where the receptionist passively tells us to take a seat. After what seems like hours, a doctor finally makes her way to us.

"Hello, Adam Hinkley?"

Jessie and I stand to meet her. "Yes, hi. Is Isabela alright?"

Her nod makes my knees feel like jelly. "We were able to pump a lot of the alcohol from her stomach, and she's getting fluids now. She'll probably feel pretty rough for a day or two, but she'll be fine. I'd like to monitor her for a few hours, then if she does well, you can take her home."

Wiping my hands over my face, I ask, "Can we see her?"

She nods, asking a nurse to lead us to Isabela's cubicle. The second I pull back the curtain, my vision blurs with tears. I've never seen her hooked up to tubes like this before. I didn't realize how fortunate I've been that I haven't had to truly fear for her safety before now. She's asleep, and the slow up and down movement of her chest is the most comforting sight I've ever seen.

I sit next to Jessie in silence, and soon, she's snoring in the chair next to me. While I'm grateful that she cares so much about Isabela and most likely saved her life, she really should be asleep in her bed. I'm sure she has classes tomorrow. I call an Uber, nudging her awake when it arrives.

"You need to go get some sleep. I promise I'll have Isabela call you when she's feeling better."

She glances toward the bed, standing on wobbly feet. "O-okay. As soon as she can. Promise?"

I agree before walking her outside to the Uber. After getting a coffee, I return to Isabela, sitting next to her bed and holding her hand as I wait for her to wake up.

IX: NARWHAL DOME
ISABELA

Beep. Beep.

I hear myself groaning, but the only thing I can focus on is that my stomach feels like it shriveled up and died.

"Isabela? Are you awake?"

Adam. He's here.

After he told me my entire life was a sham, I texted Chad for the address of the party and picked up Jessie. All I remember are the shots.

I don't want to open my eyes. I can't look at him yet. My mind still refuses to wrap around the fact that he's my...oh, God, I can't even think it.

My throat feels like sandpaper. When I try to say, "Yes," all that comes out is a mumbled mess.

His lips press against my forehead. "You scared the shit out of me last night."

Finally, I push open my eyes to find the room dark besides the light from the bedside lamp.

He hugs me tight, and my whole body screams in pain, making me yelp. "Shit, I'm sorry, I'm just so happy you're okay."

"Water," I croak.

He fills up a plastic cup as a nurse walks into the room. "Oh, good, you're up. Dr. Franks said you're free to go once we get all the paperwork in order." The nurse checks my vitals, saying they're where they should be before leaving me and Adam alone to get ready for checkout. I can barely look at him, and all I want to do is sleep. I don't think I've ever felt this shitty in my life.

My eyes are barely staying open when one of the nurses brings in a wheelchair, pushing me out to Adam's car. There's not a single thing I can think of to say to him. Besides, my throat hurts too much to speak, so I'm grateful for the quiet car ride.

Sleep must have consumed me because when I wake up again, I'm in Adam's arms and he's unlocking his apartment door. In some ways, I feel like I should recoil from his touch while simultaneously wanting to lean into it. He carries me to my room, laying me in my bed as he kisses my cheek and whispers, "I love you more than anything. I'm so sorry."

Sunlight burns my eyelids, and I moan, rolling onto my stomach. Reaching out for my phone, my fingers wrap around a slick paper. I crack my eyes open to see the girl who's supposedly my mother. If what Adam said was true, then she abandoned me as soon as I was out of her body. I toss the photo on the nightstand and pick up my phone. It's one o'clock in the afternoon...on *Tuesday?!* That means I've been out of it for over twenty-four hours.

After struggling through a shower and getting dressed, I finally work up the courage to face my broth — Dad. Fuck, that's weird.

As I walk into the living room, his face brightens. Even knowing who he is to me, it's hard to see anyone besides my brother.

"You're up! How are you feeling?" I hate how uncomfortable this is. "Are you hungry? We can stop and eat before your surprise."

Even though I'm famished, I'm way too freaked out to eat. "What surprise? I'm really not in the mood, *Dad*."

He bristles, biting out, "We're gonna see the narwhals."

I scoff. If it were possible to simply 'see narwhals' I would have done that ages ago. "It's a nice thought, but narwhals can't be kept in captivity, so..."

"Trust me."

I laugh at his audacity. "Trust you? That's cute."

He points toward the apartment door. "Just go to the fucking car."

I roll my eyes while walking down to the parking

garage, groaning at the sun shining so ridiculously bright.

We go to a drive-thru for burgers, eating in awkward silence until he pulls up to the aquarium. I know for a fact there's no way any actual narwhals here, yet I humor him as he buys our tickets.

Once we're inside, I see the poster on the wall. *Unicorns of the Sea* is showing in the dome theater. My chest tightens as I follow him to the seats located in the direct center of the dome.

As much as I'm trying to see him as the person he says he is, it's impossible to look at him like a father, and after what happened between us, I don't ever want to.

He clears his throat, shifting in his seat. "How are you feeling?"

Other than a bit of a headache, physically I'm okay. Emotionally, however... "Pretty fucking pissed."

He glares at me, deepening his voice. "Do you remember what happened at the party?"

"I remember trying to drink away the fact that I've been lied to my whole life and that I fucked my father," I snap quietly enough for only him to hear.

He reaches down and squeezes my thigh, leaning forward with blazing eyes. "I know you're angry, and you have every right to be, however, getting so trashed that you're no longer safe is unacceptable." I try to push away his hand, and he responds by digging his fingers deeper into my leg. "Something could have happened." The way he's looking at me puts a crack in my rage.

He's more than angry. He's scared. "Please, Isabela. Promise me you'll be more careful."

The lights darken, and he looks so close to breaking down, that I nod to appease him. "Fine, I promise."

He releases my leg as the room becomes an underwater simulation. It's insane how real it looks. A narwhal swims belly up over my head to meet a large pod to my right. They are huge creatures; the tusk alone can get up to ten feet long on some males. The narrator rattles off facts that I already know in a soothing voice. They really are mystical; there's so little we've actually learned about them. I cover my mouth when two males cross their tusks right in front of me. It looks like I could touch them.

Out of the corner of my eye, I see Adam staring at me. As irate as I am with him right now, this is really sweet. I keep going back and forth over how I should handle this and if I'm even capable of forgiving him or my...grandparents.

Once the show ends and we walk out to the car, I tell him, "Thank you. I really enjoyed that."

He gives me a sad smile as he unlocks the doors. "I'm glad, Bella Boop."

I despise how uncomfortable things are between us now. I have so many thoughts going through my mind, though, the ones rising to the surface now are about the girl in the photo. "What was her name? My mother?"

He sighs and looks in the rearview before answering. "Amaya." Glancing over to me, he sighs. "We were thirteen. We had no business having sex much less a kid. Her parents pushed for an abortion, but you know how Mom and Dad are. When I couldn't take care of you, they did. They *are* your parents. This doesn't change that. For what it's worth, we thought we were protecting you."

I really am trying to understand. I'm nineteen and can't imagine being a parent. At thirteen it would have been impossible. "I want to get it, okay? I just need time."

"That I can give you."

As soon as we get back to the apartment, he tells me to call Mom. "Go easy on her. She's a wreck over this."

Sunday night I was so furious, I blocked her number. Today, I'm not sure what I feel, so I let her talk and try to hear her out as she sobs her apology. I hate it when she cries. I know they love me, all of them, but I also loathe that they deceived me my entire life. Once I finally calm her down, I tell her I love her and hang up to meet Adam in the kitchen.

Unsurprisingly, he's pouring himself a drink. "You want one?"

"Sure." I lean against the counter and cross my arms.

He throws back his shot and sighs. "What's it gonna take for us to get back to normal?"

Normal? What does that even look like? "I don't know if we'll ever get back to that, although you can start by not lying to me again."

He nods, and I don't understand why my eyes go to the crotch of his basketball shorts. The bulge is defined, and now I know how impressive he is under there. I unintentionally cross my ankles as the memories of him thrusting into me try to overwhelm my thoughts.

"Do you have any questions? I'll answer anything."

"Where's Amaya?

He rubs the back of his neck, glancing up to the ceiling. "Last I heard, her and her family moved to Daytona Beach. I haven't spoken to her since you were born."

"Did she ever want to see me? Even try to be part of my life?" As the question falls from my lips, I'm unsure if I want the answer. My whole life, I thought I was a surprise...not a mistake.

"I hurt her, Isabela. I'm sure her absence in your life had a lot to do with you being part of me. Try not to take it personally. She was a kid."

Honestly, I don't know if I'd want to meet her. Regardless of when I have children, I don't think I could ever let them go. She chose to not be a part of my life. That's on her. I don't care what Adam did. I suddenly realize my life could have taken a much darker turn, and I have him and my parents to thank for it.

"Is there anything you haven't told me? Are there anymore lies?"

He grips the counter's edge, and I think he's going to ignore the question until he finally says, "I'm still struggling with how I see you now. I...I don't know how to stop it." Looking up to me, his eyebrows scrunch over his shame filled eyes. "I don't want to want you, Isabela."

I wish I could kiss away the pain he's feeling, but I know exactly what he means. I don't want to want him the way that I do either.

X: GOODBYE
ADAM

The small, heartbroken smile on her face somehow makes my chest ache and my dick hard at the same time. I fucking hate this. She walks to me with slow steps.

"I don't regret being with you." Inching closer, she takes my hand. "I know it never should have happened, and yet I still want you."

Releasing me, she slowly touches the obvious erection in my shorts. I need her to stop. This can't happen again. Telling myself to move her hand does nothing when I reach out to grab the back of her neck and crash my lips to hers. She moans into my mouth, breaking any resolve I may have had.

"This is the last time, Isabela. It has to be."

She nods, kissing my neck as she undoes my pants. Her body slides down mine to the floor, and my cock lurches at the thought of feeling her mouth again. I drop my head back, groaning as her tongue licks my shaft. When she takes me in her mouth, she goes as far as she can before gagging. She looks so damn hot doing this.

Everything about this is one hundred percent obscene. Even though our relationship is unconventional, she is my daughter. I thrust between her lips, whispering under my breath how perfect this feels.

I have to stop this. Gripping her hair, I take her off me, nodding for her to stand up. She obeys, and we don't break eye contact as I find myself undoing the button of her tight denims. I tug on the fabric, kissing down her legs.

Standing to my feet, I nip at her neck as my fingers grip the elastic of her panties. "Sit on the counter. I want to kiss your pussy." Her cheeks flush as her underwear falls to the floor. She does what I ask, revealing her swollen, delicious looking clit peeking out from between her lips. I grip her thighs, lowering my head between her legs. My tongue darts out to taste her, and at first, she slowly rolls her hips, thrusting against my tongue, but after a while, she pushes down on my head and grinds against my face.

"Oh, my God, Adam..." I take her engorged bundle between my lips, and she gasps. "Fuck, your mouth... I'm gonna come."

I squeeze her legs and savor her taste, knowing I won't ever be able to do this again. I don't stop until the pulsating of her entrance vibrates against my tongue with her orgasm. She shakes above me, moaning out her pleasure. My hands reach out to grab her waist and move her to the edge of the counter. "This is the last time." At this point, I'm not sure if I'm saying this for her benefit or my own.

She kisses me roughly before giving me a coy grin. "Then let's make it count, *Daddy*."

The comment should turn me off, yet my cock twitches at the term of endearment. "Don't call me that," I snap even with a sick part of me hoping she does so again.

With a knowing smile, she grabs my dick to guide it inside of her. Her hips rotate, showing me that she knows how to fuck better than she should.

I suddenly don't want our last time to be on the kitchen counter. Gripping her waist, I pick her up, and she wraps her legs around me. I keep myself inside her as I carry her out of the kitchen. Her arms hug my neck, and she doesn't waste a single second, bouncing her body as I walk her to my room.

I lay her down on my bed, kissing every inch, memorizing every curve. There's no way this could work between us. I should be grateful I was able to have what I got. I just can't shake the solemnness that things won't ever be the same again.

My thrusts are slow and gentle and somehow, it's more intense than it ever has been.

"I love you, Adam," she whispers between her gasps. "I always will. I promise."

Slipping into consciousness, I flutter my eyes open and reach across my bed for Isabela. She fell asleep in my arms last night. My fingers find only empty sheets until a piece of paper *crinkles* beneath my palm. I sit up in a panic, feverishly scanning over the words.

Adam,

I know, a paper note? What is this? 2004? I just really felt like what I had to say didn't belong in a text. The most important thing I want you to know is that I love you, and I'm happy that we were able to be together the way we were. I will never regret it, and I will never forget it, but I don't know how to deal with what I'm feeling, and it will be impossible to figure it out living with you. You have always been there when I needed you. Right now, though, I need some time. I forgive you for lying to me, and I understand why you did it. I'm going to crash with Jessie for a few days, so I'll be safe. I love you so much, Adam. More than I should. See you around.

XOXO,
Bella Boop

I stare at the words for I don't know how long, hating myself for driving her to this. Like her, I'd never want to change what happened between us. Even if I could, it's likely that I would repeat history. I loved having her here.

Picking up my phone, I find her contact. My finger hovers over the call button before I sigh and drop it on my bed.

She asked for time. It's the least I can do after everything.

XI: MAJOR CHANGE
ISABELA

TWO MONTHS LATER...

My keys *jingle* in my hand, and I grab my bag when Jessie walks in, kicking off her sandals. "Heard anything yet?" she asks.

"I swear you'll be the first to know."

She's only being supportive, but her asking about it twice a day puts me on edge. A few weeks ago, I met with my academic advisor about changing my major from marketing and communications to fine arts. I'm still waiting to hear if I got accepted into the program, so I haven't informed my parents of this decision yet. Although Adam inspired me to follow my dreams, I'm terrified I'm making a huge mistake. I pray it works out as well for me as it did for him. "I'm gonna run to the market. You need anything?"

"Nah, I'm good... unless you want to grab me a matcha from the coffee shop?"

I grin at her. "You got it." She lets me stay here the nights I can't deal with my parents and never makes me feel like a burden, so I'll get her as many matcha lattes as she wants.

On the way to my car, I re-read the last text from Adam.

Adam: I love you so much, and I miss you like crazy. Please stay safe.

I haven't responded because I know he was probably drunk since he sent it at two o'clock in the morning, plus everything I want to say would only make this whole situation worse. We've only seen each other once since I left, and it was even more painful than I'd imagined it would be. We had to fight so hard not to touch each other inappropriately that we could barely hug. I hated it.

Not living with him has done nothing to satiate my desire for him which proves that leaving was the right choice. Even if it was one of the hardest ones I've ever had to make. There's no way it can work between us, and being there with him would have made it impossible to end things. I know I hurt him, which was the last thing I wanted, so I have to believe that my choice was the right one.

I haven't been able to bring myself to sleep with anyone since Adam. It's as if I'm scared it will make it seem like a dream or that it never happened, and I'm not ready to erase him yet.

DECIET

Once I arrive at the market, I make my way to the feminine products. I take a big breath as I scan through my choices. Some of these are fucking expensive. This isn't the first time I've had to do this. Remembering to take my birth control every day isn't my strong suit, and being in college is stressful, so my period whacks out all the time.

With some vegetables and a jar of grapefruit juice, I drive to the gas station. Obviously, I love Jessie, but there's no way I could take a pregnancy test at her dorm without her asking a million questions and I'm definitely not doing it at my parent's house. She knows I haven't hooked up in sixty-three days—I'm counting—and she gives me shit about it. She'd have too many questions, and I never told her about me and Adam. I walk to the bathroom and pull the box from my purse.

After peeing on the little tab, I stare in the mirror for the three minutes it takes to show the result. I'm psyching myself out. There's no way Mother Nature would be that big of a bitch. Closing my eyes, I take a deep breath before looking down at the test. My skin instantly beads with sweat and my breathing becomes shallow. As my heart pounds in my chest, two bright pink lines stare up at me.

No. This can't be happening. I stare at my reflection in horror as the information soaks into my brain.

"Fuck."

BOOKS BY CHARITY B.

Series: Candy Coated Chaos (Sweet Treats #1)
Sweetened Suffering (Sweet Treats #2)
Cupcakes and Crooked Spoons (Sweet Treats #3)

ABOUT CHARITY B.

Charity B. lives in Wichita Kansas with her husband and ornery little boy. She released her debut series, the Sweet Treats Trilogy, in 2018 and is constantly working on her next release. She has always loved to read and write, but began her love affair with dark romance when she read C.J. Robert's The Dark Duet. She has a passion for the disturbing and sexy and wants nothing more than to give her readers the ultimate book hangover. In her spare time, when she's not chasing her son, she enjoys reading, the occasional T.V. show binge, and is deeply inspired by music.

For more on me and my books, visit www.charitybauthor.com or join the Facebook reader group Charity B.'s Broken Babydolls.

Printed by Amazon Italia Logistica S.r.l.
Torrazza Piemonte (TO), Italy